IVY

By
Alex Martin

Book Six

The Katherine Wheel Series

ACKNOWLEDGEMENTS

Writing this book entailed vast amounts of research. Always my husband, Phil, was at my side whether it was visiting Caen War Museum and seeing the dreadful images on display, poring over the map and lanes of Normandy to find obscure corners on which to base a scene, visiting Bayeux and marvelling at its cathedral, he was there. Phil has given patient support through the more technical side of formatting, researching and has provided a constant, willing ear as I thrashed out the complex plot.

Our son, Tom, has also been a stalwart support throughout this series. His brilliant mind has given many insights especially with structural edits and exciting brainstorming sessions.

My author friends, Judith Barrow and Thorne Moore, have listened, critiqued and advised all the way through with the empathy that only other writers can provide.

Thanks to Jane Dixon-Smith of www.jd-design.com for the fabulous cover work

Deep appreciation must also go to the Bayeux Tourism Office for their courteous and patient help with my research. The Caen War Memorial were very helpful in guiding me to research resources. I have read more books and watched more films on World War Two than I can count and there are many websites who have generously given information. Finally, sincere thanks to the ATA Museum for their help and the splendid experience of flying a simulated Spitfire.

"Sleep thou, and I will wind thee in my arms. So doth the woodbine, the sweet honeysuckle, gently entwist the sweet ivy."

From William Shakespeare's 'A Midsummer Night's Dream'

Ivy continues the story begun in Woodbine.

CHAPTER ONE
NORMANDY, FRANCE
31 DECEMBER 1941

If Lottie thought she'd see more of Thierry Thibault after they'd given in to the fierce attraction sizzling between them, she was sadly mistaken. Far from visiting again, Thierry disappeared.

Not much had happened after Thierry's last visit just before Christmas. As her most important contact with the burgeoning Resistance movement, the local schoolteacher had left a couple of rifles and a wireless for her to hide and passionate kisses on her lips. The guns lay treacherous and silent in the deepest cellar of the medieval farmhouse at Le Verger, but it was a rare moment Lottie forgot they were there, or the man who had brought them. She still knew almost nothing about him, except the feel of his mouth on hers, the fire in his blue eyes behind his horn-rimmed spectacles and his determination to rid his beloved France of the scourge of German occupation.

Lottie kept busy on the smallholding, aware of the danger its owner faced every day in sheltering her from the Nazis. The taciturn Bernadette Perrot had grudgingly provided refuge when Lottie and Bernadette's granddaughter, Françoise, had fled from the German invasion of Paris. Since then, Lottie had been forced to adopt the name of Charlotte Perrot, fictitious cousin to Françoise, to avoid deportation to one of the dreaded labour camps in Germany.

On the last day of 1941, Lottie grabbed the ancient bike from the barn at Le Verger and cycled into the village. She was damned if she'd wait any longer to see Thierry, despite his earnest plea for her to stay away – to stay safe.

She sped along between the high, bare hedges of the Normandy lanes, as alert as ever to the risk of discovery, but when she reached the entrance to the village she felt more impatient than scared of the German soldier guarding

1

the bridge over the river. She snatched back her forged identity card from him, eager to be on her way to the boulangerie nestled amongst the terraced houses and shops that surrounded the pretty village square beyond. The Mairie, its handsome stone walls now hung with two huge Nazi flags emblazoned with swastikas, stood opposite the boulangerie, so Lottie skirted around the big linden trees in the centre of the square to avoid inquisitive German eyes.

Madame Leroy, the baker, confirmed Thierry Thibault's absence. "But, no, mon petit chou, no-one has seen the young teacher. As soon as the school holidays came, he left with a big suitcase and hasn't come back." Madame Leroy screwed up her eyes, so they almost disappeared into the layers of fat around them. "Have you a message from Jean at the mill?"

To her annoyance, Lottie felt herself flush. "Um, no, not really. Just wondered if there was any news?"

"You know the Americans have declared war on Hitler after Japan bombed Pearl Harbour? You understand what it means?"

Lottie nodded. "Yes, of course I do. We're not alone anymore."

Madame Leroy patted Lottie's shoulder. "Eh, we shall beat these German bastards with American firepower on our side. Come, I'll make you coffee and close the shop for the rest of the morning. I've sold all the bread anyway."

Madame Leroy bustled Lottie into her warm kitchen where the range pumped out heat into the clean, bare room. "It's only ersatz but it will be warm. You look frozen with the cold."

Lottie warmed her hands before the fire, blazing away behind its iron grille. "My nose feels like solid ice." She gave a false laugh.

Madame Leroy didn't look as if she was fooled for a moment. She ground the roasted roots of dandelion and chicory in her coffee grinder. The handle whirred round at

2

surprising speed. "What is bothering you, little one? It's not just the war, is it?"

Lottie rubbed her hands together till they tingled. "I'd rather not say."

"Is your concern for Monsieur Thibault becoming personal?"

Lottie's face went hot again. "No, I'm just a bit bored. We see no-one at the farm and my curiosity got the better of me. Monsieur Thibault seems to be the one with all the news, that's all."

"Drink your coffee, if you can call it that." Madame hefted her considerable weight on to a chair that looked far too fragile to support it.

Lottie sipped her bitter brew, grateful for the warm sensation as it made its way down to her stomach.

Madame's spindly little chair creaked ominously. "I rely on Monsieur Thibault for the news too." Madame Leroy sighed. "Sometimes it's better not to know what's happening."

"What do you mean, Madame?"

"I have a niece in Paris. She's been carrying messages too, just like you. I haven't heard from her since November. She always gets in touch for Christmas. Usually she visits here and has a good feed over the holidays, but I've heard nothing. Not a word. I've sent letters but there's no reply. I think she's been sent to a German camp, or maybe worse."

"Oh, Madame, I'm sorry."

"Well, you keep yourself safe, little one. Better to be bored than dead."

"But you don't know she's dead, do you?"

Madame gave a little shiver. "Not officially, no, but I feel it. Here." Madame Leroy placed her plump hand across her voluminous chest. "'Nacht und Nebel', the Boche call it, though we're not supposed to know about it."

"What does that mean?"

3

"'Night and fog.' People disappear quietly and unseen."

Lottie suppressed a shiver of her own. Could this have happened to Thierry too?

Madame Leroy frowned. "And mind what you say in the village. If you are fond of a certain person, don't let it be known. Someone might rat on you – put two and two together – and if one of you gets caught, then so will the other. So will I for that matter, but I'm old, my husband is long gone and I have no children. I don't care what happens to me, but I'm damned if I'll let these Nazis stamp all over my village. I was born in this house. It's the one thing I have left. They won't take it from me."

Madame Leroy took an unbroken baguette from the table and tore a piece off. She dipped it in her drink. "And there's something else. People are writing to the Boche, trying to get in with them. Collabo's like that snake Marchand."

"The butcher is a collaborator?"

"Yes, him. Well, it's his wife, really. She's always had it in for me. Marchand had a thing for me when I was younger – much younger." Madame Leroy gave a little chuckle. "I wasn't always fat, you know."

"Madame, you are not fat now."

"Charlotte," Madame Leroy waved a finger, "do not insult my intelligence. Madame Marchand hates my guts and if she suspects for a minute that I'm involved in the Resistance, she'll make sure the Germans know. Bitch."

Lottie was shocked, she'd never heard Madame Leroy say a bad word about anyone.

They both looked up at the window as a large German army truck hurtled past.

"It's early for troop movements." Madame Leroy heaved her bulk from the chair and went to the window.

Lottie got up and joined her, pressing her nose to the glass, making it cold again.

4

"I knew it!" Madame Leroy went to the door and opened it, letting in the frosty air.

"Knew what?"

Madame Leroy looked directly at Lottie. Her usual kind expression had been replaced by a new, flint-hard look. "It's that little widow, Madame Levy, you know, the dressmaker?"

Lottie nodded.

"They've stopped outside her house. Looks like Madame Marchand has done her worst."

Horrified, Lottie looked past her friend towards the little terraced house, one of the many clustered together around the square. Four German soldiers got down from the lorry and went inside.

"Madame, what is happening?"

"Oh, my God, I don't know. I hope against hope it's not what I think."

Lottie gripped her friend's sturdy arm and kept her eyes trained on the blue front door, left wide open by the soldiers.

Suddenly, the four Germans came through the door; they held a small, slight woman who was struggling and screaming, flailing her arms towards the inside of the house. One of the soldiers grabbed her by her black hair; she wore no hat or even a coat against the bitter cold. Two other soldiers went back in the house and brought out a child each, still wearing their pyjamas.

"Dear God, not the children, please don't take the children!" The delicate-looking mother was screaming at the top of her voice now. Other doors around the square were opening a crack, white faces peered out.

Two of the soldiers lifted the distressed woman into the back of the truck. It looked effortless. Each man was twice her size. Two thin arms reached out from behind the dark green flap and she leaned out, stretching her hands towards her small children, now crying pitifully.

In turn, a soldier picked up one child, then another, and almost tossed the children up to their mother. Lottie watched, barely able to believe her eyes, as the small woman gathered her children to her chest and the flap fell back, hiding them from view. The soldiers had already climbed back inside the lorry and it drew away quickly, its engine thundering through the square, slowing only for the narrow bridge over the river, before fading into the distance.

The doors around the square shut equally quickly, including Madame Leroy's.

Lottie found she was shaking from head to foot. "But where will they go? The children…"

"They'll take them to a camp somewhere. Madame Marchand let it slip to one of her customers someone else she 'knew' in Caen had gone to somewhere in Germany. And it could only have been the Germans who told her – now, I ask you, why would they do that, if she wasn't collaborating? She's walking around looking so damn smug. I don't know how I'll stop myself from slapping her pudgy face if she comes in here to buy bread off me." Madame covered her eyes with her plump hands. Through them, she said, "And where was our Mayor? Why didn't Monsieur Voclain tackle those German pigs, eh?"

Lottie was silent. She looked away from the hatred so clearly etched on her friend's face and stared instead at the cheerful flames dancing in the range, but all she saw were the pale, frightened faces of the little boy and girl as they were hurled into the back of the lorry.

When she turned back, Madame Leroy was staring morosely into her empty cup. "What did Madame Marchand stand to gain from this betrayal, Madame?"

"Oh, nothing specific, I dare say. She's always been a Jew hater and, forgive me, an arse licker. She thinks the Boche will win and she wants to get in with them. She's too ugly to flirt with them so she's feeding them young pretty Jewish widows and their defenceless children. Spiteful cat."

"Oh, Madame, what has become of the world?"

6

"Evil has taken it over, child."

Lottie noticed that Madame Leroy was shaking too. She got up and hugged her comforting warm body.

Madame patted her back while Lottie cried out her shock. When Lottie looked up, she saw that the older woman's face was equally wet. Madame released her and rummaged in the drawer of her sideboard until she found a couple of handkerchiefs. She handed one to Lottie. "Here, dry your eyes, little one. We must be strong. Stronger than ever, yes? We must use our fear to fight these bastards."

Lottie blew her nose and nodded, willing her trembling to stop betraying her. "Madame, do you think, um, that Monsieur Thibault is in danger?"

Madame Leroy patted her hand. "He'll turn up. He's very resourceful, that one. He's probably gone to see his old associates in Paris. I'll bet he's living it up and having a good time."

Lottie wasn't sure if that idea was worse than Thierry being in trouble.

She stayed long enough for Madame to bake a couple of loaves from yesterday's dough, and took hers, still hot, and put it in the basket on her bicycle. Steam rose from the baguette into the chilly air, its aroma unmistakable, but no-one questioned why she was the only one with freshly baked bread on this New Year's Eve. The square was still silent. A couple of women walked towards her. When Lottie said good morning, they wouldn't meet her eyes but kept theirs downcast. They looked defeated already. Lottie felt angry at their bent, averted faces but then, perhaps they had Jewish connections? Did they think it would be them or their children next?

She climbed on her bike, fuming, not at the two silent women but at their Nazi occupiers. This was how they kept people obedient. Terrorised them, set them one against another. Clever.

She pedalled up to the sentry on the bridge. It was all she could do not to spit in his face. She handed over her

7

identity card. He looked younger than her, impossibly young. This time, she looked into his eyes; they were blue, rather beautiful, but hard and stony. What in heaven's name did the Hitler youth *do* to these lads to make them so inhuman, so unfeeling? She took her papers silently and remounted her bicycle.

Lottie willed her legs to work. Her whole body felt leaden and stiff. She remembered what Madame Leroy had said about using the fear and the anger to make you fight. Thierry was like that. He'd foreseen all of this from the outset.

What if the soldiers came for her? Found out she was an enemy alien with false identity papers? Or someone like Madame Marchand realised that Françoise's little boy, Bertrand, had a Jewish father, one who had already disappeared silently in the night? Le Verger was very isolated. No-one ever called except Thierry, but was anywhere safe?

Should she have gone back to the sanctuary of her home at Cheadle Manor in Wiltshire? Lottie remembered the dreadful argument with her mother over Granny's will. Cassandra had been so angry when Lady Smythe had bequeathed the estate solely to Lottie, bitter words had passed between them. Lottie now regretted everything she'd said. She missed her real family so much, including her sister, Isobel, and her best friend, Al Phipps. She'd thought she was in love with him, then he'd declared his love for Isobel, adding to the sense of rejection that had propelled her to Paris, but she could see now that it had simply been a girlish infatuation. The way she felt about Thierry Thibault was an altogether grown-up affair. And, if she had returned to England before the Nazis had blocked all routes out of France, she would never have met him.

Oh, where was he? She would fight with a lot more courage if he was beside her. Had it just been the heat of the moment, that kiss? She remembered, as she had so often since, the feeling of his lips on hers, the urgent searching of his tongue in her mouth, how she had longed for it to continue and how abruptly he had left immediately afterwards.

CHAPTER TWO
CHEADLE MANOR, ENGLAND
DECEMBER 1941

Isobel Flintock-Smythe and her mother, Cassandra, sat together over their simple breakfast in the small kitchen of West Lodge. The little stone gatehouse guarded the entrance to their real home, Cheadle Manor, now requisitioned as a hospital for wounded soldiers and therefore out of bounds to its owners unless the medical staff gave them permission to enter.

Isobel was usually too busy as a Land Girl on the farm estate to mind very much. She'd astonished everyone by signing up for a job that involved manual labour from dawn till dusk. As a child, she'd been delicate and artistic but her love for gardening and animals had persuaded her that joining the Women's Land Army would be the best way to serve her country while it was at war. Tall and blonde, sensitive and willowy, no-one had foreseen Isobel milking cows or driving tractors in the rain, but she had surprised herself and everyone else by enjoying the tough, outdoor life. However, the posting in North Wales had been miserable and it had been a relief to come back to Cheadle Manor and work at Home Farm but then, if she'd not been away, she would never have met the charming Geraint Lloyd.

Isobel hesitated. She glanced across at her mother. Cassandra looked as elegant as ever, but her hands were red and chapped from housework. Isobel picked up the letter that had arrived in the morning's post. "I think I will go to Geraint's for Christmas after all."

"Really?" Cassandra looked at her daughter, surprise widening her hazel brown eyes.

"Why not? He's sent me such a warm invitation and I quite fancy a little luxury over the holidays. It would certainly make a change from mucking out the cowshed at

Home Farm. His place sounds divine. Want to come with me? He's extended his hospitality to us both."

There was a moment's hesitation before her mother replied. "I think not, darling, though it would be heavenly. Every year, I hope Lottie will be in touch for Christmas. I couldn't bear it if I missed a telephone call, even though I know the chances are remote after all this time with her being trapped in France. Only God knows where she might be." Cassandra cleared her throat. "And I think I should stay here and be on hand if the hospital needs me."

"That Dr Harris is far too demanding." Isobel sipped her tea, annoyed it was cooling so quickly. She got up to tend the range. It constantly needed feeding with coal and they both kept forgetting to bank it up.

"Oh, I don't mind. He is so hardworking and kind."

Isobel caught a new inflexion in her mother's voice. "Is that right?" She paused, coal scuttle in hand and looked around at Cassandra, shocked to notice that her mother was wearing lipstick.

"Still, I would prefer it if you could come, Mummy." Isobel shucked coal into the greedy furnace.

"Do you really feel in need of a chaperone, Bella? I've never met a more gentle and respectful man than Geraint Lloyd. I'm sure you will be quite safe with him, and probably very pampered."

Isobel laughed. It still didn't shift the stone in her heart. Only Al Phipps could do that. "Yes, he will spoil me rotten."

"Al isn't coming home for the holidays, then?"

Isobel shut the metal stove door. Her hands were smudged with black coal – again. "He never said."

It was Cassandra's turn to look sharply at her daughter. Isobel turned her face away and washed her hands at the butler sink, watching the dirty water swirl down the plughole with fierce concentration. Whenever she thought of Al, and it couldn't be more than twenty times a day, she remembered his last letter and his excitement at the prospect

11

of going to the pub with Miriam, whoever *she* was. Was she one of those female ATA pilots he'd said were so glamorous?

She dried her hands on the damp tea towel and spread it to dry above the range. "Well, I'll just have to go alone, then, won't I? I'll write to Geraint now and tell him I'm coming."

"Can Farmer Stubbs spare you?"

"Yes, one of his sons will be home on leave. Mrs Stubbs is over the moon about it."

"Oh, that's lovely. I'm happy for her. Oh, how I wish we knew where Lottie was and if she is safe. I'd give anything to have her here with us." Cassandra's eyes misted up. She drew a deep breath and smiled at her daughter. "I'm sure Geraint will be very pleased to see you, darling. Have you made up your mind to accept his marriage proposal? You realise you will be signalling that you are seriously interested in marrying him if you do go, and it wouldn't be fair to raise his hopes with false pretences."

"I...I don't know, Mummy. I think it will help me make up my mind."

"I hope so, Bella. It must have been hard for him this last year, waiting for your answer all this time." Cassandra placed her cup down carefully on its saucer.

Isobel nodded. "Yes, I'm very aware of that."

She went through to the little sitting room. It was freezing in there as neither of them had lit the fire yet. All these fires were so much effort. Isobel wondered how on earth the staff at the manor had kept them going in every bedroom and reception room all those years when she was growing up within its graceful old walls. She hadn't even noticed at the time. It would be good to be looked after again, if only for a few days. There were lots of things she loved about her new life as a land girl at Home Farm, but the daily grind never relented.

Isobel snatched up some paper and a pen and took them into her bedroom, slipping under the welcome warmth of her bedcovers while she wrote her reply to the man who loved her so much. If only she could bring herself to feel the same way, all her mother's many financial and security worries would be over – if you discounted the war, which was, of course, impossible.

She rattled off her reply before she changed her mind, threw on her coat and shouted out to her mother. "I'm off to the Post Office. Do you want anything?"

But her mother had gone out. Cassandra's earlier words of caution floated through her head, amplifying the doubts that clouded it.

Out loud, Isobel muttered. "It's nonsense. I'm only going on holiday. Geraint won't expect anything more. I'm not signalling anything."

Isobel jumped on her pushbike, crammed a hat on her head against the cold, drizzling rain, and pedalled as fast as she could into the village of Lower Cheadle.

CHAPTER THREE
THE KATHERINE WHEEL GARAGE, CHEADLE,
ENGLAND
DECEMBER 1941

Al Phipps stepped off the train and sniffed the air of his hometown. No aviation fuel to pollute it here. It was a perfect Christmas Eve. The pavements he'd trodden to Maidenhead station in the dark pre-dawn had been rimed with frost, but he'd watched the ice melt away in the winter sunshine through the train window. Travelling through the early morning had reinforced his sense of excitement at the prospect of going home for Christmas.

He hadn't told a soul he was coming. He couldn't wait to see his family's faces when he walked through the door. He wasn't quite sure why he hadn't written to tell Isobel of his return. Some deep instinct had held him back.

He shifted the weight of his suitcase to his other hand, remembering the presents inside. His kid sister, Lily, would love that miniature plane. She was such a tomboy and kept wishing she was old enough to fight too. Al was grateful she was only twelve years old and couldn't.

He emerged from the station in Woodbury to see his village bus waiting outside. He broke into a sprint.

"Luck's on my side today!" He gasped to the conductor as he paid for his ticket.

"Yes, you've only just caught us. I hope the luck stays with you, mate. Are those wings on your cap? Thought the RAF was a lighter blue?" The conductor reeled off the ticket from the machine hung around his neck.

Al took the ticket and handed over some coins. "That's right, it is. I'm in the ATA."

"What's that when it's at home?"

"Air Transport Auxiliary. We ferry the planes and the pilots around to different aerodromes. Keeps the whole thing ticking along for the boys in the RAF."

A girl in the seat opposite looked across at him with admiring eyes. The girl next to her giggled.

Al knew his uniform made him look good, with its ultra-dark blue coat and cap, blue shirt and black tie. He was proud of the golden eagle and the ATA insignia on his peaked cap too. He'd worked hard enough to get it, starting out as just a driver and slaving through all those exams and lectures. He smiled back at the two young women, flattered to see them laugh and blush.

By the time they'd covered the five miles to his mum's Katherine Wheel Garage, he'd found out they were called Elsie and Nora and lived in the next village beyond Upper and Lower Cheadle. He declined taking them to the next tea dance in Woodbury. There was only one girl he'd be dancing with this Christmas.

He turned away from the giggling pair and stared out of the window, not seeing the familiar countryside but Isobel's fair face, her cornflower blue eyes framed by her flyaway blonde hair. With her tall and slender figure Isobel would be - would always be - his perfect partner.

He hopped off the bus before it had even stopped moving and walked the two hundred yards along the London Road to his parents' garage. It was impossible for anyone to ignore the collection of buildings but their hoardings advertising his dad's vegetables, the petrol station and the sale of cars had all been taken down for fear of invasion.

Behind all that stood the rubber factory, where his mum was manufacturing components for the army at an increasingly rapid rate. A steady thrum from inside its bulky exterior confirmed that production was in full swing. He walked past the petrol pumps and into the garage shop.

"Al!" His father, Jem Phipps, dropped the pen he held in his one good hand and extended it to his son.

"Hello, Dad, how's things?"

"Why didn't you tell us you were coming?"

"I wanted to give you a Christmas surprise!"

15

Jem pulled him into a hug and said, his voice muffled by Al's new ATA overcoat, "You've certainly done that." His dad's false arm dug into Al's side, he squeezed him so hard.

Jem stood back to look at him. "My word, son, you do look smart. Wait till your mother sees you."

They walked together towards the factory; their conversation drowned out by the noise as soon as they entered the huge space.

Al couldn't spot his mother at first, there were so many new people working on the production line.

"There she is!" Jem pointed with his good hand to where his wife was bent over a machine with a huddle of girls watching her.

Al smiled. His mother's red headscarf, knotted over her forehead but never quite containing the black curls underneath, was familiar and distinctive. As if sensing his gaze, she looked up. Katy Phipps had the sort of bone structure that film stars craved. Although she looked older and more tired than when he'd left, she was still beautiful and her pansy-blue eyes lit up at the sight of her son, making the years melt away.

As soon as she saw him, she waved and shouted, "Al! By all that's wonderful! Just give me one minute and I'll come over." She gabbled something to the little crowd of women around her.

To Al's amusement, he found several pairs of eyes trained on him. He stood up straighter in his uniform and touched his cap to them all. Giggles and smiles came hurtling back.

Katy shooed the group back to their workbenches and came over. "Wasn't going to get much sense out of that lot once they'd clapped their eyes on my handsome son!"

Al's mother almost crushed the breath out of him with her hug.

"Hello, Mum. Blimey, you look busy – so many new girls!"

16

"Yes, and don't you go distracting them! Have you got leave? Can you stay for Christmas? Have you flown solo yet?"

The questions kept coming as they walked to their home behind the factory shed, where their bungalow nestled, screened from the factory and garage among some trees and a hedge of evergreen laurels.

Jem opened the door. "I'll put the kettle on."

"Are you hungry, Al?" His mother followed them into the kitchen.

"Starving!"

They all laughed.

"Oh, dear, I'm not sure what we've got." Katy stood with the fridge door open, looking completely at a loss.

"Is that our Albert come home?" Agnes, Katy's mother and Al's grandmother, shuffled into the room. She leant on a walking stick and her face was all droopy on one side.

"Gran?" Al went instantly to her side.

"Give us a kiss, lad." Al put his arm around the elderly woman and kissed her soundly on her wrinkled cheek.

"You alright, Gran? What's with the stick?" Al guided her to her favourite armchair in the corner by the fireplace, noticing that the open grate had been replaced with a modern two-bar electric fire.

Jem came over and switched it on. There was a smell of burnt dust while the bars reddened.

"Blooming thing." Agnes nodded at the fire. "All these new contraptions. Not the same as a real flame."

"How have you been, Gran?" Al could see his beloved grandmother's health had deteriorated.

"Oh, not so bad, young man. You don't want to hear about my troubles anyway. I want to hear about your adventures. Have you really been up in the sky in one of those airyplanes?"

17

Al looked across at his mother, who shook her head and mouthed, "Leave it, tell you later."

He nodded quietly and sat down next to his grandmother, holding her hand and telling her, as best he could, how thrilling it was to be up in the air.

His mother, never a keen cook, had found some bacon and eggs and was frying them on the electric stove. The smell made his stomach rumble. His dad set the table and cut some bread into thick slices.

"So, you're a real pilot now?" Jem passed him a slab of bread, after they'd all sat down at the table.

"That's right." Al showed them the stripe on his sleeve.

"What's it like, you know, up in the air with nothing to support you?" Jem poured out tea into four mugs from the big brown teapot.

"It's the most amazing feeling, Dad. You can see all the fields down below like a miniature patchwork."

"How do you navigate?" Katy sipped her tea, her own food untouched.

"You have to find a landmark, like a church or a lake, and calculate your distance. It's really difficult if there's rain or low cloud. Had some close shaves, I can tell you."

"Tedn't natural. Should leave it to the birds." Agnes grumbled.

"Oh, we go a lot higher than the birds, Gran." Al gobbled his lunch. "Where's Lily, by the way?"

"She's over at Maggie's house. She'll be back for tea." Jem cut another slice of bread.

"I can't wait to see her face when she sees what I bought her for Christmas." Al gulped the last morsel of food. "Listen, I'll tell you more about the ATA later, but I really want to go and see Isobel. Her Christmas present is even more special."

He got up, reached for his overcoat and made for the door.

"Don't you need your bag, son?" Jem laid down his knife and fork.

"It's not a big present – not in size at any rate. Mind if I borrow the car?" Al patted his inside pocket and winked, as his family exchanged meaningful nods.

Before they came up with questions that might delay him, he was out of the door. He grabbed the keys from the hall table and almost ran out into the yard.

He jumped in behind the wheel of the baby Austin Seven they kept as a run-around and turned the key in the ignition and pulled the starter button. The little car purred into life. Al grinned. His mother might not be the best cook in the world, but she sure as hell could keep an engine running as smooth as silk.

Al put the car into first gear and pointed it in the direction of Cheadle Manor. When he reached the lodge house by its formidable gates, he had to remind himself to stop and park there, not outside the impressive façade of Isobel's childhood home. Instead, here he was, knocking at the door of the much humbler abode where his mother had been born.

No servant answered the door; it was Cassandra herself, owner of the manor house, who responded to his knock.

"Al! How lovely to see you, my dearest boy! My goodness, how handsome you look in your uniform." Cassandra kissed him on both cheeks.

He took off his cap and smoothed down his wavy chestnut hair. "Hello, Aunt Cass. You look well yourself." Cassandra Flintock-Smythe wasn't a blood relation but the two families had become so close over many years of ups and downs, both his mother and Isobel's had become like aunts to each other's children.

A faint flush bloomed on Cassandra's face at his compliment, but it was true, Cassandra looked better than he'd ever seen her, younger somehow.

"Come in out of the cold, Al. I've a fire in the parlour. No need to show you the way, you are more familiar with this house than I am! How is your grandmother, by the way? I was so sorry to hear about her stroke."

Al followed her inside. "Ah so that's what it was. I could see a big difference in Gran, but Mum didn't have a chance to tell me about it."

Cassandra kept up her commentary, as she ushered him into the small sitting room where his grandparents used to sit with their many children and grandchildren gathered around them. The furniture it contained was now much more refined and expensive, but the bones of the small house were good enough to do them justice.

At Cassandra's invitation, Al sat by the fire. He held out his cold hands to the blaze. "Where's Bella? Grafting away up at Home Farm, I suppose."

Cassandra didn't immediately answer him. Instead she went to a small table in the corner where some cut-glass decanters sparkled in the last of the winter sunshine. The amber liquids within them glinted in the bright rays. "Sherry? Or would you prefer whisky? Yes, let's have something fiery to warm us up. I think there'll be a frost tonight, the sky is so clear."

Already, Al's carefree mood had begun to ebb at this onslaught of jittery hospitality. He accepted the tumbler of spirits but kept his eyes focussed on his hostess, who was looking decidedly jumpy. "Aunt Cassandra, something's up. Where is Isobel?"

Again, Cassandra didn't reply but sat opposite him on the other elegant fireside armchair. She didn't lean back against its silky brocade but perched on the edge of the seat. Her knees were so close to the fire, Al feared she might scorch them.

"The thing is, Al dear, Bella didn't know you were coming home for Christmas. In fact, she was surprised not to have heard anything from you for weeks."

"You wouldn't believe how busy I am in the ATA. Never get a minute to spare."

"I'm sure. I know the hospital keeps me pretty much occupied."

"Yes, war doesn't allow anyone much free time."

"Quite." Cassandra sipped her drink and made a face. "Goodness, I rarely drink Scotch. I'd forgotten how strong it is."

"Aunt Cassandra. Please put me out of my misery. Where is Bella?" Al hadn't touched his drink.

Cassandra put hers down on the little antique table by her chair. Al remembered it always being at Isobel's grandmother, Lady Smythe's, side when it was housed in the big drawing room up at the manor, laden with the sweets that had killed her.

Cassandra cleared her throat. "Isobel isn't at Home Farm, Al."

"Then, where is she?"

"She's having a little, um, holiday."

"Holiday?"

"Yes, in north Wales."

With a thud, the proverbial penny dropped like a lead weight into the pit of Al's stomach. "North Wales, I see. Where that Lloyd feller lives?"

Cassandra nodded.

"How long will she be away?"

"A week, I think."

"A week? I only have three days leave." Al got up and paced the short distance between the fire and the window. He came back and stood before Isobel's mother. "I won't see her at all then."

Cassandra looked up at him. "No, I don't think you will."

"And, please, tell me the truth. Is there an understanding between them? Has she caved in to his promises of wealth and luxury? Or is he just painting another portrait of her to drool over?"

21

"Al!"

"Well, honestly, what do you expect me to say? You know I love her! I thought she loved me just as much, so what the hell is she doing, gallivanting off to stay with that man? And you're not there with her – are they *alone* together? Are they already married?"

"No, of course they're not married! Bella wouldn't have done anything so serious without telling you first. You know that."

"Do I? *Do I?* I didn't know anything about this bloody jaunt to north Wales. How could she go without telling me? For God's sake, he's almost old enough to be her damn father!" Al swigged his whisky back in one go, enjoying the scorching sensation at the back of his throat.

"Now, don't get upset, Al. It's just a visit. I'll tell Isobel you called round when she gets home."

"That is no consolation whatsoever." Al put his hand in his pocket and pulled out a ring box. "I was going to give her this, but it sounds like Geraint bloody Lloyd has got there before me. And I'll bet his will be a lot more valuable."

"Al…I…" Cassandra trailed off.

"Don't bother seeing me out, as you said, I know this house very well, and I thought I knew your daughter, too. Seems I don't know anything about her after all. Goodbye, and merry Christmas."

Al slammed the ancient door of the gatehouse shut behind him and climbed back into the Baby Austin. He started the engine and reversed savagely into the grass lining the driveway before skidding off back between the majestic gateway and out on to the London Road. He zoomed past The Katherine Wheel Garage at breakneck speed and turned off towards the downs instead. He only stopped when he reached the apex of the largest hill. There, he cut the engine and stared out at the distant view, before it misted over, and his eyes couldn't see anything anymore.

CHAPTER FOUR
NORMANDY, FRANCE
JANUARY 1942

Lottie made a point of finding out when the school term restarted and went back to the village on the first Saturday afterwards. She went straight to the school, a few eggs in her basket as a token excuse for the German sentry at the bridge and didn't care who else saw her. She cycled right up to the school door, looking neither to right nor left, and rapped on the wood with bare knuckles.

Thierry lived above the school rooms in a small apartment. When she heard him clatter down the stairs, her heart lurched with relief to know he had returned; that he was still alive! She straightened the head scarf covering her dark hair and waited. She caught sight of him peering through the little window to the side of the door and she smiled. Seeing her, he made a grimace of annoyance instead of smiling back, and she knew then she was wrong-footed.

The door opened. Thierry stood before her; his forehead creased into a frown. He looked tired.

"Hello, Thierry."

"Mademoiselle Perrot? What brings you here? I left no message at the boulangerie." His frown deepened.

"No, you did not and that is why I am here. Where have you been? You disappeared at Christmas without a word." She wouldn't give in to tears and bit her lip.

"Did anyone see you this morning?" Thierry glanced beyond her.

"If they did, they didn't stop me or even notice. They think I have eggs to deliver." Lottie cast her hand over the basket strapped to her bike.

"You'd better come in – but you can't stay long."

Lottie grabbed the bag of eggs and crossed the threshold.

Thierry didn't ask her upstairs to his living quarters, but he shut the door behind them. Lottie, torn between anger

23

and desire, wished he would open up his arms again and enfold her, like last time.

"Charlotte, I…" Thierry ran his hands through his blond hair, leaving it standing up in a state of mock alarm.

She had practised a civil, polite enquiry all the way over to the village. Now she was here, her mind went blank. She, who as head girl at her private boarding school back home in England, had given speeches to a packed hall. She, the sole owner of a substantial estate in Wiltshire. What would Thierry think of her if he saw her at Cheadle Manor instead of dressed as a simple French country girl? He knew her as the granddaughter of a widowed smallholder; a girl who milked goats, dug the fertile Normandy soil, picked apples in the pretty orchard. Thierry had no idea of her aristocratic background or the family who had pleaded with her to return to them before the borders closed.

Thierry turned abruptly away and ran his hand across his brow, but it remained wrinkled. "I can't tell you where I've been, it would compromise your safety. It's enough for you to know that Jean Moulin is trying to coordinate all members of the resistance and I'm helping. I can't say more, I shouldn't have said so much, but you deserve to know. There will be more risks ahead, if you are prepared to take them, to free France."

"Of course I am! How could you doubt me?" Her anger was winning the battle, she felt nearer to slapping him than kissing him now.

Thierry reached out his hands, then dropped them suddenly and looked away, not meeting her eyes.

Lottie took his hand and drew him towards her. For a moment, for one delicious moment, he squeezed hers back and let his blue eyes behind their horn-rimmed spectacles rest on her face, scanning its details as if memorising it.

"Charlotte, we can't do this." He dropped his hand. "I can't fight if we are close. I couldn't send you on a mission or go on one myself if I let myself love you. We're at war. It's not a game and it's going to get much, much

24

bloodier before we're through. God! I don't know if we will get through. I have lost many of my Parisian friends already. They've gone to prison, been tortured, and some have even been shot. No one knows what's going to happen. All I know is, I can only risk my life if I'm free. I would lose my courage if, if…"

"If what?"

"If we became lovers."

Despite all his warnings, Lottie could not suppress a flicker of hope at this admission, "Is that what you want to be – my lover?"

"Oh yes, of course I do. You feel it too, don't you?"

Lottie nodded, barely able to restrain her longing to kiss him.

"Well then," he laughed, looking relieved, almost happy, "Well then, my love, we must be good soldiers now and lovers later, no?"

"But what if there is no 'later'? We would have wasted our youth and love for nothing."

"Not for nothing, Charlotte. For everything." He took a step back. "Please, let us never talk of this again, not while the Boche are trying to crush France. If we win, if we survive, ah then…let us talk of nothing else."

Lottie reached out for him. "Thierry…"

"No more, Charlotte, no more. Give me your eggs and I will give you some money, so you have an excuse to be here, but then only get messages from the boulangerie. We must put our personal feelings aside and do what's right." He held out a couple of coins in the palm of his hand.

Lottie handed over the paper bag of hen's eggs. Their hands touched briefly in the exchange and an electric charge ran up her arm, making her feel more alive in that moment than at any time in the rest of her life. She looked at him, but he was resolute.

"Go now, Charlotte. Please, or I will not be able to resist you."

It took all Lottie's willpower to turn around and walk out of the door, but she did it somehow. She fumbled with her bicycle and climbed on to its saddle in a daze, her sight bleary, but her heart pounding in the knowledge that Thierry Thibault loved her.

CHAPTER FIVE
CHEADLE MANOR, ENGLAND
JANUARY 1942

Isobel was relieved to see her mother's car waiting for her outside the train station. She was so weighed down with packages and cases, the bus would have been a monumental struggle. And it was freezing cold. The sky threatened snow; its gun-metal clouds lay heavy, pressing down on the smoking chimneys of Woodbury. Even as she left the station and walked to the car park, a few tight little flakes of snow fluttered down, and one settled on her eyelashes. She wished she'd worn a brimmed hat now instead of just a scarf.

Isobel hurried over to the car with her baggage banging against her legs. Her mother couldn't have seen her, or she would have got out to help.

"Cooee! Mummy! Over here."

At last, her mother stepped out of the car. Having not seen her for a week, Isobel was struck by how well she looked. Instead of her normal drab brown hat, she wore her peacock blue one with the feather, usually only seen on special occasions. Maybe this was one. It felt a bit like it. It seemed to Isobel she had been away for far longer than just one week.

"Isobel, darling. Here, let me take some of those bags." Cassandra kissed her daughter. Isobel felt the unfamiliar imprint her mother's lipstick had left behind and a whiff of her favourite cologne.

Cassandra opened the boot of the old Sunbeam saloon and together they piled in Isobel's cases and boxes.

"Surely you didn't have this much stuff when you left?" Cassandra laughed as she got behind the driver's wheel.

"No, but Geraint was determined to give presents to everybody. He's so generous." Isobel turned away from her mother's direct gaze and looked out of the window. "I think

27

the snow is going to settle, don't you? It's coming down fast now."

"Yes, we'd better get home. I've kept the engine running to keep warm, that's why I couldn't leave the car to help you all the way."

Isobel let her mother concentrate on the driving after she skidded on some ice leaving the station car park.

"It's getting dark already and it's only three o'clock. It's so hard to see without proper headlights these days." Cassandra squinted through the windscreen.

They drove the five miles back to West Lodge in silence, mirroring the hushed countryside blanching white around them. Isobel could see that Cassandra was struggling to follow the contours of the familiar road and progress was painfully slow. By the time they got home, the tyres were leaving black lines in the deepening snow and the short afternoon had darkened into night.

"Brr…I hope the fire's still alight. Come on, Bella. Let's unload as quickly as we can and get warmed up."

Isobel's mother bundled up some bags and scurried inside the lodge house. Isobel followed with the heavier cases and plonked them down in the tiny hallway.

"Shall I put the kettle on, Mummy?"

"Oh, blow that, let's have something stronger! My nerves are wrecked after that awful drive on the icy road in the dark. Come on into the parlour while I rescue what's left of the fire."

Soon, they were settled by the hearth, each with a stiff drink in their cold hands. "I think I've stopped shivering now. Happy new year, darling."

"Your good health! Do you think it will snow for ages and cut us off?" Isobel clinked her glass against her mother's.

"Oh, lord, I hope not. There's hardly anything in the larder. I went to Katy and Jem's for Christmas dinner. Luckily Jem cooked it with Agnes supervising. Katy and I were relegated to peeling the Brussel sprouts, where we could do least harm."

Isobel laughed with her. "I'm glad you had a good time. I was worried you'd be lonely."

Cassandra shook her head. "Oh, not at all. I had a lovely time at the Phipps's and, um, Dr Harris saw in the new year with me. Just a quiet evening by the fire, while he was off duty, you know."

"Did he now? Doesn't he have a home to go to?"

"As it happens, no, he doesn't. His wife was killed in the Blitz on London in September 1940 – one of the very first raids. They didn't have any children."

"Ah, I see. That explains a lot."

"What do you mean?"

"Nothing. You seem to be spending a lot of time with him, that's all."

"He's lonely, Bella. I know what it's like to lose your partner, you know that."

Isobel smiled. "Of course, Mummy, I'm glad you've found a friend."

"Yes, yes, I have." Her mother gazed at the flames. The coal had caught properly and gave out a fierce heat. "Now, tell me all about your visit to Geraint's home in the mountains. I want to hear every detail."

Isobel laughed again and settled back in her comfortable armchair. "I hardly know where to begin. Every day was full of wonderful things."

"Was it? What's his house like?"

"Oh, it's beautiful. It's not as old as Cheadle Manor but built in the Arts and Crafts style I admire so much."

"Oh? Not a family seat then?"

"Oh, no, I think it was built around the turn of the century by Geraint's father."

"And did you meet his father?"

"Yes, but he's not well and keeps to his room mostly. Apparently, he never fully recovered from his heart attack last year."

"Oh dear, poor man. How about Geraint's mother?"

"Oh, she's lovely. So genteel and elegant and very kind to me. Of course, with his father so poorly, we were quite quiet but that suited me. You know I'm not much of a one for big parties."

"So, how did you fill the time?"

"Do you know, it simply flew by! Geraint took me to see his factories. They're enormous paper mills. It's a fascinating process, you know. I learned so much. He owns other factories too, but we didn't go to those, there just wasn't time. Then we went to some art galleries and he bought something for you." Isobel went to get up to fetch something from her bags, but her mother stopped her.

"Leave it for now, Bella. Tell me more about your visit."

Isobel described the beauty of the house, made from the local limestone, its elegant gables mimicking the mountains seen from every window; the exquisite art on the walls; the wide selection of books in the large library; how she had played on the grand piano for his parents, who'd been an enthusiastic, if small, audience. How she and Geraint had walked on the mountains when it was dry, and he'd taken pictures with his new camera.

"Pictures of you, I suppose?" Cassandra smiled and added more coal to the already bright fire.

Isobel felt herself flush, and it wasn't from the heat of the blaze. "Well, yes, but also the stunning views. Oh, Mummy, it's incredibly beautiful there. The scenery is much more dramatic than our gentle downs, although I love them too, of course, but the distances you can see! It makes you feel you're on top of the whole world. I forgot all about the war, except when we went into Liverpool and saw the dreadful bomb damage."

"And, forgive my asking, dear, but is it somewhere you felt you could live permanently?"

"Possibly."

"Did he ask you to marry him again?"

"He didn't mention it all week, just as he'd promised, but I could see he wanted to. His mother spoke to me though. She told me he'd been in love before, when he was my age, but the girl had died of tuberculosis. She said that's when Geraint went travelling and his mother hoped he'd find someone to love while he was away but if he did, he never told her or brought anyone home – not until he met me. Oh, Mummy, what should I do? I know he would love me forever and always be kind but…"

"You don't really love him."

Isobel's eyes flew to her mother's. She shook her head. "I still love Al."

She watched as her mother's face paled and hardened, looking more like she remembered it through her childhood when her mother had been wracked with grief for her dead father.

"If I married Geraint you would have no more problems, would you? We'd have enough money to maintain Cheadle Manor, pay off all those debts, restore the estate to its former glory and everyone who depends on it, I know we could. With one word, I could do all of this."

"Bella…there's something I must tell you." Cassandra shifted in her chair uneasily. She took a deep breath before continuing. "Al was here at Christmas. On Christmas Eve to be precise."

"Al was here? Why didn't you telephone me?"

"He only had three days leave and he would have been gone before you could get back. There didn't seem any point, and anyway, I thought it was up to him, rather than me."

"But I haven't heard a word! Is there a letter for me? Did he leave anything for me, a note or something?" Isobel half got up to make for the door, but her mother stopped her a second time.

"No, nothing."

"Not even a Christmas present?"

Her mother compressed her lips and shook her head.

31

Isobel slumped in her chair. Al had been here! And she didn't know anything about it. She would never have gone to Geraint's if she'd known. In those few seconds she realised exactly which man she loved.

"What did he say? Did he say why he hadn't told anyone he was coming?"

"He wanted to surprise you."

"Was he angry I wasn't here? Did you tell him where I was?"

Cassandra nodded.

Isobel put her hands over her face. How stupid to have gone away! Who was she fooling, thinking she could love anyone else? Poor Al. But why hadn't he left a note? Had he come home to tell her he'd fallen for the glamorous Miriam? Oh, if only she'd stayed!

CHAPTER SIX
NORMANDY, FRANCE
MARCH 1942

By early March, the hot topic Bernadette brought back from the weekly market was of the allied bombing of the Renault works at Billancourt, Paris. The three women had sat down to their usual lunch of soup, bread and cheese in the big farmhouse kitchen.

"What is the point of the British destroying our car factories?" Bernadette was incensed about it. "Isn't it bad enough we have the Germans parading their jackboots on our doorsteps?"

"I suppose so the Boche don't build more cars for their war effort. They're in charge of the factories now, don't forget." Lottie lifted the soup pan back on to the hob of the range.

Françoise spooned some soup into the open mouth of her baby son. "I can't bear to think of it. More people will be killed, just like Papa when the Germans bombed his Citroën factory in Paris. All this destruction. I hate it, I hate this war!"

Lottie looked from one woman to another and made her decision. "Bernadette. I know you didn't want me to talk about that delivery…"

Bernadette's shrewd blue eyes locked on to hers. "No, definitely not."

Lottie continued, unabashed. "Nevertheless, I have something in the barn that would make all our lives easier."

Françoise stopped feeding Bertrand and stared at her old penfriend. Only when her little boy started crying for more food, did she turn back to him.

Bernadette held up a calloused hand in warning. "Not when Françoise is here."

"What's going on?" Françoise frowned.

Lottie smiled at her friend. "It's nothing to worry about, honestly. It's just that I have acquired a wireless set.

We could listen to music and get the news before the gossips have twisted it."

"How…?" Françoise raised her eyebrows.

Lottie smiled. "Never mind how, Françoise. Wouldn't you like some entertainment of an evening?"

Françoise smiled back. "Well, yes, that would be lovely!"

Bernadette looked as sour as her cooking apples.

Lottie finished her meal and stood up. "I'll go and get it."

She ran to the barn and scrambled up the ladder. The radio was where she had left it a couple of months ago, wrapped in sacking under a pile of hay. She blew the hay off the top and lifted it up in its hessian shroud. Feeling more excited than she had since seeing Thierry, she bundled it to her chest and went down the ladder with ungainly haste.

"Look!" Lottie placed her burden on the other end of the big kitchen table and whipped off the sack. The radio looked dusty. Françoise handed her a clean cloth and Lottie hurriedly wiped its surfaces, wondering why she had left it so long before using the damn thing.

"Plug it in, plug it in!" Françoise had caught her excitement.

Lottie bent and unplugged the lamp in the corner and took the wireless set across to the wooden trolley next to it. She inserted the two-pin plug into the socket, praying that it would work.

She turned one of the knobs on the front. "Listen! It's still alright!" Crackles and whistles gurgled through the mesh in the centre of the Bakelite box. Lottie twizzled the other dial backwards and forwards, trying to find a station.

Bernadette and Françoise came over and stood transfixed before the radio.

Lottie twirled the knob until the sound of violins floated into the room.

"Music! Oh, it's heaven to hear something civilised again!" Françoise grabbed Lottie by the waist and swung her around.

"Huh, noisy contraption." Bernadette went to the baby, who had started to cry again. "Set the little one off now."

"But Bernadette, we'll be able to get the news at last. Won't that be worth it?" Breathless from dancing, Lottie grinned at her hostess. At last, they were connected to the wider world, to the bigger fight. Perhaps even to Britain!

"You can turn it off while we have our dessert in peace." Bernadette slammed down some bowls on the table and began to ladle out some rice pudding from the range oven.

They ate their puddings in silence. Lottie fumed at the delay in getting news. As soon as Bernadette went outside to check on the goats after their meal, Lottie left clearing up the dishes and put the wireless on again. This time, she managed to locate a station the announcer called 'Radio Paris'.

"Oh, what a difference this radio makes!" Françoise waltzed about the kitchen while the strains of Strauss's *'Blue Danube'* filled the room. Bertrand giggled in her arms as he bounced. Lottie, sitting at the table scraping carrots over a bowl of cold water to make a steamed pudding for later, laughed at their joyful dance.

When the last chords of the waltz finished, Françoise, now out of puff, joined her and settled the baby on her lap, giving him a piece of raw carrot to gnash against his sore gums and then helping Lottie by grating the carrots she'd already cleaned.

"What's this tune?" Lottie stopped her scraping to listen.

"Sounds like *'With My Girlfriend'* but the words are different."

They both stilled their busy hands to concentrate on the music.

35

"Are they singing about England?" Lottie couldn't catch all the words.

"Yes, I think so, and something about the BBC."

Lottie got up and went over to the radio, picked up a pencil and jotted down the lyrics of the simple song.

> '*In the garden of England, deception has flourished.*
> *All the liars of the world speak on the BBC.*
> *As the radio waves welcome it, they tell good lies'.*

"That's outrageous!" Lottie was fuming and switched off the wireless. The mention of the 'garden of England' took her right back to Cheadle Manor. What would Granny have said to this accusation if she'd still been alive?

"Hey! I was enjoying that. Oh, now you've made Bertrand cry. How could you, Lottie? That's the tune of a lovely song, it was *'With My Girlfriend'*, just as I thought."

"Didn't you hear the words they were singing? It had nothing to do with anyone's girlfriend, I can tell you. Listen to this." Lottie read out the words she'd scribbled down.

"Is it true? We haven't listened to the BBC yet – do they tell lies?"

"No! Can't you see, that's the whole point. The Germans must be running Radio Paris, stupid. Haven't you noticed how most of the music is from German composers?" Lottie flung down her pencil.

"Can't say I have, no."

"Oh, Françoise! Sometimes you drive me crazy! This is propaganda put out by the damn Boche."

"Well, I like it. I like hearing decent music again and so does Bertrand." Françoise pouted and picked up her little boy.

"Well, from now on, we're going to listen to the BBC!"

"You can if you like, but you won't catch me listening – it's against the law. If you go putting that on, we could all get rounded up and sent to one of those awful camps." The baby started to whimper. Françoise patted his back. She looked upset too.

Lottie took a deep breath. She could see Françoise was genuinely frightened. "I must listen to it, Françoise, I won't tell you why, but I'll be careful, I promise, and anyway, who would know?"

"Why must you? You're not…oh, Lottie, you're not one of those crazy resisters, are you?"

Before Lottie could answer, Bernadette came in. She looked cold and grumpy. She slipped off her muddy sabot clogs and put her feet into her warm carpet slippers. "What's all this loose talk?"

Françoise turned to her grandmother. "Lottie wants to listen to Radio Londres. She doesn't care that it's forbidden! She'll put us all in danger. You must stop her, Grandmère. Please, it's too big a risk."

"It's a risk we shall have to take, Françoise." Bernadette put a match to the oil lamp, flooding the kitchen with yellow light. She looked directly at her granddaughter.

"But Grandmère, think of little Bertrand."

Bernadette's reply surprised Lottie. "Yes, think of him. Think about his Jewish father. Think about all the other Jews who are being taken away. A dear friend of mine, old Doctor Hoffman, was seized the other day. He's riddled with arthritis and they wouldn't even let him take his cane. He's never hurt a fly in all his long life, and he did many good turns, some to me when I had young children. It's time to grow up, Françoise. We must get rid of the Boche before they get rid of us. We must all take risks from now on, even you."

Lottie let out her breath.

As March blew itself out with a gale and Easter approached, Lottie's resolve not to see Thierry weakened. She was determined to go to his school before the end of term and thought donating eggs to the children for the festivities might serve as a good enough excuse. She didn't tell Bernadette of her idea. The older woman would never condone giving away her produce for free, even if it was Lent.

Her feelings were conflicted at the thought of seeing him again. At times, the knowledge that Thierry loved her, sustained her. At others, it was infuriating. Why hadn't she said more last time she'd seen him? Why had she acquiesced to keeping apart? Why couldn't they love each other and to hell with the consequences? What if they did die? What would have been the point? And yet, if she was captured and tortured and betrayed him, that would be worse, but she had to see him again or she'd go mad.

All these questions buzzed through her head as she cycled as fast as she could between the hedges and ditches that lined the lanes. She only slowed down when she saw a new control post outside the village, manned by four soldiers instead of the normal one or two.

"Halt! Papers please."

Lottie dismounted and fished out her identity card. It was now as battered and worn as she could have wished and looked far more authentic than when Thierry's friend, the enormous Pierre, had forged it. Her French was much improved too - she had even cultivated a local accent. For once, she carried no contraband, having had no commissions issued by Thierry. So, it was a shock when one of the soldiers pulled her off her bike to search her.

"What is this? Why are you searching me?"

38

"New orders. We're searching everyone who enters or leaves the village."

He gave her back her identity card. She snatched it from his fist and shoved it into her pocket. She didn't wait for his permission but climbed back on her bicycle and pedalled away towards Thierry at the school. By the time she arrived, the children were out in the yard, playing as carefree as if there were no soldiers monitoring people's movements.

And there was Thierry. His blonde head covered in its usual black beret, his spectacles catching the glint of the meagre sun trying to pierce the grey clouds.

Lottie leaned her bicycle against the school wall and entered the yard carrying her basket. When Thierry first saw her, his face, so serious before, lit up with a wide smile.

He walked towards her. Lottie's heart, already beating fast from her ride, began to gallop.

"Mademoiselle Perrot. It's good to see you. It's been a long time."

"Monsieur Thibault. Good day to you." She didn't reach for him in front of the children, but her hands itched to hold him. She shoved the spare one into her pocket. "How are you?"

"I'm well." The smile left his face. "I was going to go to the boulangerie today."

"You have a message?"

Thierry looked around quickly to check no-one was listening. Lottie doubted anyone could have heard their low conversation over the children's noisy game of catch. She could barely hear his voice over the screams herself; although, he stood so close, she could feel the warmth from him.

"An instruction."

"Oh?"

"It's the radio. I need to come and set it up for you. It's time we had a gathering of an evening."

It was Lottie's turn to check for eavesdroppers now. "I've already got it going myself."

"Well done!" Thierry looked impressed. "Have you been listening to Radio Londres?"

"No, just Radio Paris, so far. It's hard to find Radio Londres. There always seems to be so much static."

"Ah, I see. You need to change frequency all the time to listen to De Gaulle and the Free French, but believe me, it's worth it. There's some important stuff being broadcast but they don't keep to the same location in case the Boche find it too easily."

Some soldiers marched towards the school gates. Thierry pulled her away to the covered part of the yard, under the eaves of the outside corridor. "I will call at the farmhouse very soon. We will need to reposition the wireless somewhere more hidden perhaps. I need to set it up. I'll bring Pierre."

"But I must tell you something…"

Just then, the soldiers entered the yard. Suddenly, the children's shouts quietened to a hush. They huddled together in groups and watched as the four Germans approached Thierry and Lottie in the corner.

Lottie saw the soldiers heading for them and took her cue. "Here are the eggs for the children, Monsieur Thibault. Be sure they paint them with pretty colours for Easter." Lottie spoke loudly and held out her basket in full view of the soldiers.

Thierry spoke his response clearly too. "Thank you, Mademoiselle. These eggs are a kind gift and will keep the children happy for hours."

They both turned towards the soldiers, now standing before them. Thierry turned to face them. "Can I help you?"

"What is in that basket?"

"This?" Thierry held up Lottie's wicker basket and lifted the muslin cloth covering the eggs.

"Give it to me!"

The soldier seized the basket by the handle and upturned it. All the eggs tumbled out and smashed on to the courtyard. The muslin floated down and stuck to the wet mess.

Lottie's hands flew involuntarily to her face. "How could you?"

The German soldier scrabbled about in the bottom of the basket. He looked at his comrades and shook his head. "Nothing. He turned back to Lottie. "It seems your hens will have to lay more eggs for your Easter celebrations." He shoved the empty basket into her body. "Here, take it back."

He turned to Thierry. "We are still watching you."

A muscle flexed in Thierry's jaw, but he said nothing, just stared, unblinking, at the young German.

The German stared back, as if waiting for Thierry to crack. When he didn't, he grunted to his fellow soldiers and they gave the Hitler salute, turned and marched off in a strict formation that Lottie thought farcical in a schoolyard of children.

As soon as the soldiers had disappeared, Thierry's youngest pupils rushed to his side, clutching at his trouser legs and his coat. Some of the little girls were crying. All of them looked scared.

"How dare they intimidate the little ones." Thierry muttered to Lottie.

"And break all my eggs." She looked at the ground. With so many French mouths hungry it was cruel to see the yolks and albumens of the eggs pooling on the ground, mixing with the dirt. "I'll help you clear it up."

"That is kind, thank you. I must see to the children. Come on now, you lot. No tears, please. Playtime is over anyway." He picked up a bell on the windowsill and rang it lightly. "Form into rows, children, just like you always do."

The children shuffled into file. "Right, in you go. Hang up your coats and sit at your desks. I will help

41

Mademoiselle clean up the broken eggs and be there in one minute. Off you go!"

Lottie shook her head. "No, you go to them, Thierry. I can manage the mess. They need you. All I need is a mop and a bucket."

He reached out then and touched her arm. "Thank you. You are very good. I will come to the farm soon. It will be night-time, so look out for me?"

Lottie gave him a wobbly smile. "I will, but Thierry...." Too late, he had already disappeared inside the school and shut the door. Lottie found a bucket and mop in the outhouse and cleaned up the debris using water from an outside tap.

It wasn't until she was cycling home that she realised she hadn't told him about the extra Germans on the control post.

They didn't stop her on her way back but nodded her through. The two baguettes sticking out of her basket appeared to provide enough evidence of the reason for her trip.

That evening, after supper, when Bertrand was asleep in his cot upstairs and all the chores had been done, the three women sat down to hear an entire concert of Beethoven's Pastoral Symphony. They each listened rapt to the music. Lottie stole peeps at Bernadette who forgot to disguise her foot tapping in time to the beat. She'd closed her eyes and was pretending to sleep but that rhythmic shoe gave her away.

Françoise listened with eyes opened; sometimes they misted up and she wiped away a tear with the corner of her apron.

Lottie followed Bernadette's example and shut her eyes too; she didn't want to look at the over-familiar shabby kitchen with its crocks of stores, its sheaves of herbs hanging in the ceiling, the cracked jugs on hooks above the stone sink, the lines of limp washing hanging above the big range. Lottie wanted instead to remember the pastoral glories of her native Wiltshire.

As the chords trilled around her, they evoked the birds who lived in the trees at Cheadle Manor, the babble of the river flowing between its banks, the willow fronds swishing in its green water. She imagined she was back home again, wandering through the grounds of her old home, all the familiar landmarks unchanged and steadfast. Lottie pictured the grey stone walls of the house, with its three gables pointing skywards, the wide terrace at the front and the steps leading so gracefully down to the sweeping drive that curved down to West Lodge, where Al's mother, Katy Phipps, had grown up. She wondered how he was, indeed where he was, what he was doing. Was he still working at his mother's garage and factory, or had he joined up like so many young men? Pray God he was still alive. That thought jerked her back into the present with a jolt.

She opened her eyes, shocked to find she was still in this French farmhouse in the middle of nowhere, in the middle of a war that never seemed to end. It was hard to sit still after that, hard to imagine herself back in Wiltshire and very hard not to want to see her dear mother and sister. The longing gave her a physical ache in her chest. Lottie got up and put the kettle on the hob. She had to do something, anything, or her feelings would overwhelm her.

Sleep proved elusive that night. Images of home kept intruding on her attempts to relax. It had been so long since she'd seen her family. Long enough to recognise how much she loved them. Not the same way as this new love for Thierry that had consumed her every waking thought for months. Was this the real thing; the sort of love romantics sang about? She'd never felt like this about Al. This electrifying sensation of being fully alive, every cell zinging with energy at his touch. Was that what she had interrupted between Isobel and Al that day in the nursery? If so, she was sorry for it now, for that feeling was the most wonderful thing she'd ever experienced. Now, far from feeling jealous of Isobel and Al's love for each other, she could only wish them well; hope they would each survive this treacherous war and have a happy future together.

And, deep down, she knew that was what she too wanted, with Thierry Thibault and no-one else. At last, she relaxed and fell into a deep, peaceful sleep.

Lottie felt full of energy the next morning and went about her chores singing. Bernadette and Françoise seemed more cheerful too. The sun augmented their mood by shining brightly through scudding white clouds. Everywhere seemed freshly rinsed by the short sprightly showers that punctuated the brightness of the day but never blotted it out for long. Lottie could smell spring in the air and wondered how she'd not noticed how fat the buds on the apple trees had grown.

The day flew by in a flurry of washing brought on by the energising weather. The three women worked together in the small stone washhouse over the washtub and iron. By nightfall they were all tired, but the house smelled renewed and fresh, as if winter had been washed out of it together with the dirty laundry.

"Let's see if there's another concert on, shall we?" Françoise turned the radio on.

They caught the end of the news bulletin. The announcer said, in thrilling tones, "England, like Carthage, will be destroyed!"

Lottie fumed at the lying, aggressive words announced over a public airway. "We'll see about that! How dare they! This is nothing but a propaganda machine." She got up. "I'm going to find Radio Londres."

Then the crisp orderly notes of Bach flowed through the homely kitchen.

Françoise held out her hand. "Oh, please don't change the station now, Lottie."

Lottie gave up and returned to her seat, fuming.

"Is this German too?" Bernadette riddled the fire with her back to Lottie, so she had to strain to catch her words over the music.

"Yes, I'm afraid it is, damn them."

Bernadette turned around. "Suppose it's alright, if you like that sort of thing."

"Oh, I love it!" Françoise sat back on the settle by the fire and put her feet on a stool. "Reminds me of home. Papa loved to listen to Bach on the radio. It's funny, I never thought I would miss him, but I do, far more than Maman."

"Have you heard from Mireille at all?" Lottie resigned herself to listening to the exquisite music and tried to find a more comfortable way of sitting on her hard chair.

"Not a single word."

"Pah! You're better off without that traitor. She might be my daughter, but she's betrayed us all going off with that fat pig of a German." Bernadette picked up her knitting and the needles clacked together out of time with the beat of Bach's violins.

"I bet she's living it up in Paris, though. That German officer looked pretty high-up to me." Françoise sighed. "I long to wear a pair of silk stockings again and I would love to get my hair done properly in a salon."

Lottie smiled. "I think you would have to pay a very heavy price for that, and I don't mean in cash."

"Oh, I know. It's just that this war is so dreary."

"Well, at least it's springtime again. It's been such a lovely day." Lottie looked out of the window. "And it's getting dark much later now, I'd better close the curtains."

A shadow, darker than the twilight, moved outside. Lottie held her breath. "Listen! I think there's someone out there."

"Where?" Françoise sat upright, her eyes wide with fear.

Bernadette laid down her knitting and swivelled round to face the door. Lottie got up and switched off the radio. If it was Germans, there was no point displaying their

45

wireless. It wasn't illegal to own one yet, but she'd still rather they didn't know they had a set, even if they were listening to Radio Paris, their wretched propaganda machine. She threw some of the clean sheets she'd just ironed over the Bakelite set.

They all listened to the sudden silence.

"Are you sure you saw something?" Françoise whispered.

"You must have imagined it." Bernadette too spoke in low tones.

Lottie went to the door. "I'll check." She opened it a crack and peered out. A shadow separated itself from the wall that divided the yard from the orchard.

"Who's there?" Lottie spoke into the void.

"Only me. Don't tell me Charlotte Perrot is frightened?"

"Thierry!"

She couldn't help it. She quickly shut the door behind her and ran towards him, grabbed his hands and pulled him close for a kiss. For a few seconds, he kissed her back with all the passion she could have wished. So much for keeping apart!

"Oh, Thierry. It's so good to see you but why have you come? Aren't you afraid of being seen?"

"Of course. I don't mind admitting when I'm afraid." He laughed and kissed her nose. "I tried the barn, but it was all locked up for the night. Your curtains weren't drawn so I could see into the house. You all looked very contented. I'm sorry to disturb such a tranquil scene."

Lottie chuckled. "I'm a lot more contented now you're here."

He squeezed her hands but before he could say more, the kitchen door of the farmhouse opened wide and light flooded the yard, exposing them in its oblong beam.

"Who is that, Charlotte? Who is there?"

Lottie tugged at his hand. "Come on, you'd better meet Bernadette. Brace yourself."

46

CHAPTER EIGHT
ENGLAND
APRIL 1942

Far below him, Al could see tips of green on the trees squaring off the fields into a neat patchwork. Signs of spring at last. When he was flying over countryside like this, he often reflected how you'd never think there was a war on. The seasons rolled from one into another, just as they always had; crops were sown, mown and harvested in the normal way. Probably more so, as more and more land was being carved up to feed the hungry, import-starved nation, but you couldn't really see those subtle incursions from the air.

With his bird's eye view, he knew the serenity below was an illusion. Flying over the bombed cities revealed the devastation of Hitler's blitzes. There was no denying that Britain was under siege when you saw the extent of the damage in those urban areas, with whole streets reduced to rubble, factories flattened, fires still burning and spewing black smoke from bomb sites.

Since going home on Christmas Eve, an engagement ring in his pocket and his heart on fire with excitement about seeing Isobel, Al had done nothing but work, work, work. He didn't mind, either. For one thing, he was as determined as the next man to see off the Krauts but also it meant he didn't have time to think too much.

He'd had one letter from Isobel. One. He'd written to her first, demanding an explanation of her absence; insisting that she explain why she had gone to Geraint Lloyd's bloody great mansion in the Welsh hills without even telling him. He was still angry, all these months later. No-one would have known, at least Al hoped not. He joined in with the general camaraderie at White Waltham. It wouldn't do to let the side down by moping about when everyone was working just as hard; when tragedies were quietly absorbed and mopped up, but the grieving staff carried on regardless. Everyone had their sad story to tell. Sometimes accidents did happen, pilots were lost, but more often it was second-hand. Someone's wife, mother, sister, brother or father had been killed, wounded, bombed out of their homes or fighting on foreign soil, blown up in some ship on the Atlantic or Pacific oceans. The whole bloody world was at it since Pearl Harbour got bombed in December. None of them had heard from Lottie since 1940, two whole years ago. Was she the victim of one of those RAF bombing raids?

If you didn't keep cheerful, keep going, sometimes Al thought everyone would all come tumbling down together.

Today, he was ferrying a Spitfire up to the Midlands. He'd been doing a lot of that lately, sometimes going as far north as Scotland. He loved flying this little plane; it was still his favourite. He hadn't yet got enough hours to try for something bigger. A lot of ATA pilots were ferrying bombers which were then flown over the channel by the RAF to decimate a German city. The RAF had been targeting Hamburg lately and the Luftwaffe were retaliating by bombing the most beautiful cities in England during their so-called Baedeker raids. So far Woodbury was untouched, but Al feared for its beautiful cathedral.

He tried not to think about the devastation caused by the RAF on German families. A lot of people said it served them right – that they'd started it and the ruination of the most historic towns in England only hardened opinion – but Al was damn glad he didn't have to put his thumb on the trigger button to release a bomb on streets and houses with families inside.

And that brought his thoughts back to Isobel and that one letter she'd written.

"Dearest Al,

I'm sure you were surprised to find me not at home at Christmas. If I'd known you were coming, I would never have gone to Geraint's."

Al remembered how it had smarted, the way she had written Geraint, not Mr Lloyd, not anything remotely formal. Geraint. What a stupid bloody Welsh name that was. He'd never heard of anyone called anything so daft.

"Thing is, I needed a little break from all the farm work and Geraint is so kind."

Oh yes, Al could imagine exactly how 'kind' Geraint had been. Rich as a king, twice as handsome, but old as the hills he lived amongst.

"I did some painting while I was there. The Welsh hills are stunningly beautiful, and Geraint has the most wonderful studio, full of paints and brushes and the best paper I've ever used. We went for long walks and then came back and worked in the studio together. It was a very quiet holiday. Geraint's father wasn't well, so it wasn't all wild parties! His mother is nice - gentle and kind, like her son.

It did me good to get away, have time to think about things, you know.

The hospital takes up a lot of Mummy's time these days, that and her Red Cross work. She still gets very upset about Lottie. We both miss her more than ever and wish, more than anything, we could find out if she's alright.

Farmer Stubbs had an order from the Ministry of Agriculture to plough up his water meadow by the river – do you remember? Where we used to have picnics. I got the short straw and had to do the ploughing on the old Fergie tractor. I kept thinking of us as children there. Seems a long time ago now, doesn't it? It will be so upsetting when there is wheat instead of wildflowers come the summer. Unbearable, really.

49

This war has made us all grow up all-of-a-sudden and I must think about what the future holds, Al. Think what to do for the best – for Mummy and Cheadle Manor and everyone who relies upon it.

Please write and tell me your news, Al. I'm so sorry I was away when you came home.

Take good care of yourself, won't you?
Love, Bella."

He knew the words off by heart, he'd gone over and over them so many times. Ferrying planes here, there and everywhere meant there was many a long evening and night in some dreary digs with too much time to fill. The letter was grubby now and frayed at the edges.

'*Love, Bella*' – she used to sign off with kisses and *all* her love. And what did '*thinking about the future*' mean, exactly? Marriage to that geriatric business tycoon and spend the rest of her days painting flowers?

Below him, Al could see the aerodrome tarmac. At least he wouldn't have to land on grass today, like he did at White Waltham. The wet spring had turned the runway into a quagmire. He tipped the wing and began to circle, ready to land, glad to focus on the mechanics of flight instead of whatever the future held.

He made a good landing, the Spitfire was such an easy plane to fly, and signed off the chit. There was only one bloke left in the office. "You'd better get on the bus into the nearest town. Afraid you're stuck out tonight, mate. Your Spitfire is the last plane in today."

Al looked out at the darkening sky and knew he had to admit defeat.

The clerk shut his ledger. "Not much left to eat in the mess now, neither. Suggest you find a pub. The White Horse is supposed to be alright. It's where we always send the ATA pilots."

Al walked past the mess and ARP huts, the hangar for the taxi aircraft and the muddle of other buildings and shelters that comprised the aerodrome, to the waiting bus near the front gate by the periphery wire fence.

"White Horse is it, son?" The bus driver looked as tired as he was.

"Seems so."

"Climb on board, then. You're the last one tonight."

Al sat down in the seat behind the driver. There were a few other people on the bus, but he didn't feel like talking after he'd nodded his hello. They all seemed to be ground crew who knew each other anyway.

He got off outside The White Horse pub and waved goodbye to the bus driver. The streets were deserted and black as pitch. His footsteps echoed on the wet pavement. Inside, the pub smelled of the usual stale beer and cigarette smoke. Al went up to the bar and lit a Woodbine.

He flicked the match on to the rough wooden floor and took off his cap. "Pint of bitter and a room for the night, please."

"You're in luck, mate. There's only one room left. It's a bit small, mind, not much more than a box room. That do you?"

"I'm so whacked I'd sleep on this bar." Al drew on his cigarette.

The barman laughed. "No call for that, lad. Here's your pint and the key to the room. ATA, aren't you?"

"That's right. Cheers." Al sipped his brew and brushed the froth from his lip with the back of his hand.

The barman wiped a wet glass dry and put it on the shelf behind him. "Got another one of your lot here tonight."

"Oh yes? Might be someone I know."

"A young lady, it is. I expect she'd be glad of some company. She's over there tucked behind the inglenook. Looks proper lonely, if you ask me." The barman winked and dried another empty glass.

Al looked over towards where the barman had nodded. In the corner of the smoky room, he could see someone in the same uniform, but she had her head turned

51

away. It looked like she was trying to avoid some unwanted attention from some blokes in working clothes, their cloth caps still on their greasy heads. He got up and went over to her.

The young woman turned around, a frown on her face. "I told you, I'm quite happy sitting on my own."

"If I'd known that, Miriam, I wouldn't have come over." Al put his pint down on the table in front of her.

"Al! Am I glad to see you!"

CHAPTER NINE
NORMANDY, FRANCE
APRIL 1942

Lottie lifted her face to the sun, blinking at its radiant beam through the apple blossom one late spring morning. The orchard had never looked lovelier. The flowery branches almost touched each other with their pink petals, making the perfect canopy overhead. The dappled sunlight flitted over her face; her skin soaked it up, greedy for its healing rays after the abstinence of the interminable, dark winter.

She was checking for stray eggs laid by the hens clucking around in the grass. She watched them tip up their backsides, showing off their frilly skirts as they scratched the ground, cleaning it of grubs and worms and gorging themselves on the fat harvest. Their contented clucking only added to the peaceful scene. The goats were in the next field, equally happy scrunching at the hedgerow and making the most of the spring glut.

Lottie felt replete too. She had never worked so hard or so long but also had never felt so connected to the earth, to the seasons, to the weather; understanding that a storm could undo your harvest, a lack of rain ruin your goat's milk yield; a destructive wind could knock your sweet chestnuts off their tree before they were ripe; worms might eat the apples before you'd turned them into the heady cider that would make the hardships recede through your laughter. No, she had not known then, in her previous privileged and sheltered life, what it was to be alive, really alive, knowing your hard work ensured your survival.

She listened to Radio Londres every night at nine o'clock, puzzling over the inexplicable secret coded messages and wondering what on earth they could mean. Sometimes she practised memorising them in case it was ever needed, as Thierry hinted on the rare occasions when he joined them and sat next to her on the settle, thigh to thigh.

Lottie had found her soulmate in Thierry. She could have settled down here in Normandy, in the countryside she had grown to love as much as him. She would have been happy to bear his children and put down roots in this fertile soil. It astonished her to know this.

But the Nazis had got in the way. Now, more than ever, she hated them for this. She hated them anyway for their jackbooted arrogance, their sweeping away the lives of people who didn't conform to their ridiculous notion of beauty and perfection, their irrational wicked hatred of the Jews, the Poles, the Russians; anyone, basically, who got in their way of stomping across territories that didn't belong to them. Oh yes, she hated them alright.

Above her, from the direction of the local Carpiquet airbase, four German planes roared in formation, heading for England. Their plumes of smoke cut through the azure sky, polluting it with noise and fumes. How many bombs did they carry? Every clear day they headed out, laden with bombs, to kill and maim her fellow countrymen. Sometimes she was profoundly glad of heavy rain and low cloud.

The next day at dawn, she cycled into the village and went, as usual, across the square to see her closest friend.

"It's started." Madame Leroy spoke in low tones in her kitchen at the back of the bakery.

Lottie watched as her plump friend kneaded dough with quick, fat fingers.

"What has?"

"The trials in Caen. Trials! Pah! There is no French judge presiding over our fellow countrymen but that damn Feldenkommandant."

"Oh, how can it be happening that these Krauts can hold the rule of law over us?"

"Because they're the ones with the guns."

Lottie simply nodded at this truth. The white dough looked springier now, as if it had a life of its own. Lottie thought it must be very heavy to pull around like that.

Madame Leroy grunted, whether from effort or disgust was unclear. "That Tirel girl was stupid to give the papers to her collabo neighbour, Madame Lefevre. I heard the cow had links to the secret German police. You can't trust anyone these days." Madame gave Lottie a piercing stare. "No-one – do you hear? Even the walls have ears."

"I know it, Madame."

"Never forget." Madame slapped the dough, already swollen in size, and covered it with a cotton cloth. She turned around to stoke the fire in the massive oven but froze as a shadow darkened the glass in the back door.

Lottie stiffened instinctively as Madame quietly closed the stove up against the bright flames and, with a lightness of foot that belied her weight and the poker firmly gripped in her hand, she tiptoed towards the door and stood behind it. Although it was early and the bakery had not yet opened, the April dawn had long since broken into hopeful pastels. Lottie reached for the sharp knife lying on the counter and watched, horrified, as the doorknob turned silently clockwise in its shaft.

Madame stood by the side of the door, the poker raised above her grey head, her eyes, within their folds of fat, trained on its handle.

The door opened a crack and a familiar face, a beloved face, peered into the room. Taking in the scene in one glance, Thierry smiled, slipped inside and shut the door behind him, before bursting into laughter.

Furious, Lottie cried out. "Why are you laughing at us?"

She could see he was struggling to straighten his face. "Because you both look so fierce! I wouldn't rate my chances if either of you'd thought I was one of the Boche!"

Madame lowered her poker but thrust its point in his face, before putting it down. "Bloody cheek." She kissed him on both sides of his smiling face. "No-one following you?"

That wiped the smile away. Thierry shook his head. "No, but I can't be long. I have an important message for Jean." He looked across at Lottie. "I'm glad you're here." His eyes conveyed how much. "Did you hear a message about cutting curly leeks on Radio Londres last night?"

"Actually, yes there was one that said that."

"Aha, good. Can you get to the mill this morning?"

Lottie, resisting the strong impulse to go across the room and kiss him, remained resolutely sitting on the chair by the table. Aware of Madame's beady eyes darting between them, screwed up with speculation, Lottie nodded assent.

"Good. Tell him, 'It's on.'"

"Is that it?" Lottie had expected something complicated.

"It's enough. He'll know. Can you go now, before anyone's about?"

"Of course." She stood up.

It was Madame Leroy's turn to smile. She looked from one to the other. "I have to go into the shop for five minutes. Keep an eye on the fire, won't you?"

She quietly left the room, having given each of them an encouraging wink.

Before the door had fully shut, they were in each other's arms and exchanging snatched, passionate kisses.

Drawing breath after a few heady moments, Lottie glanced back at the door to the shop. "How did she know? You haven't said anything about us to her, have you?"

Thierry shook his head. "Didn't need to, she's no fool, but it's dangerous if our feelings for each other are so transparent. It compromises our safety and therefore everyone else's. Listen, there's a big operation on tonight. When you've visited the mill, go straight home to the farm. Speak to no-one. If we can bring this off, you'll soon find out what we've been up to."

"Can't I do more?

"No. It's all in hand. I'm not even directly involved myself, just a link in the chain. I must go. No-one must know I've been here. Even this is risky. I must get back to the school immediately."

"Yes, go." She pushed him away, towards the door and locked it behind him.

As if waiting for the sound, Madame Leroy returned. To her surprise, she hugged Lottie hard against her soft bulk. When she released her, Madame nodded and looked at her through misty eyes. "Take even more care, from now on, mon petit-chou. You have much to lose."

Lottie left shortly afterwards, the first baguette of the day still hot and fragrant in her bicycle basket. The control post on the bridge didn't stop her. Either the soldier had just begun his shift, or he'd been up all night; in either case, he was barely awake and let her pass unmolested. She pedalled past him at the most sedate pace she could manage. As soon as she was out of sight, she forced her muscles to pump harder, speeding along the lanes between the hedges and careering wildly down the hill to the river valley where the flour mill nestled. When she relayed her brief message to Jean, his little black eyes narrowed until they were almost slits, then he clapped her hard on the shoulder and kissed her forehead.

"Thank you, little one, now go quickly, and tell no-one else what you have told me." He turned her round and shoved her gently in the back towards her bike where it leant against his rickety gate as if drunk. "Go on! And remember, not a word to a living soul."

A couple of nights later, Lottie heard the hoot of an owl near the farmhouse. Knowing this to be Thierry's signal, Lottie, always listening out for him, let him in.

He turned first to the oldest woman in the room. "Good evening, Bernadette."

"Humph."

"Good evening, Françoise."

"Hello, Thierry. Come to listen to the radio?"

"Yes, I'm hoping to hear some good news."

"I'll leave you to it. This young man's past his bedtime." Françoise mounted the stairs with Bertrand in her arms.

"Huh, good news is in short supply." Bernadette heaved herself up from her armchair and plonked the kettle on the hob. "Tisane?"

Thierry nodded. "Thank you." He took off his black beret and trench coat and laid them over the arm of the settle where Lottie sat.

"Charlotte?"

Lottie moved up on the settle to make room for him but left her hand palm down on the wood. Thierry took the hint and slid his over hers, interlinking the fingers.

Bernadette had just served up her favourite lime flower tea when the music faded, and the newsreader made his announcements.

The newsreader intoned. "*A dozen soldiers of the Wehrmacht and other servicemen on leave were killed today when the Maastricht to Cherbourg train was derailed by sabotage at Airan while travelling between Mézidon and Caen.*"

Thierry leapt up, spilling his tea and shouting. "Yes! We did it!" He pulled Lottie to her feet and danced around the kitchen.

"So that was what was 'on'!" Lottie laughed with him as they cavorted around the cluttered kitchen.

A wail from upstairs drew Françoise back down to the kitchen, muttering, "No need to wake Bertrand," before she returned to cajole him back to sleep.

"It's a good job Françoise didn't hear you admitting your involvement, Thierry." Lottie looked at Bernadette sitting by the fire. To her amazement she was laughing too and, most extraordinary of all, clapping her bony hands together.

Thierry stayed to hear the Radio Londres nonsensical messages but, as soon as they were over, stood up and said he must get back to his flat over the school.

He bent down and kissed Bernadette, who uncharacteristically patted his back and smiled all over again. Lottie had never seen her smile twice in one week, let alone in one evening.

"Say goodnight to Françoise for me, Bernadette?" He put on his beret and shrugged on his overcoat.

"I will. The baby must have kept her upstairs which is just as well. It's been a good day, teacher." Bernadette dismissed him with a nod.

Outside in the orchard, Lottie and Thierry dawdled till they heard Bernadette clomp upstairs. There was a bench under the oldest apple tree, made from one of its sisters. It had become their friend. Between kisses, they talked about what they'd heard.

Lottie laid her head in the convenient crook of Thierry's shoulder. "So, the Germans are minus twelve soldiers, hey?"

He stroked the nape of her neck where her dark hair curled upwards. "It's a good, round number."

"I hope there won't be reprisals."

"There will be. God knows how many."

She looked up at him. "Take extra care, won't you?"

"Of course."

"Were those messages from Radio Londres tonight about the sabotage of the train at Airan?"

"The other ones about curly leeks were."

"But Thierry, it all sounds like nonsense, it's hard to tell which message is important."

"Most of it is. Puts the Boche off the scent." He sucked the lobes of her ears.

Lottie groaned with pleasure and inhaled the night air. "Scent. Can you smell the apple blossom?

"I can smell you."

They pressed their bodies together. Their lips urgently searching for more.

"Charlotte, you are making me crazy." He pushed her away, took a deep breath. "We must control ourselves."

She grabbed him back. "Why"

"Because…oh Charlotte, my darling, because…"

She kissed his neck.

He got up and retreated two feet away from her. "Because we are at war, because we cannot please ourselves, because…"

Lottie paused. Her breath was coming thick and fast and her heart pumped blood loudly in her ears. She dragged her eyes away from his earnest face and looked instead at the apple trees, their few latent last buds opening into shy flowers, silvered by the moonlight. She remembered that frightened Jewish family in Jean's barn; the slewed broadcasts by Radio Paris; Madame Leroy's horror about her niece's suspected expulsion to the hated camps; Françoise's fear every time she heard of the Germans' interrogation of anyone Jewish; that dreadful explosion at the Citroën factory that had denied Françoise her father's security. Oh, so many things to remember, to resent, one piled on top of one another: the children in the school intimidated by German soldiers marching through their playtime; Thierry's dear face bruised by their fists; that little Jewish widow and her poor, terrified children as they were snatched away to who knew what ghastly fate.

Lottie stood up, shoved her hands in her coat pockets, took a deep breath of the cold night air, and turned back to face the man she loved.

"You are right, my love, I'm sad to say." She gave a little smile.

He put his hand out to comfort her.

"No, I mean it, you are right." Lottie couldn't stop the tears that ran down from her eyes to her chin. "We must rid ourselves of this filth that pollutes us. They are truly evil. One day, I hope, one day…" she gulped down her tears.

60

"One day, Thierry, my love, we will have time to love each other, but until that day, we must not be swayed by anything, anything at all, that might stop us getting rid of this wicked occupation."

Thierry remained two feet away from her. "It's true, that's absolutely true. Today, we have won a little tiny battle but not the war. We must fight now with every sinew we possess. But, know this, my beautiful girl, if we come through this, I will never, ever, let you out of my sight again."

She reached out her hand to touch his arm, but he had already merged into the trees and the black night swallowed him up.

CHAPTER TEN
NORMANDY, FRANCE
MAY 1942

To Lottie's complete surprise and delight, Thierry turned up again the following evening. Her pleasure at seeing him quickly evaporated when he relayed the news.

"Two detainees at Caen prison have been shot by the Boche. Up against a wall in a closed courtyard."

"What excuse did they give?" Lottie felt cold.

"Do they need one anymore?" Bernadette folded her arms.

Thierry pulled off his beret and stuffed it in his pocket. "Simply for being Communists. Apparently, that's enough these days. Of course, it's all to do with derailing the train."

"We knew there would be reprisals." Lottie sat down at the settle, hoping he'd join her.

Thierry nodded. "That's not all. There's a new notice up. Joy is now forbidden in the form of sport, spectacles or festivals; all the cafes and restaurants must be shut by six o'clock – even though we run on German time these days - and the curfew now starts at seven thirty of an evening."

"But Thierry, it's already eight o'clock!"

He grinned at Lottie. "It's worth the risk to see you."

Bernadette cleared her throat noisily and turned away to poke unnecessarily at the already bright fire.

Lottie was hoping, despite her brave words only the night before, Thierry would seize the opportunity to come and sit by her on the settle, but he stayed standing in the middle of the room and his face rapidly returned to its former solemn state.

"There's more. In St Germain-en-Laye they have ordered the killing of thirty so-called malefactors – by which they mean Communists or Jews."

"On what grounds?" Bernadette turned back to face him.

"Because of the train derailment. If they can't round them up within three days, they're upping it to eighty murders plus the deportation of a thousand others to just as certain a death, though perhaps slower, to the Eastern camps."

"What about in Caen?"

"God knows. They're brewing up for more there, I'm sure."

"So many!" Lottie clutched her stomach; it felt like it had been punched.

"However, I have some good news, although you might not agree." Finally, Thierry sat down, but not next to Lottie; he took a hard chair by the table. "We're going to do it again."

"Do what?" Bernadette and Lottie spoke together.

Thierry shrugged. "Derail the train. Can't let the bastards win."

"But the reprisals!" Lottie was shocked at this news.

"Isn't it just going to escalate the killings?" Bernadette went to the table and sat next to Thierry.

Thierry spread his hands. "What would you rather do? Roll over and have them walk all over us?"

Lottie got up and joined them round the table. "What can we do?"

Thierry reached out and clutched her hand, squeezed it hard. "Can you be a lookout? I'm directly involved this time and will be laying the fuses."

"Of course."

"She is too young." Bernadette looked from one to the other.

"Levassseur was twenty-two when he died yesterday." Thierry's jaw was set.

Lottie took a deep breath. "I'll be careful, Bernadette."

Bernadette grunted. "You'd better be."

63

Lottie squirmed on the hard, damp ground. A stone dug into her shinbone and she moved her leg to one side to avoid it. The limestone chipping, a spillage from the train track, rolled noisily down the embankment and settled at Thierry's feet. He looked up from uncoiling the fuse wire, scowling, and shook his head in annoyance. Lottie cursed; it would have been better to let the sharp edges of the stone cut her leg raw rather than compromise his safety. She lay still, holding her breath, but nothing happened, thank goodness.

She watched Thierry work away below her, his fingers quick and sure. She fingered the trigger of the rifle laid out in front of her, wishing her own hand was as confident.

The moon silvered the landscape, picking out the metal train tracks as they snaked around the bend towards the tunnel. Other men were busy inside it, laying the sticks of dynamite. The train was due just after dawn, before the curfew lifted. That would be the dangerous time, they had agreed, as they had cycled together the thirty kilometres here in the sunlit hours to join the others. Thierry had wobbled at first on his ancient pushbike, borrowed from a parent at his school. He'd joked that he hadn't ridden one since he was a child.

Lottie had forgotten her choking fear for a few moments as she laughed at him huffing and puffing along the road in anything but a straight line. "It's all about balance! Look ahead, not down, and fix your eyes on something in the distance. Just focus!"

Thierry, for once at a disadvantage, had sworn. "Just focus, she says! Huh." But it had worked and soon he was keeping pace with her and they sped along, side by side, in the May sunshine.

"How good this feels." Lottie glanced across at him.

"Yes, doesn't it?"

"If only we were going on a Sunday picnic."

64

Thierry grimaced. "This is going to be anything but a picnic."

After the curfew had fallen, they had spent the short summer night sheltering, with five other resistance fighters, in a work-shed alongside the track. One of the other men had picked the lock and replaced the padlock on the door handle to look as if it was still firmly shut. Thierry had hidden their bicycles in the lean-to on the side of the wooden hut and the others had parked a delivery van in the lee of the hut towards the woods. They had dozed fitfully on the earthen floor, taking it turns to keep watch. Lottie still had bits of the greasy dust in her hair and hoped it wouldn't show once the sun came up and they had to cycle all the way back, past a couple of sentry posts they couldn't avoid. The group of Communists had brought a rifle for each of them. Lottie listened carefully while Louis, their elderly leader, had shown her how to use it.

A rustling sound startled her. It was coming from the trees behind her. Moving gingerly and very slowly, she rolled sideways towards the noise and pointed the rifle in its direction. A calm descended upon her and her fingers, so uncertain before, became still and steady as they rested on the trigger. Suddenly, a bird flew out of the hawthorn tree, flapping its wings and making such a racket in the pre-dawn chilly air, it sounded as loud as if her gun had actually fired.

Another bird squawked alarm and its cousins answered from a different tree. Lottie narrowed her eyes and peered through the sight along the barrel of the old rifle. She scanned the whole copse of trees that ran parallel to the train track. Her lips compressed into a thin line of concentration; every muscle tightened, ready for action.

A fox crept stealthily along the tree line, its eyes darting to left and right, its nose twitching at her scent. It stood for a moment, staring in Lottie's direction, then slunk off and disappeared between the tree trunks. Lottie let out her breath. Several pairs of wings from the tree branches fluttered back into repose. Silence returned and she let her shoulders relax. After several minutes, she carefully turned around to check on the fuse-laying operation. The other men, all strangers to her, all Communists, were walking back towards Thierry, bent double, their boots almost silent on the grass verge. They joined Thierry who fiddled with the detonator. She couldn't catch the terse, whispered exchanges. They seemed to be arguing. How stupid! This was no time for debate. Eventually, Thierry handed over the square box to a smaller man, bent with age, who withdrew into the bushes next to the trainline. The others dispersed up into the trees and Thierry joined her up on the embankment.

"Damn fool!" He muttered as he joined her.

"Aren't we all?"

"Old Louis insisted on pulling the plunger himself. It's the most vulnerable job. Once the dynamite ignites, he'll be closest to the wreckage and his old legs can't clamber up this steep incline as fast as a younger man's."

"Did you want to do it?"

"It would be more sensible."

"Louis is right. He's had his life. Ours is still ahead." Lottie could have kissed Louis for his sacrifice, but Thierry was fuming.

"He'll never get away quick enough."

"It's his choice, Thierry."

They lay there for an hour or more. The birds began to sing the morning into life, unaware of the drama they were about to witness.

The sun displaced the pale moon, its stronger light exposing them to anyone who cared to look up from the track. With mutual silent consent, they slipped back behind the grassy slope and retreated to the cover of the trees, where they had left their bicycles.

Lottie felt the train first through the faint trembling of the earth beneath her. She clutched Thierry's arm and made him lay a flat palm against the soil. He looked at her and nodded. Then she heard it chugging along. After a few more moments, the noise of the engine became muffled as it entered the tunnel.

The dynamite exploded a split second later and the earth beneath them shuddered with the aftershock. There was a horrible screeching sound of metal on metal from the wheels skidding on the tracks. Louis's grey head appeared a little way off and urgent hands reached out hauling him up the embankment.

"I must look!"

"No, Thierry! You heard the explosion. We know it's worked." She reached for him but only caught the leg of his trousers as he scrambled up the grassy slope.

"I must see if the train caught it!"

Lottie snaked forward on her stomach after him and peered over the ridge. Great plumes of smoke poured out of the tunnel and through a hole in its roof where the bricks had blown right off, leaving an open hole to serve as a chimney for the choking black whorls of spent fuel and burning carriages.

"Eh, voila, you scum!" Thierry whooped, shaking his rifle at the wreckage.

"Shut up! Come back down."

Lottie slithered back down the slope and Thierry, after a second's hesitation, followed her on his backside.

She ran for the trees, slinging her gun across her back on its strap and grabbing her bicycle. The ground was rough with clumps of couch grass dotted about. She pushed her bike along its bumpy surface, looking round to check Thierry was behind her. The others ran towards the butcher's van that took the best local meat to the Germans at Carpiquet airbase every week. The van stood waiting, hidden by the work-shed in the opposite direction, its insignia roughly covered up with a canvas cover, strapped around its roof and sides, its two back doors now wrenched open by Louis for his companions to pile inside. The driver, Sebastien, was already at the wheel and revving the engine. The van sped off before the back doors were fully shut.

Thierry had caught up with her now. "We could cycle between the train tracks - it would be quicker."

"Don't be crazy! They'd spot us a mile off." Lottie caught her foot on a tree root. Sharp pain shot through her ankle.

"Ouch." She halted suddenly and the solid tyres of Thierry's decrepit old pushbike rammed into her knees, making her fall to the ground.

As Thierry stooped over her, shots rang out in the direction of their Communist friends.

"Oh my God! They've spotted them. We haven't killed all the Krauts, then." Thierry pulled her up to her feet. "We must run, my love. Can you?"

Lottie put a tentative foot to the ground. Again, the pain shot through her calf muscle. She nodded.

"It's not broken, is it?"

She shook her head. "No, just a sprain. I'll manage. Come on!"

The gunshots sounded louder, nearer now. They dragged their bikes and plunged into the woodland as a bullet whistled over their heads.

"Merde! They must have seen us."

"No, I don't think so." Thierry looked back. "We are out of sight - they are just shooting randomly. They don't care if an innocent farmer takes a hit too. Bastards."

A little path, well-trodden by wooden sabots and working boots appeared in the distance and they headed straight for it. "Must be for the railway workers."

"But won't it lead to the station?"

"Doesn't matter." Thierry leapt on to his bicycle seat and started peddling like mad. "The more people we're amongst, the better.

The pain in Lottie's ankle diminished fractionally when she got on her bike and took the weight off her foot. It was agony to push down on the pedal with the injured leg but hugely satisfying to be able to go much faster away from the sound of the bullets and the guttural shouts of the enraged German soldiers.

"We can't be seen carrying rifles." Thierry glanced across at her.

"We might need them!"

"No, chuck them away into these bushes."

Lottie put one foot to the ground, her good one, wriggled the rifle from around her torso and threw it as far as she could into some blackberry bushes.

They cycled fast for a couple of kilometres before ending up at the messy end of the local train station amongst the engineering sheds. There was a swarm of German uniformed soldiers milling about on the platform ahead.

"Thierry! Look! They are searching for us."

"This way." Thierry veered off away from the shield of the enormous sheds down a narrow pathway at the back of some workers houses.

Sweat beaded Lottie's forehead under her hair. Although she had abandoned her rifle, she had a stitch across her chest where its strap would have been. "We need a story. What have we been doing? There's bound to be a sentry post on the edge of town."

"We can say we were going to my parents' house in Caen to tell them we're engaged." Thierry grinned at her.

"Really?"

"Why not? That's what I would like to do."

"Honestly?"

Thierry took one hand off his handlebars and laid it on his chest. His bicycle veered into the middle of the narrow lane. "Never said anything truer or closer to my heart."

"But you haven't asked me to marry you yet!"

"Will you?"

"Do you really mean it?" Every bone and sinew in Lottie's body had been aching and willing her to stop cycling but now she felt no pain anywhere, not even in her sprained ankle.

Thierry stopped smiling and looked at her solemnly. "I do."

"Then, yes, oh yes, please."

His face broke out into that transformative grin. "I'm the happiest man alive!" He zoomed ahead and stuck both his legs out to the side.

Lottie laughed and, for a moment, forgot they were on the run from lethal soldiers with guns. The sound of tyres screeching around a street corner from the direction of the town quickly reminded her of the real situation.

"Come on! Pedal faster. We must get to the first road check before word gets out." Thierry pulled his legs back in and stood up on the pedals as the little lane rose before them.

Lottie was feeling the effects of yesterday's long ride. It was hard to ignore the cramp in her thighs as the gradient increased.

The path broadened out and joined a proper road. Ahead stood a sentry hut and two armed guards tramped the short distance from one side of the road to another. A red and white striped wooden barrier divided the two men and barred their way all too effectively.

They both slowed as they approached the guards. "Halt!"

One of the men held up his hand, his palm flat and vertical. The other soldier shifted his rifle to his shoulder and pointed the barrel at Thierry.

Lottie was sure her ankle had swollen to twice its normal size, but she was determined not to betray her pain by as much as a flicker.

One of the soldiers barked. "Papers!"

Thierry pulled out his identity card easily from his top pocket, but Lottie's fingers were clumsy, and she fumbled with hers.

"Papers! Schnell!"

"I…I'm sorry."

The barrel of the rifle shifted to her, making her hand even more unsteady.

"What is the problem? Why can't you find your card?"

The soldier stared at Thierry hard, looking at his picture and back at his face far more times than was necessary.

"What is your business?"

Thierry stepped in front of Lottie. "We're on the way to Caen, to visit my parents."

"You!" The soldier ignored him and carried on staring at Lottie. She felt herself flush to the roots of her hair; hair she knew carried the marks of that greasy work shed floor. Did she have mud on her boots and grass on her clothes? Why hadn't she checked? What a fool! She'd been too busy gloating on her first proposal of marriage from the man she now adored, standing steadfastly beside her. She looked at him; his eyes implored her to speak while her numb fingers fiddled with the buttons of her coat.

"It's, it's true. We're going to my boyfriend's house. We've just got engaged, you see."

"Humph. What's the address of his parents?"

Thierry piped up. "140 Rue du Marché."

The soldier wheeled round. "I didn't ask you!"

Lottie nodded. "That's right, Rue du Marché. I haven't met them before, you see, so I'm a little nervous."

"You're getting married and you've never met his parents before?"

"It's all been rather sudden." Lottie trailed off, knowing she sounded pathetic. She attempted a smile.

"Where do you live?"

Lottie wondered why he didn't just wait until she found her papers. "At my grandmother's house, on the other side of Caen, on the way to Bayeux." She was babbling now but still managed to keep things vague.

The other soldier, a younger man, was looking her up and down, his eyes resting on her chest, as it rose and fell far too rapidly. He licked his fat lips.

Lottie looked across at Thierry. That tell-tale muscle tightened in his jaw. "Look, we're going to be late. My parents will be worried."

"Tough. Get off your bikes. We'll find your papers for you."

The younger man made a beeline for Lottie and lingered over his body search, his hands following her curves far too slowly, his face, already ugly, not enhanced by a leery smile.

"Get off her!" Thierry brushed the other man's hands away.

As soon as he'd said it, the younger man did indeed drop his hands but only to pick up his rifle which had hung slack against his body while he frisked Lottie. He lifted it up quickly, put his finger on the trigger almost casually, and pointed it at Thierry's heart.

"Please!" Lottie touched him on his arm. "He didn't mean anything!"

She shoved her identity card at him in desperation and he lowered the gun to take it.

Before he had time to read her card, an army jeep roared up to the sentry post and a German officer, identifiable by his peaked cap and gold insignias, jumped out.

"Never mind these yokels! The train has been derailed again! We're on the lookout for a van, covered with canvas, seen driving away from the train track." The man barked out a description of the butcher's van their colleagues had used.

Lottie looked at the younger soldier whose stubby, probing fingers had left an imprint on her clothes and mind. He jerked the rifle away, signalling them to go and handed them back their papers. Thierry took his calmly. Lottie tried not to snatch hers, still unread, and slipped it back in her pocket, buttoning the clasp of her coat slowly and carefully. Using every ounce of discipline she could summon up, she climbed sedately back on her bicycle and followed Thierry's under the barrier the soldier lifted.

They didn't speak until they'd rounded the first bend and were out of sight.

Lottie spoke breathlessly. "I thought they'd never let us go."

"Me too. My God, that was close." Thierry slowed his speed and drew alongside.

"Is that really the address of your parents? Was it wise to tell them?"

"Of course not! What do you take me for?" Thierry shrugged. "They do live in Caen, it's true but there is no Rue du Marché, as far as I know."

"I did wonder." Lottie let out a long sigh.

"They're on to the others though."

"I know, but Sebastien knows all the back lanes. They'll be alright."

"Maybe we should get off the main road ourselves."

They cycled on in silence until they found a smaller lane running parallel to the main road to Caen.

"I think we should avoid the city."

"But we said we were visiting your parents. Shouldn't we stick to the same story?"

"I don't think we're important enough for them to open a file on us and take notes." Thierry looked tired now but nowhere near as tired as she felt.

They reached a village just south of the airport by lunchtime. "Come on, let's take a break." Thierry jumped off his bicycle and pushed it towards a little café on the main street. Lottie followed suit and couldn't help hobbling.

"Is it painful?" Thierry sat down at the little table outside.

"A bit." She couldn't lie.

They drank a glass of water under the shade of a chestnut tree. It all seemed so quiet, so normal, like an innocent cycling holiday before the war, when the world was still sane.

"I'll cycle with you to the farmhouse. You look all in, Charlotte."

Lottie didn't decline his offer, even though it was a risk. As they neared the airbase, another road check barred their progress. Too tired to be nervous, Lottie handed over her papers nonchalantly. It seemed to work. The bored-looking soldier returned their identity cards without comment, barely glancing at the contents. Could they really be getting away with it?

As they mounted their bikes, the butcher's van drove up, unmistakably that of their fellow saboteurs by its brand name emblazoned on the side, the canvas cover must have been discarded along the way. Lottie thought the simple disguise pretty unconvincing and knew a moment of real fear as the soldier insisted the driver dismount to present his papers.

Thierry gave Lottie a quick, sharp look.

"Butcher for the airbase." Sebastian saw them and his face blanched in recognition. The soldier who'd found them so uninteresting screwed his eyes up as he looked from one to the other. His hand had been on the barrier, ready to lift it but the sudden shrill of the telephone stayed his hand. Another soldier called out to him and replaced him at his post. This man's face was old and hard and bore a scar down one cheek, still livid and unhealed.

"Wait here," was all he said.

Lottie noticed Thierry quietly get back on the saddle of his bicycle and did the same, keeping one foot to the ground. She looked across at Sebastian. He looked very ill at ease and nervous. She willed him to be strong, but beads of perspiration were breaking out on his young face. He took out a filthy handkerchief and mopped his forehead with hands that anyone could see were shaking.

They listened to the guttural German coming from the sentry box from the soldier within, the field telephone clamped to his ear under his helmet.

"Heil Hitler!" The conversation appeared to be at an end.

The soldier came back out, his face set and his mouth grim. "Arrest these people!"

At once, Sebastian leapt back into the butcher's van and drove it straight into one of the soldiers, breaking the barrier clean in two, and knocking him flat on his back, his gun shooting bullets uselessly into the sky.

Immediately, Thierry placed his other foot on the pedal of his bike and rode it straight into the other soldier, barrelling him out of the way and making him fall to the ground. Lottie didn't hesitate but jumped on her bicycle and pedalled as hard as she could. The van quickly overtook them, and somebody opened the back door wide. The van chicaned from side to side, but big strong hands shot out to grab them.

"Stop the van!" Louis shouted. "Get off your bikes and climb in!" Lottie and Thierry leapt off their bicycles and let them crash to the ground.

The van screeched to a halt and burly arms hauled Lottie up inside.

"Go!" Thierry was pushing her from behind.

Shots fired out again. She looked back. One of the soldiers was upright again. He staggered but didn't stop shooting. Two men in the van fired back and shot the soldier in the chest and he fell down in a heap. Lottie flung herself inside the van amongst her new friends then, like them, reached out for Thierry. Many hands pulled at his, including hers. Then she felt him shudder and release his fingers on her forearm.

"He's been hit!"

"Quick! Pull harder! Pull!"

Somehow their combined efforts drew him inside and they shut the doors. Bullets rained on the metal, shattered the glass windows.

"Drive! Fast as you can!"

Marcel Le Grand, a small man despite his name, peered out of the back of the van through the broken window and then suddenly fell back against another man.

"Oh, mon Dieu! Marcel's taken a hit in the head."

Blood streamed from the side of Marcel's brow. His mouth, slack with surprise, was open, like his staring, lifeless eyes.

Lottie began to shake.

Sebastian, who had been looking behind in horror, pressed his foot to the accelerator and the van lumbered away.

"Where can we go where we won't be followed?"

Immediately Lottie thought of Bernadette's isolated farm. "Le Verger!"

"But if they follow us, you'll be arrested."

"I know a back way." Sebastian muttered. He slewed the van off the main road, down a rough track through a thick forest of oak trees.

"You need a doctor, Thierry." Louis bent over Thierry's leg, which was bleeding profusely all over the floor of the van.

Thierry had gone white. Lottie grabbed his hand and squeezed it but there was no response.

"He's passed out."

"But he's still alive, not like poor Marcel."

"At least we got the guard, maybe both of them. That's two more to us."

They bumped along the track, bashing their shoulders against the wall of the truck.

Louis took out a flat silver flask. He took a swig and then jerked his head towards Thierry. "Lift his head."

Lottie got behind Thierry and raised him up. Louis put the flask to Thierry's lips. "Drink, my friend." Some of the alcohol dribbled away from Thierry's closed mouth but then it opened a fraction, and a little went in. He coughed and opened his eyes and looked straight into Lottie's.

"It's alright, Thierry. We're not being followed." Lottie smiled at him.

"Yet." Louis muttered, passing the flask around.

"I'm getting out here." A burly man in dungarees spoke. "I have to work on the railway tomorrow at Vaucluse. I don't want to be connected with this."

Sebastian put on the brakes. "Go on then, Gaspard, but it's a long way out of the forest."

"I'll walk all night."

Louis opened the door and Gaspard, who was tall and wide, almost fell out.

"I don't think Thierry can walk far." Lottie almost whispered to Louis.

"No."

"Can you get to Bernadette's farm, Sebastian?"

"I can try but there will be roadblocks everywhere by now. They'll see our tyre tracks too."

"How far is it?"

"Only one kilometre, going north, I think" Sebastian started off again.

They drove for about ten minutes before the sound of another engine alerted them all to their pursuit.

"Bastards have found us."

Louis laid a hand on her arm. "Get him out, Charlotte. Go to your farm and seek refuge there with Bernadette. She'll know what to do."

Lottie nodded.

Louis held the door open. "Good luck, little one!"

"Come on, Thierry. We've got to jump."

Thierry groaned and sat up.

Louis glugged some more cognac into Thierry's mouth, making him gulp. "Ready, girl?"

Lottie sat behind Thierry and put her arms around him. Then she pushed them both out of the van using her legs against the floor, now sticky with his blood. They rolled into a soft landing in the leaves to the side of the track.

Lottie scrambled to her feet, acutely aware of the sound of approaching vehicles. "Come on, my love. You have to stand up."

Thierry, now grey, nodded. He put one arm around her shoulders. His weight almost unbalanced her. She gripped him around the waist, pulling his hip against hers. There was a small clearing to their left with a great stand of blackberry bushes scrambling across it.

"We're going to hide behind there. Quickly, now."

The sound of the pursuing engines got louder, nearer.

Thierry put his wounded leg to the ground and cried out in agony. Lottie could hardly bear to witness it. Her own foot wasn't feeling great, but it was nothing to his injury. Still that engine sounded closer. They must be following the tyre tracks of the van.

The bushes were only ten feet away. She had to get to them, even if she had to drag all six feet of Thierry there. How could they possibly make it in time?

Thierry straightened up. "Sounds like a motorbike. Maybe two. I'll just have to put weight on my leg, or we'll be riddled with bullet holes."

They hobbled and dragged each other across the short distance. By the time they reached the blackberry bushes the motorbikes could be heard roaring towards them. With a howl of pain, Thierry threw himself headfirst across the prickly heap of shrub and Lottie jumped with him. They crashed to the forest floor just as two motorbikes screamed past, the soldiers riding them bent low over the handlebars. Leaves and mud sprayed out from behind them, flinging dirt in Lottie's scratched face - but they didn't stop.

She and Thierry lay there for quite a while, not talking, scarcely breathing. When Lottie dared to look, she could see that Thierry had again passed out. After half an hour an army truck drove past at a slower speed than the powerful motorcycles. Lottie peeped through the thorny branches to see it sway between the tree trunks following the tyre marks and disappear.

When she was quite sure it had really gone, that they hadn't been spotted, she ventured to lift Thierry's trouser leg. White bone glistened through the broken skin and she had no idea what to do.

The hot afternoon sun filtered through the leaves of the trees. Birds trilled in their branches, squirrels busied themselves running up and down their trunks but neither Lottie nor Thierry moved for at least an hour.

She had to get help. Bernadette would know what to do.

She shook his shoulder. "Thierry?"

Eventually he stirred. "Yes?" His voice was thin and reedy.

"I have to get help. You can't walk on this leg. I must get my bearings, find the farm, find Bernadette. I could bring the donkey and cart back for you."

He shook his head. "They will see you."

"No, I will wait until dark."

"Then you will be breaking the curfew." His voice was so faint.

"I'll think up something to say."

"No, I'll walk. Find a stick to make a crutch."

"No, Thierry." Lottie felt his forehead. It felt cold and clammy at the same time.

"I insist." He looked at her. His eyes were so blue without his glasses.

She gave in and got up. It took her about ten minutes to find a staff strong and stout enough that hadn't rotted. "Here," she held it up to show him. "And look what else I've found."

At last a smile. "My spectacles!"

"Their glass caught the sun. It was easy to see them."

"Thank you, Charlotte." He sat up against a tree trunk and put them on with trembling fingers. Somehow regaining his sight seemed to have given him strength.

"That's much better. It's hard to focus in the shade of the trees."

Lottie leaned in and kissed him. "Very handsome but I don't want you looking at me right now."

"Why ever not?"

"We need to bandage that leg and my camisole is the only thing that I can think to use." She turned away from him and quickly took off her coat and jumper and finally, her vest. She put her outer clothes back on and returned to his side.

Gingerly, she pulled up his trouser leg, trying not to gag at the mashed-up flesh of his calf. "I have no idea what I'm doing but it has to be a good idea to staunch the blood."

"Yes." He groaned in pain as she bound his leg up tightly with the white cotton top. "Now, try this crutch for size."

He held the stick in one hand, and she hauled him up with the other, wincing with him when he bit his lip rather than cry out. Again, he slung an arm across her shoulder but this time he took a lot of his own weight by leaning on the improvised walking stick.

"It's working, Charlotte. I don't need to put my foot to the ground now."

"Take it steady, you've lost quite a bit of blood."

He nodded. They moved off, each limping and hobbling slowly along.

Thierry nodded at the sun. "Look it's slipping west. This must be the forest to the east of Bernadette's farm. If we follow the sun, we should be going in the right direction."

"Right then, let's march, soldier."

They didn't talk much after that.

81

Evening shadows cast pillars of black against the forest floor by the time they had reached the woodland that connected the forest to the farm.

Lottie sniffed. "Woodsmoke."

Thierry grunted. He could barely shuffle along now.

"Look, Thierry, sit down here, my love. I can almost see the farmhouse now. My leg is much better." He was too exhausted to question her lie.

She was alarmed when he immediately acquiesced and slumped back against the bark of a huge oak.

"This is a good spot. It's the biggest old oak around, so I can easily find you again."

He didn't reply. He'd fainted again. She kissed his damp forehead, the blond hair now matted with sweat. Lottie ran towards the farmhouse, ignoring her complaining ankle, using the pain to spur her on.

CHAPTER TWELVE
WHITE WALTHAM AERODROME, ENGLAND
MAY 1942

Al signed the logbook in the office and handed over his chit. He'd delivered three planes in twenty-four hours and was glad to stop.

"Fancy a quick jaunt down the pub, anyone?" Al had finished his shift for the day, but the daylight was still bright and the evening warm. He couldn't face going back to his miserable digs just yet.

Miriam giggled. "I fancy *you*!"

"Saucy!" One of the other pilots looked up from the logbook he was writing in and winked at Al.

Al had that familiar sinking feeling he had every time someone made a comment about him and Miriam. He laughed his embarrassment away and put his cap back on. No one else seemed interested in going to the pub.

Miriam took out a mirror from her handbag and applied lipstick to her full lips before getting up from behind her desk. "Ooh, looks like it's just you and me, Al."

"Come on then." Al was glad Miriam didn't grab his hand. The less they looked like a couple, the better.

"It's such a lovely evening, isn't it? May is my favourite month of the whole year, even when there's a war on." Miriam took off her cap and shook out her wavy brown hair.

Al made a point of not looking at her but steadfastly straight ahead. "Yeah, it's nice. How about we walk to the Bell?"

"It's more than two miles!" Miriam looked a bit cross.

"I could use the exercise, you know, wind down a bit."

She smiled up at him. "I can't refuse you anything, Al. You should know that after our time in that dreadful pub in the Midlands. What was it called?"

Al didn't really want to remember but the name was embedded in his memory. "The White Horse."

"That was it! What a dump. Still, we made the best of it, didn't we?" She did put her hand in his now.

Al shook his away. "My palms are all sweaty in this hot weather. Funny how you always get a bit of a heatwave this early in the year."

"Please yourself. Anyone would think you were ashamed to be seen with me."

"Oh, don't be offended, Miriam. I'm just a bit hot, that's all."

"You're telling me." She giggled again but it grated on Al's nerves. "You're a bit jumpy tonight. Have a close shave or something today?"

"Um, just tired, that's all. Could use a day off." Al picked up speed, regretting his invitation to take this pretty young girl out for a drink. Regretting even more the fumbling encounter they'd already had in that dowdy Midlands pub. He couldn't blame Miriam for it. Too much beer, too much loneliness, but most of all, sheer fatigue had all combined to lower his and her defences. Trouble was, she wasn't Isobel. Oh, how different that would have been. He wondered what she was up to. Whether she'd seen Geraint again.

"Are you listening to me, Albert Phipps?"

"What? Sorry, I was miles away."

"I can see that."

They walked on in silence for quarter of an hour and then broke it together.

"Did you…?"

"Are you…?"

They burst out laughing.

"Sorry I was cross, Al. It's just that I get the feeling there's someone else."

Al was unprepared for such a direct challenge. "I..I..um."

84

"I can see that hit the mark. Who is she?" Miriam stepped up her pace and marched on briskly.

Al lengthened his stride. "I'd rather not talk about it, if you don't mind."

"Please yourself."

Al was glad when the pub came into view. Built in the fourteenth century, all low-slung beams and whitewash, The Bell was the favourite haunt of everyone who worked at Waltham. He hoped there would be other members of the ATA network to mingle with as he opened the heavy wooden door.

"What can I get you?" The barman smiled at them.

"Pint of bitter, please. What would you like, Miriam?"

Miriam's attractive face was still stony. "Half a shandy will do me."

"Right you are." The landlord pulled the tap for the beer. Al took a sip of the froth from the top of his pint; he was thirstier than he'd realised. He passed over some coppers.

The barman checked the change and turned his mouth down at the corners. "Need another threepence, my lad."

Al fished in his pocket and found a threepenny bit. "It's gone up again, has it?"

"Sorry, mate, but at least beer's not rationed."

Al grunted. "Yet." He turned back to Miriam.

"Shall we sit in the garden?" There was a corner of the pub's leafy surroundings that the ATA crowd had made their own. Al still hoped for some company.

"Alright." Miriam took her glass and lead the way outside.

To Al's dismay, there was no-one he recognised sitting on the wooden benches scattered around on the grass. They sat down at a table on their own.

"So, why don't you want to talk about it?" Miriam lit up a Woodbine and blew smoke into the warm air.

85

Al looked at the ring of sticky red lipstick on her cigarette filter. "About what?"

"This girl you can't stop thinking about."

Al suddenly felt irritated. It wasn't anyone's business but his own. He didn't want to explain about Geraint in particular. How could anyone understand the unusual relationship between his working-class family and Isobel's aristocratic one? Everyone would think he was on the make – trying to get in with the toffs by marrying into one of its exclusive families. Maybe he'd never stood a chance anyway. He was sure Aunt Cassandra would prefer Isobel to marry one of their own and preferably a rich bloke loaded enough to rescue Cheadle Manor. The more he thought about it, the more he was certain he'd never make the grade. Bloody Geraint Lloyd would, though. He'd fit the bill perfectly.

He looked at Miriam's big brown eyes, so firmly focussed on his face. "There isn't anyone. You're imagining things. Got a light?"

CHAPTER THIRTEEN
NORMANDY, FRANCE
MAY 1942

When Lottie reached the farmyard, the hens scattered away at her lopsided gait, squawking their indignation at being disturbed. She clutched the stone walls for support, afraid the dizziness would overwhelm her before she reached Bernadette. She stumbled forward to the back door and lunged at the latch, bashing it down with her hand in a frenzy. The door gave way into the kitchen. Bernadette jumped up from her fireside chair.

"Why the hell have you been so long?"

"Followed…soldiers…Thierry…woods…wounded …shot."

"Shot?"

Lottie nodded. "Can't walk."

"So, he's alive? Where is he? Speak up girl!"

Lottie waved her arm in the direction of the woods at the back of the orchard. She still couldn't get her breath. Her lungs heaved with the effort.

Françoise clattered down the wooden stairs. "What's happening?"

Bernadette answered. "She's been on a sabotage."

"What?"

"Don't look so shocked, child. We've tried to shield you, but you have to get involved now."

Françoise's pretty faced paled as she looked at her friend. "Oh, Lottie, you look awful!"

Lottie nodded; she was quite sure she did. She reached for a chair, missed and collapsed onto the floor.

The big kitchen seemed to be spinning around her. Feminine hands grabbed her and pulled her on to the settle by the range, always alight, even in May.

"Get water, Françoise." Bernadette had taken charge. Lottie thanked God for that. "And put a slug of Calvados in it, a big one."

87

Lottie was only vaguely aware of the movements of the other two women. Soon, a mug of water appeared before her blurred vision and Bernadette held it to her lips. The spirit it held bloomed into fire on its way down to her stomach and her eyes cleared. She drank the whole mug down gratefully and looked up at Bernadette standing before her, hands on hips.

"What have you done to your ankle? It's swollen." Bernadette swooped down and felt it.

"Ouch!" Lottie jumped at the pain.

"Françoise! Get comfrey leaves from the herb garden and a bucket of water from the well so it's cold. Hurry!"

Françoise scuttled away.

Lottie leaned back against the carved wood of the settle. "Oh, Bernadette, never mind about me. Thierry's been shot in the leg. I think it's broken the bone." Lottie shivered. "You can see the bone." A wave of nausea welled up and she retched, stopping the bile from rising by putting her hand over her mouth.

"Calm yourself. Is the bone sticking out?"

Lottie shook her head. "No, it's just the calf muscle is all cut so you can see it."

"Where is he?"

"In the woods. The biggest oak tree nearest the orchard. He can't walk. We made a crutch, but he's spent and in agony. The bone needs setting or something, I don't know." Now a lump in her throat competed with the nausea.

Bernadette fetched an enamel basin. "Here. If you're going to be sick, use that."

Françoise bustled in with a basket of leaves and a bucket of water.

Bernadette nodded approvingly "Good, Françoise, put them there. Blanch the leaves briefly. The kettle has already boiled."

With brisk, efficient hands, Bernadette undid the tight laces and prised Lottie's shoe off her swollen foot and stripped off her socks. Lottie looked down at her leg. Even after Bernadette's gentle washing, her ankle remained red with rapidly blackening bruises and looked almost twice its normal size. The older woman dunked the hot leaves in the cool water and wrapped them around Lottie's lower leg.

"Muslin, Françoise. In the drawer." Bernadette nodded her granddaughter towards the big dresser and Françoise brought back the cloth.

Within a few short minutes, Lottie's leg was bandaged up in clean white linen and her foot rested on cushions raised on a low stool.

"Thank you, but Thierry? He could be bleeding to death out there!"

"I have but two hands, child." Bernadette got up and smoothed her skirt. "Françoise, come with me."

Lottie tried to get up. "I'll come and show you where he is."

"Stay there. We'll find him."

The two women left; Bernadette muttering something about the donkey and the old sledge they used to haul firewood; Françoise complaining bitterly about risking everything for the 'stupid Resistance'.

The wave of nausea passed but the lump in Lottie's throat grew until tears flowed. She held the rest of the muslin cloth to her face and sobbed into it. She wiped her eyes and blew her nose before yielding to the warmth and security of the fire.

Sounds of scraping wood against stone and the clip-clop of hooves woke her half an hour later. Dusk had fallen while she had dozed off and the birds were announcing evensong in a full-throated chorus.

The door swung open again.

"Can you stand now?" Bernadette held it wide.

Lottie nodded. "I can try."

"Good. He's heavy."

Outside in the yard, Thierry lay prone on a sledge attached to the donkey's harness. Françoise was unhooking it. Lottie got up and tested her weight on her ankle. Already it felt better. She limped over and helped take the weight of the wooden pallet as they lowered it to the ground.

"Drag it into the kitchen and let's have a look at him."

"It won't go through the door, Bernadette."

Bernadette looked at the door, then back again and nodded. "You're right. We'll have to carry him."

Thierry groaned. Lottie went to him. "You must stand, my love. Come on, I'll help you."

"Where are we?"

Lottie was so relieved he was conscious. "We're at the farm. You're going to be alright. Give me your arm and let Françoise take the other."

Together, the two girls hoisted him upright.

"Here, let me take him. You must rest your leg. Open the door instead." Bernadette put her arm around Thierry's shoulders, and he stooped down to accommodate her height.

Lottie held the door wide, while the other three hobbled inside the house. They plonked Thierry down on the settle that Lottie had recently vacated.

Bernadette looked serious when she cut his trouser leg away, took off the makeshift bandage and exposed the wounds. She shook her grey head. "This needs a doctor."

Françoise went outside to deal with the donkey. A few minutes later, she came running back. "There's a truck in the road. It's stopped but its engine is running. I think they might come up our lane!"

"It must be the Germans! They're the only ones with fuel!"

"What can we do?"

Bernadette and Lottie exchanged looks. Together, they said. "Cellar."

"No." Thierry heaved himself more upright. "If they find me, you'll be shot."

Lottie went to him. "Shut up. There's no time for arguments. Give me your hand."

"But…"

"Do as she says. We have maybe two minutes at most. There is a hidden cellar beneath the main one." Bernadette took his other hand. "Françoise! Stall them as long as you can. Say anything but keep them at the door – and make sure you answer the front door, not the one to the kitchen here."

Françoise looked terrified but nodded and slammed the kitchen door shut and rammed the lock home.

Bernadette picked up Lottie's bloody camisole and stuffed it in the pocket of her apron. "One, two, three!"

Lottie and Bernadette heaved Thierry to his feet and half carried him to the cellar door.

"The steps. Oh Bernadette, how will we manage?"

"Listen. The truck is coming nearer. Can you hear it?"

Lottie felt cold. The sound of a vehicle was getting closer. They'd never do it in time.

Thierry shifted his weight, took more on his good leg. The stone staircase yawned before them.

Bernadette pushed past him and went down the first step, holding out her arms. "You," she still never used Lottie's name even in these dire circumstances. "hold him from behind. Thierry, use your good leg to take the weight."

Thierry yelled with pain as he lowered his broken leg down.

Bernadette frowned. "No, we'll have to carry him."

Lottie knew they couldn't do it. "Go on your bottom, Thierry. Shuffle down."

Thierry sank down on to the steps while Bernadette took his legs and Lottie held his back from scraping against the stone. In this way they reached the floor of the cellar, just as loud bangs were heard battering the front door.

"Quick!"

Bernadette and Lottie left Thierry slumped against the wall. Blood oozed out on to the floor from his leg. His face was sickly pale. The two women heaved the wooden barrels to one side to reveal the hidden trap door to the lower cellar and Bernadette yanked it open.

"He'll never make it down the ladder." Lottie glanced down at the gaping hole.

"He must or he's dead anyway. We all are."

With that, Thierry threw himself on to the cellar floor and crawled to the open hatch. He dragged his injured leg after him, using the other leg and his arms to propel himself along. He looked exhausted and his face was streaked in dirt and sweat. A trail of blood followed him.

Lottie heard voices; loud, guttural, barked commands. The front door was open. She could just make out Françoise's timid voice replying.

"You go first." Bernadette jerked her head at Lottie.

"Me?"

"They'll take one look at your leg and be suspicious. Go on, girl."

Lottie quickly descended the ladder and reached up to Thierry, who was already sitting at the top, one leg hanging uselessly down into the cavity. Using his arms, he launched himself downwards and slithered to her open arms and lay there against the wall, inert and unconscious. Blood pooled around his leg.

Seconds later, the trap door slammed shut above them and they could hear the scraping of the barrels going back over it. Without the light from above, they were plunged into absolute darkness.

Then silence, before Bernadette's clogs hammered again above them, joined by the squawking of an outraged hen.

"What on earth…?" Lottie spoke to herself in the blackness.

Heavier boots could be heard clomping through the house still higher above them. Shouts accompanied their tramp up the main stairs and more distant scraping sounds came from the bedrooms.

They must be moving the furniture. If only she could see. If only she could talk to Thierry. She wasn't even sure where he was in the pitch black. She was terrified to move in case she hurt him even more.

Lottie crouched at the foot of the ladder, her ears straining to hear above the thud of her heartbeat.

The squawking stopped suddenly, quickly followed by the thunder of army boots clattering downstairs and, above the cacophony, came the wail of baby Bertrand from upstairs.

There were more German commands shouted out and then the upper cellar door burst open.

A man's voice with a thick foreign accent shouted loud enough for Lottie to hear him clearly. "What is going on here? Why is there blood on the floor, old woman?"

Bernadette answered them in a strong voice. "I've just slaughtered a chicken. Cut its throat. They always bleed everywhere. That's why I do it in the cellar and hang it up. See? There's the bird on that meat hook. This floor is easy to clean."

A moment's silence. Lottie shoved her fingers in her mouth to staunch the scream that wanted to escape from it. She bit her fingers so hard it hurt. She clutched the ladder instead and focussed on the pain her teeth had caused in her hands.

There was the sound of a scuffle and then of someone falling to the floor. Heavy feet roamed around the floor above, stamping, moving things. Not the barrels, please God, not the barrels.

More boots on the stairs.

A different man spoke. His voice was deep and severe with an edge of authority to it, but his German was clear and simple enough for Lottie to understand. "What is happening here?"

"This old bitch has killed a chicken." Lottie could only get the gist of the answer, but she understood the officer's next command.

"What are you waiting for? Bring the chicken with us. There's nothing here. The Kommandant says we have to search every farm along this blasted road. We're wasting our time. The woman is too old to be much trouble and the one upstairs couldn't swat a fly, let alone blow up a train."

"Hey, roast chicken for supper, eh, lads?"

Boots clattered, male laughter rang out, then faded. Lottie heard the front door slam shut and an engine thrummed to life in the yard. Gradually, its mechanical sound drifted away. Lottie became conscious of the pain in her ankle and the wobbliness in her knees. She shuffled sideways and groped for the wall. As soon as she touched it, she ran her hands down until she found Thierry. She slumped to the floor next to him, carefully keeping her back against the wall so she wouldn't push him over. When she reached the floor, she ran her hands over his chest, very gently. When she found his heartbeat, she rested the flat of her palms against his body. His breath rose and fell in quick, shallow snatches.

Lottie lay her head against his shoulder. "Oh, my dear love."

CHAPTER FOURTEEN
CHEADLE MANOR, ENGLAND
MAY 1942

Isobel and her mother sat around the fire in their little parlour at West Lodge one evening in May. Isobel was dog-tired. There was so much to do at Home Farm at this time of year. It was a full-time job just keeping the weeds down on the crops. Then Mrs Stubbs announced the cheese-making season must begin now their spring calves had weaned and the fat content of the cow's milk had risen enough. Lambs needed castrating and tailing. And then there was the smelly job of muckspreading. Isobel studied her hands as she listened absent-mindedly to the news. Every nail was broken and rimed with black dirt, no matter how much she scrubbed them. Would they ever hold a paintbrush again?

"Sorry, Mummy, what did you say? I was miles away."

"I had a letter from Aunt Rose in Boston today."

"Oh yes?" Isobel had never met her father's sister. She knew she had visited Cheadle Manor once, before Isobel had been born. Lottie had described her as a smiley, plump young lady, rather quiet but kind. Lottie said she had been eclipsed by her American grandmother, a tall, beautiful blonde woman but having never met either of them, it meant little to her.

Cassandra read from the page in her hand. "She says that your Aunt Cheryl and your grandfather were killed in a road accident. Apparently, they were on their way to the hospital where your Aunt Cheryl worked as a doctor, and your grandfather had an appointment for his dementia."

"I'm sorry to hear that."

"I know. It's strange how things turn out. Your grandfather was a dreadful bully, all fire and brimstone. He gave your Aunt Katy a terrible time when we stayed there."

"Really?"

"Oh yes, horrible man, I'm sorry to speak ill of the dead, but he cut your father off without a penny and made sure none of his wife's money came to Douglas either, after she died. Cheryl was awful to Katy too and not much better to me. Oh, it's a long time ago but I'm glad Rose has survived them. She has five children now! Can you believe it?"

"That must have been very hard for you and Daddy. About being cut off, I mean."

"Oh, it was, my darling. Sometimes, I think, your father wouldn't have died – you know – been so reckless that day racing at Brooklands if..." Cassandra pulled her cardigan together and fiddled with the buttons.

"Oh, Mummy. Do you really think so? If I was you, I'd hate them for that."

"My dear girl, do you think I didn't?" Cassandra turned her face away to put another log on the fire. "I know it's an indulgence to light the fire this late in the year, but the evenings are still chilly. It's a constant chore with only wood though. I wish we could get another coal delivery."

Isobel just nodded, not wanting to add to her mother's obvious distress and taking the hint of a change of subject.

Cassandra got up and switched on the radio. "Let's see what's happening in the world today, shall we? I've talked quite enough about the past."

Isobel leant back against the brocade armchair and shut her eyes, letting the bulletin about torpedoed U-boats and the Japanese invasion of the Philippines wash over her.

"Oh, listen, darling. Winston's making an announcement. Apparently, it's the second anniversary of his premiership. And what an incredibly hard two years it's been."

Isobel opened her eyes and sat up. Cassandra dialled up the volume and they both concentrated on the Prime Minister's lisping, sonorous words.

"And I warn the German government, we shall treat the unprovoked use of poison gas against our Russian ally exactly as if it were used against ourselves and, if we are satisfied that this new outrage has been committed by Hitler, we will use our great and growing air superiority in the West to carry gas warfare on the largest possible scale far and wide against military objectives in Germany. It is thus for Hitler to choose whether he wishes to add this additional horror to aerial warfare."

"Oh, Mummy! Not poison gas, surely? Aren't all these bombs and torpedoes horrible enough?"

Cassandra put her hand over her mouth and shook her head, looking very distressed.

"Are you alright?" Isobel reached out to her mother.

"They gassed our boys in the last shout, darling. It was ghastly. I saw what it did to them. I can't bear the thought of it happening again."

The Prime Minister finished his announcement and there was a short silence between them after Cassandra switched off the radio. The ringing of the telephone in the tiny hall broke it with its shrill command.

Isobel got up. "I'll go, Mummy. It's probably the hospital demanding even more of your time and you look all-in. I'll tell them you're not available."

Cassandra nodded, then said. "If it's Dr Harris, tell him I'll call him back."

Isobel smiled. "Understood." She went out into the narrow hallway and picked up the telephone receiver. Even that felt heavy, her arms were so weary.

"Hello? Cheadle 241?"

"Is that you Isobel?"

It took Isobel a moment to recognise the voice at the other end. "Geraint?"

"Yes, it's me. How are you?"

"I'm alright, bit weary but okay. It's not like you to call, Geraint. Is something up?"

97

"Yes, I'm afraid so. My father died today."

Isobel slumped down on to the dining chair next to the small telephone table. "Oh, dear, I'm so sorry."

"It happened quite suddenly in the end. Just slipped away in his sleep, but Mother is still very upset."

Isobel stared at a stain on the faded wallpaper. "Of course, she is. You must be, too?"

There was a pause before Geraint continued in a strangled sort of voice. "I must admit, I am."

He sounded terribly upset. Before she had time to think, Isobel heard herself say. "Do you want me to come?"

"Would you? Just for a few days?"

It was his gratitude that did it. "Of course. I'll stay through the funeral. It's always such a difficult time. I'm sure Farmer Stubbs will understand. The Land Army can find him a substitute girl for a short while. I'll make some phone calls and ring you back. Might be tomorrow before I can make arrangements."

"I would love to see you, Isobel."

"Leave it with me. Give your mother a kiss from me."

"I will. Goodbye."

Isobel replaced the receiver. What had she done? Running straight to Geraint's side? Anyone would think she and Geraint Lloyd really were engaged. Anyone who attended his father's funeral definitely would.

CHAPTER FIFTEEN
NORMANDY, FRANCE
MAY 1942

The scrape of the trap door opening woke Lottie. A square of light illuminated the cellar, casting shadows against its rough walls. She had no idea how long they had been down there since the German soldiers had left. Time had no meaning in utter darkness. She lifted her head and cried out in discomfort from the crick in her neck. Her whole body was stiff and numb. With sudden recollection, she reached for Thierry, felt for life in his chest and was profoundly relieved to feel the beat of his heart.

Bernadette came down the ladder with the nimbleness of a much younger woman, holding an oil lamp.

Lottie blinked at the bright light and shielded her eyes from it. Usually, she complained the lamp wasn't bright enough in the kitchen and told Bernadette she should use the electric one, but Bernadette hated the harshness of electric lightbulbs. Even she would surely admit they could do with one now.

Once her eyes had adjusted, Lottie could see that Bernadette's right eye was swollen and cut underneath.

"What did those brutes do to you?"

"It's nothing."

"It's not nothing. I heard someone fall when the soldiers were swarming all over the cellar above us. Did they hit you?"

"Maybe. Never mind that. How's the young feller?" Bernadette was already kneeling in front of Thierry.

"His heart is still beating but his breath is too shallow. That means it's serious, doesn't it?"

"Possibly." Bernadette placed her workworn fingers delicately on Thierry's neck.

"Are you feeling for a pulse?"

"Ssh, be quiet."

Lottie watched silently. She rubbed her legs where they had gone to sleep, desperately willing them to return to normal so she could be useful.

Bernadette loosened Thierry's shirt at the neck, then turned to his leg, lifting the trousers to see the wound. "We'll need hot water with lavender oil in it. Bring clean cloths, a bottle of iodine and the antiseptic cream. And bring the long butter pats – both of them."

"Butter pats?"

"Just do it."

Lottie dragged herself upright and wiped the matted hair from her eyes. Her legs still tingled but they were working. She took one last lingering look at Thierry and then mounted the ladder. Up in the top cellar she saw the blood all over the floor. Did the red congealed liquid belong to Thierry or the poor chicken Bernadette had sacrificed for him? Bet the Boche enjoyed scoffing that, the greedy pigs.

She wasted no further time in speculation but climbed the stone steps up to the kitchen. Françoise was nowhere to be seen. She must have gone to bed. Lottie looked at the clock. It was gone midnight. The curtains were closed, and Bernadette's hated overhead electric light illuminated the room, enabling her to easily find the items she'd requested.

She relieved herself in the outside WC first and sluiced her hands and face over the kitchen sink. How would they manage this practical problem with Thierry down in the cellar? She'd think about that tomorrow. Lottie gathered up the bandages and the other things into a basket and took them, with the bucket of hot water, back down to the lower cellar.

"Good. Leave them there. Now, fetch the cognac – yes, the good stuff – and a glass of drinking water. Hurry, girl."

Lottie did as she was told, despite her complaining ankle, and was back in a matter of only a few minutes, but already Bernadette had cut off Thierry's trouser leg and had washed all the blood off his skin.

He seemed to be asleep. Please God he was.

"Bernadette – he's not moving – he's not….?"

"He's fine. He's strong. Now, I'm going to pull the flaps of skin back together, but first I'm going to dose it in iodine and it's going to sting like hell. Go to his other side. Your job is to give him as much cognac as he can keep down while I work. Is there much in the bottle?

"It's half full."

"Good enough."

Lottie poured some cognac into the glass. "What about the fracture?"

"It's not too bad. One of his leg bones is broken but it's not out of place. The bullet must have gone through the flesh and just glanced off the small bone in his calf. There's no sign of the bullet inside, which is good. The other bone, the bigger one, looks sound, as far as I can tell."

"Can you set the broken one?"

Bernadette nodded. "I think so. I've done this on a young goat before and it worked."

"Not from a bullet wound, though?"

"That's irrelevant."

Lottie went quietly to Thierry's other side with the bottle of cognac and the glass.

"Ready?" Bernadette pulled out the bottle of iodine from her apron pocket and took up some of the cotton sheet Lottie had brought. She ripped it into strips and opened the iodine bottle.

"Remember, this will wake him up with a jolt. Be ready to hold him still and get him as drunk as you can. It's important he doesn't thrash about while I'm working."

"I understand."

Bernadette nodded and poured iodine on to the cloth in her hand before placing it on Thierry's leg.

"Hold his shoulders."

101

"Aaargh!" Thierry opened his eyes as the iodine hit his raw flesh and reached out with his hands.

"Be still, Thierry!" Lottie locked her eyes on to his. "Drink this. We're cleaning you up and it will hurt. Be brave, mon coeur."

Thierry looked back at her, his eyes wide with pain and fright but he sipped the drink and swallowed. Fresh beads of sweat broke out on his forehead and he looked down at Bernadette's hands working away on his bloodied, mangled flesh. Then he leaned back against the wall, shut his eyes and mouth tight.

"Give him more booze." Bernadette didn't even look up. She was pouring iodine into the wound now.

Thierry squirmed in agony and reached for the bottle of cognac, ignoring the glass tumbler. Lottie held it for him, and he swigged it straight down in thirsty gulps.

"How much longer do you need, Bernadette?" Lottie couldn't bear to watch him enduring the torture.

"Just let me get on with it." Bernadette was deftly pulling any flaps of skin she could back into their right position but there was still a gaping mash of raw tissue exposed, the skin around it now coloured a violent yellow from the iodine. She took the jar of antiseptic cream from her capacious apron pocket and smeared a yellow paste over the wound.

Lottie could feel Thierry's body relax a fraction as the tissue was no longer exposed to the air. By the time Bernadette had bandaged it up, he'd passed out again. The cognac bottle was virtually empty too.

"Hold these either side of his leg."

Lottie took the wooden paddles they used to make the butter pats and held them as Bernadette directed, while she strapped more bandages around Thierry's calf to keep them in place.

"Now, we must raise his leg. Go upstairs and get the cushions off the settle. At least three, do you hear?"

102

Lottie nodded and scrambled up the ladder, wincing at the pain in her ankle from the constant running up and down. Thierry was still out for the count when she returned, but he had a better colour now. A fragment of hope settled around her heart as she placed two of the cushions under his leg and one between his back and the cold wall.

"We'll need to improvise a bed, get him off this damp floor and keep him warm, if he's to have any chance." Bernadette was gathering up the detritus of the operation.

"Yes. What do you suggest?"

"Get the mattress off one of the beds in your attic. And bring it down here. Can you manage alone?"

Lottie nodded.

"I'll get blankets and a pillow and give you a hand down the cellar steps. We'll leave this lamp down here for him."

Within half an hour, they had Thierry ensconced on the makeshift bed. He hadn't regained consciousness, so they'd had to drag him on to it. Now they were both exhausted.

"Leave him now, child. You need to rest."

"I'd rather stay here with him. He might wake."

Bernadette was silent for a moment. "Alright. If you're here, you can make sure he doesn't try and move about. Bring another mattress down but you need to eat something first. Come."

After a bowl of soup and some bread and cheese, Lottie felt a little strength returning. Bernadette helped her bring the second mattress down and they made up another bed on the other side of the cellar to Thierry, who appeared to be sleeping soundly. With a jug of water and the oil lamp, Lottie declared herself comfortable.

"Humph. Stupid to be down here in the damp when you could be snug in the attic, but it's up to you and, as I said, perhaps it's just as well. I'm off to bed. God knows, it'll soon be dawn. I'll get Françoise to do the milking. She did it this morning while you were out. By the way, did you blow up the train?"

Lottie grinned, then yawned. "We certainly did."

"Good."

Bernadette turned and climbed the ladder once more, shutting the trap door behind her.

Lottie climbed into bed, fully dressed. She left the oil lamp burning on its lowest setting and turned to face the man she loved. Here they were, both beaten up but alive and sleeping next to each other for the first time. She had never imagined their first night together would turn out like this. Then she shut her eyes and fell asleep to the sound of his rhythmic breathing.

When she awoke again, Lottie had no idea if it was morning or not. The lamp had run out of oil and they were once again plunged into pitch darkness. She lay on her bed, adjusting to the situation. Her other senses were more acute than normal, perhaps to compensate for being blinded. The cellar, although surprisingly dry, smelled of damp. She repelled the thought of how far beneath the soil they lay, interred below worm depth. Lottie flexed her ankle, it felt much better. She reached down to find the swelling had virtually gone. Then she heard some movement above her and listened, trying to discern if it was friend or foe.

The kettle sang out its whistle. It must be morning. She heard voices, both female. Even Françoise was up and about; it must definitely be morning.

Lottie turned onto her side and felt for the earth floor. She drew up her knees and crawled over to where she thought Thierry also lay, feeling with her hands. She felt the edge of his mattress and hoped she was moving upwards with her exploring fingers, and not going anywhere near that messed-up leg.

She gasped when a bigger hand clutched hers. "Good morning, Charlotte."

"How did you know it was me?"

104

"I'd know you anywhere. Even in this utter darkness. Kiss me?"

She located his mouth and placed hers over it. The kiss was long and deeply reassuring. This man had plenty of life left in him.

Lottie lifted her head. "I'm going to find the ladder and open the trap door. Then we'll be able to see."

"Is it safe?"

"I think so, I can only hear Bernadette and Françoise speaking above."

"Be careful."

Lottie got up and crawled around the cellar, feeling for the base of the ladder. "Ouch!"

"Are you alright?"

"Found the ladder with my knee."

She orientated herself with its framework and climbed up. At the top, she pushed open the trap door. It was heavy and she was working against gravity but with two hands and her shoulder pressed against it, she managed to shift it. Thankfully, Bernadette must have moved the barrels out of the way.

"Oh, it's such a relief to see a bit of daylight! Good job the barrels aren't still on top and Bernadette's left the door open to the stairs, thank goodness." Lottie breathed in the extra oxygen and looked back at Thierry, still lying on the bed. He was pale, but not grey any more.

"I'll go and get Bernadette. Could you eat something?"

He nodded and attempted a lop-sided smile. It was enough. She turned and trotted up the cellar steps, delighted she could almost bear her weight evenly on both legs.

"Good morning, Bernadette. How are you, Françoise?" The two women were bustling about the kitchen as if it was a normal morning and there wasn't a fugitive in the cellar.

Françoise was wearing one of her pouts. "I'm really tired, if you really want to know. I've had to milk the goats

105

again and I've been up all night with this little man. He wouldn't settle after those blasted soldiers ransacked the place and now I know why. Look – Bertrand has finally cut a tooth, see?"

Françoise poked a finger in Bertrand's little mouth and opened it to show Lottie the tiny speck of enamel poking through what looked like a very red gum.

"Congratulations, Bertrand. We must tell the tooth fairy." Lottie smiled at the little boy who clapped his tiny hands. How fast children grew up.

"Hungry?" Bernadette was cracking eggs into a pan.

"Starving, actually."

"Eat yours here, then we'll take some down to that young man of yours."

"Um, he might need a bucket to, um, you know, first." Lottie felt herself flush.

"Françoise? Take the old enamel one down, would you?"

"Me? But…" Françoise looked annoyed.

"I'm cooking breakfast. Just leave it there for him. He'll know what to do. You don't have to stay and witness it, girl."

"But how will he manage, lying down?" Lottie had already wondered about this mundane aspect of things.

"I'm sure he'll work it out. Go on, Françoise."

"Bloody Resistance. Putting our lives at risk." Françoise muttered under her breath, but she got up and fetched the tin pail and disappeared down the cellar.

Lottie was already tucking into a fluffy cheese omelette by the time she returned, looking rather pink.

"That teacher has a dreadful sense of humour." Françoise leaned over Bertrand and wiped the boiled egg off his face.

Lottie laughed. This remark made her deliriously happy. Dying men didn't crack jokes. She looked around at Bernadette whose own mouth was twitching at the corners.

106

"What's wrong with his leg, anyway? He was bleeding like a stuck pig when we brought him from the woods last night."

"Never you mind." Bernadette turned to Lottie. "Finished? Here, take him this." Bernadette handed her another plate with an omelette on it. "Take a tray and a pot of coffee."

"You've made real coffee?" Françoise undid the straps that secured Bertrand in his chair and lifted him up.

"It's a special occasion!" Lottie picked up the laden tray.

"Huh! One rule for us, and another for him, is it? Well, you needn't think I'm traipsing up and down those stairs every time he needs a pee. He's not my boyfriend." Françoise pushed the chair in and her bottom lip out.

Lottie didn't answer, she was already at the top of the cellar stairs.

Thierry managed his breakfast, sitting up on the makeshift bed. He drained his coffee cup in one go and drank another straight after.

"So, I'm in your grandmother's farmhouse, then?"

Lottie nodded. "Yes, Le Verger. Bernadette Perrot is my, um, grandmother. She's the one who fixed your leg, do you remember?"

"Vaguely. I remember drinking an unwise amount of very good brandy."

Lottie laughed. "It was the only anaesthetic to hand."

"So, what's the damage? Will I walk again?"

"You may joke, but it was, *is,* pretty serious, Thierry. You were shot in the leg when we were clambering into the van by the sentry post."

"I certainly remember that bit but not a lot about how we got here. You must have been very brave."

"Not brave, just desperate. Sebastian drove most of the way and then we staggered on together through the forest. It was Bernadette and Françoise who thought of the donkey and sledge contraption to bring you the final stretch to the house."

"Were we followed?"

"I don't think so. The van was. I don't know if the others were caught. Soldiers searched this house as part of a general sweep. We were both down in the cellar by then. You'd bled all over the upper cellar and Bernadette had the brilliant idea to cut a chicken's throat and spray the poor creature's blood all over the place, so they thought it was from that."

"What happened to the chicken?"

"The bastards took it away for their supper."

"Humph. They would. It seems I owe Bernadette a very great deal."

"Yes, you do."

"And your pretty friend, Françoise, has a child. It compromises their safety to keep me here." Thierry downed the last dregs of coffee.

"I can't see an alternative. You can't go back to the village in a splint and besides, you will already be missed and therefore linked to the train sabotage." Lottie took his empty cup and put it on the tray.

Thierry gave a half-hearted grin. "Went up like a rocket, didn't it?"

Lottie couldn't smile back. She hated all this destruction. "Yes, more men died yesterday."

"But they were the Boche!"

"I know, but still men who have mothers, sisters, maybe even children of their own."

"Charlotte, we have no choice but to fight. You can see they are getting more brutal by the day. There's barely enough to eat, especially in Caen. Here, you are sheltered by Bernadette's resourcefulness – the hens, the goats, the fruit and vegetables – but believe me, there are others who are almost starving. I see it every day at the school."

"What's going to happen to the school while you recover?"

Thierry gave a short laugh. "Well, at least I won't have to listen to the children singing *'Maréchal nous voila'* anymore. That sticks in my throat. Pétain is a yellow coward who sold France out to these bloody Nazis. He has an easy life in safe Vichy. As to your question, I have already made arrangements with the wife of the mayor, Madame Voclain. She used to teach before she married. Once she hears I've disappeared, she'll take over, assuming the Boche agree. She is on our side, too, though she doesn't tell her husband that."

"This war is splitting families apart."

"I know, but think, Charlotte, it is bringing others together. I would never have met you, had the Germans not invaded."

"It seems some good will come of it all."

He leaned forward and kissed her.

They both froze when they heard footsteps above, but it was only Bernadette descending the ladder.

"How are you this morning? Have you much pain?" She felt Thierry's forehead with the palm of her hand. "Hmm, no fever."

"My leg does hurt, I can't deny it, but it's not throbbing, and I feel well. A little shaky, perhaps, but I enjoyed your omelette, Madame Perrot, and the coffee was excellent. I haven't had a proper cup of coffee since the last time I was in Paris and that was stale stuff from the black market, not nearly as good as yours."

Lottie smiled at the fleeting look of pleasure that flickered across Bernadette's weather-beaten face. "Got it off my daughter before she bunked off with that fat Kraut."

Thierry frowned. "Your daughter is with a German?"

"Oh, don't fret, teacher, we won't split on you. My daughter may be a traitor but she's miles away in Paris. Haven't heard from her since she left, and I doubt we will. Never a backward glance from that one."

Bernadette took the tray from Lottie. "Come on, you. The farm hasn't started to run itself just because we have a visitor."

Lottie got up from the floor. "Of course. I'm coming."

"See you later." Thierry gave a little wave.

"Sleep. That's the best medicine for you, young man." Bernadette made for the ladder.

Lottie looked back before she started her own climb. Thierry's eyes had shut already.

CHAPTER SIXTEEN
NORMANDY, FRANCE
MAY 1942

Lottie had never started a day with kisses before. How had she ever managed to get by without that warm tingle on her lips? For once, for a short while, she forgot about the war and sang as she went about her chores. The May sun shone brilliantly, matching her mood.

She collected the eggs from the hens, their flock now minus one, and brought them inside. Françoise sat at the table shelling haricot beans. The shrivelled pods yielded the little cream-coloured beans willingly into a blue patterned basin, pinging against the china like bullets. It was a job Lottie loved but Françoise looked anything but happy.

"Masses of eggs today. The hens are laying well." She put her basket down on the counter next to the sink.

"Oh yeah?"

"Hmm. Cassoulet for supper?" Lottie sat down at the table and picked up a bean pod.

"If you can call it that without pork or duck."

"I'm sure it will be delicious, anyway."

"The Boche even got that chicken last night." Françoise missed the bowl and a bean shot towards Lottie, hitting her in the chest.

"Hey! Don't shoot me." Lottie picked it up and lobbed it into the basin.

"I'm tempted sometimes, I really am." Françoise didn't give an answering laugh.

"What have I done?"

"I said Bertrand didn't sleep all night because of his tooth when Bernadette was there but those horrible German soldiers picked up Bertrand from his cot." Françoise's voice caught on a sob. "Yes, they picked him up and they shook him - all because of you and your boyfriend!"

Lottie's hands stilled. "What?"

111

Françoise nodded. "And they asked me who his father was. Said what black hair he had and how dark his skin was. They said, 'Have you given birth to a dirty Jew?' Of course, I said, 'no' and they put him back but not before they scared him half to death. What if they'd asked for his papers?"

"Well, you've registered him as Bertrand Paget's son, a true Frenchman if ever there was. You'll be alright but it must have been very frightening. I'm so sorry."

Françoise nodded again and sniffed. "Yes, and I know, Lottie, oh, I know, I wouldn't be able to stand their questioning if it came to it. I'm not brave, like you. And if anything happened to Bertrand, oh, I don't know what I'd do!" The beans were abandoned in search of a handkerchief.

Lottie got up and put her arm around her friend. She rubbed Françoise's back. "I'm so sorry, Françoise. This wouldn't have happened if I hadn't got involved with the resistance."

Françoise stopped crying and looked at her through bleary eyes. "No! It wouldn't! You are putting us all in jeopardy with your stupid games."

"It's not a game, Françoise! Can't you see? If we don't fight these bastards, it will get worse. Listen, the Americans are in the war now. It's only a question of time. We'll win, I know we will. You heard de Gaulle the other day on the radio. He's rallying the Free French. People have to…" Lottie stopped, realising Françoise didn't know about the train sabotage and she was right, she wouldn't stand up to questioning. It was better she didn't know. Ever. "People are fighting all over France, stopping the Germans getting everything their own way and we must fight too, Françoise, we really must."

"Why must we? We can get by, here on the farm. No one ever calls, except your stupid teacher friend. We've got enough to eat, just about. When I've been in Caen with Bernadette to the market, you can see how hungry everyone is in town. They're even rationing the bread there now."

"But don't you see? That's exactly *why* we must fight them! It's only going to get worse if we don't resist. They will cut our food supplies more and more. The government, that cowardly senile old fool, Pétain, is giving the Boche millions of francs for the privilege of having them trample all over France. People, like poor Madame Levy and Bernadette's old doctor, are disappearing all the time! For God's sake, your David disappeared in Paris - don't you remember?" Lottie took a deep breath. "Can't you see, dear Françoise, that even little Bertrand won't be safe unless we get rid of these bastards, once and for all?"

"But you can't get rid of them! How are you going to do that?"

"I don't know but I'm damned well going to try."

"You're not even French, for God's sake!" Françoise was getting hysterical; she was almost shrieking.

Lottie swallowed. "No, I'm not, but we're allies – friends! We've got to stick together. Can't you hear the aeroplanes going overhead from Carpiquet all the time? Where do you think they are taking their bombs? To England, you idiot! Everyone's fighting. Everyone's suffering. Can't you see? We must fight back – for the children, for the future, for Bertrand."

Françoise broke down into tears and leaned her head into Lottie.

Bernadette came into the kitchen, Bertrand on her hip, clutching a bunch of primroses in his fat little fist.

"Maman?" It had been his first word and was still his favourite.

Françoise looked up at her son, her face blotchy, her eyes still shedding tears. "Oh, my baby!"

"What is all this?" Bernadette scowled at Lottie and then at Françoise. "Pull yourself together, child. You'll upset your son."

Françoise mopped her streaming eyes with her apron and reached for Bertrand.

113

Bernadette handed him over. Françoise took the flowers from his chubby hand and went to the sink where she shoved the delicate stems into a vase she filled with water, one-handed, Bertrand clutched firmly in the other, his legs wrapped around her waist.

"What's going on?" Bernadette spoke softly to Lottie.

"The soldiers were rough with Bertrand last night; said he was a Jew."

Bernadette was silent. She went over to Françoise and, for the first time in Lottie's presence, kissed her granddaughter on the cheek. "Take the boy into the garden, Françoise. It will do you both good to get some sun on your faces. I'll finish the beans."

Quietly, Françoise nodded and disappeared into the sunlit yard outside.

Bernadette sat down at the table and picked up a bean pod.

"You must be exhausted, Bernadette." Lottie did the same and the beans once again pinged into their pretty china basin.

"Can't be helped. It's best she doesn't know about the train."

"I was thinking the same thing, but it won't be easy. She already knows Thierry's in the Resistance – and so am I - if the Boche come calling again and asking questions."

"Yes, all the more important she knows nothing more."

"Agreed, but she knows Thierry is in the cellar and he's wounded. How do we explain that?"

"I don't think she'll ask for more information. She knows she'll crack. Listen, the sooner we get him out of here, the better."

Lottie felt cold. All the excitement of waking up with Thierry, the lingering taste of his kisses, disappeared in that moment. Bernadette was right. He couldn't stay here.

114

"I'll go into the village. See if I can make arrangements for him to get away."

Bernadette nodded. "Do you think you'll be recognised?"

"It's possible, but I don't think so. Depends if they put two and two together. The first soldier at the sentry post didn't look at my papers and the second one, nearer here, didn't even glance at them."

"Still, best you don't go into the village for a while. Can you think of another way?"

"I could try someone else. I won't say who."

"That's sensible. Is it too far to walk? How's your ankle today?"

"Oh, God, yes! I forgot I lost my bicycle and we abandoned our rifles too, but my leg is tons better, thank you."

"Leave it a day or two. Wait till the bandage is off and the heat about the train has died down."

"If it ever does. I'm dreading the reprisals. They were terrible last time."

From then on, Lottie treasured every moment spent with Thierry. Every second counted. She knew he had to go, and soon. He said as much the next time he opened his eyes.

"You will have to contact Pierre. He'll get me out of here."

"Yes." Lottie looked at the floor.

"I don't want to leave you either, Charlotte."

"Can't I come with you?"

Thierry shook his head. "It would be too dangerous."

"It might be dangerous for me to stay here if they remember who I am from seeing me at that guard post."

Thierry frowned. "Good point."

Lottie's heart lifted. "So, I can come with you?"

"No."

"Why not?"

115

Thierry's frown deepened. "Must I spell it out? My chances are slim, with this wound. Can't you see that?"

"Then you must stay here until you can walk again."

Thierry shook his head. "That could take weeks, even months. I'm not putting you and your family in jeopardy."

"They're not my family and they are already in danger but because of me, not you."

"No, Charlotte. Absolutely, no."

"But it's not fair! I'd rather take my chances with you than stay here. What's the point of me staying? And I could help you on your journey – carry things, make up a story, pretend I'm your nurse, all sorts of things!"

"Yes, you would do all of that for me, wouldn't you?" He stroked her cheek.

Lottie nodded.

Thierry did look torn for a moment and his eyes clouded with doubt.

"Please?"

She heard the sound of Bertrand's baby giggles from above them. It seemed to make up his mind.

"No. I'm sorry but my decision is final. I shall come back for you, my love, I promise. I want you to go to Jean at the mill tomorrow. Is your ankle up to it?"

Lottie sniffed. "Yes."

"Good. Tell him what's happened and that I need Pierre to organise an escape to the unoccupied zone in the south."

"So far away?"

"Listen, you don't need to know more. Trust me?"

Lottie shrugged. "Seems I have no choice. I could shackle you to the walls, I suppose."

He laughed and drew her to him, flinching when she brushed against his leg but still holding on to her tightly.

"I love you, Charlotte Perrot, whoever you really are."

CHAPTER SEVENTEEN
NORTH WALES, UK
MAY 1942

Geraint Lloyd clung to Isobel the minute she stepped off the train in Wrexham. The platform wasn't crowded but still she looked around to see who was watching them and found every pair of eyes trained on their embrace.

Geraint released her. "I'm so glad to see you, my dear."

Isobel felt dismayed at this open display of affectionate need. She wasn't sure she could fulfil it. Wasn't even sure she should have come.

She answered with a smile rather than words.

Instantly, Geraint withdrew a little and dropped his arms. "You must be tired from the journey."

"Actually, it was quite restful, just sitting watching the countryside glide by." Isobel picked up her cases.

"No, no. You don't have to carry them. I'll get a porter."

"Really, there's no need, my farm work has strengthened muscles I never even knew I had." She tried to laugh.

"I insist." Geraint hooked a finger at a man in uniform who'd been hovering nearby. He gave him some coins with a nod. "The car's waiting for us out the front."

Isobel and the porter obediently followed Geraint's tall, immaculately tailored frame out through the archway and into the car park in front of the small station.

Silently, she clambered into the front seat before realising there was a chauffeur at the wheel. His face was professionally impassive, but a muscle twitched at the corner of his mouth. Embarrassed, she climbed back out and into the rear of the large limousine. Geraint quickly joined her, and she hoped he hadn't seen her mistake. She knew he

117

would be too polite to comment if he had and somehow that made her feel even more awkward.

The big car moved smoothly forward on to the main road. Isobel looked out of the window at the distant mountains. "I half expected snow on the tips of the mountains, even in May."

Geraint gave a stiff smile. "We are not such a foreign country, you know."

Isobel felt corrected and ill at ease, something she'd never experienced in his company before. She looked across at his face. He looked tired. Shadows under his grey eyes made him look older. For the first time since she'd met him, he looked his age. Twenty years older than her.

She looked away back at the mountains and the foothills that led up to their glorious summits. "It's so beautiful here."

He reached out and took her gloved hand in his. "Much more beautiful, now you are amongst us."

They didn't have to drive very far before the car swept into the driveway of Geraint's elegant house. The door opened as the tyres whispered to a halt outside the front door. The majestic entrance opened to reveal the butler, who descended the wide steps and took charge of their luggage.

"Thank you, Evans. Take Miss Flintock-Smythe's luggage up to the east guest room, will you?"

"Certainly, sir. Would the young lady require refreshment?" He stood aside so they entered the panelled hall before him.

Isobel grabbed the opportunity for some time alone. "Oh, yes, please, Evans. Would it be too much trouble to have a cup of tea in my room?"

Geraint frowned. "But Mother is expecting you in the drawing room for tea."

"Oh, yes, of course. Silly me."

"But, please, settle yourself in your room first, if you would like to."

"Oh, no. I'll come straight into the drawing room and see your mother." Isobel handed her coat, hat and gloves to the butler's waiting hands and submitted to an immediate audience.

"Mrs Lloyd, how lovely to see you but I'm sorry about the circumstances." Isobel kissed the wrinkled cheek of Geraint's mother, whom she found sitting by a blazing fire in the elegant drawing room.

"I'll ring for tea." Geraint pulled the bell cord and the hard-pressed Evans appeared immediately.

Mrs Lloyd sat back down. "We'll have tea in here, Evans. And bring some Welsh cakes for Miss Flintock-Smythe."

The butler shut the door behind him.

Isobel had forgotten how convenient it was to have servants to do your bidding. She sat down on the sofa opposite Mrs Lloyd and Geraint sat next to her, close enough for their hips to connect through their clothes. "I was so sorry to hear about Mr Lloyd." Isobel discreetly shuffled a little further away.

"It's strange. We all expected it but it's still a shock when it happens." Mrs Lloyd dabbed at the corner of her eyes with an embroidered handkerchief.

"Yes, I'm sure."

"How was your journey, dear?" Mrs Lloyd tucked the tiny square of linen into her silk sleeve.

"Oh, quite slow but straightforward. I was saying to Geraint, at least it gave me a rest." Isobel smiled.

"A rest?" Mrs Lloyd raised her eyebrows.

"She means from the farm work, Mother. Had you forgotten Isobel is a Land Girl?"

"Do you know, I had? So enterprising." Mrs Lloyd glanced down at Isobel's reddened work-worn hands, now gloveless and exposed, their history of hard graft clearly visible on the rough skin.

Isobel tucked one hand inside the other on her lap. "Have you set a date for the funeral?"

119

Geraint answered for them both. "Yes, it's to be next Tuesday."

"The local church?"

Mrs Lloyd handled that query. "Oh, no, dear. Chester Cathedral is our chosen venue."

"Goodness, are you expecting a lot of people to attend?"

"Naturally. Geraint's father was an important figure in local business. We would have preferred Liverpool Cathedral, but it's still not finished - because of the war - you know. However, Wrexham is Roman Catholic so it wouldn't suit us, but Chester is perfectly adequate. I don't mind it being over the border in England as it will be convenient for those attending from further afield. Ah, here comes the tea trolley."

Isobel had felt hungry on the train but, although the Welsh cakes were excellent, they tasted dry in her mouth.

Geraint and his mother drank only tea but pressed her to have another little pancake.

"Oh, no, really. I'm not that hungry. Actually, I am rather tired after all. Would you mind if I went upstairs for a little rest before dinner?"

Geraint stood up immediately. "Of course, you're tired. Come, I'll show you to your room." He held out his long, elegant fingers. Isobel could think of no way to refuse them and placed her palm in his hand. "Thank you."

They mounted the graceful staircase. Its oak balustrade was echoed in the extensive wooden panelling surrounding it. The effect was warm and pleasing, but to Isobel's sensitive mood, also slightly claustrophobic, giving her a sense of confinement.

"This is your room, dearest. I do hope you will be comfortable." Geraint opened a door off the large landing and held it wide.

Isobel walked inside. "Oh, I'd forgotten how charming this room is, thank you."

Geraint came in with her but before he could shut the door behind them, Isobel forestalled him. "Actually, I need to freshen up, after the journey, you understand."

"Oh, of course. Excuse me. I just wanted to give you this."

Before she could stop him, Geraint leaned in and kissed her on the lips. Only lightly, a fleeting brush of his whiskers, no more, but he'd never done that before. Not ever.

When the door shut behind him, Isobel flopped on to the luxurious silk cover on the large bed. Her mother had been right. Everyone now assumed they were a couple, including Geraint. And there was no way she could leave before the funeral at the cathedral. A cathedral! The whole population of north Wales, Cheshire and even Liverpool must be attending. And there she'd be, standing beside the grieving son, as if she was already his wife.

CHAPTER EIGHTEEN
NORMANDY, FRANCE
MAY 1942

Thierry slept a lot that day and the next and Lottie slept in the other makeshift bed nearby at night, careful to bring candles, and a torch as well as the oil lamp down to their hidden tomb. She never wanted to experience that pitch blackness again with the cellar ceiling pressing down on her, unseen, oppressively heavy, and threatening to suffocate her. Neither could she bear not to be near him.

They talked when he was awake. About everything. Their past lives, their families, their hopes for the future. Lottie had never relaxed with anyone like this, never trusted anyone so deeply, not even Al or Isobel.

On the third day, she could put off the trip to the mill no longer. Her ankle no longer pained her. She had no excuses left. Thierry was brighter now and awake more than asleep during the day. He was hungry too and desperate for fresh air.

"Come up to the kitchen, if your leg will let you. It needs testing." Lottie didn't know how he withstood the claustrophobia of the deep cellar.

Thierry shook his head. "I couldn't move fast enough if someone came."

"Then how on earth do you think you'll manage getting down south?"

"I'll cope."

"You'd do a lot better if I came with you."

"Don't start that again, Charlotte. Get off to the mill and give that message to Jean."

Lottie sighed. "Alright, if I must. I'll bring you some food first."

Upstairs, she plated up a chunk of bread, some dried sausage and a good wedge of cheese and added a bowl of chicory coffee. When she took it down, Thierry was already

122

sitting up in bed. "Thanks. I'm starving. I think that must be a good sign."

"Yes, I'm sure it is but that means you'll be going sooner rather than later."

"Think of Françoise's little boy."

Lottie couldn't argue with that. "Enjoy your meal. I expect I'll be a couple of hours. It's about five kilometres each way."

"Let's hope they don't have a search warrant out for you. Keep safe, my love."

His words rattled around her head all the way to the mill. She jumped every time she heard anything. A flock of birds, a cat fight, distant sounds of a car; everything sounded louder and more alarming than normal.

Although it had taken her only just over an hour to walk the distance to the mill, it had felt three times that long. But there it was, nestling in the valley, hunched over the rushing river, its waterwheel churning round and round, propelling the huge millstone inside the old building.

She almost ran down the hill in her relief. She had to bang loudly on the door above the sound of the gurgling water but in the end, Jean poked his ugly head through the ancient framework.

"Oh, it's you."

Did no-one use names around here? Was it just because of the war or did all the locals address each other as 'you?'

"Yes, it's me."

Jean looked furtively over her shoulder. "Don't come into the mill. Let's go around the back, behind the wheel."

"Does everyone get this warm welcome?"

Jean shut the door of the mill behind him. "Things aren't the same after, you know, what happened."

"You mean the train?"

"Ssh, mademoiselle!" Jean darted his beady black eyes around his yard. "Come into the barn. You don't have a bicycle?"

"No, I lost it running away."

"Just as well. They've clamped down on those now. Can't even push one along outside of curfew hours and the penalty is harsh if you're caught."

Lottie followed him into the vast barn where the Jewish family had sheltered up in the vaulted rafters. She wondered where they were now but didn't dare ask Jean with him in this mood.

He turned to face her. "Well? What do you want?"

"It's Thierry. He's wounded and hiding in our cellar at the farmhouse."

Jean nodded. "I'd heard he got shot. You know the others were captured?"

Lottie's heart thudded in her chest. "No. Did they find the van?"

"Yes. They're all in prison in Caen. God knows how many others will be shot or deported now. A thousand were sent to the camps afterwards and thirty shot. It's only going to get worse."

"Oh God, I'm sorry. I didn't know it was as many as that."

"Now you know why I'm jumpy. And my cousin in Caen saw one of our own police roughing up a Jewish doctor at the station. An inspector. Punched him in full view of everyone and called him a dirty Jew. Said the same to some Communists who were there too." Jean spat on the ground. "Even our fellow Frenchmen are turning against us."

"What happened to the doctor?"

"Took him as hostage with a load of others to the camp at Royallieu. They don't stay there long before they ship them out to some other Godforsaken camp further east. There was a notice in the paper yesterday saying that if all those culpable for the train sabotage are not arrested by

124

midnight on the twelfth of May, many more from the same background will be executed."

"From the same background – what does that mean?"

"Jews, Communists, you know, the ones they call 'dirty'."

"Oh, why do they hate them so? They're just people."

"That's exactly it. The Nazis don't see them as people at all. They're looking for any excuse to round up more, so everyone is on the lookout for the saboteurs to avoid more arrests. You must keep a low profile and trust absolutely no-one."

"Dear God. What have we done?"

"In their warped minds they reckon it's the only way to stop a similar crime happening again but, of course, it suits their purposes to have an excuse to eliminate more 'undesirables'."

Lottie nodded. Her hands had gone all clammy. "Can you get a message to Pierre?"

Jean grunted assent.

Lottie spoke quickly, urgently. "Thierry wants to try for the Unoccupied Zone down south. He says Pierre will know what to do."

"Did you get stopped on the way here?"

Lottie shook her head. "No. Didn't see a single German."

"Good. Stay away from the village. They know a girl was involved. I'll tell Pierre. Go now…and don't come back for a long time, understand me?"

"Yes, Jean, I understand." She pecked him on each of his stubbly cheeks and left it at that.

Lottie returned through the barn door and stepped across the slippery wooden bridge spanning the rushing river. The hill climbed steeply from the mill up to the main road, but she kept up her pace. Her ankle was niggling her to slow down, but she ignored it. She fished her scarf out of her pocket and tied it firmly under her chin. Not much of a disguise. She'd have to think about that, especially as she was wearing the same dress as she'd worn on the day of the sabotage. It all depended on whether the guard at the first sentry post remembered her face and gave out her description, and others linked it to her identity cards or not. Maybe they'd got wounded and were now in some distant hospital. She hoped to God they were dead.

Lottie pounded along the rough tarmac for a while and then her nerves prompted her to walk through the trees lining the road instead. Here, she felt a little safer. Her shoes made no sound and the shadows cast by the leaves gave her shelter. She heard a car approaching. Only the Boche had petrol. She hunched over to keep her head down, and quietly walked deeper into the woods, crouching behind the wide trunk of a sycamore tree as the noise of the engine got louder. Lottie peeped out as the vehicle passed. A swastika flag rippled on the bonnet of the army car, but she couldn't glimpse its passengers. She waited until she couldn't hear it any more before venturing out. She broke into a jog, slowing only now and then to listen out for more cars. Instead of going along the lane to the farmhouse from the main road, she took a longer, more circuitous route through the woods and came out at the back of the orchard, just as she had done with Thierry on the night of the train sabotage. What were they thinking when they'd blown it up? Had it really been worth it, despite her defending it to Françoise?

At last she could see the apple trees emblazoned with pink blossom, unperturbed by the threat imposed by these vile occupiers but innocently opening their buds to the spring sunshine, just as they had always done.

Lottie undid the knot of her scarf under her chin and shook out her black hair. She felt more frightened now, after seeing Jean's very real fear. She never wanted to let Thierry out of her sight again and yet it must be done, and urgently.

She took a deep breath before entering the house.

126

Françoise was clearing away the lunch things and Bertrand was playing on the floor banging a spoon on a metal saucepan and making a huge din. "Oh, you're back."

"Yes, am I too late for a bite to eat?"

Françoise shrugged. "Please yourself. We had cabbage soup, just for a change. I think there's some left."

"Thanks."

"Not going down to lover-boy first?"

"Has he had some?"

"Oh, yes, Bernadette gives him top priority." Françoise clattered some bowls into the sink, almost breaking them.

"She's been very good and so have you, Françoise. He'll soon be gone, I promise."

Françoise turned around, wet hands on hips. "Thank God for that, the sooner the better."

"I know." Lottie ladled some soup into a bowl, but her appetite had faded. "Maybe I will go and see him first."

She clattered down the stone steps to the first cellar and lowered herself down the ladder backwards to the one beneath.

"Hey, you," Thierry rewarded her with a loving smile.

"How are you feeling?" She kissed him briefly on the mouth.

He treated her to one of his grins. "Much better after that."

"I've given Jean the message for Pierre. He's pretty scared."

"Don't blame him. Any news?"

Lottie nodded and reached out for his hand. "Thierry, the others were all caught."

"Damn!"

"Yes, bad luck for them."

Thierry frowned. "And for us. They might talk. Where are they?"

"In the prison at Caen but the worst of it is, that innocent hostages have also been taken to the camp at Royallieu. Everyone's on the lookout for us to avoid more arrests. They've given until the twelfth of May to find us before they drag other Jews and Communists off the streets who had nothing to do with it. Oh God, Thierry, was it really worth it?"

Thierry fell silent. He ran his hands through his hair. "I must get up. Start using this leg. The sooner I'm out of here, the better."

"I'm not so sure. I think it would be better to wait until they stop looking for you, maybe leave it till after the twelfth."

"Did Jean say anything else?"

"No, well, except to tell me not to go there again. You see, I'm useless around here. I would be much better going with you."

"We've talked about this, Charlotte, and the answer will always be 'no'."

Lottie gave up and took his empty tray back to the kitchen. She still couldn't face the soup and poured the contents of the bowl back into the pan on the stove. There was no-one about, the others must have gone outside somewhere. She ripped off a piece of bread – they were back to Bernadette's tough sourdough – and smeared it with goat's cheese and honey. She washed it down with plain water. She couldn't enjoy it; she just needed fuel.

Bernadette came in with a basket of spinach on her arm. "Here, wash these leaves, will you?"

Lottie took the basket.

Bernadette nodded at her. "I'll make a quiche with it tonight."

"That'll be nice."

"That man of yours needs iron."

"Yes. I heard today they are on the lookout for us both and more hostages will be taken if we are not found

128

before the end of the week." Lottie took the jug and glugged water into a bowl.

"You mean people suspect you personally?"

"Not me, unless the guard remembered my name, but Thierry will be missed at the school and they took more notice of his identity cards. He even gave an address for his parents in Caen, and, although he made that up, they still live in Caen. It's inevitable he will come under suspicion." Lottie plunged the spinach leaves into the cold water.

"Who knows he's been coming here?"

"Madame Leroy, Jean at the mill, and Pierre."

"Too many." Bernadette dragged the kettle across to the centre of the hob, where it was hottest, and spooned dried lime flower leaves into her earthen teapot. "What about the other saboteurs?"

"All caught and imprisoned in Caen." Lottie swished the grit off the spinach. "I've left a message for an escape to be organised."

"Don't tell me who with. The less I know the better and, for God's sake, tell Françoise absolutely nothing at all. Understand?"

"Of course. I wouldn't ever do that."

"Do you know when you'll hear from this person?"

"Not a clue, only that the message will be delivered soon."

"Right, best get him fit then. Time he was up and about. The danger of infection has passed." Bernadette poured boiling water into the teapot.

"But not the danger of him being found here." Lottie lifted the spinach leaves out of the water and placed them carefully in a large sieve to dry.

"No, but we'll hear anyone before we see them, and Françoise can be a lookout. It's time that man had a wash." Bernadette's lips twitched in what Lottie assumed was meant to be a smile. "It's getting smelly down in the cellar."

"Believe me, I had noticed."

"Hmm. We'll bring the tin bath in here this evening and Françoise can go upstairs to listen at the front bedroom window where she sleeps anyway. I'll set it up with you and then go in the yard to keep watch while you wash him."

"Me?"

"Oh, for heaven's sake, it's obvious you're in love with him. You're going to see him naked at some point, it's only natural, but don't do anything that will get you pregnant. We've enough to contend with. One child is enough to protect."

Lottie flushed to the roots of her hair. "I wouldn't dream of doing anything like that!"

"You'd be surprised how quickly these things can happen. You're no better than the rest of us, wherever you're from. Right, take this tea down to him and tell him what he's in for."

That evening, after Françoise had stomped upstairs and banged her bedroom door shut, Bernadette and Lottie helped Thierry to his feet. The deepest cellar ceiling was so low he had to stoop beneath it as he limped to the ladder.

"Can you bear weight on that leg?" Bernadette followed closely behind him, watching his progress through her shrewd eyes in the lamplight. "Otherwise we'll have to work something out for getting up that ladder."

Thierry tested his leg.

Lottie saw a spasm of pain shoot across his face, but his leg held. "Maybe we could put another piece of wood underneath his foot and lower the splints so they support it?"

Thierry looked at her appraisingly. "We seem to have an engineer in our midst, but I think I can do it without such ingenuity."

"Good, get on with it then." Bernadette jerked her head up to the trap door.

Thierry laughed, then frowned as he mounted the wooden ladder.

"Take the strain with your arms." Lottie encouraged him from above.

130

"I will but they are weaker than normal. Never mind, here I come." Thierry heaved himself up, rung by rung with his hands, and hopping his good leg up to the one above until he reached the top.

Lottie held out both arms and steadied him as he emerged into the higher cellar. He clutched at the big barrels lining the wall while he got his breath back.

"That's the worst bit over." Bernadette was swiftly clambering up behind him, holding the oil lamp. "Come on, the stone steps will be much easier. Grab the rope handrail on your left there."

Again, Lottie went first, looking behind her as Thierry took each step one at a time, resting at each one. How on earth he thought he could manage to escape to the Unoccupied Zone in this state was beyond her.

Finally, they reached the kitchen. Steam rose from the tin bath in front of the range. The clean smell of lavender filled the big room and a towel was draped over one of the chairs next to it.

Bernadette put the oil lamp down on the table in the centre of the room and switched off the electric light above. She fiddled with the curtains, making sure no light escaped. "Can't be too careful. Right, can you manage between you? The soap is home-made. It's all we have but you'll be a darn sight cleaner afterwards. Don't let your wound get wet. I've left fresh clothes on that chair there. They belonged to my husband. He was bigger built than you and a little shorter but at least you'll look like a farmer not a damn teacher in his posh togs."

Thierry stroked the stubble on his chin. "Have you a razor?"

Bernadette shook her grey head. "I have, but I think it's best you let your facial hair grow."

She turned to Lottie. "Shout out if you need me and I'll bang on the door if I hear anything." Bernadette closed the back door behind her.

They were alone. Lottie felt suddenly shy, as if she was with a stranger, but it was quickly dispelled when Thierry pleaded for a chair.

"Oh, of course, sorry." She pulled one out from around the table and set it before the fire and he lowered himself down on it.

"This is a bit awkward, isn't it?" He grinned at her.

"You'll feel marvellous once you've had a wash. Come on. Let's start with your sock. There's only one so it'll be easy." Lottie knelt in front of his chair.

Thierry lifted his good leg and she drew his sock off. "Sorry you have to do this; I'll bet it stinks."

"So do mine, some days."

He stroked her hair. "I wish this was our wedding night and I was undressing you."

"Don't, I won't be able to…"

He drew her towards him and wrapped his arms around her. "I should wait until I smell a little sweeter before I do this."

Lottie yielded to his kiss; lost herself to it. After a while, when their breath had quickened, Bernadette's warning voice sounded in her ears and she withdrew a little. Instantly, Thierry released her.

"What's wrong?"

"Nothing's wrong, Thierry. It all feels so right but…I promised Bernadette I wouldn't do anything silly."

"Silly! When I kiss you, it feels like it's the only sane thing that's happening in my life right now." Thierry ran his hand through his hair. "But she's right. I'm beginning to realise that she usually is, however brusquely she might say it."

Lottie smiled. Her lips were all shaky and quivered before she spoke. "I know. She's a wise old witch. Come on, off with your shirt and let's get you in the water before it's stone cold."

"I can do it. There's nothing wrong with my arms except lack of use." Thierry reached behind him and pulled his shirt off, flinging it on the floor.

He unbuttoned his flies and Lottie turned away to fetch the towel. "Here, put this over your lap and I'll pull your trousers down."

Thierry hitched himself up and Lottie, with some difficulty, dragged his trousers over his leg, carefully drawing the sawn-off trouser leg over his splint.

"I'll do the next bit and save your blushes." Thierry wriggled his pants off under the towel. "That's it. I'm in my birthday suit. Bring another chair alongside and I'll use that to hold onto."

He tucked the towel around his waist and got up, balancing most of his weight on his good leg, and hobbled over to the bath. Lottie held him under his armpits from behind as he lowered himself into the water, discarding the towel as he did so. She was dismayed at the rush of desire that thumped through her when she touched his bare skin and saw the beauty of his body before it disappeared under the water.

He leant back against the tin rim of the bath, his face damp with sweat from the effort and his wounded leg propped up on the edge of the tub. Lottie tried to make sense of the confused feelings of new sensual yearnings jumbled up inside her with a motherly tenderness at how pale he looked - and failed.

Lottie swallowed and picked up the flannel Bernadette had put ready. "Is it very painful?"

"I can bear the pain of my leg better than I can control my feelings for you." He reached out and cupped her chin in his hand. "Come closer, please?"

Lottie dipped the flannel in the fragrant water and began to wash his chest. "I think this is probably close enough."

"Not nearly enough." He kissed her again, deeper and longer. Only when the water crept up her sleeve on to

133

the rest of her dress did any other sensation displace the overwhelming longing Lottie had to rip off her own clothes and dive right into the tub with him and to hell with the consequences. Her common sense had long since departed and all Bernadette's sensible words of advice were obliterated by the overpowering urge to cave into doing what every cell of her body was craving.

Then, very gently, Thierry pushed her away. He was panting slightly, as was she. He plunged his head under the water and stayed there so long, she became anxious. When he came up for air in a huge rush, water cascaded over the rim of the bathtub, soaking the few parts of her clothing that had so far remained dry.

"Give me that revolting looking object Bernadette claimed was soap, would you?" Thierry frowned but then laughed. "Oh, Charlotte, you are damn near irresistible."

Lottie gave a shaky laugh. "No one has ever said that to me before! I was always the ugly duckling in our family."

Thierry began to scrub himself vigorously. "I do not believe that."

Lottie laughed again. "It's true. If you saw my sister, you wouldn't give me a second glance. She's fair in every way and not short, unlike me."

"If you talk like that, I shall have to kiss you again and then where would we be?" He splashed water over his face and began to soap his neck.

"I'll do your back." Lottie shuffled round on her knees behind him. He gave her the soap. It didn't lather much. She rubbed it on his back and round his neck, his ears, dwelling far longer than necessary over each delicious curve but keeping well out of kissing range.

After he'd washed his hair and other areas she dared not venture, Lottie used the jug to rinse the soap from his head. Then Lottie helped him stand up and held out the towel, standing discreetly behind him. He sat on the chair to dry himself and she brought over the rough clothes that had belonged to the long-dead Monsieur Perrot. Once he was dressed in them, he did look different but probably not nearly enough. The glasses were a dead giveaway.

There was a sharp rap on the door and Lottie almost tripped over the bath in fright.

Bernadette walked in. How had she known he would be dressed by now?

"All done?"

"Yes, and I must thank you for your husband's clothes. I feel I should labour on the farm to repay you, Bernadette." Thierry towelled his blond hair.

"Humph. If you were sound in wind and limb, I'd hold you to that." Bernadette looked him up and down and then shook her head. "You are still far too recognisable. You'll need new papers and we'll have to dye that yellow hair of yours. Are those spectacles really necessary?"

"I do need them, it's true, but I can manage without for a short time if I don't have to focus on anything too distant."

"That's good. You don't see many farmers wearing glasses." Bernadette swooped down and picked up the soap and the jug they'd used for washing his hair.

"I'll clear up, Bernadette." Lottie took the jug and began to empty out the tub into a couple of buckets.

"See these?" Bernadette held out a bowl of black walnuts. "Turns hair darker. We'll do it tomorrow. I'll put them into soak overnight."

"Good idea, thanks." Thierry folded the towel over the back of the chair. "I feel much better already."

"Warm yourself up by the fire before you go downstairs again. We've kept that leg free of infection so far. Don't want you catching cold now." Bernadette helped Lottie drag the almost empty bath to the door and out into the yard where they tipped it into the drainage channel and took it to the wash house to hang against the wall.

"When can he take off the splints, Bernadette?"

"I'm not sure, best leave them on as long as we can. When is his contact coming?"

Lottie shrugged. "I don't know. We just have to wait."

"I was thinking, those papers of my son's. He can use those."

"But that would mean linking him directly to the farm, if he…if he was caught."

Bernadette screwed up her grey eyes. "Good point. Maybe not, then. He'll have to find the name of some other young man who died too soon. There's plenty to choose from these days."

Bernadette went up to bed soon after that and Lottie went towards the cellar to follow suit.

"Charlotte?" Thierry stopped with his hand on her arm.

"Yes?"

"I think it best if you go back to your normal bedroom now."

"But why?"

"Can't you guess? I wouldn't be able to restrain myself now I'm feeling so much better. I look across at you sleeping, and I want to join you in your bed but so far, I haven't been strong enough. Now that I am, it wouldn't be fair to you if we…"

"Oh, I see. You have a very high opinion of your charms."

"It's not *my* charms I'm worried about."

Lottie flushed at the compliment. "But, Thierry, I don't want to waste a minute of our time together. You will soon be gone and who knows when I'll see you again?"

"I know." He used the chair for leverage and stood up to kiss her.

They went down the stairs very carefully. Lottie was pleased at how much more easily he was moving. "I think you are getting more confident on your pins."

"Yes, now I know it can take a little weight, I can use it more."

Lottie passed him the oil lamp once she saw Thierry had safely reached the floor and closed the hatch behind them. She joined him at the bottom of the ladder. "We're alone again."

"I'm growing to like it like this."

"Me, too." Lottie stepped closer, so their bodies touched.

"If you come any nearer, I shall no longer be a member of the Resistance."

Lottie chuckled. "I'm going to suspend my membership for tonight, if you will."

Thierry reached out and stroked her hair. His eyes searched hers. "I have nothing with me to protect you from any consequences if we make love, Charlotte."

"There are risks with everything. We could die tomorrow. You could be killed going south. I could be deported to a labour camp. There is no such thing as a risk-free life."

"But…"

She kissed his lips before he could finish the sentence. "Let us live, and love, while we can."

He pulled her to him fiercely, his arms pinning her to his chest and kissed her till she was breathless. Lottie undid the buttons on his rough shirt. She longed to touch his bare skin once more. All the desire she'd felt washing him welled up again, more intense than before, as she pulled his borrowed shirt off him and kissed his exposed chest.

Thierry unfastened her dress, opened it and let it fall to the floor, where it lay in a heap, unnoticed by either of them. He kissed her throat as he slipped down the straps of her flimsy camisole and gently took it over her head. He cupped her breasts, kissing them gently all over until she groaned in ecstasy. Soon, they were both naked and he drew her to the bed on the floor.

Thierry slid on top of her. "I'm fast reaching the point of no return, my love. Are you quite sure you want to do this?"

Lottie didn't answer but pulled him inside her. She felt a fleeting stab of pain before the sensation was drowned out by sheer pleasure as he moved within her. Lottie felt her skin was melting, her body fusing with his until she no longer knew where the boundaries were between them.

Here, in this deep cave burrowed into the earth, no-one could hear their cries of sensual delight as they abandoned themselves to the desire they had suppressed for so long. Cold though their refuge was, they were damper than the cellar walls when they finally exploded into each other and clung together tightly, exhausted by their shared passion, perspiration pearling their skin, hearts pounding, their breath exchanged and mingled, exhaling in quick gasps.

Stunned by the experience, it took Lottie some minutes to regain her ragged breathing as she lay in Thierry's arms, cocooned in a warm, tingling sensation of utter peace.

They lay together in silent harmony until Thierry shifted his wounded leg and winced in pain.

Lottie stroked his face. "Are you alright?"

"I can honestly say I have never felt more right, my love. Ah, Charlotte. I adore you!"

"I love you too, Thierry."

Lottie lay back and disentangled her legs from his good one, so he could be more comfortable.

"First time for me." Lottie nibbled his ear, savouring the taste of him and her sensation of complete bliss.

"Me too." Thierry stroked her shoulder where it connected with her neck.

Lottie propped herself up on one elbow. "Really? I thought it was different for men."

"Not all men are like that, Charlotte."

138

"I'm glad."

"Me, too."

"Can we do it again, now we're no longer virgins?" Lottie giggled softly.

"I think we should, it's only right." Thierry chuckled back. "A little more slowly, this time, so we really get the hang of it."

They slept deeply that night. Lottie didn't even feel anxious when the lamp gave out and she woke in pitch darkness. While she could hear Thierry's heart thumping a steady rhythm next to hers, she was in the safest place in the whole world.

The next morning, when a sharp rap on the hatch jerked them awake and someone flung it open, they got up and lit a candle to dress by.

"I think we're meant to go up, as the trap door has been left open." Lottie straightened her dress. Would she look different to a keen observer like Bernadette this morning? She felt different enough. Thierry, now fully dressed in Monsieur Perrot's rustic outfit, grabbed her around the waist.

"One big kiss before we join the others."

Lottie had no hesitation in complying with his request.

Thierry drew away eventually. "We'd better go upstairs before I get too carried away and pin you to the bed for the rest of the day."

Laughing, Lottie turned and clambered up the ladder in a happy haze.

They ate breakfast alone; the others were already out in the garden. "Ah, Thierry, if only this was our farmhouse and we were starting every day together like this."

"Don't torture yourself with wishes."

Lottie cut some more bread. "It's not torture to wish you could stay forever."

"It is to me." Thierry turned as Bernadette came through the door.

"Finished breakfast, you two?"

Lottie nodded. "Just about."

"Good. It's time to complete his new look." Bernadette had the walnut hair dye ready in an old pudding basin, its porcelain cracked with age, on the huge oak buffet. She picked it up slapped it on Thierry's blonde head before combing it through, without any polite preamble. She even pasted some on his eyebrows. Thierry suffered her attentions in courteous silence.

"Goodness, you do look different and your beard is coming on too. Lucky for you that your facial hair is darker than the hair on your head." Lottie found the transformation both alarming and reassuring. "Leave your glasses off. Yes, it's really good. You don't look like Thierry Thibault anymore."

"Go and sit in the sunshine to make it set." Bernadette waved him outside.

"But…"

"I'll keep watch." Lottie smiled at him as she followed him out of the door. "The sun will do you good after days in that dank old cellar."

"Be vigilant then. I'm terrified I'll bring trouble to this kind family." Thierry sat on the bench under the apple tree where they had so often sat before.

"Then you must do what Bernadette says. Here, use this staff you had before if you need to get up." Lottie wandered off towards the lane to check for unwanted guests. She hugged the memory of last night to her as she meandered towards the road, pulling seed heads off the tall grasses and inhaling the sweet scent of the May blossom. After half an hour she did see a man walking towards her, but it wasn't a German.

"Pierre!"

Pierre raised an enormous palm in greeting. "Good morning, mademoiselle."

140

She held out her hands and kissed him on his rough cheek, standing on tiptoe to reach.

"Is he here?"

Lottie tugged him along. "In the orchard, come."

"Is that wise in broad daylight?"

"We are very isolated."

"Still, you must be very careful."

Lottie nodded. "We know. That's why I was on the lookout. Have you got different papers for him?"

"Not yet."

"We've been working on making him look like your average peasant." Lottie stood back to watch Pierre's face when he first saw Thierry.

Pierre let out a guffaw. "Very good! You certainly don't look like a teacher now."

"Pierre!" Thierry used the crutch they'd made from an oak tree branch to heave himself up.

Pierre frowned. "You won't get far like that, my friend."

"It's mending fast. Any news? What's happened to the others?"

Pierre sat down on the bench, his face grave. "They didn't wait until the twelfth. Twenty-eight hostages were shot yesterday because of the train."

Thierry thumped his good thigh. "Shit. It's hard to justify what we did when you hear that."

Lottie looked at Pierre's grave face, then back at Thierry's downturned mouth.

They were all silent for a moment before Thierry took a deep breath. "Do we know how many Germans we took out?"

Pierre frowned. "Ten killed and twenty-two wounded."

"A third of those innocents who paid the price." Thierry ran his hands through his damp hair and looked at the stained palm afterwards. "Seems it's not dry yet."

141

Pierre didn't smile. "You need papers. They are searching for you everywhere. As soon as you didn't turn up at the school, you were linked to the train incident."

"What about her?" Thierry nodded towards Lottie who was standing in the shade.

Pierre shook his head. "There's been no mention of a girl that I've heard about. It's you they want."

Lottie saw the relaxation in Thierry's face when he heard this.

He looked up at her, his blue eyes eloquent without his glasses to obscure them. "All the more reason for me to go. Can you get me some new papers quickly?"

Pierre nodded. "I'll come back this afternoon with my camera and take a photograph of your new look and then I'll go straight to the forger. We should be able to organise it in a couple of days."

"And the contact for going south?"

"I'll see to it." Pierre got up. "I won't shake your hand, Thierry."

Thierry laughed. "Very wise."

Pierre smiled briefly. "What about a name?"

"If I'm not being looked for, use Charles Perrot." Lottie ventured.

Thierry shook his head. "No. It would still link me to this farm. I don't want those bastards coming anywhere near you."

Pierre hitched up the satchel he always wore. "I need a name now, to give to the forger."

"Leave it up to him, Pierre. He'll have the best idea. Tell him I'm dark and a farmer now."

"Very well. I'll see you later then."

"Thanks, friend. Take care."

The two men embraced, and Pierre loped off, his long stride quickly taking him out of view.

"I'd better wash my hands." Thierry limped into the kitchen and sluiced the dye off his hands at the sink.

"You know, your hands are a little unworn for a farm hand's. I shouldn't worry too much about the stains." Lottie gave him a cloth to dry them.

"Well spotted. Give me something to do with them. Something that will chafe!"

Bernadette was kneading dough on the table. "I need a wall mending. You can perch on a stool while you work. Working with stone and sand is the quickest way I know to roughen hands, especially if you use a bit of lime."

Thierry, who had been very solemn after Pierre's news, brightened perceptibly. "I'd be glad to repay your hospitality. Set me to work!"

Interrupted only by Pierre's quick visit to take his photograph in the goat's barn, Thierry worked diligently on the stone wall at the back of the hen house for the next two days, sitting on the milking stool, with his leg stretched out to the side. The sun was hot in the May sunshine and Lottie could almost imagine they would live here together for the rest of their days.

The nights in the dark cellar were heaven to her. They slept or made love as the mood took them, exchanging their deepest thoughts along with deeper kisses. Lottie never wanted it to end. The rhythm of the farm took over once more and even Françoise's bottom lip retreated under Thierry's irrepressible charm. Only Lottie heard the despair he felt over the tragedy of the hostages. Only she knew it wasn't just his hands that chafed at night. Although she also knew Thierry had to go to keep himself and them safe, Lottie dreaded Pierre's return.

All too soon, Pierre came marching up the little lane with his wide stride. "You look suitably tanned and hardy, I must say, Leon Durand."

"I like that name. Good solid French stock. Yes, I'll take that as a good omen that I will endure, whatever comes." Thierry mopped the sweat from his tanned face and held out a newly hardened palm to receive the little, vital documents.

143

A knot tightened in Lottie's stomach. Not long now and he would be gone.

CHAPTER NINETEEN
NORMANDY, FRANCE
MAY 1942

Things happened too fast for Lottie after that. That evening, when they were all gathered around the radio trying to listen to Radio Londres through the crackles, another visitor stealthily crept through the woods at the rear of Bernadette's orchard and knocked on the back door.

Bernadette got up and went to the window while Lottie switched off the radio and covered it with a towel. Bernadette looked through a tiny gap in the curtains then turned back to Thierry.

"A man in a cap. About fifty years old. Can't see his face."

"Let him in." Thierry limped over and stood behind the door.

A man slipped inside. He moved like a cat, liquid and silent.

Bernadette stayed by the door, after pulling the bar across to lock it. "Lucien Dubois. I should have guessed."

Monsieur Dubois drew off his greasy cap and nodded acknowledgment at Bernadette. "I'm looking for Leon Durand."

"That's me." Thierry went up and shook his hand.

"You're not Durand, you are the schoolteacher, Thibault, aren't you?"

"Never heard of him." Thierry smiled.

"Hmm. I see. Well, Monsieur Durand, you need to get ready. What's wrong with your leg?"

"It's fine. I can walk as well as any man."

"Tell me the truth. I don't want any lame dogs." Monsieur Dubois looked around the room. He seemed to take in every detail all at once.

"Very well. Bullet wound fractured my fibula in my right leg, but it's mending fast. I'm still wearing splints."

Monsieur Dubois made a very French sound of disgust. "Not good." He hunched his shoulders under his ancient leather coat. "Don't expect me to slow down if you can't keep up. Be ready tomorrow night about this time. Don't bring any luggage. Wear a coat and good shoes and make sure your identity papers are sound. I'll see you then."

With that, he made for the door. "Good to see you, Bernadette. Or maybe I should call you 'Comrade' from now on?"

"Don't push your luck, Lucien. I haven't become a Communist just because of him."

"Pity. We could use a woman like you."

"You already are! There's nothing like a common enemy to bring people together. See you tomorrow." Bernadette opened the door for him, and he disappeared back into the night.

"Come on, Françoise. Time for bed." Bernadette bustled about.

"But I'm not sleepy."

"Then read in bed." Bernadette's mouth was set firm.

"Oh, honestly." Françoise flounced out of the room.

"We'll feed you up and look at that leg tomorrow. Good night." Bernadette followed her granddaughter up the stairs.

"Goodnight." Thierry and Lottie spoke together. The minute Bernadette's black boots had left the last stair, they were in each other's arms.

"I don't think I can bear it, Thierry." Lottie whispered the words she'd forbidden herself to say out loud.

"I know, oh, I know." Thierry kissed her so passionately, he bruised her lips and she relished the pain.

"You'll be gone tomorrow."

He dropped his arms. "Yes."

"Let's make the most of tonight, Thierry. Let's be together properly, while we can."

Silently, they made their way back down to the cellar, pausing only to kiss. Lottie felt caught up in time, unhurried, golden.

She closed the trap door behind them once Thierry had lowered himself down to the cellar and lit the oil lamp. A soft mellow glow filled the gloomy space.

"You should sleep, really. Save your energy."

"To hell with that." Thierry took off his shirt and threw it on the chair Bernadette had placed in the corner.

Lottie lifted her summer dress over her head.

"Let me do the rest?" Thierry came to her and pulled her camisole up and over her head before slipping his hands down to her knickers. Lottie helped him by sliding them down her legs with her feet and then kicking them off.

"So beautiful." Thierry kissed her neck, her shoulder, her breasts. Then he sat down on the chair and Lottie helped him off with the rest of his clothes.

Without words, they drifted across to the bed and lay down together, their breath hot and quick, their hands wandering at will, exploring each other's bodies, laughing over the acrobatics needed when one leg out of four was in a splint.

Afterwards, they lay together, arms entwined, silent while their breath slowed into deep rhythmic unison.

They did sleep in the end but not for very long. They were woken by stirrings in the kitchen above. The lamp had again gone out, but Lottie never found the blackness frightening while Thierry lay beside her.

She kissed his nose and he stirred. Lottie rolled out on to the floor and groped for the candle and matches she knew lay between the two mattresses. She scrabbled about for a minute and then found them and struck a match. It was damp and took a few goes before she managed to light the candle. In the soft glow she clambered back into bed beside him and pressed her cold body into his warm one, making each of her curves meld into his.

"Thierry, will you make love to me just once more?"

"Very happy to oblige."

Eventually they tore themselves apart and got dressed.

Lottie had never felt less like beginning a new day. Her body was singing with joy; she never wanted to stop feeling like this and yet the harsh truth must be acknowledged. "Our last day together."

Thierry held her close. "It's not going to be forever."

Lottie shivered within his embrace and whispered, "I hope to God you are right."

The day passed all too swiftly, partly because they had got up so late. Françoise was grumpy, having done the milking again, but Bernadette was kind, kinder than Lottie had ever known.

They had proper coffee for breakfast again – both of them. Lottie had forgotten how good it tasted. And goat's butter on their bread as well as cherry jam. They ate alone, the others were outside, weeding the vegetables from where they had good sight of the lane through the lavender border.

"I wish I could do more to help Bernadette. She has been incredible." Thierry poured out more coffee and sniffed the aroma issuing from his cup.

Lottie smiled. "I think she must have loved her husband very much, once upon a time."

Thierry nodded. "She must have loved someone, she certainly understands."

"I'm sure she'll get me to work out my penance, once you're gone. She's taken a shine to you. And you a teacher too."

"What's wrong with being a teacher?"

"Didn't you know? You poach children away from the land into far off cities of wickedness."

"Ah, the sin of education."

148

Lottie helped Thierry mix up more mortar after their luxurious breakfast and he took great pride in finishing the low wall enclosing the chicken run. It took all day, a day Lottie never wanted to end.

Bernadette came and inspected it as the evening shadows cast their markers across the orchard. "Hmm, not bad, for a teacher."

Thierry and Lottie exchanged smiles and tried not to laugh.

"What's so funny?" Bernadette scowled from one to the other.

"Oh, nothing."

Bernadette shrugged. "Right. Time to go in for supper and then we must check that leg before Lucien Dubois comes."

Supper passed, like the rest of that sunny day, much too swiftly for Lottie. Françoise cleared the table with unnecessary clatter and Bernadette made Thierry sit on the settle to examine his leg, which she propped up on the milking stool from the barn.

Lottie brought the oil lamp over and held it high, fascinated to watch the splints come off and expose the wound underneath.

Bernadette washed off the yellow paste so delicately Thierry didn't even wince but also watched with great interest.

"Humph. It's done well." Bernadette sat back on her haunches.

"It's fantastic! Look at how the skin is already knitting back together." Lottie couldn't believe her eyes at the healing that had taken place.

"What's in that yellow stuff, then, Bernadette? Miracle powder?" Thierry stroked his shin tentatively.

"That's for me to know. My mother's recipe. Never fails. Plants are powerful healers." Bernadette rinsed out the cloth in the basin. "Now, teacher, I want you to try standing without the splints."

149

"Are you sure I won't undo your handiwork?" Thierry shifted forward on his seat, ready to stand up.

"It is a risk, but you'll be less noticeable if you can manage without."

Thierry leaned on Lottie's shoulder and stood up. He put his foot to the floor very tentatively. "Ouch!"

"Sit straight back down. I thought so, it's a pity but it's too soon. The bone might fracture again. Never mind, I've made some new splints. Here." Bernadette reached behind and brought out some pieces of planed wood that had been wrapped in a cloth. "It's good, solid oak and I've sanded it down so it's as smooth as silk. See? I've curved them to fit round your leg."

"Bernadette, you're a genius." Thierry reached over and kissed her on the mouth.

"That's quite enough of that. Hold still, young man." Bernadette looked pleased, just the same, as she wound a fresh cotton strip around his lower leg and then rolled a thick woollen sock over the bandage. "You," she nodded at Lottie, "hold the splints just so, while I bind them."

Soon, Thierry was standing up again, without grimacing in pain, and testing the weight.

"Very good. Now, I have got these boots with wooden soles. Everyone's wearing them these days because they can't get the leather. We'll slide his leg with the splints inside and that will not only hide them but they will act as support for each other. The wood will take the weight instead of your foot." Bernadette jerked her head towards Lottie. "She gave me the idea."

Thierry submitted to the boots and strode about the kitchen, almost evenly.

"Marvellous! I'm good as new, Bernadette! You know, you should have been a doctor."

"Humph. The old ways are the best. And here's a walking stick to go with it." She looked at Lottie. "Let's get this mess cleared up. It's nearly time."

150

Lottie, distracted by the excitement of the operation, looked at the clock, shocked to see it was nearly nine o'clock already. She looked at Thierry and found he was staring right back at her. He smiled and nodded. He knew. He felt the same. She thought she might choke on the lump in her throat and busied herself gathering up the paraphernalia strewn about the settle.

She had barely finished when there was a soft knock at the door.

"I'll go." Françoise went to the window and pulled back the curtains a fraction. "It's Monsieur Dubois again."

She opened the door and Monsieur Dubois came in, the shoulders of his coat and his cap wet with rain.

"Good evening. Are you ready, son?"

"Hello. I'll just get my coat." Thierry shook his hand.

"I told you to be ready." Lucien Dubois looked seriously cross.

Bernadette stepped in. "We had to dress his leg, Lucien, but it's much better. He'll be able to walk almost normally now."

"Good, he'll need to. A limp and a stick are very conspicuous, but this rain is good. The Germans don't usually prowl about in bad weather unless they have to."

"I'll get your things." Lottie made for the cellar and Thierry followed her to the top of the stone steps.

"Stay there, Thierry. I'll still be quicker than you, even with your new splints."

"Kiss me first, darling, please." He grabbed her and crushed her against his chest.

She pulled back. "We mustn't keep him waiting."

"I love you, Charlotte."

"I know." Lottie turned and bolted down the stairs and then the ladder. She came back with his coat and beret. He was already back with the others in the kitchen.

Monsieur Dubois looked even crosser. "This is taking too long! Have you got your papers?"

151

Thierry held them out for inspection.

"Scuff them up a bit, make them look worn."

Thierry rubbed the little cards against his rough coat.

"Time to go." Monsieur Dubois nodded at each of them in turn. "Say nothing to anybody. Nothing, do you hear? You never saw me," he looked at Thierry, "and you never saw him either."

Bernadette nodded, her face as solemn as his. "Understood, Lucien. Off you go, young man. Keep safe."

Thierry kissed her wrinkled cheeks. "I will." He kissed Françoise the same way. "Give my love to Bertrand too?"

Françoise nodded and touched her cheeks where he had kissed her.

Then he turned to Lottie and whispered in her ear. "Goodbye. I'll see you again, I know it, my love."

Lottie leant forward and kissed his mouth, just briefly, just enough to savour the taste of his lips one last time. She couldn't speak but pushed him gently towards the other man, who looked more impatient than ever at this further delay.

Thierry went to the door, his step almost level, and opened it. Monsieur Dubois walked through first, and Thierry looked around at the three women. He blew them each a kiss before disappearing into the rainy night. The door shut behind him. Lottie began to run to the window to watch him go but Bernadette stopped her.

"Leave it, child. Let him go. Lucien might be a Communist but he's also a countryman. He knows his way about even in the dark. Your man is in good hands."

Lottie slumped on to the settle and stared into the flames burning in the range. She felt torn in half; she would never feel whole until he was with her again. She remembered the night before when their bodies were completely united. Whatever came, even if it was a child,

152

she would never regret last night. She made a silent prayer that it wouldn't be all she would ever have of him.

CHAPTER TWENTY
WHITE WALTHAM AERODROME, ENGLAND
MAY 1942

"Another Spitfire for Prestwick, Al." There was a new girl in the office. There seemed to be a new one every week, operations were expanding so fast.

"Another one? Why are they all going so far north?"

Judy raised her eyebrows. "Haven't you heard? It's for the American aircraft carrier. '*The Wasp*' it's called."

Al shook his head. "Daft name for a big ship like that."

"I know! Let's hope these Spitfires can deliver a good sting off its decks."

"Do we know its destination?" It was the fifth Spitfire Al would have flown to Prestwick in a week, and he wasn't the only one.

Trixie, the girl in charge of the rota on the next desk, lowered her voice. "I've heard it's off to Malta, but I think it's hush-hush."

Al frowned. "Thought it had already gone when we took a load up there before? The RAF gave the Krauts a bit of a licking, I'd heard."

Judy signed his form. "It's come back for more. Finish the job off, so to speak."

"Okay, mum's the word. I'll be off then." Al picked up his chit and went out into the bright sunshine in search of his plane. At least there was no hanging about this time of the year. What a difference the weather made. It had been a penance waiting for the rain to clear sometimes over the long winter.

Up in the air, he felt free. He looked around to check there was no other aircraft in the vicinity. Then he put the Spitfire into a spin, 360 degrees, just to shake himself up a bit, even though it was against all the rules. There was no other feeling like this. He felt invincible. Fair weather clouds presented no obstacle but mere wisps of white fluff to glide through. He played with being invisible by disappearing into a cloud formation for a few seconds. There was no-one to tell him what to do up here, and, apart from delivering the kite on time, no-one to confuse or upset him. No Miriam clinging to his arm at a dance; no Isobel to turn his heart over.

He'd telephoned his parents last night. They were alright; more than alright, his Mum had said. Making a packet out of the war with four new girls signed on at the factory only last week. His Dad was in the Home Guard and they'd been issued with proper rifles. All well and good. Then he'd asked about Bella. Might as well have been a bomb dropping.

He swooped up into the clouds again, diving into their soft billowing anonymity, sheltering within their secret, soft, concealing folds. He didn't want to land this plane anywhere. What if he just flew on into France? What would Isobel think if he was shot down, killed or captured? Would she care? Miriam would. He ought to put a stop to their affair. He didn't love her. The longer it went on, the harder it would be to finish it. She'd already started on about what they'd do after the war.

After the war. As if it would ever bloody end.

And his mum had said Bella was in north Wales again. Lloyd senior had popped his clogs. No doubt Geraint would now be even richer than before and even more keen to marry. What would Bella do? She'd refused Al's offer of marriage, saying she was too young. Why didn't that apply to Geraint Lloyd? Or did his advanced age cancel her youth out? He'd a good mind to turn this bird around and fly over the 'beautiful Arts and Crafts manor house' Bella had talked about in such glowing terms.

He'd do it! He was going to fly right over Chester anyway. Al focussed on the map beside him. They were allowed to mark where the balloon barrages and defended areas were now, and he knew the name of the village next to

155

the house. Surely, if it was that bloody magnificent, he'd be able to pick it out?

He swung west till he located the River Dee then pointed the nose of the little aeroplane northwards until he found the lake that Bella had described so vividly. He could see the curve of the huge Mersey river curling through the docks of Liverpool in the distance and the mountains of Snowdonia to the west. It must be here somewhere.

He was too high. He took a sharp dive towards the earth, ignoring the protests of the engine.

Bella was right. It was beautiful countryside. The smoke of Liverpool didn't penetrate these moors and mountains, or the villages tucked between them in the snug valleys. With a pang, he understood why Bella, who loved the countryside, loved anything beautiful, would be tempted to live amongst this grandeur; that she would find it inspirational for her painting and even her happiness. This sweeping majestic landscape, coupled with the ease Lloyd's fortune would provide, meant Isobel would not only be secure herself, but so would her beloved mother, together with Cheadle Manor and all its dependants. Isobel adored her mother. Relieving her of the burden of the financial debts the manor struggled under would be a massive incentive.

But what about Lottie? She was the real owner, the sole owner of Cheadle Manor, after all. Would she ever return? God, everything was so damned uncertain these days. This bloody war had brought nothing but chaos. Isobel would never have met Geraint Lloyd if she hadn't been posted up to this Godforsaken windswept part of the world.

He abandoned the attempt to find the Lloyd residence. Suddenly, he didn't want to know anymore, to locate its exact position in this fierce, pristine landscape. He veered east recklessly, tipping the wing too sharply. The engine whined as it compensated for the sudden change in direction. A part of him wanted to point the nose directly at the ground and lance it. Then the black thought lifted as

156

swiftly as it had come. Ashamed of himself, he remembered the RAF pilots who were waiting to fly this incredible machine. He didn't know what Malta looked like, but everyone had heard what a hard time they were having in their strategic position in the Mediterranean. His life didn't matter, perhaps, but this game little fighting machine did.

He eased back the throttle and adjusted the wing tip. The Spitfire always had a tendency to yaw to the right. He corrected the balance and regained his course above the Welsh borders, heading north. He could clearly see the bomb damage at the port of Liverpool inflicted during the blitz last year. Poor bastards. They were sitting ducks alright, with the Mersey so easy to identify and all those ships waiting to sail from its docks. He leaned down to get a better look out of the cockpit side window. Vast areas of the city had been reduced to rubble; wiped out. What was he on about? There were people down there who'd lost everything, including their lives. He gave himself a mental shake and resolved to shelve his love life until after the war, should he survive it.

He'd give Miriam the elbow when he got back. He'd do it gently. He'd be kind. But he couldn't go on like this, whatever Bella decided about her own future. He couldn't go on living a lie.

Lottie's period was late. She didn't know if she was sad or happy about it. She ached for Thierry rather than his child. It was the man she needed, not a vulnerable infant.

Having watched Françoise give birth and raise a child without a father, she had no illusions about how hard it was. Françoise was more uneasy than ever about little Bertrand as a new edict had appeared forcing all Jews to wear a fabric yellow star on their clothing, so they were easily identified as aliens.

Lottie gazed at Bertrand, who was asleep on a couple of rugs on the grass nearby. Françoise had put him under some dappled shade in the orchard by the old bench and Lottie was nearby, feeding the hens. Their contented clucks didn't seem to bother the sleeping child. Lottie rubbed her belly; how would she cope if a new life had germinated within her? Was it really morally defensible to bring another soul into this twisted world? What did their German overlords think about illegitimate children anyway? She couldn't contact Thierry to tell him if she had conceived a child. She had no idea of his whereabouts or any way of knowing if she'd even see him again.

Lottie sat down on the bench where she had so often sat with Thierry. Was he already out of the Occupied Zone? Could he walk properly on that leg? Was he still in France or had he fled into Spain? Or simply dead? Would she feel it if he was killed?

Other murders had taken place since he'd left. Eleven communists had been shot in Caen and she was sure there were many more executions elsewhere. They'd even arrested twenty people who'd had the temerity to throw wreaths at the monument to the dead back in November in Caen. Bakeries were forced to shut on Sundays and Mondays now and bread was rationed along with everything else. She had no bicycle to go and find out more from Madame Leroy, even if she dared to leave the farm.

Françoise walked across the yard and joined her. She looked at her peaceful son. "He looks out for the count. It's learning to walk that's so tiring."

"You'll need eyes in the back of your head soon, Bernadette says." Lottie patted the seat. "Come and sit down for five minutes."

Françoise smiled. "Thanks. It's good to stop."

Lottie looked at her friend and picked up her hand. "Look how strong your hands are now, Françoise."

"Careworn, you mean. Gone are the days of nail polish and perfume. Sometimes I wonder if we'll ever see Paris again."

"I prefer your hands like this. They look capable and caring."

Françoise guffawed. "Chapped and sore from work most of the time. Still, I have come to love this farm and my grandmother isn't a bad old stick really."

"She's fantastic, Françoise. You should be proud of her."

"I am, actually. She's a lot more impressive than my mother, for all her glamour. This war has taught me so much, however hateful it is."

"I know what you mean, and I think I owe you an apology."

Françoise raised her eyebrows. "Whatever for?"

"All those patronising lectures about David. I know what it is to fall in love now and how easy it is to take risks in the heat of the moment."

Françoise's blue eyes widened. "Did you and Thierry, you know?"

Lottie nodded. Unconsciously, she stroked her stomach. "Yes, and I'm sorry I was such a pompous idiot to you. It's impossible to stop when you get swept up in all the emotion, isn't it?"

Françoise squeezed the hand she still held. "Do you think you are pregnant?"

"I don't know. I'm a bit late – just a couple of days."

"What will you do, if you are?"

"I don't know that, either. Part of me wants to have something of Thierry if he never comes back, and let's face it, the odds are against it. Another part of me wants to get back to the fight, without anything or anyone holding me back. I hate these Nazis so much."

Lottie cried when the blood came two days later. Cried and cried and cried. Françoise heard her and came up to the attic.

"What is it?"

Lottie grabbed a handkerchief and wiped her eyes. She blew her nose and sniffed, took deep breaths before she could reply.

"No baby, after all."

"Oh, Lottie! No wonder you're upset." Françoise sat down on the bed beside her and put her arm around her friend.

Lottie leant into her shoulder as more tears fell. "I didn't really want a baby. I just want him!"

"I know; there, there." Françoise patted her back until Lottie regained control.

She sat up. "I'm fine, honestly. It was as if he was still with me while I thought, you know, before…"

"You don't have to explain. And I've been thinking, I owe you an apology too."

"Oh?"

Françoise gave a half-hearted laugh. "I was so fed up when Thierry was here, seeing you were so much in love with each other, and I know I was really grumpy. I was just jealous of your happiness. I still think of David, you know. Every day. I look at Bertrand searching for some likeness, little quirks he had, the way he would smile with his big brown eyes. Then I remember what a rat he was for disappearing without leaving me word. And then I almost hate him."

"This bloody war."

"Yes." Françoise sighed. "I expect he's dead now. So many are. I've given up hope. It's easier that way."

"Maybe I should too. The chances of Thierry surviving are close to zero."

"At least we are still friends, have each other?"

Lottie threw her arms around her friend. "Absolutely."

Lottie's physical pain passed with the days, but her soul remained bruised. Françoise kept to her word and the two girls became much closer. Bernadette looked approvingly at them as they shared the chores and the childcare more evenly.

Lottie was helping her hoe the rows of vegetables in the kitchen garden one afternoon a few days later. The weeds had responded to a recent fall of rain with rampant growth.

Bernadette handed her the secateurs. "You and Françoise seem to be getting on better."

"Yes, it helps."

"Well, that's something, at least. I was talking to one of the fishermen from the coast at the market yesterday. Seems the Boche are building a wall where he used to keep his boat. Poor bugger can't get near it now."

"Why not?"

"Germans have taken over the whole of the shoreline and everyone has been moved inland to stay with friends or family, if they've any left. Some of them are starving. I gave him the last of the leeks."

"So, they're not allowed to fish at all?"

Bernadette shook her head. "No, can't get to their boats. Seems the Nazis have taken over the hotels on the seafront too. The whole area is no-go because they've

161

reinforced the 'Zone Interdite' border north of the Route Nationale. Like it's a foreign country or something."

"What? The whole area is just for Germans?"

"Not entirely, just near the beaches, but of course that includes the fishing fleet. That's where they are setting up this so-called 'Atlantic Wall'. Barbed wire everywhere, he said, and a huge gun is planned at Longues-sur-Mer."

"No expense spared then."

"That's right. Hitler can find the money for killing machines, but he can't let our fishermen catch the food their families rely on." Bernadette spat on the ground. "Filthy pigs."

Lottie thought for a moment. "They'll need more men, surely, to build something as big as that? The place will be swarming with even more soldiers soon."

"Not necessarily. I've heard they are setting up a work camp on this side of Bayeux."

"Where are the workers coming from?"

"No idea, but I'll bet the Boche will drag them in from somewhere. Just hope it won't be farmworkers, there's barely any left. I'm glad I have you two girls to help me out on the farm."

A couple of weeks later, they heard disturbing news on the radio. Pierre Laval, Minister of Information and Interior, spoke directly to his people over the crackling wireless set.

Françoise had been chattering on about Bertrand learning to talk but Bernadette stopped her clacking knitting needles and held up one hand. "Be quiet. This is important."

Lottie hadn't been doing anything except daydreaming and making imaginary shapes from the fire flames. At first, she found it hard to concentrate, as the politician intoned his policy objectives through the wire mesh of the Bakelite box.

"We, the French Government, wish to re-establish normal and trusting relations with Germany and Italy. Indeed, a German victory is to be welcomed because, otherwise, Bolshevism would establish itself everywhere."

"German victory? What is the man on about?" Lottie was shocked out of her reverie by this announcement.

"Over my dead body. I don't like the Commies any more than he does but that's ridiculous." Bernadette had abandoned her knitting and sat on the edge of her chair to listen as Laval went on to request volunteer workers to go to Germany in return for the release of prisoners-of-war held there.

"That's blackmail!" Lottie stood up and leaned closer to the radio.

Françoise went pale. "They wouldn't make me go, would they? I mean, I have a child. Oh, they wouldn't make me go too?"

Bernadette shook her head. "It'll be men first, I dare say. Don't worry, child."

"Don't worry? That's easy for you to say, you're too old to be called up."

Lottie paced the kitchen. "But listen, didn't you notice? He's not calling people up - he's asking for volunteers and using the release of the prisoners-of-war as bait. Just imagine, if you had a brother over there, how would you feel if you didn't come forward to release him? That is clever; clever and really wicked."

She stopped her pacing and turned to Bernadette. "Do you think they'll force people to work for this Atlantic Wall that they're developing on the coast?"

Bernadette spread her hands. "Can they force people? As you say, he's asking for volunteers. I heard the Germans are using their own soldiers to work on the coastal defences but who knows? So many people have already been displaced from their homes and livelihoods. One thing's for sure, the Boche will do just as they like."

163

CHAPTER TWENTY-TWO
CHEADLE MANOR, ENGLAND
JUNE 1942

Isobel leant her head against the train window. She didn't care if she left a smudge of powder against the thick glass. It wouldn't be the first. She'd be glad to get home and take off all this stupid make-up. She looked at her reflection, distorted by the rattling vibration of the train as it sped back southwards towards her home.

She'd painted her lips fashionably scarlet for the funeral. Mrs Lloyd had taken her into Chester to buy new clothes for the occasion, brooking no argument about the expense. She'd then marched her into Boots, the chemist, for cosmetics Isobel didn't want. Foundation, powder, lipstick, even rouge. Isobel thought the result made her look like a painted doll. Geraint had looked pained when he saw her descend the wide oak staircase, dressed all in black, a hat with a spotted veil over her face, the make-up too vivid underneath its net.

She'd felt like a mannikin dressed up for the shop window of the cathedral. Painted to conform to Mrs Lloyd's ideal of a daughter-in-law, ready for inspection by the great and the good of the county.

Geraint had given her his arm when they'd entered the packed cathedral. With so many eyes watching her, she felt she'd had no choice but to slip hers inside the crook of his and concede to solemnly marching up the aisle at his side. Hundreds of pairs of eyes bore into her back. Isobel had adamantly refused the fur coat Mrs Lloyd had wanted to buy her, protesting it was far too expensive for one occasion and in this battle she had won. The cashmere tailored coat they'd finally agreed upon, like her hat and dress, had been made up for her in relentless black. Deep mourning for a man whose company she had only experienced for one week, for most of which he'd been incarcerated in his bedroom. She must have spent all of five hours with him in his entire lifetime and she felt a complete hypocrite.

Geraint ushered her in to the front pew. The family, as was always the custom, were the last to arrive, swiftly followed by the coffin. Mr Lloyd's corpse was encased in deepest ebony. The coffin's highly polished silver handles were held by six pallbearers walking in slow ponderous, everlasting steps up to the altar.

Isobel, who had never felt so healthy and strong as during these last couple of years as a Land Girl, felt weak and faint. The geometric patterns on the tiled floor made her eyes ache. She studied the ornately carved wooden pews instead, but she still faltered when she stood up to mark her respect with the rest of the congregation. Geraint was quick to put his hand under her elbow, exerting a gentle yet firm pressure to hold her upright.

Isobel blinked and tried to focus on the almost black coffin laid tenderly down in front of her through the ridiculous spots of her hat net. They were enough to make anyone feel dizzy.

The service passed horribly slowly. Eulogy after eulogy issued forth from the pulpit as the worthy merchants of Liverpool spouted their praise of Geraint's father in a show of solidarity, celebrating the wealth created by their generation. Many of the elders had been Victorians, whose forebears had made their fortunes on the backs of slaves imported in their thousands through the port of Liverpool on the death ships from Africa. Isobel knew little of worldly affairs, but she knew about that. Lottie had told her about it in great indignation when she discovered the history of the British Empire in her usual forensic desire for the truth. It seemed Isobel wasn't the only hypocrite present.

Geraint left their pew and went to the pulpit to give the last of the speeches. "It is a very sad day for me and my family." He nodded directly at Isobel when he said this. "Today, we lay my father to rest. I hope I can live up to his excellent example and carry on the business in the same

165

exemplary manner my father brought to the many projects he accomplished." Isobel didn't listen to the rest. The sense that her future was being mapped out for her was too overwhelming. She didn't want to hear the details.

After an interminable time, they followed the coffin to the churchyard and stood in incongruous sunshine as Mr Lloyd was interred in the consecrated ground. Her black clothes absorbed the heat of the sun, now at its zenith. Isobel quietly perspired under the expensive material and longed to fling off the distressing black net that bounced spots in front of her eyes. She looked across at Geraint. He still looked his age, perhaps even older than he actually was. Lines from his nose to his mouth etched the pale skin either side of his greying moustache. The mouth itself was closed tight shut and turned down at the corners. After he sprinkled some Cheshire earth on the coffin, he drew out an immaculate white handkerchief and blew his nose.

Chastened, Isobel reached for his hand and squeezed it. Geraint looked down at her with deep emotion in his grey, kind eyes and nodded his acknowledgement of her compassion. Isobel smiled at him, then caught the gaze of his mother who was observing them closely, enveloping her in a net much bigger than the one on her elegant hat.

Eventually the Bishop, for he it was who had presided over the massively well-attended event, closed the proceedings with a blessing and the crowd dispersed.

Geraint once more took Isobel's arm into his and patted her hand. "Nearly over, my dear. Just the refreshments at The Grand Hotel and we will be able to go home. I'm so glad you are here, Isobel. I'm not sure I could have got through it without you."

The gathering at the lavish hotel had passed in a blur. Isobel had been introduced to more people than she could ever remember. She'd smiled at them all, shaken their hands, listened politely but only just managed to resist the intense desire to run away.

166

CHAPTER TWENTY-THREE
WHITE WALTHAM AERODROME, ENGLAND
AUGUST 1942

Al was delighted to be made up to a Class III pilot after the Spitfire deliveries to Prestwick but less thrilled at Miriam's reaction when he'd told her he wanted to cool things off a bit.

"But why, Al? You do like me, don't you?"

They'd been in the pub garden again, sitting on their own under the shade of a tree. Miriam had sat next to him on the wooden bench and kissed his neck between his collar and hairline.

Al pulled away. "Don't do that, Miriam."

At first, she had laughed. "Don't be silly, no-one's looking at us."

"It isn't that."

"Does it make you hot under the collar?" Miriam laughed more loudly and then a couple of people did turn and look at them.

Al shifted to a separate chair. "Keep your voice down."

"Oh, Al, it's not like you to care." Miriam took a Woodbine from the packet on the table. "Want one?"

"No thanks. Thing is, I've something to say."

Miriam blew smoke into the air and looked at him. Al tried not to notice the expectation and hope in her brown eyes.

"Ooh, you're not getting all serious, are you?"

"Yes, as a matter of fact, I am."

"I'm all ears, Al." She stubbed out her cigarette, even though it was hardly used, and put both hands on the table, reaching for his.

Al shoved his hands in his pockets. He cast his eyes over the crowded pub garden, hoping for inspiration. The

167

skin under his hairline and on his palms prickled with sweat. "Blooming hot weather, isn't it?"

"Oh, for heaven's sake, Al, don't talk about the weather at a time like this."

"No, sorry. Um, it's just that, with the war and everything, being so busy and stuff, I don't think I can go on seeing you."

Miriam's face was a picture. Just like in the films, her jaw dropped in comical dismay. Except Al wasn't finding the situation the least bit funny.

"You what?"

"It's not you, don't think that but, thing is, I love someone else. Someone at home. I'm not sure she loves me anymore but until I can stop loving her, I can't love anyone else." There, he'd finally said it. He'd been trying to find the words for a whole month.

"You don't mean it. You can't mean it! I don't believe you. Why've you been carrying on with me all this time then if you love this other girl so much?" Miriam's eyes weren't soft anymore but sparking with anger.

"You're right, I shouldn't have done. It just sort of happened that night in the Midlands. We were both so tired and fed up and I should never have taken advantage of you like that."

"I should think you did take advantage too, Albert Phipps. Well, I've never been more deceived by anyone in my life!" She was almost shouting now.

There were plenty of heads turned their way now. Al got up and turned his chair so they couldn't see his face and sat back down again.

There were a few laughs at that, and one young fellow came across and spoke to Miriam, ignoring Al entirely. "Is everything alright, Miss? Only, you look a bit upset."

Miriam's chin wobbled. "Oh, you are kind. I am a bit."

The young man turned to Al. "You want to watch your step, mate. Upsetting a nice young girl like that."

"Shove off, won't you? I'm not going to hurt her."

"How do I know that?"

"Because I said so, alright?" Al stood up and put his hands on his hips. "Why don't you mind your own business?"

The young man, who was a good deal shorter and slighter than Al, turned back to Miriam. "You sure you're alright?"

Miriam nodded. "Yes, honestly, I'm fine. He wouldn't hurt a fly. It's only words."

"If you're really sure, but I'll be just over there, and remember, there's plenty more fish in the sea." He winked at Miriam.

"Thanks." Miriam gave him a half-hearted smile and her admirer, after giving Al a hard stare, mooched back over to his friends. They slapped his back and welcomed him back into their circle with more guffaws.

Al ground his teeth. He wished he'd chosen somewhere more private for this tricky conversation.

Miriam lit another cigarette with shaky hands. She didn't offer one to Al this time.

Al studied her red nails clamped around the white stick. They were beautifully filed and tapered. Inspiration struck. "You're a good-looking woman, Miriam. Anyone would be proud to be seen with you. I'm sure you'll find someone else, someone better."

"Not better, Al. Never that. I thought you were going to ask me to marry you."

"I know. That's why I had to say something. Should have said it before."

"Yes, I think you should have. It wouldn't have hurt so much but then, we'd not have had our time together, would we? And it's been good times, hasn't it, Al?" Her voice was pleading, needy.

He decided not to tell the truth, so he nodded instead. "Yes, it's been great, Miriam, but it really is over. Let's face it, the war's not getting any easier and we're run off our feet. Now I'm a Class III I'll be doing the taxi runs on the Avro's, I expect, and never have a minute to myself."

"That's true." Miriam was one of the administrative staff and dealt out the operations rota.

"Maybe it would be easier if I asked for a transfer."

Miriam shook her head. "You don't have to do that. I won't embarrass you."

Al took his hands out of his pockets again. "But people will talk."

Miriam blew smoke into the air and looked away from him. "They'll soon forget about us. There's a war on."

"You're terrific, Miriam, do you know that?"

"Oh yes, so terrific, you're finished with me."

"We could still be friends, couldn't we?

"I don't know, Al. I don't think it would work." Miriam stubbed out her second half-finished cigarette. "I'll be off then. No, don't get up. I'd rather walk back on my own. Be seeing you."

As she walked past the other table, a couple of the blokes gave her a low wolf whistle. Miriam smiled at them and picked up her pace.

Al stared at his pint, then downed it in one go. He walked the other way, through the pub and out of the door.

CHAPTER TWENTY-FOUR
NORMANDY, FRANCE
MARCH 1943

Lottie stretched out in her bed in the attic. She'd already got up and opened the shutters, braving the cold just to see the daylight. It was almost the equinox, with the days and nights as long – or short, depending on how you looked at it – as each other. At last, the long dreary winter was over. Today, the frost had finally melted, and green shoots poked their spearheads through the soil, searching for the sun.

She wasn't sure she could endure another winter like the last. Those endless winter nights sleeping all alone, and the constant hunger. She'd relived every second of every minute when Thierry had shared this ancient farmhouse with her and the two other women, who now seemed like family to her. It had been so long since she'd heard from her own blood relatives. Sometimes she struggled to remember their voices, or even their faces, and that shocked her.

She clung to the vague hope that Thierry would somehow manage to contact her. Some days, the longing for news overwhelmed her completely and she would have to find a quiet corner in which to weep.

It hadn't been so bad in the summer. At least they'd had enough food then. Late in the autumn, German soldiers had come to the farm. Lottie had fled upstairs but watched from the windows under the attic gables as they tore around the place, raiding the stores. They'd taken all the carrots, parsnips and potatoes from the clamp, the apples and pears from the barn, so painstakingly kept separate in neat rows so they wouldn't spoil, and now tossed any-old-how into a sack before they threw it into their army truck. Lottie had learned enough about apples to know they'd be spoiled within the month.

The hens had flown up in the air in outrage, their feathers flying around them, as they were swept up by meaty hands and crammed too tightly into crates. Lottie had watched as Bernadette stood there in her yard, silent and immobile as a figure carved in stone, while her poultry flock and stores disappeared. The pillaging was over in a mere quarter of an hour.

But the soldiers hadn't found the lower cellar. That night, the three women had opened a bottle of Calvados to dull the rage, which was all the soldiers had left behind, along with the rejected goats and the donkey. It appeared they preferred horses to donkeys and creamy sweet cow's milk to the lighter, pure-white milk the nanny goats provided. Most of the local farms could provide plenty of both as Bernadette was unusual in keeping goats but that's why her cheeses sold so well - or used to.

But staying in bed brooding would do her no good. Lottie was awake now. She and Françoise took it in turns to milk the goats these days and it was her morning off. On past winter morning lie-ins, she'd wriggle back down under the covers and try to blot out the freezing cold, the memories and the fear, but the sunshine was too bright, too insistently energetic today.

She got up and pattered across in her thick socks to the mirror between the two empty beds opposite and looked at herself in the broken pane. Her hair was short now, the curls springy and close to her head, defiantly shiny, in spite of her meagre diet. It made her look optimistic, which she wasn't. She'd got Françoise to cut off her hair after Thierry had left. If the Gestapo did look for her, it would be for a girl with longer hair in a pretty summer dress. She never wore a skirt now but used old trousers left by the long-dead Charles Perrot. It was more practical when you were working like a man. She held his old coat around her thin waist with baler twine and covered her head with one of Bernadette's old woollen scarves tied tight under her chin when it was cold. No-one would mistake her for a posh young English girl now. She even thought in the local

French dialect most of the time. It was a good ruse to keep the loneliness at bay.

She dressed and went downstairs.

"You're up late this morning." Bernadette was at the sink, scraping out a saucepan.

Lottie wasn't sorry she'd missed their normal breakfast together. "Is it alright if I grab a slice of bread?"

Bernadette grunted. "Looks like you'll have to. Make the most of it, there's not much flour left. I'll have to use ground chestnuts soon."

Lottie hacked off a chunk of the tough bread, made mostly of rye flour they'd had in the bottom cellar. She tried to take a bite, but it was too hard. It was a wonder she still had teeth in her head.

"Mind if I heat some milk?"

"Mix it half and half with water." Bernadette wiped her hands on a tea towel. "The oldest nanny has dried up. I've written to Monsieur Berger to see if she can mate with his billygoat but he's killed it for meat. I think we'll have to do the same with the old girl."

"Oh no! Surely not?" Lottie dunked her bread in the hot milk mixture. The goat's milk had quite a tang with only hay and no fresh grass for the goats to eat but she'd got used to it and hardly noticed. She couldn't bear the thought of murdering the gentle creature that had provided so many other breakfasts.

Bernadette sucked her teeth. "Can't keep her going forever. It's another mouth to feed."

"How is the hay holding out?"

"Not well but we should just about have enough if we have one less goat. She's past her time. I'll do it soon and you'll have to help me. We'll get a bit of meat off the old girl. She'll need some long cooking; she'll be tough as old boots, but it will be nourishing, especially for the child."

Lottie, appalled at this grisly prospect, stopped eating and glanced at Bernadette, noticing how tired she looked; how her skin sagged under her chin and her wrap-

173

around apron now seemed far too big, as if it could accommodate two of her. "Come and sit down, Bernadette. Share a cup of tisane with me."

"Do you know? I think I will." Bernadette sat down heavily on the chair next to Lottie.

Lottie got up and pulled the kettle across to the hottest part of the range. "Lime flower?"

"Please, and let's have some honey. At least those German bastards didn't take my bees. Too cowardly to risk a sting."

The two women sat together in silence while they sipped their soothing brew.

Lottie spoke first. "No frost today for the first time in ages."

Bernadette nodded. "No."

"So, spring is on the way." Lottie stirred more honey in her drink.

Bernadette heaved a sigh. "I suppose so." She rubbed the back of her hand across her forehead.

"What's up?" Lottie had never seen her hostess so down.

"Nothing and everything. I'm not sure it's worth going to the markets anymore. The Boche buy everything in sight at a ridiculous discount, and I hate to feed them but they're the only ones with any cash, and even then, they don't always pay up. I've no vegetables to take, no eggs. There's just the cheeses and not enough milk at the moment to have enough surplus to make them. What we're to do for money, I don't know. The price of everything! A franc doesn't go far these days, especially on the black market and that's the only way you can get most things."

Lottie wanted to pat her hand but didn't dare. Bernadette might be feeling low, but she never welcomed open gestures of affection. "Can you sell your cheese on the black market when the goats yield goes up?"

Bernadette shrugged. "Maybe. The goats need to be mated if they're to produce more."

174

"We've enough. We'll get by. We've seed from last year we can sow into the vegetable patch and there will be greens in the hedgerows before long."

"I know but…Oh, never mind me."

"Is there something else bothering you, Bernadette?"

Bernadette darted Lottie a quick look with her flinty grey eyes. "I didn't tell you, but I took the cart into the village yesterday, on the way back from the market, to get the ration cards and to see if I could get some flour off Madame Leroy."

"Oh, how is she? I do miss my chats with her."

"Hmm, she asked after you too. She's alright; fed up, like the rest of us." Bernadette grimaced, it might have been a smile, Lottie wasn't sure, it wasn't something she saw very often. "Not so fat as she was."

"Did she have any flour to spare?"

"Not a single grain."

"Well, that's not surprising."

"She doesn't even bake every day now, just Wednesdays and Saturdays, she said, so I couldn't buy any of her bread, either."

Lottie's stomach rumbled at the memory of the buttery croissants she used to eat in Paris. "Surely, that isn't all that's given you the blues?"

Bernadette fiddled with the spoon in her bowl. "It's Françoise. Seems Madame Marchand, the butcher's wife, saw Bertrand when Françoise was in church. I told her not to go, that it wasn't worth the risk, but she insisted, even though she's not bothered before. She seems to have decided that if she prays hard enough, Bertrand will be safe. Stupid girl, it's done the opposite and put the child in danger."

"Danger? What sort of danger?"

"It's his dark colouring. And that horrible film, the 'Juif Suss', was showing in Caen last week. Seems our butcher and his wife went to see it. Everyone else I talked to

175

was revolted by it and say it's made them turn against the Boche, but those two rats are even more convinced that the Jews are a breed apart, dirty and to be despised." Bernadette rose to her feet suddenly. "Well, I tell you, I despise *them*!"

Lottie drew in her breath sharply. "Oh, God! I remember Madame Levy and her two little children. I saw them being taken away to the camps. They pulled her hair almost out of her head. And Madame Leroy said then it was Madame Marchand who'd informed on her. She was sure of it."

Bernadette poured herself more tea. "Yes, she keeps her finger on the pulse, that one, you can be sure of it, alright."

"What can we do to protect Bertrand?"

"Keep him out of sight. I'm going to ban Françoise from taking him to church for a start. If we need anything from the village or Caen, you'll have to go or come with me and Françoise will stay on the farm from now on."

"Of course, I will. The Germans will have forgotten all about the train by now."

"I doubt that, but they may have forgotten about you."

"We must protect Bertrand, at all costs."

"Not at all costs, child." Bernadette squeezed her shoulder in a rare display of emotion.

Lottie took a chance and patted her hand after all.

A couple of weeks later, Lottie was out in the vegetable patch again, hoeing the soil ready for sowing. They'd had some welcome sunny days and the earth had dried out enough to be worked. Soon it would be Easter. She remembered how Farmer Stubbs had always planted his seed potatoes on Good Friday. If only they had some, she would willingly dig the soil. At least there were young nettles for soup now.

It was warm work, and she took off her old jacket and rolled up her shirt sleeves, another legacy from her deceased French namesake. The sun had some genuine warmth in it. How quickly the seasons changed, even if nothing else did.

Footsteps on the lane made her look up in alarm. It sounded like big, male boots. Her heart began to pound. She stopped her scraping and raised her hoe in defence, pointing its sharp edge towards the oncoming intruder. When Pierre rounded the bend, she cast it aside in relief and ran towards him. She hadn't seen anyone but Bernadette, Françoise and Bertrand for months and months.

"Hello, Pierre!"

"Hello, Mademoiselle Charlotte. How are you?" Pierre reached her quickly with his enormously long stride and kissed her warmly on both cheeks, then gave her a third for good measure.

"I've brought a couple of rabbits for Bernadette to breed from." Pierre held up a wicker basket and Lottie peeped in through the bars on the front.

"That's a great idea, Pierre. I was thinking about rabbits but I've no idea how to trap them and, surprisingly, neither has Bernadette."

"Charles always did that for her."

"Of course. Well, we are very glad of them."

"Put them to work and they'll provide you with plenty of babies before you know it." Pierre winked. "Système D."

Lottie laughed. "Yes, the famous French 'Système D' of getting by any way you can. Well, they will certainly help us 'make do'. Let's take them to show Bernadette. She's in the washhouse doing the laundry." Lottie turned to go back to the yard.

"Wait. There's something else."

Lottie's pulse quickened. "Oh?"

"We need a messenger. I haven't seen you around on your bicycle?"

"No, I lost it after the train sabotage."

"If I get you another, are you willing to work for us again?" Pierre scanned her face with keen eyes.

She looked up at him. He was at least a head taller than her and she had to look into the sun to see him. Lottie shielded her eyes and nodded. "I'd like nothing better."

"Thought so. There's talk going around that the Allies are forming a plan to liberate France. We've a base at Falaise where they are getting air drops of ammunition and guns. It's up to us to bring them here and we need everyone to help. Here, take these rabbits for now. I'll be back in a week."

With that, he handed over his cargo and departed.

Lottie picked up the crate of rabbits and took them into the washhouse. Françoise and Bernadette were up to their elbows in scummy water at the stone sink.

"Look what we've got!" Lottie held up the rabbits.

Bernadette shook out a shirt, slung it in a basket and came over to peer inside the wicker crate.

"Who brought these?"

"Pierre."

"What's his price?"

"No money but he wants me to help out again. He's going to find me a bicycle."

Bernadette's grey eyes narrowed. "Do you really want to?"

"If Thierry is fighting in the south, I want to do the same here."

Bernadette flung her hands up in despair. "Then God help us all."

Françoise stopped her wringing and stared at Lottie. "How can you be so selfish as to endanger us all again?"

"What's dangerous is the bloody Boche. The sooner we get them out, the better. We know from the radio that they've lost Stalingrad and Pierre says there's talk of an Allied plan to liberate us!" Even as she spoke, hope, so long suppressed, surfaced in Lottie.

"Liberation from the Nazis?"

178

"Really?"

Lottie nodded. "It's only rumours but I'm going to do anything I can to help. I'm sorry if it frightens you, Françoise. I understand about Bertrand but it's true. The worst possible thing for Bertrand's future is if the Nazis stay lording it over us in France. Remember the Republican motto that de Gaulle quoted on the radio? *'Liberté, Egalité, Fraternité!'* Isn't that what you want for Bertrand?"

"I don't know, I suppose so." Françoise looked decidedly unconvinced.

Bernadette stomped back to the sink and plunged her brawny arms back into the water. "Humph. In the meantime, you can put those rabbits in the old chicken house. Make sure the run is secure before you release them."

Undaunted, Lottie did as she was told. She went around the circumference of the chicken run, mending any holes in the wire before she let out the two rabbits. Then she went to the orchard and picked some dandelion leaves for them. The rabbits were curious creatures. They investigated every inch of their new territory before settling down to munch on the leaves. Lottie knelt down and watched them.

Unlike her new furry friends, her cage had just been lifted.

She didn't even have to wait a week for Pierre's return. This time, he brought another crate with four young pullets inside, but he wasn't carrying them. The basket was strapped to a bicycle he pushed along beside him. "Thought Bernadette might appreciate having hens again."

"Oh, that's marvellous, Pierre! She will be pleased, and I'm delighted to have a set of wheels."

Pierre smiled. "I want you to visit Madame Leroy at the bakery as soon as you can. She's the contact with Falaise."

"This is getting better and better!"

"It's also serious, mademoiselle, and not without risk."

"I understand that, Pierre, but I've been cooped up here since Thierry left."

"It's not a game, little one."

Lottie started to bridle at his tone. "I'm an adult, monsieur, just like you."

"I beg your pardon. If you get news of a delivery, tell Jean at the mill and he will contact me. There's a code which Madame Leroy will tell you about. Now, we need places to stash some things. I must talk to Bernadette about that."

"She's in the orchard. Let's take her these birds. She'll be delighted with them."

They walked together, Lottie wheeling the bicycle, towards the apple trees.

Bernadette turned around at their approach. "Hello, Pierre. What's that you have?"

Pierre unstrapped the basket from the bike and showed her the hen pullets, while Lottie pointed to her bicycle.

"I'm glad of the hens, I must say." Bernadette didn't even mention Lottie's new means of transport.

Lottie left them to it and wheeled her metal steed back into the goat's barn. Pierre met her in the yard. Lottie shut the barn door behind her. "What did Bernadette say?"

"She'll do it, but she called it blackmail and said I was bribing her with the baby hens."

Lottie laughed. "But that first omelette will taste wonderful."

"You'll have to wait a few weeks for that."

"It'll be worth it."

Pierre kissed her cheeks again. "I must go. Good luck."

Lottie watched his tall, bony frame lope back down the lane until he rounded the bend, out of sight.

Bernadette joined her in the yard. "Got me roped in now, hasn't he?"

180

"Aren't you glad though? Deep down?" Bernadette's stern face didn't fool Lottie.

"Maybe. We must all do what we can, but I worry about Françoise. It's good you have a set of wheels again because I'm keeping her within sight from now on."

"Perhaps it would be best not to tell her about the cache when it comes?"

Bernadette nodded. "Agreed. The lower cellar is ideal, and Pierre knows it. I can't deny them use of it."

Lottie tried the bicycle out the next day, it being a Wednesday and a baking day at the boulangerie in the village. She couldn't suppress her excitement. It was sheer joy to pedal along the lanes again. The sense of freedom was so exhilarating, but she was glad of the high hedges that afforded her the cover of their burgeoning green leaves.

She didn't recognise the guard at the control post. He barely looked fifteen and his face was covered in acne. He looked too nervous to challenge her when she gave him her best smile. A nasty red flush made his spots inflame when he handed her papers back to her.

Lottie went over to the Mairie to collect their monthly allowance of ration cards. As she mounted the steps, she tried not to look at the swastikas obscuring its lovely stonework, or she might have been tempted to rip them down.

She walked inside and entered the door marked 'Office'.

There was no Frenchman to answer her enquiries. The Germans had taken over here too. The soldier looked well-fed, complacent. She hated him on sight.

"Yes?"

"I need to collect my ration coupons."

"Identity papers?" He held out his hand imperiously and took the bundle of cards. He scanned her image. "Your photograph should be in profile, mademoiselle. It's a new rule. I'm surprised you haven't changed it already."

"I've not been out much through the winter."

181

"Why is that?"

Lottie shrugged in what she hoped was a French way. "It was cold, and I kept to my farm."

"So, who collected your ration cards?"

"My grandmother."

"Not too cold for an old woman then?"

"I was doing the heavy farm work."

He sucked his teeth. "You will have to fill in some forms with the SNS."

"Sorry?"

"The SNS - you know – The National Statistics Department in Caen."

"Do you mean I can't have my coupons today?"

"I will have to go and check. Wait here."

"Oh, I see. Thank you."

The soldier got up, sighing heavily and scraping his chair. He went out, leaving the door open to the corridor. On a table behind his desk lay the ration coupons. Piles of them.

Lottie remembered a conversation she'd had with Thierry. 'If you see coupons, just take them, but don't get caught.'

She looked around her, went to the door and peeped down the corridor to left and right, looked out of the window. There was no-one. She went around to the table on the other side of the desk and helped herself to about twenty coupons. She didn't read what they were for, just grabbed them and stuffed them in her basket. She was just covering them over with a cloth when a shadow fell across the floor. Lottie whirled around.

A well-dressed, middle-aged woman stood in the door frame, staring straight at her. She seemed to take everything in with one glance. She entered the room and quietly shut the door behind her.

"What are you doing?" The woman spoke in a cultured voice in French.

"N…nothing."

"Are those food coupons?"

182

There was no point denying it, so Lottie nodded.

"Hide them quickly then."

"You're not going to denounce me?"

"You look hungry." The woman looked back at the door as they both heard heavy footsteps approaching. "Be quick! Cover them up and get this side of the desk."

The woman stood aside as the soldier returned, looking irritated. He looked at Lottie's hands fumbling in her basket. Lottie held her breath. Time stretched in the next few seconds of silence.

"Good morning, soldier." The woman inclined her head but didn't smile.

The soldier looked surprised to see her. He saluted. "Madame Voclain."

The telephone on the desk shrilled out. Lottie let out her breath.

The soldier walked to his desk and picked up the receiver. "Ja?" He frowned in concentration as he listened to the caller and shook his head. "Bleiben Sie dran." He seemed to remember Lottie was still standing in front of him. Tutting, he took one ration card from each pile and shoved them across the desk at her, then waved her away.

Not waiting for verbal confirmation, Lottie picked them up and put them in her coat pocket and bolted. Madame Voclain followed her out into the corridor.

"Thank you, Madame!"

"Say nothing, Mademoiselle." The woman stared at Lottie intensely. "Absolutely nothing, understand? As the mayor's wife, I still command a shred of respect, but the smallest mistake could change that. Go now." She looked at Lottie's basket where the coupons lay under her cloth. "Eat well this month at least."

Outside, the delightful smell of fresh bread drew her to the boulangerie where a long queue trailed out of the shop. Finally, she reached the counter.

"Mon petit chou! How nice to see you!" Madame Leroy looked delighted to see Lottie again.

Lottie whispered. "Don't make too much fuss, please, I don't want the attention."

Immediately, Madame Leroy lowered her voice. "One baguette only per person."

Lottie handed over her bread coupon. "What time do you close, Madame?"

"Twelve o'clock, unless the bread runs out beforehand."

"I'll come back then." Lottie said under her breath.

Madame Leroy took the hint and looked over her head at the woman behind Lottie. "Next please."

The woman elbowed Lottie out of the way. "Let me get my bread before it's all gone."

Lottie walked back to the square. She looked across at the school. If only Thierry was still inside, teaching the children. She remembered the mayor's wife. Wasn't she supposed to have taken over?

Lottie went to the butcher's shop next. Madame Marchand was serving at the counter, while her son was slicing through a skinned rabbit in savage lunges with a cleaver almost as big as the animal, at the back of the shop. Much as she longed to splurge all her illicit coupons in one go, when it was her turn to be served, she just bought a few sausages and some pork belly. There wasn't much too choose from anyway. Soon, they would have goat on the menu at the farm. She still couldn't face the thought of that.

Madame Marchand looked at her with suspicious, red-rimmed eyes. "Haven't seen you around much lately? What have you been up to?"

"Just working on the farm. There's no man to do the heavy work anymore, so I have to do it. Bernadette's not getting any younger."

Madame Marchand seemed to accept this as she wrapped up the meat with fat fingers and slapped it on the counter. Lottie used her legitimate ration coupon to pay. She would give the others to Bernadette to spend in Caen where

184

there was less risk of gossip or pass them on to Pierre so he could barter them for guns.

The clock struck twelve. German time of course. Really, it was only eleven o'clock, but Lottie was still famished. She returned to the bakery and went around the back and let herself in.

Madame Leroy's kitchen was wonderfully familiar. As comforting as the woman who owned it.

Soon Madame Leroy came bustling in from the shop and wrapped her arms around Lottie as if she was her own long-lost child. "Sweet girl. Oh, how lovely to see you." She kissed Lottie twice on both cheeks. "I have some soup and some spare bread. Share it with me?"

"Oh, Madame, I can think of nothing nicer."

Madame Leroy chuckled. "It will be good to have your company, chérie."

Madame Leroy's soup was leek and potato. "How did you get potatoes – and cream?" Lottie scooped up the delicious mixture voraciously and immediately held out her bowl for more.

Madame ladled out more soup. When she sat down, she tapped her nose. "Bread makes for easy bartering, but you have to know the right people."

Lottie scraped out her bowl with the fragrant fresh baguette. "It's absolutely heavenly."

"More? There's still a little left in the pan."

Lottie shook her head. "I'd love to, but I might be sick if I have any more. It's been so long since my belly was full."

Madame Leroy laid down her spoon. "I understand, chérie. So many go hungry but it's much worse in the towns."

"I haven't been anywhere – not since Thierry left."

"Have you heard from him?"

Lottie sighed. "No, not a word. I'd hoped you might know something. He was shot in the leg, you know, and walked with a limp. His chances weren't good. Oh, I'd give

185

anything to know if he was even alive." Suddenly the rich soup didn't sit so well in her stomach. Lottie swallowed down the acid rising up in her gullet and broke off another piece of dry bread to squash it down.

"Hmm, but he's a tough one. He'll be alright, I'm sure of it."

"I hope you are right, Madame. Who's running the school now? I'd heard it was the mayor's wife, but I saw Madame Voclain just now, in the Mairie."

"Yes, she took it over for a short while but now it's some young girl from Caen. A plain little thing, timid as a mouse but very good with the children."

"Well, that's the main thing, I suppose."

Madame Leroy shifted in her seat. "You know she's one of us."

"Who, the mousy schoolteacher?"

"No, Madame Voclain."

"Ah, I did wonder. She, um, she helped me out just now. I stole some coupons when the soldier was out of the office."

"Good for you! They'll come in handy."

"Do you need some?"

Madame Leroy laughed. "No, not me, mon petit chou. You can see I'm in the right job. Keep them for Françoise's little boy."

"Tell me about Madame Voclain."

"I shouldn't really, the less said, the better. Just know that she hates her husband, and the Germans he sucks up to, in pretty much equal measure. Do anything to thwart either of them."

"Why does she hate the Mayor?"

"I'm surprised you asked, living with Bernadette."

A vague memory surfaced in Lottie's mind. "Oh yes, Mireille had a thing with him years ago, didn't she?"

Madame Leroy nodded. "She certainly did. Flaunted it all around the village too."

"But he married his fiancée and Mireille was packed off to Paris, wasn't she?"

"Yes, but not before Madame Voclain, or Veronique Laurent as she was then, was publicly shamed by it all. Of course, she was pregnant by then and had no choice but to marry the rotten philanderer. Oh, everyone knew the whole story when she walked up the aisle, especially as Mireille was in the congregation – and wearing bright red!" Madame Leroy laughed.

"I can see that would have been very awkward."

"I'll say! I shouldn't laugh really, Veronique is a good woman underneath all that bourgeoisie nonsense, and she's had to put up with Monsieur's wandering ways ever since. Well, she has her son to show for her forbearance. Nice young man."

"What's his name?"

"Emile, in memory of her father. He died of a heart attack soon after she married. No coincidence, if you ask me!" Madame Leroy snorted, then looked pensive. "Is Françoise sure of who her father is? Could be that she and Emile are half brother and sister."

Lottie raised her eyebrows in astonishment. "Gosh, I never thought of that! But no, Françoise is too young to have been fathered by Monsieur Voclain, unless Mireille sneaked back to the village."

Madame Leroy shook her head. "Oh, no. Bernadette sent her off with more than a flea in her ear. She only came back twice. Once for the wedding and once for her father's funeral, probably to see what she'd get."

Lottie remembered the first time she'd seen Bernadette and the hostility between her and her daughter when they'd first arrived. "Well, she's back in Paris again now but this time with a Nazi."

Madame Leroy shrugged. "Typical. People don't change."

Lottie wiped her mouth with the linen serviette Madame Leroy had provided. "Is there a message for Jean?"

She smiled. "It feels like old times to ask but I wish we didn't have to."

"I know. This war drags on."

"You've heard the rumours about the Allies planning to liberate France?"

Madame Leroy nodded. "I'll believe it when it happens. Now, tell Jean we expect the bread to rise at the next full moon."

"I will. Not sure he'll give me the warmest welcome. It's months since I saw him, and last time he told me not to come back too soon."

"Oh, he's a curmudgeonly soul but you can rely on him if you're in a hole, believe me. We'll need somewhere to store the 'bread'. Pierre said something about your place?"

Lottie smiled. "He doesn't waste time, that one. Yes, Bernadette has agreed to the use of our cellar."

"Good. That's sorted then. You'd better get off to the mill. It's been so lovely to see your young face again, mon petit chou."

Lottie kissed her warmly and left quietly. She didn't get stopped by the bridge and sailed on past, revelling in the freedom the bicycle gave her. It was an ancient old contraption, but Pierre must have cleaned it up as it worked perfectly. It had no gears, but the wicker basket was capacious, perhaps it had been a delivery bike years ago. Lottie loved it.

She zoomed down the valley to the mill and leant her bicycle against the wooden railings of the bridge over the mill race. Jean emerged from the barn, carrying a sack of flour.

"Hello Mademoiselle! Good to see you."

"Hello, Jean." Lottie suffered the mandatory kiss of the cheek and didn't breathe in until he let her go. Jean wasn't much of a one for washing and running a mill was sweaty work. "I'm glad to hear it."

Jean chuckled. "Oh, never mind me. I was rattled after the train sabo. Is this a social call or have you news?"

Lottie relayed her message.

Jean grunted. "Tell Madame Leroy I'll add the yeast at the right time."

Lottie mounted her bicycle again. "I will. Let me know if you want more help. We have some space in our cellar for storing the 'bread', Bernadette says."

"Aha. Good to know."

"Bye, then." Lottie willed her legs to pump her up the hill. She'd forgotten how steep it was.

CHAPTER TWENTY-FIVE
CHEADLE MANOR, ENGLAND
APRIL 1943

Isobel missed driving the tractor. The old Fergie was a reliable machine that she had come to call her own, but Farmer Stubbs insisted the petrol ration must be kept in reserve for the harvest. They were out in the top field, with Ida and Nellie, the two enormous shire horses, ploughing the rich earth before planting it with potatoes.

Isobel walked by the horses' heads, giving them encouragement while Farmer Stubbs walked behind with the small plough. "That's it, Nellie. Good girl. Come on, Ida." They'd reached the steep bit and the horses blew air through their nostrils, making clouds of steam in the fresh April breeze.

"Right, Miss Isobel. Time you took over. They're slower on this slope, see, it'll give you a chance to keep up."

Isobel was very fond of Farmer Stubbs, but his occasional patronising comments grated on her nerves. She'd proven herself over and over again to be as capable as any man.

"Righto." Isobel patted Nellie on her muscular neck and dropped back behind the two Shire horses.

"Get a hold of the handles like this, see. Now, you must stand to one side, so the plough can turn the earth over, or your feet will get in the way."

Isobel did as she was told and gripped the handles of the plough which were uncomfortably wide apart – built for a man's arm-span.

"Gee up, girls." Farmer Stubbs rippled the reins and the two massive horses plodded on. The plough bounced on the untilled earth and it took all Isobel's concentration to hold on.

"Steady now, ease your grip, let the handles slip a bit and the plough do the work. You're not pushing the damn thing, girl."

190

Isobel stopped holding the handles so tightly and started to get the feel of the motion in her hands. "Is that better?"

"That's it. You're just guiding the direction, that's all."

By the time they reached the top of the field, Isobel was slightly out of breath.

"Now then, they'll go a bit faster downhill. Reckon you can do it?" Farmer Stubbs handed Isobel the reins. "Loop 'em over your arm, so your hands are free for the plough. These old girls know what they're doing."

"They do, don't they? Do you think they've missed the work?"

Farmer Stubbs stroked Ida's nose. "I reckon they might have done, at that. This war doesn't have many compensations but getting these old girls out of retirement is a real pleasure, I must say."

"I'm ready, if you are, Mr Stubbs."

"Let's turn 'em then." Farmers Stubbs chucked to the horses and Isobel jiggled the reins. Together, the team turned around on itself smoothly, so it was now pointing down the long decline of the field. "Right, off you go."

"Come on, girls. Forward march." Isobel shook the reins again and the horses moved off. They did walk more quickly downhill, but Isobel had the knack of it now and kept up. Her shoulders ached a bit from the width of the plough but other than that, she started to enjoy it. By the time they reached the bottom, Farmer Stubbs gave an approving nod. "I think you've got the hang of it, Miss Isobel. I'll leave you to it. I've got to go and fill in more ruddy forms for the Min of Ag."

"Oh dear. Good luck with that." Isobel turned the horses around to face uphill again. Once he'd seen her accomplish the turn, Farmer Stubbs took out his pipe and lit it - always a sign he was satisfied with her work.

Alone with the giant horses, a natural rhythm to the ploughing established itself, more from their instincts than any guidance from Isobel. She plodded up and down the big field behind them, enjoying the absence of noise from an engine. Seagulls wheeled in from the distant coast and flapped above them, swooping down to pull out a worm from the freshly turned earth. The trees were breaking bud in the hedgerows and the whole countryside was unfurling its green mantle. Blackthorn bloomed white between the green foliage. Another farming year was fully underway.

Isobel was even more relieved than usual that the winter was over. It had been long, dull and lonely. After Mr Lloyd's funeral, she had been relieved to discover that Geraint was kept very busy managing the businesses in Liverpool and had not insisted she visit again soon. His letters had disturbed her though, with their implicit air of expectation that she would, eventually, join him in the enterprise and life he now lived.

Gone was the dreamy poetic tone. No paintings spilled out of the envelopes. Her address was typed out by some minion in his office now and although it was his own handwriting flowing just as elegantly as ever across the expensive paper, the letters were brief and to the point. She always answered these missives promptly and politely with news of the farm and the hospital; how the grounds had been dug up by convalescing soldiers to provide more vegetables for the patients within her old home; how her mother was kept busy with the Women's Institute, the Red Cross and her deepening friendship with Dr Harris. She never promised to visit or even hinted at her return. Isobel hoped that, with time, he would stop asking but he never failed to include a vague invitation for her to come and stay sometime in the future. The war remained her best excuse to refuse.

An aeroplane flew overhead, drowning out the birdsong. Isobel looked up but the sun blinded her. When she reached the end of the row, she halted the horses and shielded her eyes to try and see it. Another bomber by the looks of it. So many had lumbered overhead lately, loaded with lethal packages to drop on German cities, kill more people, destroy more beautiful architecture. She hoped Lottie wouldn't be among them.

Al had written to her about it.

"Very busy these days, Bella, so, sorry if this is a short letter. Massive bombing campaign in Germany means I'm ferrying planes morning till night with not much time in-between.

We have such long working days at the moment, there's no trips to the pub anymore! Hope all's well on the farm.

Love, Al."

And that had been it. Couldn't have been briefer or more impersonal if he'd tried. She hadn't even seen him at Christmas. He never got leave. Or said he didn't. There'd been no mention of Miriam for a long time and she didn't know what to make of that.

Isobel chivvied the horses back into a walk. She couldn't think about it. Just put one foot in front of the other. That was all anyone could do.

CHAPTER TWENTY-SIX
NORMANDY, FRANCE
JUNE 1943

Lottie couldn't sleep on the night of the full moon. She lay awake for hours, listening for a plane. Eventually she got up, tip-toed down the stairs and went out into the yard. Drawn by tender memories, she gravitated towards the bench under the apple trees, and sat down.

Although it was now midsummer and the nights warm and fleeting, Lottie shivered in her nightgown and pulled her old coat around her, wishing it was Thierry's arms. She gazed up at the moon. It was a clear night, perfect for a drop. The stars sparkled in the moonlight. Was Thierry also looking up at them, wondering how she was? This same moon would also be shining in Wiltshire, silvering the pale stone of Cheadle Manor. An owl shrieked, piercing the night with its hunting cry. That, too, reminded her of home.

Lottie lay down on the bench and put her hands behind her head for a pillow, the better to contemplate the diamonds of light punching holes in the infinite indigo panorama above her. Everyone she loved was under this same big disc of a moon and not so far away, not really. If they were still alive, of course. She blinked her blurring tears away when she heard the distant drone of an aircraft. She strained her eyes to try and catch a glimpse of it in the navy-blue sky, but it was too far away. All too soon, the engine noise faded into the night. Was that the aeroplane carrying the guns and ammunition they would have to hide from the Germans? The chance it might involve her connected her to the fight, to Britain, to anyone engaged in ridding this scourge of evil the Nazis had forced on the world.

She went back to bed and fell asleep immediately. For once, the hollow feeling in her stomach had eased. She wasn't alone after all. They were all in it together, and even if she couldn't see, touch or hear them, she did have friends and allies.

The next day, and the one after that, Lottie was on the alert for a visit from Pierre but there was nothing. On the Wednesday, she cycled into the village just before midday and went straight around to the back of the bakery.

Madame Leroy was already in her kitchen, looking hot and flustered. "Honestly, it's not my fault that flour is in short supply. Some of the women think I'm hoarding it. As if I would! But I must pace the baking, or we will run out completely. That Madame Marchand accused me of collaborating with the Nazis! Talk about the pot calling the kettle black. I have to give the Boche their bread quota first, or I'll probably be shot! Doesn't mean I *want* to. Makes me sick."

"Oh dear, Madame Leroy, that's tough. Let's have some of your coffee." Lottie kissed her outraged friend on both cheeks.

Madame Leroy nodded. "Good idea and nice to see you." She set about making the dandelion and chicory brew.

"Phew! It's hot today." Lottie went to the sink and splashed water on her face. "Any message, Madame?"

"Yes, the bread is baked, tell Jean. Five loaves."

Goosepimples broke out on Lottie's wet arms. "That's excellent news."

"Hmm, keep it under your hat. Speak only to Jean. Let him organise storage and only get involved if you must. Here's your coffee."

"Thanks. You're the only one who can make it taste anything like the real thing. Our coffee has run out now. Bernadette has given up going to the markets. We only have enough food for ourselves and not enough to sell. She's even going to have to kill the old nanny goat now her milk has dried up."

"That's sad, and it'll be a hard lesson for you, my dear, but it's the same everywhere. What wouldn't I give for a decent bar of soap."

195

"Bernadette makes ours. It's not that nice but I could bring you some."

"No thanks, I'll wheedle some decent stuff off Madame Voclain. Her husband always manages to get by. He's so in love with these Nazi brutes, he can get anything he wants. She even wears silk stockings."

"That can't make her very popular."

"Bet they feel nice though. The only other one with luxuries is that Marchand woman. You can spot a collaborator a mile off."

Lottie drank her coffee down in one go. It wasn't exactly delicious, but it did resemble coffee. "I'm not so sure about Madame Voclain. I think she's playing a deep game."

"You're right, she is, but it doesn't mean you should drop your guard. Sometimes I think I don't really know anyone, anymore." Madame took their cups to the sink. "And I trust them even less."

Lottie got up. "I'll be off then."

"Yes, don't hang about longer than you have to, or you'll get signed up for the STO."

"The what?"

"Service Travail Obligatoire. Oh, didn't you know? For all the Marchand's and Voclain's secret milking of the black market, they haven't got preferential treatment for their sons."

"What do you mean?"

"They've both been called up to go and work in Germany, haven't they?"

"Oh no! But I thought that was voluntary?"

Madame Leroy grunted. "You must be joking; that was just a ruse by Laval to seduce everyone to think they still had control over their lives. No, Pétain signed it off a couple of months ago. I'm surprised you didn't hear it on the radio."

"No, I missed that. Are you sure it's compulsory?"

196

"It's compulsory alright. Luckily for you, they haven't extended it to girls. I mean, technically you could be called up, but the church would be up in arms if the Germans tried."

"But, do you mean they'll go to one of the camps?"

"I don't think so, it's more for real work. Could be anywhere. Might even be in France making bombs to drop on their own families. Imagine that. Anyone born between 1920 and 1922 is on the list. Even Emile Voclain and Victor Marchand."

"But, if they are in with the Boche, can't they get them off?"

"Seems not. Not for this." Madame Leroy sighed. "I mean, I don't like their parents much, but this is criminal. There's no knowing if they'll make it back but at least they haven't gone yet. I suppose they'll get rounded up just as if they were Jews or Communists."

"I'm so shocked, Madame."

"Eh, we all are, mon petit chou. Go now, keep your head down. Promise me?"

"Yes, Madame, I will."

"Make sure of it." Madame Leroy held Lottie's chin in her plump hand and looked at her fondly. "You're like the daughter I never had, chérie."

Lottie hugged her and left before either of them embarrassed the other.

Lottie mounted her bike and set off across the square towards the bridge and its sentry post. When she passed the linden trees in its centre, she heard someone hissing at her. Alarmed, Lottie looked to where the sound came from.

"Mademoiselle! Over here!"

Lottie peered under the dark canopy of the big trees. Nonchalantly sitting on the bench as if avoiding the glaring sun and taking her ease, was Madame Voclain. She looked cool in her sunhat and summer dress already, rather than in need of a parasol of green leaves. Lottie looked around to

197

see if she was whispering to someone else but no, Madame's heavily made-up eyes were staring intently at her.

Lottie braked, got off her bicycle and wheeled it across into the shadow cast by the leafy trees.

"Madame?"

"Come and sit with me awhile, Mademoiselle. It's too hot to be cycling at this time of day." Madame Voclain patted the seat.

The square was already deserted. Everyone had gone inside to eat their leisurely lunch. People still had the time, if not much food, to eat and the midday break remained sacrosanct in the village.

"Not having your lunch, Madame?"

"I'm not hungry."

"Then you are alone in that."

Madame smiled and inclined her head, so her broad-brimmed hat hid the top half of her lined but still attractive face. "Perhaps. But there are more important things than food."

"Not when you don't have enough. Then it's hard to think of anything else."

The older woman lifted her face, and Lottie could see worry lines creasing her forehead. "You have enough to eat on Madame Perrot's farm, though, don't you?"

"Thank you for your concern, Madame Voclain. We get by." Lottie mistrusted her level of interest.

"That's good to know. I've heard you are going to be storing some 'bread' soon."

Lottie, already alert to the oddness of the interview, was alarmed at this disclosure and decided to say nothing.

Madame Voclain put her manicured hand on Lottie's forearm, now tanned and muscular from the farm work. "Don't worry, child. I let you get away with the coupons, didn't I? Surely, that proves you can trust me? Monsieur Thibault and I understood each other very well, you know. You are fond of him, no?"

Lottie compressed her lips and her body went rigid.

Madame Voclain withdrew her hand. "I commend your discretion. Understand this, I know everything you have done so far. Everything. Now, if you do not wish me to tell my husband all about it, and believe me, he wouldn't hesitate to pass the information on to his German friends, you will help me with a small favour, yes?"

Sweat broke out on Lottie's palms, despite the deep shade under the linden trees. She looked around the deserted square, but she could only see the young German soldier pacing up and down by the bridge, looking bored. There wasn't another soul in sight. Of course, that didn't mean no-one had observed this dangerous tête-a-tête through one of many windows around the square.

Her mind raced with the implications of Madame Voclain's words. "What favour?"

Madame Voclain's veneer of politeness fell away. Under the powder, her skin looked tired and fragile. She glanced over Lottie's shoulder to check no-one was listening. In a low voice, she said, "It is my son, Emile. He has been called up to serve on the STO. He will be rounded up any day now. I…I need to find him a safe place to hide while I organise an escape to the south." She stared hard at Lottie with unblinking eyes. "Just as you did for Thierry."

"You know?" Lottie blurted out the words and instantly regretted her admission of guilt.

Madame Voclain smiled. If she'd been a cat, she would have purred. "Oh, yes, my dear, I know all about it."

Lottie dropped her gaze from the steely intensity of Madame Voclain's dark-blue eyes. She couldn't bear the triumph in them. She studied her own hands, now wet with sweat and clenched in her lap.

Madame continued, "Françoise's little boy is a handsome young fellow, isn't he? I saw them together in church the other Sunday. There has been much speculation about his absent father. Such dark skin and eyes, when his mother is so fair. It would be a shame if his papers didn't bear scrutiny. Françoise seems a rather delicate young woman. I think it would break her, if anything happened to…what's the child's name?"

Lottie mumbled. "Bertrand, like his father."

"Ah yes. From Paris, wasn't he? And conveniently dead." Madame Voclain no longer looked attractive. Her face was tight, the lips a thin line. "You see, Charlotte, um," she coughed theatrically, "Perrot, you have no secrets from me." The woman nodded slowly, her face relaxing into smugness.

Lottie wanted to slap her complacency away. Who had betrayed her to this snake of a woman? She refused to believe it had been Thierry.

"I have a cousin Emile can stay with. The southern zone is occupied too now, but the Auvergne is big enough to get lost in. So, shall we assume you are willing to help my son?"

CHAPTER TWENTY-SEVEN
NORMANDY, FRANCE
JULY 1943

Lottie was so perturbed by her conversation with the mayor's wife, she almost forgot to turn down the lane to Jean's mill. She delivered her message to him breathlessly, being in a hurry to get home and talk things over with Bernadette.

"Okay, understood." Jean squinted at her in the sunshine. "Eh? What's up, little one?"

"Oh, nothing."

"Come on, tell me."

Lottie retrieved her bicycle. "No, I'll speak to Pierre. Let's keep things simple. Where does he live?"

"I understand your need for secrecy, but don't go to his place. It's better you don't know where he lives. I'll send a message for him to visit you. Problems?"

Lottie nodded. "It's urgent, Jean. It has to be today."

"Leave it with me."

Grateful for his taciturn reassurance and lack of curiosity, she cycled home again.

Bernadette, when informed of the developments, was disconcertingly as worried as Lottie.

"I don't like this. It's not good there are more people involved than we thought. I don't trust Veronique Voclain. She's always been two-faced."

"But what can we do? It was obvious she really did know about Thierry's escape. She must be part of the network, or heaven forbid, a spy for the Boche! She's desperate to get Emile away. I wouldn't put it past her to betray us to her husband if we don't help him. And she's right about Françoise. It wouldn't take much for her to buckle."

"Hmm. We'd better prepare then."

Lottie sighed. "Yes, we have been left with no choice. I just hope we can buy her silence if we help her son.

I've left a message for Pierre to call so he can set up the escape route south."

"Good. The quicker we shift him off the farm, the better. I didn't think we'd have to do this twice."

Lottie put her bicycle away in the goat's barn. She went up to the old nanny goat who nuzzled her pockets for treats. "I wish I had something delicious to give you, old girl." Lottie stroked the long nose of her favourite goat. Then wrapped her arms around its neck. A hefty nudge of its horns was all the thanks she got.

Lottie had given up all hope of seeing Pierre that day, so she was surprised when he knocked softly on the back door after the others had already gone up to bed. She peeped through the curtains to check it was him before unlocking door.

"Thank you for coming to see me, Pierre. It's late and you've had to fit me in at the end of what I'm sure was a long day." She kissed his cheeks.

Pierre pulled off his beret and sat on the settle by the range. He looked tired and his clothes hung loosely off his long limbs. "It's true. A tisane would be welcome."

"Of course, or would you prefer a Calvados?"

Pierre gave a weary smile. "I would, if I'm honest. Where's everyone else?"

"Already in bed. We'd better keep our voices down, so we don't wake them. Bernadette can be pretty fierce if roused from her slumbers."

Lottie poured one for each of them and sat down opposite Pierre. "Madame Voclain's son has had his papers for the STO. She wants him to hide out here while an escape is arranged for him to the old unoccupied zone. Can you help?"

"You don't have to do this, Charlotte. It would be even more dangerous a second time and the Nazis invaded there in November too."

"It seems I do."

202

"But why?" Pierre drank his Calvados down in one go.

Lottie poured him another. "Our mayor is in cahoots with the Nazis and his wife will tell them all she knows about our activities if we don't. It seems she knows everything."

"The bitch!"

Lottie nodded. "Quite. She threatened other things too, but you don't need to know the details."

"That's wise." Pierre sipped from his second glass of cider brandy.

"So, can you help?"

"I'll see what I can do. The Maquis are growing in numbers in the south because of this STO thing. Young Voclain isn't the only one making a dash for it."

"I heard Victor Marchand is on the list too." Lottie took a sip of her drink.

Pierre stood up and paced the room. "It's disgusting. Taking young Frenchmen to do their dirty work for them! Isn't it enough the Boche have taken our land, our food, our crops, our money? I tell you, girl, I am so angry. All the time, I'm angry. So, yes, I will arrange it." He held out his empty glass and Lottie filled it silently.

"What about the cache of arms from Falaise, Pierre?"

"I'm not sure you should have that here as well as a boy who might not keep his trap shut."

"Fair point. Have you somewhere else in mind?" Lottie treated herself to a second measure of the Calvados. She had a warm, reckless feeling starting vaguely in her stomach.

"No, I think we'll leave it in Falaise until you're clear. There's nowhere better than Bernadette's cellar."

Lottie giggled. "The cellar beneath the cellar. The 'sous-cellar'!"

Pierre relieved her of the bottle. "I think you've had enough for one evening. Go to bed and listen out for more instructions. Perhaps go to the village tomorrow on some errand and let Madame Voclain know you'll take her boy. And don't drink any more hooch or you'll have a thick head come morning."

"Is that the voice of experience?"

Pierre laughed softly and ruffled her short hair. "Don't be cheeky to your elders." He placed his beret back on his grizzled head and slipped quietly out of the door.

Lottie dutifully cycled back to the village the next day. They were due their ration coupons anyway, so she marched boldly up the steps to the Mairie and collected them. A different German was doling them out, a younger soldier, who didn't seem the slightest bit interested in whether her profile was frontwards or sideways.

Lottie decided not to ask after Madame Voclain. She didn't want any German to associate her with the Mayor's wife. Instead, she went two doors down and knocked on the front door of the elegant detached house where Monsieur Voclain, who was also the local lawyer, had his legal offices and home.

A young housemaid answered, wearing a black dress and white pinafore, just like the ones Sarah wore at Cheadle Manor. It unsettled her a little. She almost believed her own disguise as a French peasant these days but, as she entered the tasteful hallway and sat in a Louis XIV chair, she could also imagine she was Charlotte Flintock-Smythe again, calling on a fellow member of the gentry to drink tea or play tennis. She instantly recognised this was dangerous thinking and Lottie dismissed the thought as soon as it surfaced, schooling her mind to re-inhabit her new persona.

"Monsieur is engaged with a client, mademoiselle." The maid, rather than speaking to her deferentially, looked disdainfully at Lottie, who supposed that an old coat and rough trousers, held together with baler twine, wouldn't naturally invite respect.

"It's Madame Voclain I've come to see."

"Wait here."

In due course, the lady of the house entered the hall, preceded by a waft of expensive perfume.

"Thank you for coming. Let's go through here." Madame Voclain waved her arm in the direction of the rear of the building.

They ended up in what looked like a pantry, next to the kitchen.

Madame Voclain gave an insincere smile. "I thought it best to pretend you were bringing something for the kitchen." She looked around at the shelves and took down a jar of honey at the back amongst some similar ones. "Madame Perrot keeps bees, does she not?"

Lottie nodded, anger rising in her at this woman's arrogant tone and resentment at her elegance. Madame Voclain didn't have a hair out of place in her chignon and her fingernails were painted coral pink to match her silk dress.

"Then let's say you brought this jar. It bears no name. It could be from anywhere, should anyone enquire."

Lottie grew impatient with this farce. "About Emile?"

Madame stepped closer, so the smell of her perfume grew more intense. Chanel Number Five, just like Mireille Blanchard. Lottie wrinkled her nose, now more attuned to the smell of the farmyard.

Madame Voclain whispered. "Would tonight be too soon? I think it's best done under cover of darkness, don't you?"

"What about the curfew?"

Madame Voclain frowned. "I will get Emile to walk to the woods near your farm during the day. He is in the office now, helping his father, as normal, but I'll get my husband to give him the afternoon off. He can wait there until dark."

"Does he know the way?"

205

"He's a clever boy, he'll work it out. He played there as a child in any case. He's always preferred the countryside to the town, sadly."

"Very well. There's a very large old oak near the farmhouse, towards the back. It's much bigger than the others with a large hole near the base, just above the roots. Tell him to wait there quietly. I will come for him when it is fully dark."

"What time would that be?"

"Around ten o'clock. The moon is still big, so no torches, tell him. Give him some food and water. Oh, and money. A lot. He'll need that for the journey south."

"Very well. I can do that. I presume you'll want some?"

Lottie stiffened at this insult. "No, not at all, but he will need a coat. He may have to cross the Pyrenees and there's no way of knowing when."

"I understand. Thank you." Madame Voclain surprised Lottie then by reaching forward and kissing both her cheeks.

Lottie remained unmoved. "You have left me no choice, Madame. I want your solemn word that you will not betray us at any time to the Boche. Not me, not Bernadette, not Françoise or her little boy - or the deal's off. I will not agree to helping Emile unless you give me this undertaking and shake hands on it, or I shall be forced to tell those interested about your son's illegal departure. Believe me, madame, I would not hesitate to do so if I found out later that you had told tales about us."

Madame stood back a little. She raised her eyebrows. "I think I may have misjudged you a little Mademoiselle." She held out one slim hand. "Agreed."

"Say it."

"I swear I will not breathe a word of your clandestine activities to a living soul."

"Or anything else about us. Ever." Lottie folded her arms across her chest to emphasise her words.

"Or anything else, ever. Do we have a deal?" Madame Voclain's hand was still extended.

Lottie released her arms and shook it. "We do. I will let you know when he has gone. We must think of a message no-one would guess. Seeing as I'm supposed to have brought honey today, shall we say, 'the bees are swarming?'"

"Yes, that seems suitable. I suppose there's no way of my knowing when he reaches the south?"

"That won't be up to me, Madame."

"No, no, of course not. Well, good day to you, Mademoiselle." The maidservant came into the kitchen from the hall and went straight out to the back garden carrying a basket of wet laundry.

Madame waited until the young girl had disappeared before saying in a much louder voice, "Thank you for the honey. I think it's best you go through there."

Lottie took the hint and went towards the back door – the tradesman's exit.

Madame Voclain came with her and watched her from the door frame. The maid was talking in a low voice to a young man in scruffy clothes, a bundle of white sheets scrumpled in her arms.

Lottie stopped to say goodbye, but Madame addressed the maid instead. "What are you doing, Odette? Get on with pegging out the laundry. Is that your brother, Jules?"

The maid whirled round, looking scared. "Yes, madame."

"I've told you before. He's not welcome here during your working hours."

The young man, who had been slouching against the sun-drenched wall with his back to them, turned around and gave a cocky smile. "I'm not stopping her working."

Madame Voclain went into the garden. "Well, it certainly looks that way. Your sister is busy. She has a real job, even though she's so much younger than you. You

207

should be ashamed of yourself at your age, with no proper work of your own. I've a good mind to report you for the STO."

"Alright, keep your hair on, I'm going." Jules winked at the older woman and looked at her shapely legs. "Just let me know if you want more stockings, yeah?"

Madame Voclain looked embarrassed. She turned to Lottie. "What's keeping you? Our business is done."

Jules was openly smirking now and winked again, this time at Lottie as if she was a co-conspirator in the black market. Lottie, startled by the exchange, didn't look back at the scene in the garden but unlatched the back gate and entered the village square.

The morning had grown late. She would just catch the butcher if she was lucky. The queue was only three people long and she quickly reached the counter. Madame Marchand looked grumpier than ever.

"There's only offal left."

"I'll take some liver then." Lottie handed over her coupons.

"Should have come earlier. I saw you going to the Voclain's house. Legal problems?" Madame Marchand's piggy eyes never missed a trick.

"No, actually. I was delivering honey from the farm."

"Huh, black market prices, no doubt."

"A fair price for a good product, I'd say."

"You can say what you like, but there's not many can afford to buy honey these days." Madame Marchand rolled up the newspaper over the slimy meat. Her hands were bloody from it, the nails black. Lottie wondered if she ever washed them.

"Thank you, good day to you."

"And good day to you too, Mademoiselle Uppity." Madame Marchand followed her to the door and pulled down the blind. "You got here just in time. I'm closing now."

"So I can see. Enjoy your lunch."

Lottie turned with relief to the boulangerie on the opposite side of the square and let herself into Madame Leroy's immaculately clean kitchen.

"Chérie! Good to see you. How are you, my dear?" Madame Leroy enveloped Lottie in a fond embrace.

"Glad to see you, Madame Leroy." Lottie told her friend all about the arrangement to help Emile Voclain escape.

Madame Leroy listened, goggle-eyed, to the proposal. "What a cheek! That woman always gets exactly what she wants. I wonder what Madame Marchand will have to say about it when she finds out."

Lottie was horrified at this pronouncement. "Let's hope she never does! Someone has been telling tales already. Otherwise, how would Madame Voclain have known about Thierry?"

"She keeps her eyes open, that's all."

Lottie shrugged. "She could be a spy - or playing a double game. You know, helping the Resistance while keeping in with the Germans through her toady husband."

Madame Leroy threw up her hands. "I hadn't thought of that. What is the world coming to? You can't trust even your neighbours or your mayor."

That afternoon, Lottie brought down the mattress from her attic bedroom and installed it in the cellar with some sheets and blankets. Remembering her own experience, she also placed an oil lamp, candles and matches in there on a chair. When she had finished, she looked at the empty bed, picturing Thierry lying there, smiling his warm invitation to her. She clutched at her throat which had constricted suddenly, swallowed, and quickly climbed the ladder. There was no point dwelling on it, but she wished to God she knew he was safe.

Bernadette was in the upper cellar. "All done?"

"Yes, I've made up a bed and put some lighting on the chair from the attic."

209

"It's enough. We're not running a hotel, although it's beginning to feel like it." Bernadette dragged a barrel across the trap door.

Lottie went to help her. "We'll have to tell Françoise about Emile, won't we?"

"Can't see any way around it. Let's hope it won't be for long. Let's wait until he's installed, just in case something goes wrong. No point telling her anything we don't have to."

Supper passed slowly that night. Lottie had been hungry, but her appetite faded over the meal of turnips and liver. The turnips were tough and fibrous and the liver no less so.

Françoise put Bertrand to bed straight afterwards and they listened to the radio as normal for an hour before Bernadette and Françoise went up to bed. Lottie usually stayed up a bit later to read by the fire, so Françoise didn't suspect anything unusual was about to happen.

As soon as she was sure they had bedded down for the night, Lottie let herself out into the yard and walked quickly towards the woods at the rear of the orchard with soft, silent footsteps. The moonlight made everything look black and white, as if it drained the landscape of colour but she could easily pick out the silhouette of the largest oak tree, ivy wrapped around its wide trunk. She should know where it was, she often visited it. It helped her to remember Thierry and now another, even younger man, lay waiting within its ancient embrace.

CHAPTER TWENTY-EIGHT
NORMANDY, FRANCE
JULY 1943

She saw the knife first. The silver blade caught the moonlight and flashed white. Its point was aimed right at her but the hand that held it trembled.

"Emile Voclain? It's me, Charlotte Perrot. Put the knife down, you are not in any danger."

Slowly, the vicious looking blade lowered and a face, almost as pale as the moon, peered out from behind the massive tree trunk.

Lottie smiled at the terrified young man and knelt down next to him, hoping it would make her look less threatening. "Have you been waiting long?"

Emile nodded. "Since late afternoon. I wanted to get here before the curfew."

"Very wise. Come, let's get you inside. Have you eaten?" Lottie held out her hand and he clasped it and stood up.

"Not much. Didn't have time to grab more than a piece of cheese and bread."

"Follow me. We'll put that to rights straight away."

Emile stood up and clumsily picked up his rucksack and the coat he'd been sitting on. Lottie went ahead, looking to left and right for intruders as they covered the familiar ground. She let him in through the back door, lifting the latch as quietly as she could, and barring the door once they got inside.

She had left the lamp on low and the room welcomed them in its soft glow. The clutter of everyday living in one room seemed less obvious in the low light. The fire glowed through the bars of the range and the scent of the herbs drying above it gave off a slightly antiseptic and reassuring aroma.

211

Lottie indicated the chairs around the table in the centre of the room. "Sit down. There's some soup I could warm up. Would you like that with some bread and cheese?"

"Please. My stomach's rumbling!" Emile sat at the table and gave a tentative smile. He was a good-looking boy of about twenty or so, fairly tall with dark hair and the same dark blue eyes as his mother. He'd also inherited her fine bone structure and slim frame.

Lottie heated up the soup and placed a bowl in front of him.

"So, you're hoping to head south then?"

Emile politely swallowed his food before replying. "Yes, to a cousin of my mother's, although I'm not sure how I'm supposed to get there. I don't really want to go but Mother said it would be better than working for the Nazis in Germany. People don't always come back from there."

"Quite right. You'll be safe here until someone comes for you."

"Do you know who?"

Lottie shook her head. "Not yet. We make a point of not disclosing names unless we must. We only know the next person in the chain. Keeps it safe, you understand. What you don't know, you can't say if you're questioned."

Emile looked at her with wide eyes. "Have you done lots in the Resistance then?"

"Not really, not enough, at any rate."

"Do you think I'll make it to the Maquis in the south? I'd like to join in the fight. Mother says I shouldn't, that I should lay low with her cousin in the Auvergne, but I'm determined to kill a few of the Boche before it's over."

"That's not up to me, Emile. My job is just to get you out of here."

Emile had finished his soup. He yawned.

"Come on, sleepyhead. I'll show you your quarters." Lottie got up and he followed her into the first cellar. "Now, see those cider barrels over there? Underneath is a trap door down to a lower cellar and that's where you'll

212

be hiding. It's crucial that the floor is scuffed over the line of the trap door when you come up and the barrels replaced over the opening – every time! Get it?"

Emile nodded, his eyes like saucers.

Lottie took him down to the lower cellar and lit the oil lamp. "There are candles if the lamp goes out. It gets totally dark down here but it's not too damp. I've made up a bed and here's a pitcher of water and a glass. There's also a slop bucket, should you need it. I'll come and get you in the morning when it's light. Believe me, you won't know when the dawn comes!" She laughed softly. "But don't worry. I've slept down here and it's not that bad. You can hear people moving around upstairs but for God's sake, don't come up until I fetch you in case there are soldiers or the Gestapo out looking for you."

"I understand."

Lottie held his gaze. "Good. Even if you run out of light, you stay down here until I come for you."

"Alright."

Lottie clapped him on the shoulder. "Good man. Get some rest now and I'll come for you first thing in the morning. Sleep well." With that, she mounted the ladder and closed the trap door, pushing the barrels back into place across it.

Lottie made sure she was first up in the morning. Dawn broke early at this time of the year and she was downstairs as soon as it was light, fully dressed. She filled the kettle and put it on the hob before going down to the cellar and lifting the trap door. "Everything alright down here, Emile?"

It was pitch black in the cellar. A rustle of bedclothes told her Emile was still alive. "Is it morning at last?"

Lottie laughed. "It certainly is. Why didn't you light a candle?"

"Couldn't find it in the dark after the lamp went out. I think that was the longest night of my life." Emile got off

213

the mattress and stumbled towards the square of light cast by the open trap door.

"Come on up and have some breakfast."

Emile clambered up the ladder and followed Lottie into the farmhouse kitchen. "The WC is outside by the chicken run." Lottie nodded towards the door.

Emile lifted the bar off the door and disappeared. His hair was still tousled and his eyes sleepy when he returned but by then, Lottie had a bowl of milky ersatz coffee waiting for him with the last of Madame Leroy's excellent bread.

Emile flopped on to a chair and tucked in. Bernadette clomped downstairs and greeted him with a brief nod. Emile immediately stood up and bowed his head to her. "Thank you for letting me stay here, Madame Perrot."

"Humph. Your mother gave us little choice in the matter. Keep quiet and out of harm's way." Bernadette began to make some more chicory coffee.

"I could help on the farm, if you'd like?" Emile stayed standing behind his chair.

Bernadette shook her head. "We're supposed to be keeping you hidden, lad."

"Keeping who hidden?" Françoise came downstairs, Bertrand on her hip, and stopped on the penultimate step. "Oh! Who are you?"

Emile turned to her and smiled. "Emile Voclain. I'm staying here for a while. What a lovely little boy! What's his name?"

Françoise smiled back. "Bertrand. He's almost three now. Say hello to the nice gentleman, Bertrand."

"Hello, monsieur." Bertrand looked solemn.

Emile went over to him and kissed him on both cheeks. "I'm glad there's another man in the house, Bertrand."

Bertrand thought for a moment and then held out his chubby arms. Emile took him onto his hip as if it was the most natural thing in the world. Lottie and Bernadette

214

exchanged glances when Françoise didn't object, and her smile widened. Emile sat back down with Bertrand on his lap, who seemed completely at ease with the stranger.

Françoise sat next to them, her eyes fixed on Emile's face, while he chatted amiably to her son. Bernadette slapped the pan of ersatz coffee and the rest of the bread down between them and coughed loudly. "Breakfast."

"I'll see to the goats, I've had mine." Lottie took herself off to the barn and told the goats all about the stupidity of love at first sight, but they weren't really listening.

By Wednesday, with no sign of Pierre, Lottie took matters into her own hands. "I'm off to the village, Bernadette. We can't go on like this."

"Yes, do go. Bertrand is getting far too attached to the boy."

"And he's not the only one." Lottie watched as Françoise laughed at something Emile had said to Bertrand. The three of them were in the yard feeding the rabbits, who had now produced a family of young kits. They didn't even look up when she shouted her goodbyes from the bicycle.

Lottie went straight to Madame Leroy's to see if she could shed light on why no-one had come for Emile.

"Come in, chérie, and shut the door quickly behind you. Put your bicycle out of sight round the side, so no-one knows you are here." Madame Leroy looked furtively over Lottie's shoulder.

"What's all the secrecy?"

"Soldiers have been knocking on doors. See that truck over there?" Madame Leroy had gone to the window and stood to one side so she couldn't be seen by outsiders but still had a good view of the square. Her house stood opposite the butcher's and the German army truck was parked a couple of doors down. Some soldiers were banging on the door of the Marchand's shop, which had already shut for lunch.

215

"Is it for the STO?" Lottie peered over Madame Leroy's shoulder.

Madame Leroy nodded. "Must be."

The door of the butcher's shop opened, and Madame Marchand stood at the doorstep, a tea-towel in one hand and her pinny wrapped around her large waist. She looked flushed and hot, as if she'd been cooking.

They couldn't hear what was being said but Madame appeared to be blocking the soldier's entrance to her house. They both gasped when one of the men used the butt of his rifle to knock her sideways. Madame Marchand fell back against the wall and they marched past her.

Lottie clutched Madame Leroy's hand and gripped it.

A few minutes later, they watched as Victor Marchand was pushed towards the street in front of the two soldiers. Madame Marchand got up from the floor and tried to grab her son but missed. Victor was marched unceremoniously towards the back of the truck. Before he reached it, his father ran out of the house waving a meat cleaver at the soldiers.

"You can't take my son! I won't let you! I've been good to you, haven't I? Kept you fed? Ask your Feldenkommandant if you like. He promised me…"

One of the soldiers raised his gun at Monsieur Marchand. "Stop or I'll shoot."

Madame Marchand screamed. "No!"

"Papa!" Victor dodged the soldier's grip and ran back to his father, getting between him and the soldier's raised rifle. "Don't shoot!"

His father pushed him out of the way. "Let me deal with this." He raised the meat cleaver and lunged at the soldier. There was a crack as the bullet found its mark and Monsieur Marchand collapsed on to the ground. Madame Marchand fell on her husband's body, crying and screaming. The soldiers ignored them both, grabbed Victor by the lapel of his jacket and frogmarched him to the back of the lorry.

They signalled him to climb in by waving their gun barrels. Victor stumbled and one pointed his gun in his back. Victor climbed up into the truck. As the flap opened, they could see other young male faces all in various stages of shock for a few seconds until the tarpaulin fell back and hid them from sight.

The soldiers then turned around and marched straight to the Mayor's beautiful house set at right angles to the butcher's and two doors down from the Mairie building. They rapped on the door. It took a while to open.

Lottie held her breath, too shocked to speak. What would Madame Voclain say? Would she hold up under pressure? Had she seen the violent death of Monsieur Marchand?

When the door opened, it revealed both of Emile's parents standing shoulder-to-shoulder in solidarity in their hallway.

The soldiers said something briefly, then barged past the pair and disappeared from view.

"Oh my God, Madame Leroy! What can we do? What if they are interrogated and Madame tells the Germans where Emile is? Will they shoot the Voclains too?"

She could feel Madame Leroy's considerable bulk trembling, though her words denied it. "We must stay calm, chérie. No point jumping to conclusions. Veronique Voclain is tough and not stupid."

"Does Monsieur le Maire know where his son is hiding?"

"How should I know?"

Lottie acknowledged the truth of this with silence. She turned back to the window. Other lace curtains around the square were held back with invisible hands but all anyone could see was an open door for what seemed like hours.

Lottie looked at the clock. Only ten minutes had passed.

She looked back at the butcher's shop. Madame Marchand was prostrate over her husband, sobbing uncontrollably, but no-one came to help her.

"Oh, Madame, maybe I should go to the farm now? Oh, if only we had a telephone! Emile was out counting rabbits in the yard when I left. I should have made him stay in the cellar. Oh, why didn't I make him stay down there!"

"Look! Something's happening." Madame Leroy pointed at the Mayor's house.

"It's Monsieur Voclain! What are they doing to him?"

"I don't believe it! No, surely they can't…"

Lottie watched over Madame Leroy's shoulder in growing horror as the soldiers marched Monsieur Voclain, one of them holding a gun to his back, towards the waiting lorry, which had turned around in the interim so it was now facing the bridge and the main road out of the village.

"They can't do that! He's too old."

"He's our mayor! I've a good mind to tell them!" With that, Madame Leroy opened the door and marched across the square. She went straight up to the soldiers. Lottie watched, wishing she could join her, but she knew she mustn't draw attention to herself for Emile's sake.

Madame Leroy was gesticulating with both arms, pointing at the Mairie building then back to Monsieur Voclain. Madame Voclain came down the steps of her house and joined her.

Both women were obviously pleading the case for the mayor, who stood silently watching their efforts with the gun still firmly shoved in his back. Lottie could see the indentation of his shirt as the metal pressed against it and sweat stains weeping into the cotton from his armpits. Monsieur was a tall, thin man. He bore no extra flesh on him. Lottie could easily imagine his discomfort.

The soldiers listened impatiently to the two women. Then the one in the peaked cap shook his head and turned away to his soldiers indicating that Monsieur Voclain should get in the truck and pointing to his clipboard.

The two women clutched at each other as Monsieur Voclain, assisted by those already in the lorry, heaved himself up and sat next to the butcher's son, Victor Marchand. The soldiers quickly climbed in the front of the truck and drove away. A minute later, all that remained was dust swirling in the July sunshine and three shocked women staring at the body of Monsieur Marchand.

CHAPTER TWENTY-NINE
NORMANDY, FRANCE
JULY 1943

Lottie pedalled back to Le Verger as fast as she could. As soon as she reached the yard, she slung her bicycle against the stone wall that Thierry had built and ran into the kitchen, whose door stood wide open to the hot sunshine.

"Bernadette! Françoise!" she yelled at the top of her voice.

There was no-one. Was she too late? Had the Germans got here first? Panicked, she ran down the steps to the cellar, then down the ladder to the lower one. Nothing. The place was deserted. Lottie ran back upstairs, checked all the bedrooms. Still not a soul in sight. Frantic, she went to the window on the landing and looked out over the yard towards the orchard.

Then she saw them. Emile and Françoise were carrying the old chicken ark between them and Bernadette was following, holding little Bertrand's hand and pointing instructions. Small, half grown apples clustered on the leafy branches of the trees around them and daisies bloomed at their feet, their clean, white faces upturned to the sun. A scene of bucolic serenity.

Lottie slumped against the window frame. An immense fatigue swamped her, and she slid down against the wall to the floor and shut her eyes. Instead of the idyllic family group she'd just seen, she saw Monsieur Marchand's blood staining his own doorstep; saw how it congealed in the sun and left a trail, already turning brown, when other villagers pulled his heavy frame back inside his butcher's shop. She rubbed her hands across her eyes to wipe the image away, only to see the face of Monsieur Voclain; stony, grey, with deep lines emphasised in his sallow cheeks, and even deeper sadness in his brown eyes behind

220

his wire spectacles as he gazed, probably for the last time, at his once-beautiful wife.

Emile! She must get him out of sight. Lottie stood up, feeling rather dizzy, stumbled back down the stairs and went back out into the brilliant sunshine, blinking at its brightness.

Before running to the orchard, she peered down the lane to check no-one was approaching. She reminded herself she would hear a lorry before she saw it anyway. She ran full-tilt to the orchard and was so puffed out when she reached the others, she couldn't get a word out.

"Emile!" she gasped.

"Yes? Oh hello, Charlotte." Emile gave his charming smile. "We're moving these young birds on to the grass. They seem to love it."

Bernadette turned around and saw Lottie. "What is the matter with you? Why are you running? What has happened?"

Lottie had a stitch. She clutched at her side and pointed towards the village. "Soldiers…round-up."

"Did they come for Emile?" Françoise came towards her, gathering up Bertrand into her arms.

Lottie nodded, trying to control her breathing. "Yes."

Emile turned away from the young chickens pecking at the grass. "What happened when the Germans realised I wasn't there?"

Lottie leant a hand on the reassuring steadiness of an apple tree trunk. "Emile, you must hide. They've…I'm so sorry…they've taken your father instead of you. They seemed to buy your mother's story that you were away staying with a cousin in the country, but they insisted they had to meet their quota, so they took your father instead."

"What? But my father is the mayor!" Emile looked as if he'd been punched in the stomach. Françoise went to his side.

221

Bernadette turned to Lottie. "What about Victor Marchand?"

"That's the worst of it. His father went at the soldiers with a meat cleaver and…" Lottie gulped, "they shot him."

"They did what?" Emile's young face had blanched white.

Bernadette stood very still. "Is he dead or wounded?"

Lottie looked at her straight in the eyes. "He's dead. Madame Marchand was distraught."

"And Victor?" Bernadette's grey eyes narrowed.

Lottie shook her head. "They took him away."

They stood in shocked silence, then Bernadette started to shoo them towards the house. "Come, inside, Emile. They could be looking for you even as we speak. You'll have to stay in the cellar from now on. We've been taking too big a risk, letting you wander about outside. You'll stay there, take your meals there, everything, until we get you away."

Emile looked at Françoise rather than Bernadette and reached for her hand. Lottie walked behind them and saw how their fingers interlocked in a tight handhold. Françoise didn't even have eyes for her son, who was enjoying riding on Bernadette's stout hip and throwing the daisies he'd collected, one-by-one, onto the verdant carpet beneath their hurrying feet.

Once inside the cool of the house, Bernadette shut the door and put the bar across it.

"I'll take Emile downstairs, Grandma." Françoise still held Emile's hand.

"Very well, but I'm sure he could manage by himself." Bernadette plonked Bertrand down on a rug and gave him some old toy bricks she'd found that had belonged to her daughter.

"Here, take some fresh water with you." Lottie poured some water into a jug and gave it to Françoise.

"Thank you." Françoise and Emile left the room quietly together, their hands still firmly entwined.

Lottie collapsed on to the settle. "Oh Bernadette. It was horrendous this morning and now we have Françoise to worry about too. She has a tendency to fall in love much too quickly."

Bernadette nodded. "It's an unfortunate turn of events. You must contact Pierre. Why hasn't he come already for the boy?"

Lottie shrugged. "No idea. I'll go to the mill right away, it's the only way I can get a message to Pierre – unless – could you contact Monsieur Dubois?"

"That's not the way we're supposed to operate, is it? Try to get a message to Pierre first. Now you must eat something; you look awful. It won't help anyone if you faint from hunger on the way." Bernadette plated up some cheese, bread and shelled a few walnuts to go with it.

Lottie didn't feel much like eating but she knew she must and gobbled the food down as quickly as she could.

"Take a couple of apples as well." Bernadette gave them to her. "Don't stay out longer than the curfew."

Lottie mounted her bicycle and sped off down the lane towards the mill.

She found Jean loading hay from a cart into the open barn. A sorry-looking horse stood in its shafts.

"Eh, hello little one." Jean leant on his pitchfork.

Lottie got off her bicycle but, as Jean was dripping with sweat, she submitted to the mandatory kiss with her face averted from his ripe odour.

"Jean, how are you?"

"Alright. The bloody Germans took my cart horse. This poor old mare is all I have left." He nodded towards the miserable creature whose head hung down wearily.

"Poor horse. Maybe she needs a drink. She's standing in full sun."

Jean shrugged. "You could be right." He went to the dejected horse, undid the shafts and lead her to a stone trough in the shade.

The mare drank greedily. Jean tied her up under a tree and came back. "Seems you *were* right."

"Listen, Jean. Pierre has disappeared. No-one has come for our 'friend'. I must contact Monsieur Dubois directly unless you know what's happened to Pierre?"

Another shrug, this time of denial. "He had contacts all over the place. Anything could have happened. I know he was involved in daubing 'death to Hitler' on the train of STO deportees in Caen. A futile gesture, if you ask me, and not worth getting arrested for, but he's incensed about the STO. Maybe he has been arrested and is in jail."

"How can we find out?"

"Best not to try. I'm sorry, little one. I can't help you. You know where Dubois lives, don't you?"

"Yes, Bernadette told me."

"Then go, and good luck." Jean picked up his pitchfork and turned back to lifting the hay from the cart into the barn.

Feeling dismayed that Pierre could have been arrested and was now in trouble, Lottie turned her bicycle around and pedalled off in a new direction, south of the village on a lane she hoped would avoid it. Bernadette had given clear instructions on how to find Monsieur Dubois's dairy farm but Lottie, already exhausted and shocked from the murder she had witnessed only that morning, found it hard to think straight. She knew she had to head north of Le Verger, but she dreaded using the main road and undergoing the scrutiny of a random control post.

She looked up at the sun, still bright in the sky on this warm July day but already beginning to slide westwards, as she knew she must. She turned her bicycle towards it and kept pedalling. After half an hour she came across the train line. She followed Bernadette's instructions and bore right, keeping to the track until she reached a bridge over the railway line. It was very small, barely wide enough for a cart and mercifully unguarded. Heartened by finding this important landmark, Lottie walked her bicycle up the steep slope and then mounted again and swooped down the other side. She looked at the line of woodland in front of her and saw the track she was looking for in the gap opposite the bridge. Bernadette had said the farm was a short way off to the left after about a kilometre.

Grateful for the cover of the trees, Lottie cycled on, ignoring her aching muscles and alert for any sign of German troops in the area. In fact, the countryside here was tranquil. You would never imagine there was a war on in this quiet spot, except when a couple of German bombers flew overhead bearing northwards towards England. A pair of gates appeared, and she stopped. Yes, there was a pond on the other side, just as Bernadette had said. This must be it.

The gates were locked, and she had great difficulty lifting her heavy old bicycle over it and bashed her shin painfully in the process, but she dared not leave it where it could be seen. Her leg was bleeding slightly but she wasn't going to stop now.

She cycled up the narrow, rutted track until she saw a cluster of buildings in the local stone. The sound of mooing cattle came from behind and, as Lottie entered the yard, Lucien Dubois strolled into it from the opposite direction, preceded by about twenty cows, all heavily in milk.

He saw her immediately and frowned. "What are you doing here? Don't you know it's forbidden?"

"I had no choice." Lottie leaned her bicycle against the stone barn.

Lucien left his cows and came over. "What's happened?"

"Pierre's disappeared and I have another person hiding in our cellar who needs to get to the Auvergne. Could you arrange it, like you did before?"

225

A cow urinated behind Lucien, adding more fluid to the already mucky farmyard. "Who is it?"

"Can anyone hear us?"

Lucien shook his head. "I live alone since my wife died."

Lottie wondered why he didn't hide people here instead, if it was only him here, but then realised that he probably did. "I'm sorry."

Lucien shrugged. "It happens. So, who is it?"

"Emile Voclain. They did a round up for the STO, but he escaped to our place before the soldiers turned up. Have you heard about Monsieur Marchand?"

"No? What's that damned collabo been up to this time?"

"He's dead. The Germans shot him when he went at them with a meat cleaver."

"Why the hell did he do that? Thought he was well in with them?"

"It wasn't the local Boche but some lorry with different German soldiers. They took Victor at gunpoint in the STO round-up."

"Oh my God."

Lottie looked down at the ground. A rivulet of slurry flowed across towards them and pooled around Lucien's boots.

"When did this happen?"

"Only this morning. By chance, I was there and saw it all. It was dreadful, Monsieur Dubois."

"Lucien." He pressed her arm with his strong, brown hand. "Emile must get away quickly. Unless, do you think we should leave it until the fuss dies down?"

Lottie shook her head. "No, the Boche apparently believed the Voclains' story that their son had gone to see a cousin in the country in the Auvergne, but they took his father instead to make up the quota."

"What? But he's the Mayor! And he's cooperated all along with the Nazis!" Lucien looked genuinely shocked at this, even more than at the news of Monsieur Marchand. "Monsieur Voclain won't survive a work camp. Do you know where they were destined for?"

"No, no-one does and the soldiers who rounded people up weren't ones I'd seen before. They didn't bother to make enquiries, just bundled the men away. They didn't care."

"It's just a number to them but the village has lost two men who were on their side. So stupid! And what's happened to Pierre?"

Lottie swatted a fly away from the congealing blood on her shin. "Jean said he thinks Pierre was involved in daubing graffiti on the train with the last consignment of STO deportees at Caen station and has been arrested for it."

"I don't believe that. Pierre would not be so stupid as to do such a petty act of resistance and he's far too smart to be caught." Lucien shoved his hands in his pockets.

"I hope you're right. In any case, he's not around."

Lucien sighed. "It's hard to take in your news. Nevertheless, I will come for Emile tonight. Get him ready – you know the drill. Money, coat, good shoes." He gave a brief, cheerless smile. "I take it he's sound in wind and limb, unlike the last feller?"

"Oh, Lucien, do you know if Thierry made it?"

Lucien shook his head. "I wish I could tell you, Mademoiselle. Truth be told, I am but one link of a very long chain. All I know is I delivered him to the next safe house about twenty-five kilometres south of here and he made it that far."

Lottie held on to this tiny crumb of comfort as she pedalled back to the farm. She let herself into the kitchen to find Bernadette minding little Bertrand and cooking supper at the same time.

Bernadette looked up when she entered the house. "Well?"

"Pierre is missing, possibly arrested, but I went to Lucien Dubois's farm and he's coming tonight for Emile."

227

Bernadette gripped the edge of the sink and stared out of the window for a long minute. "So, they've got Pierre. I see." Her voice was tight and hard. "Go and tell Emile to get ready. Say he'll have extra rations tonight."

Lottie, now bone weary, did as she was told, speculating as to what was the real relationship between Pierre and Bernadette. Perhaps it was just their long association over their lengthy lives. Whatever the nature of their friendship, Bernadette was obviously deeply moved by his absence.

She found the barrels pushed to one side and the trap door open to the lower cellar. "You idiot, Emile! Didn't I tell you always to keep the barrels over the door?" Lottie peered down below and just caught Emile and Françoise breaking apart from an embrace. She hadn't the heart to say more.

"Emile? Come here, would you?"

Emile's face looked up at her. "Yes?"

"You're going tonight. Someone is coming for you after dark. Get yourself ready and come up to the kitchen for supper when I call you."

"Tonight? So soon?" Françoise joined him at the bottom of the ladder.

"Yes, tonight." Lottie retreated back to the kitchen and sat on the settle, gazing into the fire. She put her face in her hands to block out the dreadful images that danced in the flames. It didn't work. All she could see was Madame Marchand's distraught, shocked face as she saw her husband fall to the ground.

The poor woman, however much she'd told tales, was now without son or husband. Who would be next?

CHAPTER THIRTY
NORMANDY, FRANCE
JULY 1943

"I want you to walk with us." Lucien Dubois spoke quietly in Lottie's ear while Françoise bid Emile a teary farewell by the stairs.

Lottie was surprised at this request but fetched her heavy boots and a jacket.

Bernadette had to prise Françoise and Emile apart in the end. "Come on. It's time to go, Emile. You must not keep your escort waiting."

Emile let go of Françoise's hand and made for the door. Tired and unprepared though she was, Lottie was glad to leave Françoise behind as she was now sobbing into her apron. The door closed softly behind them. Lottie suspected even Emile was relieved to begin his journey. Then she looked at his face and saw how upset he was. She fell into step with Lucien and let Emile bring up the rear in solitude while he recovered his equilibrium.

"Why do you want me with you, Lucien?"

"I have received very bad news. Pierre has been arrested but not for some trivial graffiti on a train. Did you know he was our contact with the Special Operations Executive?"

"I don't even know what that is."

"The SOE are a British undercover outfit. They communicate with London, and therefore De Gaulle, through a radio operator, but our local circuit has been caught by the Gestapo. The whole lot has come down like a pack of dominoes."

Lottie was shocked, not least because she had no idea that fellow Britons were nearby, and no-one had realised they were her countrymen.

Lucien went on. "That's not the worst of it. Jean Moulin has been arrested in Lyons. The Gestapo tortured him so much, he died from his injuries. He was coordinating the whole country, you see, Charlotte. He and De Gaulle worked together for the Free French." Lucien spat on the ground. "Filthy Boche. They gave him such a rough time, but they got nothing out of him."

"What about Pierre?" Lottie found it unbearable to think of her tall, bony friend being beaten up, or worse.

Lucien sucked his teeth. "Caen prison. Not much hope, I'm afraid."

Lottie blinked rapidly and swallowed. After a moment, she turned back to Emile. "How are you doing back there?"

"I'm fine, thanks. Enjoying the night air after being cooped up in that cellar." Emile gave a half-hearted smile.

They walked on in silence for a while. Lucien glanced across at Lottie. "Do you think you could remember this route on your own?"

"I'm not sure. I think I'd have to study a map first."

"I will teach you how to use a compass. I think it's important that you do remember it. With the circuit down and people being tortured into saying what they shouldn't, we need more recruits for this kind of work."

"I see."

"Anyone could be next, including me." Lucien shrugged.

"Or me."

Lucien shook his head. "I don't think you've ever come under suspicion. The Boche are very old-fashioned about women."

"Yes, I've noticed that. I suppose all the German Fraus are obedient housewives."

"Not a description that would fit you." Lucien smiled.

"I should bloody hope not." Lottie reflected on this new information about other British people being close by, unknown to her. "Were you in touch with this Special Operations outfit, then?"

"Only through Pierre. So, if he talks, I'm done for."

"He won't, I'm sure of it."

"Then you don't have any idea of what these Nazis do to people. It's more than most people can bear. I'm not sure I'd stand up to it."

Lottie's first instinct was to ask for details, then she thought better of it. Ignorance wasn't exactly bliss, but she'd rather not know what was in store, maybe for her too. "What would happen to your cows if you got caught, Lucien?"

"Good question. I've an arrangement with another farmer, close by."

"That's sensible. Well, count me in as an escape conspirator if you want. Though my geography is pretty hazy."

"Believe me, Mademoiselle, by the time you've walked all the way back again, it will be etched clearly on your brain."

Lottie laughed softly. "You make the prospect so inviting."

They walked on through the night, keeping to woodland paths, well away from the beaten track and main roads. All the time, Lucien pointed out landmarks and the orientation of the stars in alignment with the compass, briefly using a torch to show her the needle each time. Lottie tried to take it all in but wished she could write it down.

After about two hours of non-stop hiking, Lottie was cultivating a blister on her right heel and an outrageous thirst. "Lucien?"

"Yes?"

"Do you think we could stop for a short break?"

"What's the problem?"

"I need to adjust my footwear. I didn't have time to prepare for this jaunt, remember? You rather sprung it on me." Lottie spotted an inviting tree root and, without waiting for his answer, lowered herself gratefully into its knobbly embrace.

"Oh, Charlotte, I'm so glad you said that!" Emile quickly joined her.

"You youngsters have no staying power." Lucien chuckled. "Thirsty?"

The 'youngsters' both nodded. Lucien swung his rucksack off his back and drew out a stoppered glass bottle. "Here."

Lottie drank first. Never had water tasted so good. She passed the bottle to Emile.

"Thanks."

Lucien was rummaging in his bag for something else. "Dried sausage, cheese and an apple each. Take it."

Soon they were all munching silently. A fox barked somewhere in the forest behind them.

"He can smell our sausage, I expect." Emile wiped his hands on his trousers.

Lottie was busy adjusting her socks.

"Blister?" Lucien watched her struggle.

"Yes, but it hasn't burst yet."

Again, Lucien dug deep into his pack. This time he brought out a tiny jar and a strip of white muslin. "Time and again I've had to use this for people heading south."

Lottie took the jar and opened the lid. "What's in it? Smells nice."

"Honey and calendula. Put a little on then stick the cloth on top. Then reverse your socks so they are dry and hey presto."

Lottie did as she was told. The effect was miraculous. She handed the little jar back to Lucien. "Thank you, that's much better."

"Good, because we must press on. How are your feet, young man?"

"I'm okay."

"Then let's go. We're just over halfway." Lucien tied the straps on his rucksack and slung it on his back and they marched on.

The fatigue of her stressful day was catching up with Lottie when Lucien stopped in a clearing in some woods and held his finger to his lips. Then he pursed them

232

and gave a low whistle. A figure emerged from the trees in front of them, darker than the other shadows in the moonlight. Obviously a countryman, judging from his clothes and rugged face, the young man shook Lucien's hand and nodded brusquely at the others. The two men muttered quietly between themselves for a minute, then Lucien turned and took Emile's arm to include him in the conversation. "This is him. Go well, young man. Keep safe."

"Thank you for your help." Emile turned to Lottie. "Thanks for everything and, you know, give my love to Françoise."

"I will. Look after yourself Emile. Come back safe." Lottie kissed him quickly and soon he and his companion had disappeared into the trees.

"So, we're not going to the safe house then?" Lottie had been nursing hopes of a hot meal and a bed for the last three hours.

Lucien shook his head. "Wouldn't stay safe for long if they had a constant stream of visitors, now would it?"

"So, we've got to walk all the way back straight away?"

"That's about the sum of it."

Daunted, Lottie rubbed her tired eyes. "I see."

"Come on, let's get started. We've about four hours till dawn breaks."

Lucien turned back the way they had come, and Lottie followed. Her legs ached, her feet were sore, and she longed for a long soak in the bath but the only way she was going to get any creature comforts was to put one foot in front of the other and repeat the process until she reached Le Verger. Lottie took a deep breath, ignored all the urgent messages her body was sending her mind to stop and rest, and plodded on.

Another Christmas had come and gone. The senior commander's wife had made a brave effort at celebrating the season, but the congealed sausage rolls and warm beer hadn't compensated for not going home. Winter had the airfield firmly in its grip and flying days were restricted to the short daylight hours.

Al was assigned the delivery of a Typhoon bomber to Belfast one particularly frosty morning.

"Check for fog over the Irish sea before you take her up, Pilot Officer Phipps." The Flight Captain stood next to him in the queue for the day's chits.

"Yes, sir."

Clare Harrington gave him his paper. She had taken over Miriam's old job. Miriam, despite her brave words, had put in for re-assignment and was now working at Thame at the new training centre. Clare was polite, mousey, quite shy but incredibly efficient. Al found he didn't miss Miriam's vivacious dark looks half as much as he'd thought.

The last year had been so busy with the bombing campaign over Germany, he'd barely had time to think about his love life. Not that he had one. It was better that way. If he got offered leave, he refused it. Al phoned his parents regularly and wrote to Isobel, but it was easier just to keep going than to delve into a load of emotional turmoil he was no longer sure he could cope with. There had been twenty-eight casualties in the ATA last year, and almost twice as many the year before. His whole approach these days was just to motor on.

Al went to see the weather report team. "What's it like over the Irish sea?"

"Should clear in an hour or two. Off to Belfast?"

"That's right. Typhoon."

"Have a cup of tea and wait it out, I would."

Al went to the canteen, past the new block of engineering buildings. The aerodrome had grown so fast since he'd joined. Now, even on this cold winter's morning, the place was bustling with engineers, mechanics, deliveries, admin staff and ground crew.

It was warm in the canteen. Condensation rolled down the inside of the windows from the steam coming from the kitchen and the tea urns. Al got a cup of tea and found an empty table. He picked up a newspaper someone had left behind and turned to the sport on the back page.

Vera Lynn belted out, *"We'll meet again, don't know where, don't know when…"* over the radio. He'd given up on the sunny day and the blue skies turning up any time soon. He lit up a Woodbine and turned the paper over to read the headline.

"Allies land at Anzio, Italy!" It screamed. Good news at last. There was a long article speculating about Churchill and de Gaulle meeting up in Marrakesh a couple of weeks ago, but it was mostly hot air and no substance. Al stubbed out his cigarette and drained the dregs of his tea.

Outside, the mist had cleared a bit. He went onto the airfield and got directions from the flight engineer about which plane was his. He climbed up into the cockpit of the single-seater bomber and got clearance for take-off, nodding to the ground crew to take away the chocks.

Up in the air, he couldn't relax as much as normal. Feeling lightheaded, he clamped his oxygen mask over his nose and mouth. The Tiffy, as the RAF chaps called her, was known for leaking carbon monoxide and the gas sneaked up on you silently, without any warning smell.

The cloud cover was dense in places, making it hard to spot landmarks. The Hawker Typhoon's trademark was its ability to fly low, so Al dropped altitude and tried to get below the heaviest of the cloud formations. At least he wasn't having to face the flak that the RAF boys had to at this altitude. There was a price to be paid for flying low over

235

the hotly contested stretch of water to the south. Today he would be flying over the Irish sea. A cold soup to crash into.

He wondered what Isobel would be doing today on the farm. She'd be out in the fields no doubt, whatever the weather chucked at her. Unless she'd gone to visit Geraint Lloyd at his posh house again. Funny, he never thought about what Miriam might be up to. He wished he could find a way to tell Isobel he'd finished with Miriam, but Al found saying anything important in a letter almost impossible. Isobel didn't give much away herself. Al felt they were just drifting further and further apart.

It started to rain, making visibility even harder. Al cruised along at a moderate speed. He'd be glad to land today with the weather closing in like this. The engine coughed and then regained its thrum. Al checked all the indicators, but it all seemed normal. He looked down at the ground. He reckoned he wasn't far from his native Wiltshire. Yes, there was Stonehenge. Couldn't mistake that.

The engine spluttered again. Sounded like a blockage in the fuel tank. Al tapped the fuel gauge. The trouble with the 'Tiffy' was her weight. Such a heavy plane was always thirsty for fuel.

Then everything went quiet. The engine stalled completely. In the ensuing silence, he could hear the fuel sloshing and rolling about in the big steel tank but none of it was coming through. Frantically, Al released the throttle but there was no response.

The heavy tail of the plane created a drag and Al brought the bird up level again, but he was losing height fast. The one thing he mustn't do was get her into a tailspin. He pulled back on the joystick again, keeping the body of the plane on an even keel and looked down desperately through the rain for a field to land in. There was one to his right, but it had been ploughed, the brown earth drilled into straight rows with puddles pooling between them. He needed grass, however wet.

Desperately, he scanned to his left. A patch of woodland stretched between the hedges. Then he saw a clearing in the tree growth showing a good expanse of green. The Typhoon was descending rapidly now. He fought to keep it level as he aimed for the only decent-sized field in sight. He felt a thud as the treetops skimmed the fuselage beneath him. The metal gave off a screeching sound as the branches scraped against the underbelly of the plane.

Damn! The field wasn't going to be long enough! Now he was almost upon it, he could see that the expanse of grass was only half the length of the landing strip at White Waltham. Al let the wheels down and tried to land the plane as if the engine was still working. There was an enormous impact as the wheels tore into the soft ground, carving it up in great deep grooves. Al pulled on the brakes as hard as he could and held her steady. The hedge opposite him rushed towards him at a terrifying speed.

He shut his eyes and braced for impact.

Farmer Stubbs greeted Isobel with an unwelcome request to do her least favourite chore one bitterly cold morning. "Best get the rest of the slurry on Top Field, Miss Isobel."

Isobel groaned inwardly. "Righto, Mr Stubbs. I'll get the Fergie out of the barn."

"Reckon it's going to rain soon. Got your gabardine?"

Isobel sighed. Farmer Stubbs was always horribly accurate in his weather forecasts. "I'll put it on before I get going."

"Reckon that's a good idea. Do what you can before it really sets in. Wouldn't be surprised if it didn't turn to snow."

"It's certainly chilly enough."

"Aye, wind's from the north, alright." Farmer Stubbs put his pipe away in his top pocket. Isobel took this as a warning.

She hooked up the muck spreader with gloved, frozen fingers. At least the rotating blades meant she wouldn't have to shovel the filthy stuff off the trailer like she'd had to in Wales. Once she was satisfied the machine was safely attached, Isobel climbed up into the driving seat and started the engine. She headed out of the farmyard, stopping to open and close gates and tighten the woollen scarf around her neck. That sharp wind was finding every crevice in her clothing.

Sure enough, she was chugging up and down the biggest field on Home Farm with her noxious trailer spewing out manure, when the rain that had begun an hour ago stiffened into sleet, which swiftly morphed into icy snowflakes. Already sodden and frozen, Isobel decided she'd had enough exposure for one day. She'd finish this load and turn tail for the fireside, or at the very least, some indoor task. Even the cows had more shelter than her during the most inclement months.

The snow melted into the wet ground, joining the muck she was spreading around to form a gooey, stinking layer on the field but she knew from experience that the worms would soon pull it down into the earth and do the really hard work of turning the soil. Even on days like this, she could find satisfaction in her job, but she wouldn't be sorry to grab a hot drink in the farmhouse kitchen before she tackled anything else.

Once she was satisfied the trailer had dispensed every last scrap of ordure, she turned the tractor back down the hill. The wicked north wind had now chilled the ground enough for the flakes of snow to cover over the brown slurry and transform it into waves of pure white snow, disguising the fertile waste with its crystals of frozen water. It was coming down fast in a blizzard now, the wind whipping up into a gale. Soon the countryside would be submerged in snow, if she was any judge, and she had the happy thought that it might lead to getting a bit of time off.

Isobel drove through the gates of Top Field, and then down the lower ones towards the refuge of Home Farm, dismounting either side to open and close them. The snow was accumulating so quickly there was already an inch of icy frosting on everything. She could barely work the catches on the gates, her fingers were so numb. Snowflakes settled on the tractor and her eyelashes and she felt a giddy sense of childish delight in watching them swirl down from the laden sky, lacing the hedges and trees with their delicate, frozen filigree.

"Hello there!"

Isobel squinted through the storm in the direction of the unseen voice, its identity muffled by the snow. It seemed to be coming from the farm, but it didn't sound like Farmer Stubbs.

"Bella! Over here!"

239

Not many people called her Bella anymore. Isobel felt a tingle spread across her skin and, despite the arctic weather, it wasn't from the cold. She put her foot down on the accelerator and the old Ferguson tractor lurched forwards over the bumpy ground.

Someone was running towards her. It looked like a man. A young man in a dark uniform who was waving wildly at her. He opened the last gate before the farmyard and then she recognised him.

Could it really be *him*? At long last? The howling wind was eddying so many snowflakes in front of her eyes, she could barely see at all.

"Al? Is that you? What on earth are you doing here?"

"Well, that's a nice welcome to come home to." Al grinned at her. His shoulders and cap were dusted with snow, his face red from the sting of the wind.

"You never wrote and said you were coming?"

Al shut the gate behind the tractor and came to stand alongside. "Got another seat up there?"

Isobel shook her head. "No, there's only one. I'm heading for the old barn over there. Got to get out of this snowstorm!"

Her mind wouldn't compute his presence. The snow seemed more demanding of her sluggish wits. All she could think was to get out of the lashing gale and away from the shards of ice pelting against her cheeks. She was grateful Al went ahead and yanked open the old door to the barn. The snow was rapidly piling up against it and she could see it took all his strength to pull the wood through the powdery drift.

Once she was inside, Isobel cut the engine and, in the ensuing hush gazed at Al, letting the fact of his presence penetrate her mind while it thawed.

"Let me help you down." Al held out his arms.

"I'm perfectly capable of getting down on my own, thanks. How do you think I've been managing all this time without you?"

"I'm sorry, just trying to help."

Isobel jumped down on to the floor and took off her sou'wester hat. She shook the snow from it and took off her gloves so she could run her hands through her hair. She felt at a distinct disadvantage. She knew she must stink of manure; her hair needed washing, but it had been too cold to bother that morning; her hands were filthy too, like the rest of her. She hadn't even brushed her teeth, having lingered in bed for a precious extra five minutes before braving the frigid delights of the rudimentary lean-to bathroom at West Lodge.

"Wow! Bella, you look marvellous. What a sight for sore eyes. I can't tell you how much I've longed to see you." Al took his cap off and banged the snow from it against his thick, smart coat before tossing it aside on to a bale of straw.

"Is that right? Why did you never come home on leave then?" Bella felt her heart was as frozen as her fingers.

Al had come forward, as if to kiss her, but he stepped back. "You know I've been busy, Bella. It's been mad, really frantic, at the ATA."

"I haven't exactly been idle myself."

"No, I'm sure."

Melted snow dripped unceremoniously from her nose and she searched unsuccessfully for a handkerchief. "Of course, I haven't had much of a social life, either. Unlike some."

"That's not what you said in your letters. What about all those trips to north Wales?"

She could feel the hot flush spreading across her cold face. "What trips?"

"You know – to that ancient Lloyd feller's place – you went there for Christmas, and his Dad's funeral. Lap of luxury it sounded like."

241

"Two trips. Two! In two years!" Isobel undid her gabardine Mackintosh and found a handkerchief in one of her jodhpur pockets. She wiped her face. Suddenly she felt more hot than cold.

Al looked even redder in the face now. "But you stayed with him, didn't you? A week at a time! At his house and Aunt Cass never went with you, did she?"

"Because there was no need, stupid! What do you think I was up to at Geraint's?"

"How should I know? You seemed pretty attached to him and all his worldly goods from your letters."

"How dare you! Are you insinuating I'm some sort of bloody gold digger?"

"If you're not, then tell me what his appeal *is* exactly?"

Al had come closer now and they had both thrust their faces forward belligerently.

Isobel wasn't aware she'd done so; she could only see Al's angry expression. "Geraint is too much of a gentleman to talk about him behind his back. Instead, why don't you tell me about Miriam's charms?"

Al's shoulders dropped. Isobel's anger deflated in a second. That was what this visit was about. He'd married Miriam and had come to tell her. She turned away, unable to look at him. Isobel felt two hands descend on to her wet shoulders.

"Turn around, Isobel." Al's voice was calm now. He pulled her gently to face him. "I finished with Miriam last year."

"Last *year*? Why didn't you say?"

"I was ashamed of myself. You know, it's pretty lonely on a winter's night when you're stuck out in some bleak spot in a town you've already forgotten the name of because it's the third one you've been to that week. We were in the same boat and took comfort from each other. That's all."

"That's *all*? It's quite a lot if you ask me."

242

"I know. I'm sorry."

"And you've got the cheek to blame me for visiting Geraint?"

"I was jealous."

"You were…?"

Al didn't answer. He pulled her closer and kissed her mouth. For a split second, Isobel longed to let go into that kiss, but the injustice of his words made her pull away.

"Not so fast, Albert Phipps. Let's get a few things straight."

He smiled at her, laughter dancing in his eyes.

"And don't you dare laugh at me!"

He laughed. "I can't help it. I love you so much and I'm so happy to see you, my darling."

Still she held him at arm's length. "I have not entered into a romantic relationship with Geraint Lloyd. I want that made quite clear."

Al schooled his face into a more serious demeanour. "Understood. I'd like to know what sort of relationship it is, though."

Isobel turned her face away, but Al cupped her chin and brought it back to look at him directly again.

She brushed his hand away. "It's a friendship."

"Yes, and…?"

"And nothing, on my part, but he does love me very much."

"Can't say I blame him for that."

Isobel frowned. "I don't know about that, but, oh, it's been so difficult. Somehow, I just wanted to help him but he, and his mother, seem to expect me to marry him after the war."

Al folded his arms across his chest. "Do you want to?"

"No! Oh, no! I…"

"You what?"

"I think you already know."

243

"Of course, I know, darling Bella. I love you with all my heart and I know, at least I think I do, that you love me too?"

Isobel sensed resistance was futile. She was still nodding and smiling when Al wrapped his arms around her and left her in no doubt of the depth of his feelings. It took quite a while for them to separate. Al drew her to the straw bale, and they sat down together on its warm, prickly seat.

"Bella, I had an accident a couple of weeks ago."

"Oh no! Were you hurt? What happened? Were you in a plane?"

"Yes, I was flying a Hawker Typhoon and the ruddy engine failed – fuel blockage. Came down in a field and smashed into a hedge."

"But you're alright?"

"Never better. In fact, I got promoted for not crashing the kite and a Certificate of Commendation into the bargain."

"Well done you!"

"Yes, but that's not the important bit. The thing is, it made me realise I might not be so lucky another time. Oh, I know I'm not in the RAF on the frontline, but quite a few of my colleagues have copped it already and the show's not over yet."

Isobel went to kiss him again, but he stopped her. "I'm here, Bella, because I don't want to live without you anymore. I've brought this." He put his hand in his pocket and drew out a piece of paper.

"What's that?"

"Special marriage licence. I'm not hanging about."

"You want us to get married – now?"

Al nodded and got down on one knee on the dirty concrete barn floor. "Isobel, will you marry me?"

Isobel didn't have to think about it. "Get up, you mad idiot. Of course, I will!"

"No putting it off, mind. I want to do it now, while I'm on leave, and I've only got three days."

244

"But how?"

"I arranged it all and the church is booked for nine o'clock in the morning!"

"You've got a bloody cheek!"

"I know, but not much time!" Albert sat back down on the straw bale and gathered her into his arms. "Are you sure, my love, really, really sure?"

"I am. What's the point of waiting, being sensible, being apart? I've been as miserable as hell, to tell you the truth, Al. And so lonely. Kiss me again."

As Lottie lifted her bicycle out of the goat's barn in glorious sunshine one February morning, she congratulated herself on another winter endured under the cosh of occupation. Little Bertrand now boasted a full set of milk teeth and never stopped talking. Bernadette had suffered a bad bout of bronchitis through January which meant Lottie had to do more than ever on the farm, as well as getting the ration cards every month. Françoise, still melancholy since Emile's departure, had shown real skill and a surprising amount of patience in nursing her grandmother through the worst of her illness. Lottie had been relieved to shoulder the burden of the farm instead of staying indoors with the invalid, who had not taken kindly to conceding defeat. Bernadette had slaughtered the old nanny goat before Christmas and Lottie had joked that her malady was the goat's revenge but somehow Bernadette hadn't found it that funny.

Bernadette had slit the goat's throat so swiftly and quietly that the animal had no prior fear. Lottie, holding the bowl beneath its gullet to catch the blood, had been dreading the occasion but the actual killing had been remarkably undramatic. It had fallen to her to gut the beast, under Bernadette's taciturn instruction and that had been far more challenging because of the smell. She'd thought she'd never be able to eat the meat, having gagged over the carcass, but by the time Bernadette had laced it with onions, thyme and sage and cooked it very slowly at the bottom of the range oven, the aroma had transformed into a savoury delight and she had wolfed it down with the others. Hunger blunted sensitivity and sharpened the appetite alright.

Bernadette, ever resourceful, had made dried sausage from the blood and what little fat the poor animal carried, and the icy winter weather had kept the rest of the meat safely preserved in the outhouse for a few weeks. It had got them through the worst time of year. Today, as she cycled into the village for the ration cards, Lottie was as hungry as ever with the abundant season of plentiful goat meat a distant memory.

The day heralded spring with an unseasonal warmth. Lottie had learned how fickle February could be in this part of the world. There would always be these few treacherous days of sunshine before the wind whipped up from the north again and withered any precocious buds that had begun to open too early. She lifted her face to the sun, willing her winter-white skin to drink in its transient rays before they disappeared behind the habitual grey clouds.

She passed the control post without incident and crossed the little bridge to the square. The butcher's shop was still shuttered. Poor Madame Marchand. However much she disliked the woman, losing both son and husband in one day shouldn't happen to anyone.

Lottie wheeled her bicycle over to the Mairie. Just as she was leaning it against the railings, Madame Voclain came hurrying across to her.

"Mademoiselle Perrot?"

"Yes?"

"How are you today?"

"Fine thanks, enjoying this sunshine while it lasts."

Madame Voclain gave a false, hurried smile and lowered her voice so only Lottie could hear it. "Mademoiselle, have you any news…" she looked around the square, "…of Emile?"

Madame Voclain whispered her son's name so softly Lottie could barely catch what she said. "No, Madame. No swarming bees have been reported to me."

Madame Voclain blinked several times. "I see. Thank you. So, no honey yet."

"No, Madame, no honey."

"By the way," Madame Voclain took Lottie by the elbow and steered her around the corner to the quiet, shaded side street, "a word of warning."

Lottie hated the way this woman made it so obvious they were talking in secret. Anyone watching them would be suspicious. She shook off Madame Voclain's hand, noticing that the nail polish at the ends of her long, elegant fingers, normally so immaculate, were chipped and worn. She looked at the ex-Mayor's wife properly. No make-up except some too-bright lipstick that only enhanced her pallor.

"What about, Madame?"

Her voice still low, Madame Voclain leaned in. "Do you remember that obnoxious brother of my maidservant, Jules Deschamps?"

Lottie scoured her tired brain. "Um…"

Madame Voclain looked irritated. "Have you forgotten? In my garden – when you brought the honey?"

Lottie's mind was blank.

"Oh, for goodness sake, girl! He offered me more silk stockings off the black market!"

Lottie simply nodded, realising that admitting this constituted a major breach in Madame Voclain's thin veneer.

"Well, watch out for him. The coward has joined the Milice."

"The Milice?"

"Yes, haven't you heard? They're not just prowling round Vichy now, but they are sneaking around in our Occupied Zone too. Believe me, they are not like the normal French police, and God knows they are bad enough. These snakes have no rules. They stop at nothing to shop their neighbours. Jules has plenty of grudges he's longing to pay back."

"But I don't know him. He has nothing on me."

"Maybe not and I'm happy for you but don't trust anyone. People are paying off old scores through the Milice. They are worse than the Gestapo because they are local and know all the gossip. They recruit young men from round here and pay them well. It means they get fed and also get off being conscripted into the Service Travail Obligatoire, unlike poor Victor Marchand and my husband."

Madame Voclain's hands fluttered up and dabbed at the corners of her eyes but there was no mascara to run from them today.

Lottie put out her hand and touched the older woman's shoulder. "Thanks for the tip-off, Madame. I will be careful."

Madame Voclain sniffed. "Make sure. Make damn sure." She turned and walked back to her own house and closed the door behind her.

Feeling a bit rattled, Lottie mounted the steps to the Mairie's office.

The German soldier at the desk nodded at the railings outside. "That your bicycle?"

"Yes."

"Can I see the documents of ownership?" He held out an imperious hand.

Lottie rummaged in her bag and took out the ragged piece of paper she'd had to sign up to in August.

The soldier scanned the page. "The tax has gone up to forty francs."

"How much?"

"You heard."

"But that's twice as much and it's all I have!"

"Can't help that. You must pay the difference now or I shall confiscate the bike."

Anger rose up in Lottie at this further injustice. She fished in her purse and handed over five franc coins, hating Pétain's pet phrase, *'travail, famille, patrie'* inscribed over them with Vichy's emblem reinforcing their alien faces.

The soldier took the money impassively and wrote out a new licence. He handed it over with her ration cards.

"But there is much less food allocated. We are entitled to more than this!" Lottie counted the vouchers in her hand.

"Not anymore, you're not. Next!"

A queue had formed behind her. Lottie stuffed the coupons into her satchel and stalked out with a stiff back. Oh, how she would like to give that complacent bastard a taste of her temper. He didn't look the least bit hungry.

The clock struck twelve and she marched her newly taxed and licenced bicycle over to the other side of the square to the boulangerie. Bearing in mind how much it had just cost her, she tucked it out of view round the side of the boulangerie and rapped on the back door.

It opened quickly. "Chérie! I saw it was you over by the Mairie. Come in, mon petit chou." Madame Leroy enveloped her in a fond embrace and Lottie nestled into her friend's comforting, soft arms.

"So nice to see you, Madame Leroy."

"What's this? Has something happened to upset you?"

"Nothing important." Lottie told her about the bicycle license, about Bernadette's chronic cough and Bertrand's incessant chatter while Madame Leroy bustled about cutting bread and slabs of cheese to go with her delicious home-made chutney. It felt good to unload into a sympathetic ear.

"Now tell me your news, Madame."

"Oh, I just keep on going, you know. The rationing of flour means I don't have to work so hard but, oh, the grumbling!"

"No-one wants to go without your gorgeous bread." Lottie smeared her slice with butter – a luxury she'd not tasted in months - then a chunk of some Pont l'Eveque cheese and smothered the lot in chutney. She bit into the tottering pile, not caring she had smeared food on both sides of her mouth. She always felt at home with Madame Leroy.

"The coast is crawling with soldiers on the other side of the main road. Some high-faluting German officer came and ordered reinforcements of this stupid Atlantic Wall they are building. There's even a work camp set up near Caen. Full of Polish and Russian prisoners-of-war. Treat them like slaves, they do. I've heard of awful things – they're half-starved and the Boche whip them if they don't work hard enough. It's disgusting."

Lottie took a sip of water. "I'm sorry to hear that. Another breed of people they classify as sub-human, like the Jews. Dreadful."

Madame gave a lop-sided smile. "One good thing though. I've heard some of the workmen have weakened the cement mixture with flour and sugar!" Madame Leroy laughed. "No wonder I'm going short of my two main ingredients, but I don't mind if it's used for that. There are plenty of French businessmen making money from selling the cement to the Boche but thank God some of our countrymen are loyal. The main road is crumbling under the weight of lorries loaded up with the nasty stuff."

"But madame, surely all these reinforcements must mean the Boche are worried about an invasion?" Lottie spoke through a mouthful of bread and cheese, unable to stop cramming her mouth with food.

Madame Leroy didn't answer but got up and shot the bolt across her back door. She drew back her lace curtains at the window a tiny fraction and peeped outside. She gave a satisfied nod, then went to the partition door that led to her shop front and locked that.

Finally, Lottie finished her meal. She sat back, replete, watching all these security measures. Madame Leroy came back to the table and sat down heavily.

Lottie wiped her mouth with the back of her hand. "Madame, what is it? Tell me all you know."

Even though she had both doors locked, Madame spoke in a low voice. "I have had contact with a new agent."

251

"British? From this Special Ops thing Lucien spoke about?"

Madame Leroy shook her head. "No, she's French, although she hinted she'd been to England. Works from Paris but she's going around the countryside looking for places for airdrops because…" a beaming smile broke in Madame's round face. "Because a big invasion *is* planned."

"What? Really?"

Madame Leroy put a finger over her mouth. "Ssh. We don't know where or when, but it's certainly planned. Do you have somewhere on the farm that could take a plane landing? A clearing big enough without trees in the middle but surrounding it for cover?"

Lottie felt a bubble of excitement competing for space in her full stomach but, try as she might, she couldn't think of anywhere at Le Verger that would suit. "Ah, madame, I wish I could say yes to that. I would like nothing more than to be involved but there's nowhere I know of. I will ask Bernadette when I get back."

Madame Leroy's face fell. "That's disappointing. I'll make other enquiries but if you do discover somewhere, come back and tell me quickly. This woman is returning soon. And, as always, mon petit chou, say nothing to anyone. With the Milice sniffing about, it's harder than ever to keep a secret – and this is the biggest one yet."

Lottie got up to go. "Don't worry, madame. My lips remain sealed."

"Ah, chérie, you have no idea the ways they can be made to open." Madame Leroy kissed her. "Go now. Be safe."

Isobel opened her eyes and blinked. She didn't know where she was. She felt very comfortable, she knew that, and in a new way she'd never experienced before. Her whole body felt relaxed and at ease, calm and warm at the same time, as if she was in a bath of deep water at the perfect temperature. A pleasure she'd not enjoyed since before the war.

Then she remembered. She turned on her side and looked at Al, still fast asleep next to her. He lay on his back, both arms flung back against his pillow. His breath rose and fell in a regular rhythm. She watched his naked chest move up and down in a peaceful, steady beat. The aliveness of him!

She wanted to stroke his body. It had given her such pleasure the night before. Why had they waited so long for this? She felt cheated and momentarily sad they'd wasted so much precious time. She spent a long time gazing over her husband's sleeping form before letting her eyes wander around their bedroom at the Strand Palace Hotel. Such extravagance! But Al had insisted.

The wedding had passed in a quick flurry of form filling, after the short ceremony at the local church in Lower Cheadle, suitcase packing and hugs and kisses from bewildered members of their families, now formally connected by their love.

Her mother had hesitated for only a moment before congratulating them when they'd come back through the blizzard of snow to announce their one-day engagement.

"Are you disappointed I'm not marrying Geraint, Mummy?" Isobel had asked the question in a low voice, covered by the noisy congratulations of Katy, Jem and Lily who had come up to West Lodge after Al had summoned them over the telephone.

"All I care about is that you love each other. I adored your father, and nobody could stop me marrying him, although they tried pretty hard. Love is all that matters, darling, and if you share that with Al, then you have my most sincere blessing. Believe me, I wish you all the happiness in the world."

Isobel gave her mother a hug and kissed her damp cheeks. "Thank you, Mummy. That means everything to me."

Cassandra held her daughter at arm's length and looked deep into her eyes. "I couldn't be happier for you. My only wish is that Lottie was here to join us. No, that's not true. I wish your father was here too. He loved both you and Al." Cassandra took a handkerchief from her pocket and blew her nose. "Now, we'd better get busy. We must organise a wedding in a very short time!"

At that point Katy had come up and put an arm around each of them. "Don't you worry about your mother, Bella. I'll see she's alright."

"Thanks, Aunt Katy."

"This calls for a toast!" Cassandra went to the drinks' cabinet in the corner of the tiny parlour. "Sherry or whisky? It's all we've got!"

"Can I have some, Mum?" Isobel noticed Lily tugging Katy's sleeve and looking delighted when her mother said she could have a very small sherry, as it was 'such a special occasion'.

When everyone had their glasses filled, Jem lifted his up. "To our Albert and your Isobel. May they be as happy as me and Katy and share many, many years together."

Everyone clinked glasses and sipped.

Katy spoke into the brief silence. "I'd like to propose a toast to absent friends. To Douglas Flintock, whom I still miss every day. Well done, old friend, and dearest Cass, for producing such a beautiful daughter to make our son happy."

"Hear, hear!"

Katy continued, "But also to dear Lottie, wherever she may be. Please God she will come home soon and be part of the family again."

Cassandra raised her sherry glass. "Thank you, Katy. You are such a good friend. To my darling Douglas and our dearest Lottie."

Jem chinked glasses with each of them. "Good health and happiness to you both."

Al cleared his throat. "And I want to say thank you to all of you for everything. I'm sorry I haven't been home in such a long time. This ruddy war has a lot to answer for but me and Bella will make the most of whatever time we have together. To us all! And...to victory!"

A ragged cheer had followed.

Isobel lay back against the pillows. And now here she was. After the briefest of weddings and a short train journey, she was in London on her honeymoon and blissfully happy.

She couldn't hold back any longer. She kissed Al on the lips, and he stirred.

As soon as he opened his eyes and saw her, he smiled. "Hello, my love."

"Hello."

Al yawned. "Did you sleep well?"

"Like a top. I think it's being Mrs Phipps that did it. I haven't slept so well in simply years."

"Mrs Phipps. Doesn't sound posh enough for you." Al ran his finger over her bottom lip, tracing its curve.

"It's perfect and don't talk rot." She bit his finger.

"Ow! That's no way to greet your husband of a morning."

"Show me another way, then."

"I'll show you something alright." He slid on top of her.

She loved the weight of him against her body; the way their skin melded together, inside and out. Soon she was gasping in delight, just like last night, and begging for more.

"You are very beautiful, Mrs Phipps." Al kissed her neck, then her breasts and she cried out with the joy of it.

"Oh, I love you so much, Al!" She nibbled the lobe of his ear and they rolled over, so she sat astride him, riding the waves of rapture until he gave a moan of pleasure, held her so tight that her body arced in ecstasy too, and then they flopped back on the bed. Isobel cuddled into him and nestled her head in the crook of his shoulder. She licked the sweat beading on his skin and traced the bones that defined his handsome face with delicate fingers.

"I'm quite fond of you too, you know." Al chuckled. "Tell you what, we'll have lunch at The Ritz today, shall we? You can get a meal anywhere for five bob in London while the war's on."

"Really? Oh, I'd love that." She heard his stomach rumbling.

"Breakfast first. I'm starving. All this nocturnal exercise has given me an appetite."

Isobel stretched luxuriously. "I never want to leave this room. I don't want to see anyone but you."

"We've got to keep our strength up." Al stroked her bottom. "Got to make the most of today. I'm back at the airfield tomorrow."

"Oh, Al, don't remind me."

Breakfast was served in the big dining room decorated in art deco style, like the rest of the hotel. They took a table in a corner.

"So many American soldiers here, Al!"

"I know. They'll make sure the food's good! I think they take ration vouchers here too, so tuck in."

They ate their fill and walked it off in the Victoria Embankment gardens. A feeble wintry sun shone through the bare branches of the leaves and glinted on the Thames beside them.

"Happy?" Al kissed her lips.

"Blissful."

"I've still got room for a slap-up lunch at The Ritz. How about you, Mrs Phipps?"

"Why not?"

As they entered the opulent hallway, Al gave Isobel a sideways glance. "Just about good enough for my wife, I reckon. Let's hope they don't work out you're with riff-raff."

"Don't be silly, Al. I'm proud to be with you. You look quite splendid in your uniform."

The waiter ushered them to a table next to a huge mirror made up of smaller rectangles of glass. Isobel looked at her smiling reflection. "Look at us, together at last."

Al laughed. "And we're legal, too."

"Yes! No-one can tell us what to do anymore."

"Except Hitler perhaps."

"Don't talk of the war. Let's ban it for today."

They ordered their food and some wine in honour of the occasion. Isobel had to prompt Al to taste the wine when the waiter poured a little into his glass and stood back, waiting for his approval. Al looked embarrassed when he realised his mistake but then took a sip and nodded at the waiter. "That's fine. Pour away."

Her husband was a quick learner. Isobel sipped her claret and cut into her lamb chops. "I shan't ever forget this day, Al."

He smiled and topped up her wine. "Yes, it's like that song, *'Putting on the Ritz.'* Saw it in a Ginger Rogers and Fred Astaire film. It's miserable going to the pictures on your own and so lovely to be sharing this with you. I shan't forget a single minute either, my love."

"Let's go to the pictures this afternoon. I don't care what's on. It'll be warm in the cinema."

"Good idea. We can snuggle up together in the dark too."

They spent the afternoon watching *'Ali Baba and the Forty Thieves'* in the Plaza cinema at Piccadilly, snatching kisses under the cover of the dim light.

"Blimey, I thought old Ali would never manage to marry Amara, did you?" Al looped Isobel's arm through his as they walked through the grand foyer before leaving the picture house.

It was raining hard outside and the pavements already had pools of water collecting at their edges, though it was hard to see without streetlights. People scurried past them holding on to their hats and brollies against the downpour.

Isobel stood on the steps of the cinema, hesitating before leaving the shelter of its porch. "It certainly had enough thrills and spills to take my mind off the war. Baghdad looked a very exotic place, not like dreary old England in the blackout. Look at the rain! Oh, I wish I'd brought an umbrella."

"Come on, let's hop on this bus and see where it takes us."

"Go anywhere near The Strand Palace Hotel, mate?" Al handed over some coppers to the bus conductor.

"You're in luck, son. It's four stops away."

Al turned to Isobel. "Oh, I'm in luck alright."

Isobel kissed him. "Me too. I never want our honeymoon to end. I'm having so much fun and sharing London with you is very heaven."

They got off the bus near the hotel and ran all the way through the pouring rain. Once inside the stylish atrium, they shook off their dripping raincoats and went straight up to their room to warm up.

"Let's not go out again tonight, Al. We've eaten so much food already, I don't really need another meal. I'd rather just stay in with you and getting around in the blackout in the rain would be awful."

"Tell you what, there's a dance on downstairs later. I'd love to twirl you round in my arms, Mrs Phipps. Show off my beautiful wife to the world."

"Oh, that does sound like fun and a good way to warm up!"

Isobel changed into the one evening dress she'd brought with her and brushed her hair, sitting at the dressing table.

Al came up behind her and watched. "That's a new way of doing your hair. I like it."

"It's called the Victory Roll. Means you don't need hairpins. Can't get them for love nor money these days. Mummy gave me her last pair of silk stockings for the wedding and I still haven't laddered them." Isobel pointed her stockinged toe out to one side to show her husband.

"If you go on doing things like that, we'll never go downstairs."

"I don't care. I don't mind if we just stay here." She smiled at his reflection above her in the mirror.

"Just a couple of dances will do us good."

Isobel stood up. "There. Do you think I'll pass muster in this old dress?"

Al did a mock bow. "Madame, you will be the belle of the ball. Blue always did suit you. Matches your gorgeous eyes."

Isobel laughed. "Come on then."

The dance room was full of American GI soldiers and the dancing was already in full swing. They had to shout to make themselves heard.

"Want a drink?" Al yelled.

"Not really, let's just dance!"

The band was playing a Glenn Miller number, *'Chattanooga Choo',* and everyone was singing along while they cavorted about in a mad, abandoned way Isobel had never seen before.

259

Al swept Isobel on to the dance floor and soon they were imitating the wild moves of the American soldiers.

"What is this dance called? It's crazy!" Al shouted at one of the couples who were tapping their feet in dance to the music and swinging each other around like footballs.

"Don't you know the Jitterbug when you see it? Where have you *been*, pal?"

Al laughed, "Not here often enough, that's for sure!"

"Say, let me take your partner and you have my girl for the next one. We'll show you how it's done."

"Oh, I don't know about that. We only got married yesterday!"

"You just got married?" The American grabbed Isobel by the waist. "Congratulations, honey!"

Isobel just about managed to gasp out, "Thanks!" before he swung her around him, then back again and twizzled her around until she was dizzy. When the band stopped for breath, so did everyone else.

"Hey, partner. You did swell but I'd better hand you back to your old man. Guess you want to make the most of your honeymoon." He winked at Isobel who returned to the arms of her husband with some relief.

Al took her hand. "I need a drink!" They left the dance floor and grabbed a couple of gin slings at the bar.

Isobel drank a great gulp of the refreshing liquid. "My goodness, this is delicious."

"Isn't it, though? I'm so thirsty, too."

They downed their drinks quickly.

"Come on, Bella. Let's show 'em how us Brits do it, now we know the moves."

But the next song was a slow one, *'Moonlight Serenade'*. Isobel felt more in love than ever as they glided round the ball room holding each other tight, cheek to cheek.

They danced for ages, interspersing their exercise with more gin slings but Al wouldn't let anyone else cut in and dance with his wife. "I'm not parting with you to another chap again."

Feeling a little giddy, Isobel looked up at the clock. "I know it's only eleven o'clock, Al, but I'd like to go back to our room now."

"Do a little dance of our own, do you mean?"

She nodded. "Yes, please."

They held hands on the way up to their room. Once inside, they kissed long and hard. Al started to undo her dress and she unbuttoned his shirt.

Isobel's head swam. "I'm a bit lightheaded from all those gins. I can't wait to get into bed. The dancing was wonderful, wasn't it?"

"Not a patch on this, though, hey?"

Isobel shook her head. "No, nothing can equal this."

The distinctive wail of the air raid sirens rent the air outside.

Al paused with her buttons. "Oh no! Not a bloody air raid tonight?"

"What are we supposed to do, Al? I've not been in London at all through the war. Don't we have to go to an air raid shelter or the underground or something?"

"We should, and there's one in the basement of the hotel. Do you want to?"

Isobel kissed him. "No. I couldn't be happier than I am this moment. Even if I die tonight, life couldn't get much better than this. Let's stay here."

She held one of his hands in hers while she reached for the light switch and turned it off with the other, plunging them into pitch darkness. Not a glimmer of light penetrated the room through the blackout curtains.

Al didn't say anything but scooped her up in his arms and lay her down on the bed. They took off the rest of their clothes and made passionate love to the sound of bombs exploding nearby. Isobel, drunk on gin cocktails and sexual abandon, ignored the whine of the bombs falling, the crash of masonry, the smashing glass, the crump of the

261

shells detonating nearby and the shiver of the building after each impact. Within the secrecy of their darkened room, they lost themselves in their lovemaking, losing all their shyness in the intense physical expression of their mutual love. When they had finally climaxed, the raid was also over. The long note of the all-clear sounded out to confirm it.

They lay silent on the bed, exhausted by their wild and wanton release, wrapped in each other's arms. Isobel felt empty, stunned by the experience, yet not the least bit ashamed. Al was part of her flesh now. She was no longer separate and never wanted to be away from him again.

Into the blackness, she whispered. "Is it always like this for everyone, Al?"

"I don't know, darling. I never thought to feel like this. I feel I've dissolved into you, that we're just one person."

"I'm glad we didn't go down to the basement with the others."

He hugged her tighter. "Me too. We've been bloody lucky, though."

"And in so many ways."

"Don't know how I'm going to leave you tomorrow, Bella."

She kissed the palm of his hand. "I'm not sure I'll be able to bear it."

"Let's sleep for a bit, tucked up safe together."

"I love you, Al."

"And I love you, with all my heart, body and soul." Al kissed her.

Isobel shut her eyes and nestled even closer to him.

CHAPTER THIRTY-FIVE
NORMANDY, FRANCE
SPRING 1944

Lottie crouched in the shadows, her torch firmly clamped in her fist, her rifle resting against her feet. She didn't want to lose either in the undergrowth at the crucial moment. The full moon silvered the leaves rustling in the branches behind her and she cursed their pretty noise. She'd been straining her ears for the sound of the plane approaching, or worse, a German vehicle bearing soldiers and guns.

She looked across the open space at Lucien who was similarly crouched down amongst the line of trees edging the field opposite her. He too, carried a gun and had shared his hefty pouch of bullets with her.

When she had come back from Madame Leroy's and asked Bernadette if there was anywhere suitable for an airdrop at Le Verger, Bernadette had cursed roundly.

"Haven't we already put ourselves in enough danger?"

Lottie had pleaded with her. "I know but there's an invasion coming. Don't you see, Bernadette? The only real way out of this nightmare is for the Allies to send the Boche packing, once and for all. Don't you want to help that happen? End this tyranny, once and for all?"

Bernadette had compressed her lips, opening them only to cough the dry hacking cough that had plagued her for months. She had gone to the sink and looked out across the yard, staring at the orchard beyond; then, she had turned around, coughed again before saying, "Very well. There is a parcel of land not attached to the farm. It lies between Le Verger and Lucien's dairy farm." Bernadette jerked her head in the direction of her apple trees. "North of here."

"Is it big enough, a good open space, enough to land a plane?"

"How should I know how much damn room you need for landing a bloody plane!"

Lottie bit her lip. "So, roughly, how many metres long or wide?"

"Look, child. You'd best go yourself and have a look. I want nothing more to do with it? Do you hear? I'm sick of all this danger and worry. Sick and tired."

And Bernadette did indeed look worn out.

"I'm sorry. I know you have been poorly. Draw me a map and I'll go alone."

Lottie had found it easily from Bernadette's directions and couldn't help but feel a tingle of fear mixed with excitement at the prospect of a plane landing in the field. Bernadette said it had been intended for a poplar plantation but neither her husband or son had got around to it and so it had lain fallow. Sometimes Lucien used it for grazing and paid her in beef. It was an arrangement that had suited them both and Lucien had raised no objection to it being used as a temporary airfield when she'd visited his farm a second time. He had objected to the visit though.

"Never again, Charlotte! You are compromising your own safety as well as mine!"

Now, on this clear starry night, Lottie's fears subsided, and excitement took over. What if there was a British person on the flight? What if they dropped an agent, not just containers? She would have so many questions to ask them! She longed to send a note home to her mother and had written several only to burn them in the kitchen range. If she was found with that on her, her cover would be blown, and she'd be shot on sight or deported as an enemy alien. No-one but Bernadette and Françoise knew her real identity - that she was English - not Jean or Lucien or even Madame Leroy. It would be stupid, so stupid to blow it now. If the invasion was successful, maybe, just maybe she would get home and see her mother again.

Her thoughts turned, as they so often did, to Thierry. What was he doing right now and where was he? Whenever she looked up at a clear night sky, she thought of him under the same stars, looking up at them and wondering about her. Would they see each other again? Was he still alive? A movement on the other side of the field caught her eye and brought her thoughts abruptly back to the present moment.

She looked across at Lucien. He held one hand up, the index finger pointing up to the sky, then cupping his ear. Lottie focussed on listening. Was that the hum of an engine? Yes, faintly at first, then louder came the sound of an aeroplane.

Lucien switched on his torch and stepped into the clearing, beckoning her to do the same. They each went to their allotted places and lit the paraffin torches they'd set up earlier into a large 'L' shape. They shone their torches, clicking them on and off, up into the sky. The darker hulk of the aeroplane could now be seen above them.

"It's spotted us, Lucien!" Even as she spoke, a white mushroom billowed forth from the belly of the plane, followed immediately by another. The two parachutes descended far too slowly for Lottie's peace of mind. Seconds stretched into minutes, hours, and all the time she was listening for the sounds of other engines as the plane pulled away and up towards the stars. So, it wasn't going to land, after all. Good job she hadn't brought that letter.

"Quick! Douse the lights." Lucien jabbed a pointed finger at the flaming torches while he ran towards the white cylinders rapidly approaching the earth.

Stumbling slightly, Lottie ran between the torches and killed their flames and pulled them out of the ground. She ran back to Lucien who was struggling to disengage the parachutes from the containers.

"They are much bigger than I imagined." Lucien freed one container and went to the other. "You fold up the parachute while I separate the other one."

The parachute was made of a silky material but rougher than real silk. It bundled up together easily but the sheer size of it made the process awkward and slow, as it billowed out of her hands in the breeze. In the hush left behind by the swift departure of the aeroplane, Lottie heard every rustle in the undergrowth and her nerves jangled as she prayed it wasn't German soldiers but only a curious fox.

She soon had a tidy collection of used torches, lamps and the two parachutes at her feet. She looked across at Lucien. "What next?"

He shook his head. There is no way we can lift these buggers between us. Each one must weigh fifty kilos!" Lucien sat back on his heels and pushed his cap back off his forehead before rubbing it.

Lottie lifted one end of the container nearest her. It was true. They'd never manage it between them alone.

"How about asking someone to help us?"

Lucien shook his head again. "The fewer who know about this, the better."

"I know, I'll get the donkey and cart from Le Verger and we'll do it in two loads."

"You still got that old animal? Not good enough for the Boche, was she?"

Lottie smiled. "No, they didn't want the goats either, but they took all our hens, but Pierre brought us some pullets and they're doing well, I only hope he is too."

Lucien grunted his assent to her wish. "Listen, it's a good idea about the cart but we'll have to hide these first. You go and get the donkey and I'll cover these in broken branches. Let's drag them to the trees first."

Lottie unfolded one of the parachutes, cursing its sleek whiteness which the moon picked out too well, and wrapped the container in it. "Here, take the straps of the 'chute and we'll pull it along."

"Good idea but hurry up!"

They dragged the parachute as far into the trees as they could. The smooth material slipped nicely on the grass

266

and they managed to get it a good way in. They were just bringing the second one to join the first when Lottie stopped.

"What's the matter, child?"

"Listen. It's a car engine."

"Hurry! Pull it to the trees!" Lucien yanked even harder on the parachute straps and started to jog forwards. Using all her strength, Lottie joined him. Feverishly, they scrabbled about in the undergrowth and threw dead leaves, twigs, fallen branches, anything they could find, over the tell-tale pale cargo.

"It's the best we can do. Listen, they are closer. Get further into the woods, as far as you can and let's split up." Lucien threw one last handful of earth over the containers.

"They're well covered now. Good luck, Lucien." Lottie darted off into the woods and ran for her life. When she felt she had reached a safe distance, she crouched behind a thicket of brambles. The ground fell away behind it and she threw herself down on the sloping bank and peeped through the thorny tangle. Two beams of light flickered between the trees across the field and she saw the shadow of a German army jeep bumping along the track on the other side of the clearing.

Already sweating from her exertions, Lottie ran her hand across her damp face. Should she stay and watch or run further and risk making a noise? The vehicle had stopped now, and a search light scanned the field. She could hardly bear to look. What if they saw a glimpse of white parachute? Or spotted the holes where the lamps had been shoved into the ground in that tell-tale 'L' shape Lucien had insisted upon? Where was he? She cast about around her, but she couldn't see him amongst the tree trunks. That was good. If she couldn't see him, maybe neither could the Boche. Lottie picked up some damp earth and scrubbed her face with it, hoping it would take the shine off her cheeks.

The soldiers were yelling at each other, but she couldn't make out the words. A tall lean man stood amongst them in a different uniform. The search light rested on his face for a few seconds as it swept in a circle. Lottie gasped out loud. Jules Deschamps, the young Frenchman who had turned traitor in the Milice, was pointing straight at her. Surely, he couldn't know she was here.

A German officer turned to the group of men and barked an order. Two of them went to the trailer at the back of the jeep and came back with something they set up as a tripod. Then they crouched down behind it before sending bullets flying out across the clearing. Lottie could see the flashes of fire as it rent the air. Lottie ducked involuntarily and lay flat on the ground, wriggling down into the earth as the bullets whined past her, before raking the woods to her right, further away. They must be doing it in case there was someone here. Had they seen the parachutes coming down? Or just heard the plane? God knew there were enough German planes issuing from the air base loaded with bombs heading for England most days. But not usually at night and not with the tell-tale circular RAF insignia on their sides.

She heard the gunfire run the length of the woods, then, as suddenly as it had started, the machine gun stopped firing. Had they given up? She risked a peep through the blackberry briars. The soldiers piled back in the jeep and lifted the machine gun back on the trailer. The engine started up and they turned around. Ten minutes later she could hear more distant sounds of gunfire.

Lottie sat up on her haunches and willed her heart to slow its rapid beating. She closed her eyes and put her shaking hands on her knees to quell their trembling. She jumped in alarm when she felt someone else's touch on her shoulder and turned around sharply, almost falling over.

"Don't be afraid, little one. It's me, Lucien."

"God, you gave me a fright."

"I know. I think they don't know we used this field. They are searching everywhere randomly. They must have heard the plane and are firing on any likely spot in hopes of killing anyone connected with it, or an agent landing."

268

Lottie stood up. "Yes, do you think they saw the parachutes?"

"I don't know. This is a remote spot. It could have been a collaborator who reported it."

Lottie looked back at the field. "Just what I was thinking."

"Did you see that bastard Deschamps with the Boche?"

Lottie nodded.

Lucien spat on the ground, but quietly. "He's got fingers in many pies, that one. Supplied a lot of people with silk stockings and food from the black market. Made a tidy profit too. He will have spies everywhere."

"What about the containers?"

"It's too dangerous to get them tonight. They're well covered. Let's get home in one piece and try again another day."

Lottie felt disappointed at this idea. "But what if the Boche find them first? They're bound to come back and scour the area in daylight."

"Too bad. It's more important you are safe."

"But…?"

"I mean it, child. Come on, let's get you home."

"I can go alone; it would be safer. We live in opposite directions."

"Can you manage alone?"

Lottie clapped him on the shoulder. "I'm sure I can. I can say I was out poaching if questioned." She lifted her rifle.

Lucien studied her face for a long moment. "Alright. Take care. I'll be in touch."

Lottie watched him stride away in the soft moonlight. She looked up at the stars, located the north star and turned away south. It wasn't far to Le Verger, only two kilometres at the most but it might as well have been two hundred ahead of her, the way she was feeling.

269

She swallowed, shouldered her gun and stepped gingerly forwards into the dark forest.

CHAPTER THIRTY-SIX
NORMANDY, FRANCE
MAY 1944

Lottie was fuming, worried and scared, all at the same time. She'd stolen back to the woods a couple of weeks after the drop, in hopes of finding the containers and removing the contents, even if it meant each item had to be retrieved one-by-one. Lucien had said they would contain guns and ammunition, food and even money, all sent from her native country and all really needed if they were to be of any use in ridding Normandy of the German curse. She retraced her route to the woods under cover of darkness, cursing the two-week wait until there was no moon.

She could only remember vaguely where they had put the precious cargo and rummaged around for an hour or two, trying to locate them, using a torch as little as possible. She eventually conceded defeat when she found a patch with many footprints in the dead foliage and bullets lodged in tree trunks left over from their narrow escape. Frustrated, she'd reluctantly turned back and trudged to the farm, her only reward being more tired than ever the next day.

As soon as it was time to get the ration cards, she pedalled to the village. The meagre allowance was doled out again but passed without incident this time. She had to show her identity papers and the licence for her bicycle, but she had learned to keep her mouth shut and made no comment, grateful not to be interrogated.

Lottie wheeled her bike over to the boulangerie, nodding 'hello' to Madame Marchand who was sitting in the sunshine by her front door. The butcher's wife looked different, as well she might. She'd lost a lot of weight and her hair had gone quite white. Lottie smiled and waved, feeling like a hypocrite, but received no acknowledgement in return. Lottie parked her bike up the alleyway to the side of the boulangerie, knocked on the back door and let herself

271

into the kitchen at the back, surprised that Madame Leroy had not resorted to locking it by now.

She sat down at the kitchen table and slumped back on the chair. This little bakery was the one place she felt she could really relax. Daft really, when Madame Leroy was the kingpin of resistance communications.

A muted babble of conversation emanated from the shopfront, but Lottie couldn't be bothered to listen to it and going to join in would be sheer folly. The less people knew about her visits here, the better. Eventually the voices petered out and she heard Madame Leroy shut and bolt the shop door.

She listened to Madame Leroy's heavy footsteps heading towards the kitchen.

Not wanting to alarm her, Lottie called out, "Coucou! Madame Leroy! It's me, Charlotte Perrot."

"Hello, mon petit chou."

They hugged fondly. "You look tired Madame."

"I am weary, it is true. I have bad news."

Lottie's stomach tightened.

"It's Lucien. After the container drop that night, German soldiers went to his farm and ambushed him on his way back. He's been arrested and tortured."

Lottie's hands flew involuntarily to her face. "We saw them. They shot at us but then they moved off and we thought we'd got away with it. That snake Deschamps was there too."

Madame Leroy looked grave. "Yes, it was Jules Deschamps who handed him over to the Gestapo. They used the water treatment on him."

"How do you know this?"

"Word gets around."

"What is this 'water treatment'?"

"Oh, child, do you really want to know?"

Lottie nodded.

"The bastards put people in a bath of freezing cold water and hold them down until they almost drown and then

272

release them, only to push them back in again before they can get their breath back."

Lottie got up and paced the room. "Do you also know if he broke, if he…said…?"

"No. I don't think he would. He's a veteran of the last war and he's tough. Since his wife died, he has nothing to live for. No children, no spouse, just like me. He told me he didn't care what happened to him. Ah, but the things these Fascists do to people, child. It's unbelievably cruel and wicked."

"Poor Lucien. I can hardly bear it." Lottie paced faster. "So, what can we do now?"

"Well, we can't use that field for an airdrop again, that's for sure. And the Boche will have rubbed their hands in glee at grabbing everything in those containers. Jules Deschamps must be feeling very pleased with himself."

Lottie nodded, too preoccupied in picturing what might be happening, had already happened probably, to Lucien, to think what to say. His weather-beaten face swam before her; the lines etched by the wind and rain and sun; the eyes hard but kind; the soul behind them, bleak and lonely. She shivered, contemplating what he might be going through, hoping it never happened to her. She wasn't confident she would be so tough. She remembered that day, so long ago now, when she and Al, Lily and Isobel had tipped their little boat over in the sluice gate on the duck lake at Cheadle Manor. Lily had almost drowned because she couldn't swim, and it had taken all of Lottie's strength to pull her up to the surface. In a flash, the memory of that first gasp of fresh air filling and expanding her lungs came back to her vividly. Please God she never experienced that again.

Madame Leroy went to the sink and washed her floury hands. "Can you eat something, mon petit chou?"

"I don't know. I know I'm hungry, but I feel a bit sick."

"Drink some wine." Madame Leroy poured out two tumblers of thin table wine.

Lottie drank a sip and felt the warm glow dissipate some of the fear clutching at her vital organs.

"Better?"

Lottie nodded and drank a little more, aware of her blood expanding in her veins, warming away the chilled sensation.

Madame Leroy put a fragrant fresh baguette and a round of cheese on the table with some onion chutney. "It's all I have."

"Thank you, Madame, you are good to share this with me."

"Nonsense." Madame Leroy cut the crusty bread. "That agent, the one I told you about who wanted the airfield?"

"Yes?"

"She also wants safe houses for her radio transmitter operator. I don't know who it is, of course, but they would only use it occasionally. Do you think Bernadette would allow it?"

"Bernadette's not as strong as she was. She had bronchitis for months over the winter and it's left her weakened."

"I'm sorry to hear that, Bernadette has always been so healthy. All those herbs she loves!"

Lottie cut into the rind of cheese. The golden insides oozed out and she scooped it up with her knife. "She's getting better all the time, but I think it's the constant fear that's undermining her health. I don't think I can agree until I've asked her."

"Fair enough. Come back tomorrow?"

"It's a deal."

After supper that night, when Françoise was upstairs putting Bertrand to bed, Lottie broached the subject of letting the radio transmitter operator use the farm.

Bernadette's response astonished her. "Of course, they can. I'm surprised you bothered to ask. You usually jump straight in without consulting me."

"That's not true!" Lottie smiled, pleased at seeing some of the old Bernadette fieriness again.

"Humph. We've run so many risks, why stop now?"

"I'll tell Madame Leroy tomorrow."

"Let's hope no-one puts two-and-two together with you going to the village twice in two days."

"That's a lot of twos!"

For the first time in months, they laughed.

The next day, at the boulangerie, Madame Leroy's welcome was subdued.

"Hello, mon petit chou." Madame Leroy poured out some red wine without even asking if Lottie wanted any. "Charlotte, I had a visit from Jules Deschamps yesterday. You know he's in the Milice now, the coward?"

Lottie took a slug of wine. "What did he want?"

"He asked lots of questions. Some of them about you. Why you came so often, that sort of thing."

"Can't we have friends during our occupation?"

"That's what I said but, oh mon petit chou, I couldn't bear it if you were arrested."

"They've got nothing on me."

"Keep it that way. What did Bernadette say?"

"Surprisingly, she said 'yes', straight away."

"That is good news."

They both looked towards the inner door to the shop as the door handle rattled.

"I'm closed for the rest of the day!" Madame Leroy shouted out. "Tch! People are so demanding these days. I don't have enough bread to sell to keep the shop open until lunchtime anymore." Madame poured herself another glass of wine into her empty tumbler and drained it in one go. Her hands were shaking.

"Madame…?"

Lottie's question was never finished. Someone was hammering on the back door now.

"Who is it? What can they want? I've put up a sign saying the bread's all gone for the day!" Madame Leroy went to the door and opened it a crack to peer out. As soon as she unlocked it, it was forced wide open and Jules Deschamps, wearing a military-style blue uniform and beret, entered the room. Outside, two German soldiers blocked the sunlight.

"What is the meaning of this? Why are you here?"

"You are under arrest, Madame Boulangère. And you, mademoiselle, can come too."

"Get your hands off her!" Lottie grabbed the young man's arm as he lunged forward, gripped Madame's plump arm and propelled her to the door. Immediately a soldier came in and shoved his rifle butt into her back, pushing her out into alleyway and then the square. In the hot sunshine, Lottie felt exposed. She looked across the square and saw Madame Marchand standing in her doorway, her arms folded across her chest, and noticed she smiled at Jules Deschamps who nodded back at her. There was no-one else around, it being midday, but Lottie could sense the many pairs of eyes watching their progress through the windows around the square.

The soldiers and the young Milician marched them up the stairs of the Mairie. A German officer was in the front office. He came out and spoke to Jules Deschamps, blocking their way in the corridor.

Lottie watched Deschamps' face blanch as the German said something to him so quietly, right in his ear, she couldn't catch the words.

The army officer clicked his heels and gave the Nazi salute. "Heil Hitler!"

Deschamps, pale and sweaty now, responded in kind. He looked relieved when the Nazi returned to his office and left them alone. Deschamps cleared his throat noisily and squared his shoulders before showing them into a room at the very back of the building, with one bench and two chairs and nothing else. Lottie noticed some dubious stains on the walls and floor and perspiration broke out on her skin. She looked at Madame Leroy who met her gaze with a fierce stare, full of meaning and behind it, love.

Jules Deschamps seemed to have regained his composure. He barked at the two women. "Sit."

The soldiers shoved them down on to the bench together, then stood either side of the doorway in the corridor, their rifles held across their chests.

Lottie wondered why they felt the need for such armed defence when she and her friend had none.

Jules Deschamps put one foot on a chair and leaned his elbow on his knee. He looked so young, almost nervous, and yet triumphant at the same time. Lottie sensed he could barely contain the thrilling power he held over them. He licked the sweat off his upper lip. "You will tell me why you meet up so often. That's two days in a row, my informant tells me."

Lottie spoke first. "We are good friends. Always have been. Madame Leroy shares what little food she has with me."

"Show me your papers."

Both women fished in their pockets for their papers and handed them over. Lottie, knowing hers were false, prayed her assessment of Jules Deschamps' lack of education was right. He didn't look overloaded with brains, just malevolence.

"So, you live at Le Verger?"

"That's right."

"And Bernadette Perrot is your grandmother?"

"Yes."

He looked up at her through narrowed eyes. "How come we never saw you growing up round here?"

Lottie swallowed. "I lived in Paris with my aunt after my mother, Sylvie, died. Aunt Mireille and Bernadette were estranged for years."

"Ah yes, that old scandal with Monsieur Voclain. Alas, he is not here to vouch for it."

"That was before my time."

Jules Deschamps acknowledged this with a grunt and handed Lottie back her papers. He turned to Madame Leroy. "But not before yours, hey?" He brought one of the chairs to the centre of the room and put it in front of Madame Leroy. "Sit on this chair, if you please."

He grabbed her roughly by the arm and pushed her down on to the wooden seat. Then, he grabbed both her arms and put them behind the back of the chair before clamping her wrists in handcuffs. Lottie winced as she watched the corners of the chairback dig into Madame Leroy's fleshy armpits.

Jules Deschamps shoved his ugly face right into Madame Leroy's. "You know a lot of secrets, I think, Madame?"

Madame Leroy simply shrugged and turned her face away. Jules Deschamps slapped it back.

Lottie gasped out loud. "You can't do that to an old woman!"

"Oh, can't I? Should I do it to a young one then?" Deschamps slapped Lottie's face in turn.

Her cheek stung and she put her hand up to it. "How dare you!"

"Oh, I dare, alright." He turned back to Madame Leroy. He looked more excited than nervous now. "Tell me about all the comings and goings to your bakery, Madame. There have been so many people in and out of your back door lately, I'm told."

"Who told you?" Madame Leroy looked furious.

It was Deschamps turn to shrug. "Does it matter?" He stood up straight, lit up a cigarette and drew on it heavily, making the end glow bright red in the gloomy room.

"What matters, Madame, is who these people are. They are not all innocent young peasant girls, now are they?"

"I wouldn't tell you if you were the last man on earth. You are nothing but scum, Jules Deschamps, you never were. If it wasn't for the Milice, you'd be sent off like the others with the STO and would be working in Germany. Perhaps that's where you belong, seeing as you love the Boche so much."

Before Lottie could register what he was going to do, Jules Deschamps brought down his lit cigarette and pressed the burning tip into the plump flesh of Madame Leroy's upper arm, through the thin cotton of her dress. Horrified, Lottie watch smoke curl up from the burning skin. Madame Leroy bit her lip so hard, blood oozed from the corner of her mouth.

Lottie jumped up. "Leave her alone, you brute!"

Jules Deschamps did lift his hand off Madame's arm and instead swung it across Lottie's face with such force, she was flung against the corner of the room. She banged her head hard on the wall before she fell down.

She looked across at the German soldiers, shocked to see them smiling sadistically through the glass window in the door. What human being could witness this and not come to the aid of two defenceless women? Lottie scrambled to her feet and stood between Madame Leroy and Deschamps, spreading her arms wide.

"Oh, do get out of the way, there's a good little girl. We're not interested in peasants who deliver a few eggs now and then." He shoved her in the belly with his boot back towards the wall. Winded, Lottie couldn't speak for a minute. She watched in horror as Deschamps rolled up Madame Leroy's other sleeve and applied the cigarette butt. This time, Madame Leroy groaned through her clenched teeth. Again, pungent smoke spiralled up from the burning flesh.

Gasping for breath, Lottie lunged forward and threw herself at the vicious young man.

He held both her arms pinned against her side. "You know, under that dirt, you've got a nice little face, for a yokel. It would be a pity to scar it for life, now wouldn't it?" He let go of one arm and, bending down, held the half-burnt cigarette up to Lottie's face.

Madame Leroy struggled to sit upright. She screwed up her face and spat a fat wad of sputum right into Deschamps' eyes. "Leave her alone! If it's me you want, I'll talk, but only if you let her go."

Deschamps let Lottie's arm go and turned to the older woman. "Really, now that's the first interesting thing you've said. Alright, she can go, and we'll talk some more, Madame Boulangère."

Lottie turned to Madame Leroy. "I'm not leaving you with him."

Madame Leroy looked deep into Lottie's eyes. "I want you to go, child. I love you as my own daughter. Go, be free, be happy. Think of me and I will always think of you, whatever happens. Understand?"

"But…"

"Please, Charlotte, do this for me."

"Come on, come on. Do what Madame said and leave, will you? I've no time for all this." Deschamps pushed Lottie hard in the back, jarring her spine.

He opened the door. "Escort Mademoiselle off the premises, will you?"

The soldiers came and stood one in front, one behind, with Lottie between them. When she looked back, hesitating, the one behind jabbed her on exactly the spot that had already been bruised. Lottie winced, blew a kiss to Madame Leroy who nodded at her, tears in her eyes, before the door slammed shut and obscured her from view.

"Outside. Think yourself lucky you're not arrested too." The older soldier shoved her as she teetered on the top step. It was enough to send her falling down them and Lottie landed on the bottom one in a heap.

The younger soldier laughed at her. "Go and dig your turnips, peasant girl!" The two men turned and went back inside. Lottie sat on the bottom step, trying to gather her wits. As she sat there, a ghastly scream emanated from the building. It must be Madame Leroy. She turned to climb the steps again, but the young soldier barred the door, still smiling. Another agonising scream rent the air. Lottie pulled at her hair. She couldn't stand it. She stood rooted to the spot staring at the soldier, unable to go or stay.

A shadow fell across the steps. A hand, not brutal this time, cupped her elbow.

"Come, come with me. There's nothing you can do."

Lottie turned around. Madame Voclain stood there, compassion showing through her make-up, under the brim of her hat. "Let's go."

CHAPTER THIRTY-SEVEN
CHEADLE MANOR, ENGLAND
APRIL 1944

"Are you going to be long in there, Bella, only I've got to dash off early this morning on the London train. This meeting of the Women's Institute has been in the diary for months, you know, and the train service is so reduced, if I miss this one, there won't be another until tomorrow."

Isobel wiped the vomit from her mouth. "Almost done."

She pulled the chain to flush the toilet and stood up to look at her image in the mirror. How could she have conceived a baby so quickly? They'd only been together for three days. She wouldn't tell anyone. Not a soul and certainly not Al. He had enough on his plate, judging by the last letter he'd dashed off in obvious haste. Her face stared back at her. Did everyone look different when they were pregnant? Her blue eyes had dark shadows beneath them and the hollows under her cheekbones looked more pronounced than ever.

Isobel filled the basin with lukewarm water and splashed it over her face. She patted it dry on the towel and looked at herself again. Better. Not only was her face clean now but it had a misleading glow from the friction of the abrasive towel. She hurriedly dragged a brush through her hair and tied a scarf over it, upside down with the bow at the top, the way her Aunt Katy – now her mother-in-law - tied it. Better again. The bright scarf made her look almost jaunty.

She took a deep breath and opened the door.

Her mother looked harassed. "Honestly, Bella, you knew I had a train to catch this morning. You could have let me go first."

"Sorry, Mummy."

"Are you alright, darling?"

"Of course. I'll make a pot of tea. Have you time for a cup?"

Cassandra looked at her watch. "Barely." She shut the door behind her, and Isobel heard her splashing about in the bathroom.

Isobel went into the small kitchen of West Lodge and riddled the fire in the range. It was almost out. She picked up the coal hod and shucked in some fuel before filling the kettle and putting it on the hob. When it had boiled, she poured the water over the tea leaves in the pot and another wave of nausea welled up. How strange that tea set her off like this. Normally she couldn't get enough of it but now its aroma turned her stomach.

Her mother came in, half-dressed, and poured herself a cup. "I'll take mine into the bedroom. I'll be lucky to catch that train! See you later, darling."

Five minutes later the front door slammed, and she heard the old Sunbeam revving into life before departing swiftly through the manor gates, just outside the lodge house.

Isobel poured the contents of the full teapot on to the compost bucket and returned to sit alone at the kitchen table. What on earth was she going to say to Farmer Stubbs?

She leaned her chin on her hands and indulged in fond memories of her honeymoon, glorying in the sensuous moments she'd shared with Al. It had been heavenly but oh, how soon it had been over! She looked up at the clock. She was late for work, really late. Thank goodness the sickness had passed now. She grabbed her coat and walked up the path, past the manor house, to Home Farm.

"I'm sorry to have to say this, Miss Isobel, but you're getting later and later of a morning." Farmer Stubbs chewed on his pipe in the farmyard. He was letting the cows back out into the field and did not look happy.

"Yes, I know, Mr Stubbs, but there is a very good reason for it. Can we talk?"

283

"You can talk while we sort these old girls out, can't you?"

"Of course." She closed the yard gate as all the cows were now placidly plodding up the lane.

"Well, then? What is it, young lady?" Farmer Stubbs took out his tobacco pouch from his fawn overall pocket, pulled out some brown threads and stuffed them in the bowl of his pipe.

Isobel hesitated, unsure of how to divulge her news. She watched as the farmer struck a match and lit the tobacco. He used a brand she liked, it was sweet and fragrant with a hint of exotic spice. She dreaded it might make her feel sick, like tea did nowadays, but as the blue smoke drifted past her nose, she found it relaxed her, like it always had. Farmer Stubbs' tobacco gave off the same reassurance as the man himself.

"I'm waiting, Miss Isobel, though, if it helps, I think I can guess what you're going to say."

"Can you? Is it that obvious?"

"I'm a farmer and a dairy farmer at that. So, yes, is your answer."

"It must have happened on our honeymoon. I hadn't realised you could conceive so quickly."

Farmer Stubbs sucked on his pipe. "Only has to happen once, doesn't it?"

Isobel felt her colour rise. "I suppose so."

"When's the baby due?" Farmer Stubbs tapped the rear cow with his wooden staff. "Get along there."

"Well, I think it should be around October."

"We'll have to reconsider your work on the farm then. Maybe get another Land Girl to help out. There's jobs you shouldn't be doing now."

"But I feel fine, once the morning sickness passes. Same as normal after that." They had reached the gate to the pasture and Isobel opened it to let the cows through.

"That's as maybe but there are risks to the unborn on a farm. We'll have to talk to Mrs Stubbs about it, and

284

you should see young Dr Benson or that Dr Harris at the war hospital up the manor."

The last cow ambled into the field and Isobel drew the gate shut. They turned back to the farm and picked up their pace, unencumbered by bovine sloth.

Mrs Stubbs, wreathed in motherly smiles, congratulated her warmly when they returned to the farmhouse kitchen. "Well, my dear, that's what you must expect if you go and get married. Let's hope this awful war is over soon and your Al can come back and you two can set up home together properly."

"Oh, Mrs Stubbs, wouldn't that be wonderful!"

After that, and for the next couple of weeks, Mr Stubbs insisted on doing all the heavy work and the daily milking and his wife wouldn't hear of Isobel doing anything remotely strenuous or unhygienic which, on a dairy farm, covered most activities.

A fortnight after her disclosure about her pregnancy, Mrs Stubbs drew her inside as soon as Isobel turned up for work. "Come into the kitchen, Miss Isobel. We've something to say."

Mr Stubbs was still sitting at the breakfast table, but it was his wife who addressed her. "We've decided you must make the baby your top priority, Miss Isobel. You can help me in the farmhouse with the jam-making and such-like. We've another Land Girl coming. Edith, is her name, and she can do the outside work alongside my husband."

Mr Stubbs packed tobacco leaves into the bowl of his pipe. "Can't be too careful, Miss Isobel."

They still didn't call her Mrs Phipps, but Isobel let that go. "Well, if you're sure?"

"Certain."

Edith was a sturdy girl from Kent, used to farm work and very knowledgeable. Not much of a talker, she suited Mr Stubbs very well and worked diligently, if rather slowly, not that the cows noticed. When Isobel's morning sickness soon grew worse rather than better, she was forced to give up her work entirely. That meant she had to tell her mother about the baby.

"But darling, that's marvellous!" Cassandra kissed her on both cheeks. "I won't hug you, I can see that would be unwelcome, as you look a bit green. To be honest, Bella, I had already guessed! It's hard to hide a secret in a small cottage with one bathroom."

"Oh, Mummy, why didn't you say?"

"I knew you'd tell me when you were ready, sweetheart, and it's a special time for a woman, isn't it? There's a sort of private joy you want all to yourself at first, as I remember."

Isobel hugged her. "Thank you for understanding, Mummy."

"Does Al know?"

Isobel shook her head. "All this talk of invasion means he's busier than ever. I don't want him worrying about me."

"Hmm, he does have a right to know."

"Maybe, but not yet."

"Do you mind if I tell Dr Harris? He could give you the once-over, or would you prefer Simon Benson?"

"I suppose Dr Harris is nearest."

Cassandra looked pleased. "I'll ring him right away. Congratulations, darling."

Dr Harris came that evening to examine her. These days, he visited every evening, but Isobel didn't mind, as she had grown fond of him. A quiet man, and a good listener, he exuded kindness and he was obviously very attached to her mother.

They went into her bedroom for the examination which was brief and professional.

Dr Harris put his stethoscope away in his case and spoke in his soft Scottish burr. "Yes, there can be no doubt that your baby is due in October. Your window for conception was very precise with your husband's short amount of leave so you don't have to be a mathematician to

286

work it out. The morning sickness will pass when the placenta takes over and you should feel much better then."

"When will that be?"

"Oh, at about four months."

"That seems ages away."

"It will soon pass but you should take it easy until then. Small, frequent meals, no alcohol and afternoon rests. I'll examine you again in June, unless you are worried beforehand. Where do you want to have the baby?"

"Goodness, I hadn't thought about it."

"The hospital isn't far away. I would be happy to deliver your child."

"Oh, yes, I see. Thank you. I'll have a think."

They went back to the little parlour and the evening passed off pleasantly on the surface, listening to the wireless as usual. Underneath, Isobel was entirely preoccupied with the prospect of an actual baby and what on earth she was supposed to do with it. After seeing Dr Harris out at the end of the evening, her mother returned to the parlour, where Isobel sat, gazing into the dancing flames in the fire and trying to imagine herself pushing a pram.

"You know, you ought to tell Katy and Jem about the baby."

"But if I do, I'd have to tell Al first."

"Isn't it time you did?"

Isobel sighed. It was obvious the baby wasn't going to remain her secret any longer.

CHAPTER THIRTY-EIGHT
NORMANDY, FRANCE
MAY 1944

Lottie, who prided herself on not being a cry-baby under any circumstances, sobbed uncontrollably in Madame Voclain's back garden.

Madame Voclain, as unlike Madame Leroy as any two women could be, did not enfold her in her arms but sat on an elegant garden chair, dispassionately watching her.

It took Lottie a full ten minutes to regain some sort of equilibrium, at which point Madame Voclain handed her a finely woven cotton handkerchief. "Please keep it."

Lottie blew her nose and drew a deep breath. The trembling took longer but Madame Voclain didn't wait for that to cease before speaking. "I'm very sorry Madame Leroy has been taken but it's unlikely she'll be shot. Once they have finished questioning her, she'll be imprisoned in Caen, I expect, along with Lucien and Pierre."

"You know them *all*?"

"I've told you a few times, I know everything."

Lottie stuffed the sodden handkerchief in her trouser pocket and sniffed. She had no idea what to say to that, so she simply waited for more.

"I shall miss your friend, more than you will ever know." Madame Voclain gave a bitter smile. "And everyone will miss her bread."

Thoughts of what Madame Leroy might be going through at this very minute while they sat in this pretty courtyard made Lottie jump up from her chair and pace its length. "So, you are part of the Resistance, after all?"

"Of course, I am. Sit down, child. I do not want to raise my voice."

Lottie ran her hands through her short hair. Her unconscious action reminded her of Thierry. He always did that when under stress. If only he were here now. She took in another deep breath and sat back down again.

Madame Voclain's voice was calm. "We can do nothing more for Madame Leroy. I hope she can withstand whatever they inflict upon her. Neither Lucien nor Pierre betrayed us, and I don't think she will, but it will be very hard."

"How can they *do* these things to people! They are not human! Deschamps isn't even a Nazi!"

"Sadly, human beings are capable of evil. If they weren't, we wouldn't be at war at all. But the fact is, we are. Now, you and I have to decide what to do about it next. You know we need safe houses for the radio operator?"

Lottie nodded; she still didn't trust herself to speak.

"Can Le Verger host a radio operator for a couple of days?"

Lottie cleared her throat. "Yes, definitely, Grandmother has agreed to it."

"That's excellent news. In which case, you will be the first. It's a woman. You will know her as Manon Fourcier who is selling stationery around the country. I'll set it up for three days' time. You can keep her in the bottom cellar, like you did with my son, Emile, no?"

Lottie nodded again. "Very well. Is there anything else?"

Madame Voclain took off her hat and smoothed her hair. She got up from the chair and walked towards her house. "No. Go now. Are you well enough to cycle?"

"I'll manage."

"I thought you might. And don't come here again unless you receive a message to do so. You will not need to come to the village so often now we have no butcher or baker."

"I'll need our ration cards every month."

"Of course - but come for nothing else. We need you to be as discreet, as invisible, as possible. Things are going to change soon, Charlotte. In a big way. Keep strong, my dear."

Madame Voclain disappeared inside. Lottie let herself out through the garden gate. She walked past the Mairie on the way back to fetch her bicycle from outside Madame Leroy's, her ears straining for further sounds of the torture that her friend must surely be enduring, but none came.

Lottie wasn't sure if that wasn't worse.

She found Bernadette in the sunny orchard sitting on the bench she'd shared with Thierry so often, under the apple trees. Before she heard her, Bernadette was sleeping. She looked peaceful – and old. When Lottie dismounted from her bicycle, Bernadette must have heard her because she sat up abruptly and blinked, rubbing her eyes.

Lottie knew better than to let on she'd caught her pretend-grandmother napping. She propped her bike against the goat's barn and sat down next to Bernadette.

"What's happened?" Bernadette's instincts were always uncannily accurate.

"It's Madame Leroy." Lottie told her everything that had transpired in the village.

To her dismay, Bernadette dropped her face in her hands and her normal steely self-control snapped.

Lottie felt panicked by this. In that moment, she came to realise how much she depended upon this woman, who wasn't even a relative but who had taken her in and treated her like one. She put a gentle arm around her shoulders and knew the depth of Bernadette's despair when it wasn't shrugged off.

Bernadette wasn't undone for long. After a couple of minutes, she did shrug her shoulders and Lottie quietly withdrew her embrace. Bernadette wiped her eyes on the corner of her flowered apron and shivered, despite the warmth of the May sunshine.

"We were at school together, you know. Louise and I."

"I never knew her first name."

290

"Really? She was younger than me, of course. Everyone is these days but when we were kids, we both loved to break the rules if we had the chance." Bernadette sighed. "So long ago. God give her the strength to withstand whatever these beasts inflict on her. My God, how I hate these Nazis!"

"I know and the Milice seem to be even worse than the Gestapo." Lottie flexed her back and rubbed her stomach where it had been kicked.

"They hurt you too?"

Lottie nodded. "Nothing significant. I'll heal. It's just bruises."

"Bastards."

"Bernadette, there's more. It seems Madame Voclain is privy to everything that's going on in the resistance."

"Oh, I know that."

"How come everyone knows everything and never tells me?"

"Because, stupid, we're protecting you."

Lottie was silent for a moment while she took this in. It *was* stupid of her not to realise that. How kind these French country people were underneath their surliness. "Then, I thank you, for everything." She reached sideways and kissed Bernadette on her wrinkled cheek.

Bernadette turned to look at her, not scornfully like she normally would, but with real warmth in her flinty grey eyes. She cupped Lottie's chin. "You're welcome, Charlotte." Bernadette stood up and shook out her apron. "Now, what else is there?"

Lottie, despite her aching bones and heart, smiled at hearing her name coming from the mouth of her taciturn hostess. That had been a long time coming.

They walked together to the farmhouse. Françoise was weeding vegetables in the kitchen garden and Bertrand was making mud pies with a trowel, squatting on the path next to her with the ease only very young children have.

291

"I swear that child grows at least a centimetre every single day." Lottie waved at them.

The kitchen seemed dark by contrast when they entered it.

Bernadette picked up the water pitcher. "I'll put the kettle on. Sit down and rest, child."

Lottie did as she was told. Her bruises were stiffening up. She felt she'd been kicked all over, and it was partly true. "I told Madame Voclain we would provide a safe house for the radio operator. Apparently, she's a woman who goes by the name of Manon Fourcier. It'll only be for a couple of days as she moves around constantly."

"When is she coming, do you know?"

"In about three days."

"That'll give your bruises a chance to heal."

"Yes, I'd like a breather before I get more."

CHAPTER THIRTY-NINE
CHEADLE MANOR, ENGLAND
MAY 1944

Isobel hesitated in front of the letterbox on the main road outside the manor gates. She still wasn't sure it was a good idea to tell her husband about the baby, but her mother was right, he deserved to know. It *was* his baby too. The last time she'd posted a letter was in the whirlwind before her marriage. She'd found the time to write to Geraint Lloyd explaining the situation before her hasty wedding but, after the excitement of her London honeymoon, had forgotten all about him. Al had already returned to work for quite a long time before she had received a reply. Geraint had been as polite and as courteous as ever, but his pain was evident in every word left unsaid between the lines of his neat, flowing script. Isobel knew Geraint would feel her rejection keenly, that he might never get over it, but she also knew she had made the right decision in marrying Al.

And this was the right thing to do now. She pushed the letter through the open mouth of the letterbox and heard a gentle thud as it hit the floor inside the bright red pillar. Instantly, she felt better. Al would be thrilled at her news. She lifted her face to the May sunshine and carried on walking down to the Katherine Wheel Garage to make her announcement to his parents. A procession of American army lorries trundled past leaving wolf whistles in their wake. She laughed up at the GI soldiers. They wouldn't be whistling at her when she was waddling along in a few months' time, so she waved her acknowledgement of the compliment and swung her long legs a bit more energetically, bucked up by their admiration.

It was good to get out in the fresh air and do some proper exercise. All she could do of a morning was lie in bed with an enamel basin nearby to retch into at horribly regular intervals. When questioned, Cassandra confessed she'd never suffered like this and Isobel wondered resentfully why it was so wretchedly different for her. Just her luck. She missed her job on the farm; missed the companionship of Mr and Mrs Stubbs; she even missed the damned cows!

She missed Al too but sometimes she felt more angry than sad at his absence. What if he never came home? In low moments, exhausted after a bout of sickness, she would fleetingly regret their impulsive wedding and its result. Her deepest fear, the one she'd expressed to Al when he'd first asked her to marry him at the outset of the war, had come true. If he didn't survive it, she would have to bring up his child alone and the prospect terrified her. Then, when the nausea subsided, she would be full of joy at the life she carried within her and gloried in their boldness in getting married spontaneously. Then she would long to see Al and share the excitement with him and feel guilty about the dark thoughts that the fear had provoked. Would her moods equalise as the pregnancy progressed? If she could only stop being sick every day! Thank goodness Al hadn't got into the RAF. There had been casualties at the ATA but far, far less than in the Royal Air Force.

She smelt the rubber factory before she saw it. It exuded a truly awful pong and the all-too-familiar nausea threatened, so she was glad she'd left her visit until well into the afternoon. The garage was far less conspicuous these days as the old advertising hoardings had gone, along with all the signposts on the roads. No-one wanted to flaunt themselves in wartime, although the initial fears about the Germans invading had faded long ago, everyone observed the blackouts and the ARP wardens made sure they did.

The noise emanating from the factory was much louder than the last time she'd visited, months ago now, and the yard was filled with a couple of parked cars and many more bicycles that Isobel assumed belonged to the ever-expanding workforce.

A young woman came out of the factory. For a split-second, Isobel thought it was her new mother-in-law but quickly realised it was Lily, looking so much like her mother they could have been twins, if there wasn't such a difference in their ages.

Lily spotted her immediately. "Isobel! How lovely to see you!" She ran across and kissed Isobel's cheeks.

Isobel hugged her back. "Goodness, Lily, you've shot up lately! Are you working at the factory too?"

"Yes, I love it! I only work weekends because of school but it's much more interesting than boring facts about trigonometry and the kings and queens of England."

"When do you leave school? Can't be long?"

"Not this year, annoyingly. Mum and Dad say I've got to stay on and finish my Higher Certificate, so I'll have to carry on next year. You'd think they'd let me off, with a war on."

Isobel laughed. "I have to admit I bunked off at sixteen and joined the Land Army."

"No chance for me. They won't hear of it. I'd much rather work full-time here. But I'm going to train to be an engineer as soon as I leave school and I'll need the higher qualification, so it's Hobson's choice, really."

"Good for you! Where is your Mum?"

"Oh, she's at the factory. We're working six days a week now. Shall I fetch her for you?"

"Are you sure she's not too busy?"

"She'd love to see you. Wait here." Lily dashed off back into the hangar and soon emerged with a smiling Katy.

"Hello, daughter-in-law! Nice to see you. I'm due for a break – fancy a cup of tea?"

"Maybe not tea, but I'd love a glass of water. It's hot for May, isn't it?"

Katy gave her a quizzical look but lead the way to her bungalow, behind the thick hedges of its garden.

Once inside, she turned to her daughter. "Lily, be a dear and get your Dad, will you? I'm sure he'd like a cuppa and would be pleased to see Isobel."

"Alright." Lily went out the back door into the vegetable garden.

"How's your Mum these days, Aunt Katy?"

"Not too good, I'm afraid. Dr Benson thinks she may have had another little stroke. She has a nap every afternoon now. He says another one might be the last." Katy sighed. "She's a terrific age though, so we must expect it, but I hope she lives to see peace again."

"I hope so too." Isobel sat down at the table.

"Sure you don't want tea?" Katy busied herself filling and switching on the electric kettle.

"I've gone off it, rather."

"Oh?" Katy sat down opposite Isobel. "Oh…I see. I'm guessing you're…?"

Isobel nodded. "That's right. Due at the end of October. Halloween, would you believe?"

"Congratulations! Does Al know?"

"I've just posted him a letter."

"What a shame he can't hear it from you directly. You could telephone him."

"I thought a letter would be best, give him time to take it in."

Katy smiled. "I'm sure he'll be desperate to see you. Has he any more leave coming up?"

"No, all leave has been cancelled because of this invasion everyone's talking about. Do you know anything about it?"

Katy shook her head. "What I know, I can't tell you, I'm afraid. We're busier than ever. We can hardly meet the demand, but I probably don't know much more than you've heard on the radio. Everyone thinks the troops will depart from Kent and go to Calais as it's the shortest sea crossing but I'm just guessing, like everyone else, and I have no idea when they plan to go." She got up and spooned tea leaves into the brown pot. "Mind you, I don't think it will be long."

"Maybe I shouldn't have written that letter to Al."

296

Katy passed her a glass of water. "Of course, you should! It's his baby too and he'll be delighted, I know he will."

CHAPTER FORTY
NORMANDY, FRANCE
MAY 1944

Lottie had slathered her bruises in Bernadette's comfrey salve, but she still ached all over. Even three days after Madame Leroy's arrest, walking was painful. She was jittery too, unable to sleep well while waiting for her visitor to arrive and plagued by images of Madame Leroy, Lucien and Pierre in prison, or worse.

All day she'd listened out for the sound of someone's approach; all day she'd looked down the lane or to the woods beyond the orchard for the slightest movement. Now, she'd given up, exhausted from expectations not met.

Being mid-May, it was late when the full dark of night descended and she was weary to her bones as she shut up the hens, her last task of a long and tedious day. The moon was waxing now, building up strength for another month and lending a pearly gleam to everything it touched. She didn't dare use a torch or a lantern to illuminate the operation and caught her trouser pocket on a piece of wire sticking out of the fence. She bent to unhook it, squinting in the dim light.

And then she heard something. It was almost imperceptible and yet distinct. Lottie had grown so familiar with the sounds of daily life on the little farm, she recognised the alien nature of this immediately. After a few second's hesitation, she carried on shutting the hen house. There was no point missing out on precious eggs, whatever was about to happen.

She sensed someone approaching rather than saw them. No further noise aided her in locating it, but she knew someone was there. The hairs on her bare arms prickled into an upright position. Lottie bent down to close the makeshift gate on the perimeter fence of the chicken run, then stood up, waiting quietly, her feet slightly apart, their soles connecting to the earth, her toes splayed and her knees slightly bent, poised to spring if required.

She listened intently to the familiar night sounds. A hen ruffled its feathers inside its wooden house; a fox barked in the distance beyond the orchard; a frog croaked a love-song from the pond in the woods; and yet she didn't hear the intruder. Without warning, a strong arm wrapped itself around her throat, pressing on her airways, pushing her Adam's apple against her windpipe, making her gasp for breath. Lottie jabbed both her elbows into her attacker, ignoring the pain from the grazes still not healed from falling down the steps of the Mairie. A grunt told her she'd found her mark, but the arm tightened further, making her choke for air. She jabbed again, as hard as she could, and twisted her body at the same time, gaining some release from the pressure against her neck. Using the advantage, she kicked backwards and was rewarded by another grunt as her boot found its mark. Another jab of the elbow and she was free.

Lottie twizzled round, fists up, throat bruised but open and sucking in the sweet night air in huge in-breaths. Dizzy from lack of oxygen, she stumbled backwards against the chicken shed, glad of its robust sturdiness at her back.

"Not bad, not at all bad, for an amateur." Even in the faint light, Lottie could see the tall young woman before her wore glasses and a tweed skirt with neat, laced brogues on her feet.

She was laughing.

Too shocked and angry to think, Lottie's hand shot out and slapped the girl's face so forcefully, the glasses slipped sideways and down her nose.

"That wiped the smile off your face!" Lottie gasped out.

Seemingly unperturbed, the woman pushed her glasses back up her nose and held out her hand. "Manon Fourcier. You must be Charlotte?"

Still panting, Lottie nodded, ignoring the outstretched hand. "Why did you do that?"

"It was a test." Manon bent and picked up a brown suitcase. "You passed." She put her head to one side. "Would you be kind enough to show me my quarters?"

Lottie opened then shut her mouth. With a curt nod, she marched towards the farmhouse, furious that she had suffered another unwarranted violent assault without due reason. "Go in there." Lottie held the kitchen door open.

Manon hesitated, looked at her questioningly behind the thick-rimmed glasses, before saying, "After you, I insist."

Lottie sighed impatiently and walked into the familiar kitchen. Manon followed behind. Lottie shut the door and made sure the curtains were tightly drawn before going to the table and lighting the oil lamp, keeping the flame on its lowest setting.

"Very good. I like the way you're careful." Manon sat down at the table without waiting for an invitation.

"I'm so pleased you approve. I wonder how we've managed this long without your supervision."

Manon put down her suitcase, so it stayed propped against her calf. "I gather I'm to sleep in the cellar?"

"That's right."

"Is there a window? I'll need to poke the aerial outside to get a signal."

"No. No window."

"Damn." Manon frowned. "I'll use one of the outbuildings then. Have any of them got a power supply?"

"You actually want my opinion? Didn't you scan and memorise the whole layout of the farm just now?"

"There's no need to be so sarcastic."

Lottie rubbed her throat. "There was no need to attack me."

"Listen, I need to make a transmission now. I haven't got time for pleasantries."

Lottie bit back her retort to that. "The only power socket is in the house."

"No battery?"

"No."

"Oh dear. Have you a socket in a bedroom?"

"No, but there is the one for the radio over there."

"It'll have to do."

Manon lifted up her suitcase and followed Lottie to the corner of the big, cluttered room. Lottie lifted the big basket of laundry out of the way and bent down to unplug the radio. She lifted up the Bakelite box and put it on the floor. "Here, use this trolley. Is it big enough?"

"It'll do but I must hurry, or I'll miss my slot. The one thing the Germans have done that's enormously helpful is to put the clocks forward by two hours, so we are on the same time frame as the rest of Europe, including Britain."

"Yes, that is useful. Have you everything you need?"

"Yes, I have done this before, you know."

Lottie ignored that remark. "Listen, I'll wait outside, and I'll rap on the window if I see anything suspicious. That way, if any Germans came, you could hide in the cellar – it's down there."

"And you'd cover for me?"

"Of course."

"Very well." Manon quickly plugged in the radio and put the headset over her neat brown hair.

Lottie, incensed at not receiving a thank you for offering to save the other woman's life, went to the door. She opened it and went outside. It took her fully five minutes to control her temper, during which time she paced around the yard, and another five minutes to realise that doing so would immediately alert anyone spying on her.

The door opened behind her, startling her overstrained nerves.

"Are you always this jumpy?" Manon came out of the house with her suitcase.

301

Lottie decided not to rise to this further provocation. "How long do you intend to stay here?"

"Keen to get rid of me already?"

"You could say that."

"I'll stay for tonight only. You've a good spot here but I don't want to push my luck with the invasion so imminent."

"I'll show you the cellar then."

They went back inside the farmhouse and down both sets of stairs to the lower cellar.

"Oh, this is excellent." Manon said when Lottie pushed back the barrels of cider and revealed the trap door to the lower cellar.

"It has been very useful lately." Lottie reached the lower floor and put her oil lamp down on the one chair and lit the candle sitting on its holder there. "There's a bed there and it's freshly made up. There's a slop bucket and a pitcher of water. It's pitch-black in here when the trap door is replaced so make sure you know where the matches are for the candle. Goodnight. I'll come down for you in the morning."

"Goodnight, and...thank you. I know how dangerous this is."

Lottie just nodded, picked up the oil-lamp and went up to bed. She got undressed and laid down on her bed in the attic. She'd looked forward to getting involved with the famous SOE network, but this Manon woman was a severe disappointment.

In the morning she went down to the cellar and found Manon already up and dressed and anxious for some air.

"Did you get any sleep?"

"Enough. It certainly is very dark down here."

"Come up and have some breakfast." Lottie lead the way back up to the kitchen.

Manon ate hungrily. She was very thin and wiry, and her tweed skirt and white blouse looked loose on her bones. Lottie wondered how long she had been living like this.

Manon wiped her bowl with the crust of Bernadette's sourdough. "I don't think it's generally known that the invasion is due next month when the moon is full?"

"I had heard vague rumours."

"It's good they are vague. The Allies will land on the beaches north of here in early June."

"Here? Good God!"

"This is top secret. The Nazis believe the Allies will land in Calais. Tell no-one, absolutely no-one, they will arrive on the Normandy beaches, do you hear?"

Lottie, still shocked at this news, just nodded.

Manon narrowed her eyes. "It's imperative you speak of this to nobody. I insist you swear to it."

"I swear. I had no idea it would be here."

"That's good to know. Now, there will be some important announcements broadcast beforehand. Do you know how to tune in to Radio Londres?"

"Absolutely."

"Right, I want you to memorise six sentences. I won't write them down; you must remember them. Can you do that?"

Lottie could feel her temper rising again. Then she remembered she looked like a French peasant girl, not the ex-head-girl of a posh school in England.

She schooled herself not to react. "I think so."

Manon nodded. "Excellent. Shortly before the landings, Radio Londres will broadcast the first stanza of Paul Verlaine's poem, *"Chanson d'automne"*, to let the Resistance know that the invasion is imminent. The first part of the stanza, *"Les sanglots longs des violons de l'automne,"* will indicate that the invasion will begin within twenty-four hours; the second, *"Blessent mon coeur d'une langueur monotone"*, will be the specific call to action. Got that?"

"Of course."

They were on the third sentence when young Bertrand clattered down the stairs, followed by his mother and great-grandmother. All three of them stood stock still on the lower stairs with a comical look of dismay on their faces when they saw their new guest.

"Who's this?" Françoise spoke first.

"Her name's Manon. She's a sales rep for stationery."

"How do you do?" Manon got up from her chair and smiled.

Lottie looked at her. It was funny how some people could do that and still look cold and unfriendly. Manon seemed to have mastered the art.

"Stationery?" Françoise scooped up her little boy and came to stand by the table. "What on earth do we need paper and pencils for?"

"Don't ask silly questions, Françoise. See to the boy's breakfast." Bernadette nodded at the stranger. "Have you been here all night?"

"Yes, and I was very comfortable down there, I must say." Manon jerked her head in the direction of the cellar steps.

"Have you had enough to eat?" Bernadette's grey eyes flickered over Manon's tall frame and its meagre proportions.

"Enough, yes."

"Would you like more?" Bernadette cut the sourdough loaf on the table.

"Perhaps another slice."

"I just gets one." Bertrand piped up. He was clutching Françoise's flowery wrap-around apron and staring wide-eyed at Manon.

"And you shall have it now, Bertrand." Lottie settled him on his chair and took a piece of bread. "Jam or dripping?"

"Give him jam, Charlotte. Keep him sweet." Françoise poured some warm goat's milk into a bowl for the child.

"Perhaps we could walk around the farm?" Manon asked Lottie directly.

Lottie took the hint and her slab of bread and they went outside.

"I didn't realise you shared the house with other women and a child."

"You mean you *don't* know everything?"

Manon had the grace to laugh. "Forgive my manner. It's living on the hoof all the time. Frays the nerves but…" she lowered her voice to a whisper. "It won't be for much longer, as I said, the Allies are on their way. That's why you must memorise the other sentences that will come through on the radio."

"Teach me while I let the hens out."

"You will need to concentrate."

Lottie started walking towards the henhouse. "I can do both."

Lottie had memorised all six sentences by the time she was milking the goats, with Manon sitting nearby.

"Good. Repeat them once more and then we're done."

Lottie did as she was told.

Manon looked at her thoughtfully behind her glasses. "Very good. Have you always lived on this farm? You don't seem quite the type."

"I think the less you know about me the better, don't you? It's the golden rule."

"Hmm. That's right. Ah well. I must make another transmission. The messages are coming thick and fast at the moment."

"You'd better wait until I've finished here and made sure the coast is clear. I don't want Françoise or Bernadette to know what you are doing."

"Don't trust me or protecting them?"

"Both. Can you wait ten minutes?" Lottie patted the goat she'd milked and moved on to the last one.

"Looks like I'll have to."

Lottie hurried through the milking. "I'll have to let them out."

"How long will that take?"

"You take this old girl and I'll bring the other one." Lottie unleashed the goats from their stalls and handed one of the halters to Manon.

"The things we have to do in wartime." Manon wrinkled her nose distastefully at the goat but dutifully followed Lottie to the meadow by the orchard. Lottie took them inside the fenced field and slipped the ropes from their necks. The goats wandered off immediately, nibbling at the tender May leaves in the hawthorn hedge. Manon carried her suitcase with her wherever she went, even when she had a goat's tethering rope in the other hand, and she now picked it up and went back towards the house.

Lottie shut the gate and followed. They bumped into Bernadette in the doorway, carrying the laundry basket.

"Washing day. We'll be in the wash house. We've got the child." Bernadette looked meaningfully at Lottie.

"You'll be busy for a while then?" Lottie nodded towards Manon's suitcase.

"It'll take two hours at least."

"Understood."

Lottie shut the door behind Bernadette. "You can go ahead. Bernadette understands what you're up to. She'll make sure Françoise doesn't. I'll stay indoors this time and watch through the window.

Manon nodded and took the transmitter back to the corner. Lottie kept her eyes trained on the yard while she listened to the tapping noise and Manon scribbled on a pad. She assumed it was Morse code, having learnt the basics at school but she couldn't make out the message at all.

When the tapping stopped, Manon quickly packed up her gear and shut the lid of the suitcase. "I have more messages for you. Are you sure we can't be overheard?"

"The others are still in the wash-house. They do all the laundry today as it's a Monday. They won't hear us here; they will be elbow-deep in soapsuds."

Manon bolted the door shut.

"Is that really necessary?"

Manon nodded. "I have news from the FFI in London."

"FFI?"

"'*Forces Françaises d l'Interieur*' – they work with the SOE in London through De Gaulle. They warned of Allied bombings targeting the coast. That might include the airbase at Carpiquet, I suspect. You'd better make a shelter."

"You mean the Allies will *bomb* us here?"

"They'll have to. They'll have to throw everything at it too, because the coast is so well guarded and there are many German troops in Caen because of the port and the estuary."

Lottie felt a quiver of fear. The thought of British bombs landing at Le Verger was a very strange concept.

Manon continued. "They also said they have developed four plans for the resistance to execute for the invasion. They are colour-coded into green, blue, and violet and the fourth is named 'tortoise'."

"Tortoise? Why isn't that one a colour?"

"I don't know." Manon looked irritated. "Perhaps because it's a delaying operation aimed at the enemy forces that might reinforce the German troops already in Normandy. You wouldn't understand, but it could be the most crucial part."

"Is that right? Clever you."

Manon brightened perceptibly, seemingly not recognising the sarcasm in Lottie's voice. "Now, let's take them one at a time and talk you through it."

"I'll try and concentrate."

"Oh, well done. Now, Plan Green is a fifteen-day operation to sabotage the rail system. Did you hear about the one in Vaucelles?"

"I know it was bombed in February."

"Earlier this month it was sabotaged by the railway workers but a member of the local Milice, Serge Fertier, who used to know and work with them, betrayed them to the Gestapo. They were shot just over a week ago. They sang the Marseillaise just before they were killed."

Lottie glimpsed some emotion behind Manon's factual report of the tragedy and softened a little towards her. It couldn't be easy, being on the run all the time. "No, I hadn't heard. We have lost some people even closer to home lately and it was the Milice who shopped the last one, a dear friend of mine."

"Yes, I know. That's why we must get these plans right."

"Okay, so what are plans blue and violet?"

Manon smiled, showing uneven teeth. "You remembered! You are more intelligent than you look."

Lottie breathed deeply and remained silent, though it took some effort. She congratulated herself on the success of her disguise and tried to concentrate on the matter in hand.

"The Blue Plan needn't involve you. It's about destroying electrical facilities and we've another team dealing with that. The Violet Plan is to cut telephone and teleprinter cables and you will be part of it. The messages you've memorised are the signals to set things in motion for each plan. I have a one-time pad to decipher the messages, but you just need to listen to the radio and then communicate with your colleagues."

"There aren't that many left."

"Madame Voclain is the main one, but I also want you to go to Jean Everard at the mill."

"So, she has been playing a double game."

"Sorry?"

"Madame Voclain. I'm glad my instincts were right about her. Um, did you meet Madame Leroy, the village baker?"

Manon met Lottie's direct gaze. "Yes, she was our other lynchpin and a sad loss."

"Do you know if she's alright?"

"She's in the prison at Caen. She's alive but," Manon cleared her throat, "she's a bit beaten up."

Lottie swallowed. "I see. Thank you."

Manon stood up. "Right, I think we've covered everything. I'm going to sleep for a bit. I shall leave under cover of darkness tonight."

"I'll come and do the trap door for you."

"Thanks, I appreciate that and, Charlotte?"

"Yes?"

"Good luck."

CHAPTER FORTY-ONE
WHITE WALTHAM AERODROME, ENGLAND
MAY 1944

"Letter for you, Phipps!" Trixie pointed to the pigeonhole Al called his own.

"Thanks."

"All done for the day?"

"I think so. I've ferried three Spitfires to Aston Down today."

"Good going. Things are certainly cranking up, aren't they?" Trixie smiled.

"Yes, think I've earned a pint. Fancy coming to the pub?"

Trixie pointed to the stacks of paper on her desk. "No thanks, I've still got piles of filing to catch up on."

Al touched his cap and set off for the two-mile walk to the pub. A constant stream of army trucks thundered past him, most of them American. He took his pint into the garden to catch the last fading rays of sunlight but there wasn't a seat to be had. The place was stuffed with American GI's.

Al perched on the low stone wall that surrounded the lawn and drank a third of his beer down in one go.

The young American soldier sitting next to him nodded hello. "Thirsty work, hey, fella?"

"You could say that. You lot don't seem that busy, though."

"Busy? Huh, we're flat-out at the base. Something big is cooking." The young American offered him a cigarette and lit it using his Ronson cigarette lighter.

Al inhaled. "Your fags taste different to the Woodbines I normally smoke."

"Oh, yeah? Do you like it?"

"It's alright. Here, have one of mine."

"Gee, thanks."

310

"Have you any idea of when you're off, um, sorry, don't know your name?" Al took a drag of his cigarette.

"My name's Gus. No, they don't tell us much but they sure as hell keep us at it. You know, long hikes through your beautiful English countryside, laden with our packs, jumping through all sorts of hoops in the training ground and stuff. And the mud and the rain – why doesn't that stop in the summer? It's no wonder the guys need some of your warm beer."

"Don't you like our ale, then?"

"It's okay but I'd die for a cold beer. You know, all golden, with the condensation running down the glass."

"Doesn't it chill your insides?"

"You must be kidding me, right?"

Just then, another GI sauntered up and claimed Gus for a game of skittles indoors.

"See you around, pal." Gus gave Al a mock salute.

"Good luck, Gus." As soon as the young American was out of sight, Al stubbed out his foreign cigarette and lit a Woodbine. Fishing in his pocket for his lighter, he found the letter he'd stuffed in there as he'd left the base. He'd forgotten all about it in his craving for a decent pint of bitter.

Al slit the envelope open and spread out the single sheet of paper.

"Darling Al,

How are you? Busier than ever, I'll bet. Do take care, won't you, my dear? There is much talk of the invasion of France here at home, but no-one actually knows anything, not even your Mum.

I'm not as busy as I was because I have given up my work at Home Farm. It seems that our honeymoon has started something as unstoppable as the war itself. We're going to have a baby, Al!

I have struggled to believe it happened in such a short time but it's definite. I saw Dr Harris yesterday and he's confirmed our child will be born at the end of October.

311

So, you've got to stay safe now, my love. Please make sure you do.

I'm horribly sick every morning and then I hate you but as soon as it wears off, I long to see you again. I know you probably won't get any leave at the moment if the number of soldiers around Cheadle – most of them Yanks – are anything to go by, but I do hope that you will be able to come home for the birth.

I hope this news hasn't come as too much of a shock. I was in two minds whether to tell you or not, but then I realised it's half your baby too! I'm planning to tell your parents very soon and Mummy already knows. Everyone was asking why I wasn't working as a Land Girl anymore so I couldn't keep it a secret any longer, much as I would have liked to preserve my privacy!

I wish I could tell Lottie my news, too, don't you?

Let me know if you're pleased or not, won't you, dearest Al? I wish I could kiss you right this minute to help you get used to the idea of becoming a father.

I'm at West Lodge a lot of the time now, if you want to ring. It would be so lovely to hear your voice, but I understand if you are busy.

All my love, your Bella xxxxxxxxxxxx"

Al looked up from the sheet of paper, expecting the world to have changed around him but it still looked the same. It was him who was different…*"becoming a father…"*. A father? What had he done? Had it been selfish to sweep Bella off her feet and insist on marrying her then and there? Why the hell hadn't he used a prophylactic? What had he been thinking? What if he was killed? Some days he was so tired at the end of a flying day he could easily make a mistake or have an engine fail, like that last time. What a fool he'd been! A mad, impetuous, bloody lunatic.

Al closed his eyes. Images of their wild abandoned lovemaking in their blacked-out room at the London hotel, with bombs dropping all around them, glass shattering above and below, and their total indifference to the mayhem came back in a rush to haunt him. Poor Bella. Throwing up every morning, giving up the job she loved, and she hadn't complained, not once.

He re-read the letter to check. Not a word of blame, no criticism, no resentment. Then he got to the line where she said she hated him every morning. And why wouldn't she? Right this minute, Al hated himself.

CHAPTER FORTY-TWO
NORMANDY, FRANCE
JUNE 1944

"Watch the skies." Manon had pointed upwards and given a little wave goodbye when she'd departed a couple of weeks ago.

Lottie had watched her disappear into the velvet night, expecting her to reappear before the invasion but she hadn't seen her again.

Now it was June, the month Manon had said the landings would happen. Every night, she leant against the door frame and looked dutifully up at the waxing moon. It would be full in a few days and Manon had hinted strongly that the Allies would use its white disc to illuminate their invasion and ensure the highest tide. Lottie tried to imagine it but couldn't. She knew so little about what was coming, only that it would be huge.

She felt strangely bereft now Manon had left. Though not an easy woman to befriend, Manon had confidence, bags of it, but Lottie had to admit she'd taken a fair proportion of that elusive quality with her.

Lottie breathed in the night air, as always there was a taint of petrol fumes from the airbase spoiling its purity. It might be almost ten kilometres away but if the wind was in the right direction, it could ruin the day with the drone of aeroplanes and the spent fuel they spewed out.

Weary from the strain of Manon's visit and all it foretold, Lottie went inside and locked up the house. She took her oil lamp up to the attic in stockinged feet and pulled off her clothes, flopping into bed, longing for sleep. And yet it eluded her. She couldn't have been more tired but the knot in her stomach tightened rather than loosened. She must talk to Bernadette in the morning, make preparations before it was too late. The time had come to forewarn the others. She went over the six sentences she'd memorised

314

and only when she'd remembered each and every word, did her brain relax into sleep.

Dawn came early in June, but Lottie slept through it. Only when Françoise clomped up the attic ladder and thumped on the wall did she wake.

"Come on, Charlotte. I've already done the milking, you lazy layabout!"

Lottie sat up. "What time is it?"

"It's gone eight o'clock already. Come on, Bernadette's in a foul mood and I need some moral support."

"I'll be down in two minutes."

Lottie still felt half asleep when she stumbled down the stairs and into the kitchen.

Bernadette set a bowl of so-called coffee in front of her. "Drink that and wake up."

Lottie tore off a piece of bread and dipped it in the warm liquid. Slowly, her brain cleared. "Bernadette, we need to talk."

"Oh yes?" Bernadette sat down and poured herself a cup of herb tea. "Has that woman come back? Is she still locked in the cellar?"

"No, but I need to tell you everything she said when she was here, there's no point in keeping it secret from you any longer. Come here, Françoise, you need to hear this too."

Françoise turned around from standing at the sink and wiped her hands on a cloth. "Why?"

Lottie drank the last of her breakfast 'coffee' down and wiped her mouth with the back of her hand. "The Allies are on their way. There's an invasion planned very soon. It's top secret, don't breathe a word to anyone."

Françoise snorted. "As if we ever see anyone."

Lottie pushed her hair back from her forehead. "I might as well tell you, the invasion will happen here in Normandy, and soon. There's going to be a lot of fighting around here, I've been told. We need to protect ourselves. We might lose electricity; we might get bombed."

"Bombed!" Françoise looked over at little Bertrand who was playing with a wooden toy car Emile had whittled for him.

Lottie nodded. "Yes, Françoise, bombed. I don't know for certain, but I've heard they are bound to fight over the airbase and if they come by sea, as Manon thinks, they'll head towards Caen which is stuffed with German troops. The coast is bound to be under attack from all directions. Bernadette?"

"Yes?"

"I think we should prepare a lot of food and water, beds, anything we might need – candles, torches, everything, and put it all in the cellar." Lottie felt better now she was organising things.

"Humph. You could be right. Françoise – peel those potatoes and boil them up. Mash them when they are cooked with some cheese." Bernadette looked back at Lottie. "What shall we do with the animals? We can't keep them down there."

Lottie frowned. "I don't know the answer to that. We'll need to milk the goats every day, won't we? I suppose they'd better stay in the barn but then they wouldn't be able to feed themselves."

Bernadette got up from the table. "They haven't that much milk anyway, having not been mated with a billy for a couple of years but all the same, they will be uncomfortable if not milked and then, their milk will dry up completely. We will have to take turns to see to them."

Françoise was busy peeling potatoes. "They'll sort themselves out if we leave the door open. Let them go to the meadow and into the barn when they want to. Same with the hens, just leave the door open."

"What about foxes?" Bernadette hated foxes.

Lottie nodded. "Françoise is right. They'll all have to take their chances and we'll have to leave it up to them to

316

sort themselves out. If we're lucky, the farm won't be at the centre of things, but we have to take precautions now and prepare for the worst."

"Ouch!" Françoise sucked her thumb. "I've cut myself."

Bernadette got up and looked at Françoise's hand. "You should be more careful at a time like this. It's not too bad. The bleeding will stop in the potato water."

Lottie gave a brittle laugh. "More protein for us!"

Françoise scowled at her. "Do you want me to slit my wrists too?"

"That's enough, you two." Bernadette retied her apron around her waist and rolled up her sleeves. "We've work to do."

By the late afternoon, the three women gathered in the lower cellar to survey their handiwork. The three spare mattresses from the attic, having been thoroughly bashed free of dust in the June sunshine, now lay on the floor, side by side. In one corner was a metal slop bucket and some neatly folded towels on a small table. In the other, stood a chair with a pitcher of water and four mugs. They had brought down one of the empty barrels and filled it with dried goods – dried apples, biscuits, walnuts in their shells, cheese wrapped in muslin, hard-boiled eggs, two loaves and three dried sausages. Françoise had baked a cake, padded out with grated carrots and sweetened with the last of the sultanas and put it, with the cheesy mashed potatoes, in separate containers on the top of the pile. A big jug of goat's milk stood in a pail of cold water with last year's wrinkled apples bobbing around it. Several bottles of cider and Calvados flanked the chair. Next to Lottie's bed, the one nearest the ladder, were stacked a few books, all dog-eared and worn. Another small table between her bed and the food corner bore an oil lamp and underneath it stood a couple of cans of spare lamp oil and a box of candles and matches.

"What about the radio?" Françoise stood, hand on hips, surveying their refuge.

317

"Won't work without power, unfortunately. Some music would be very welcome if we were stuck down here for any length of time." Lottie put pillows on each of the beds and plumped them up.

Bernadette snorted. "Be glad not to have to listen to the damn thing."

Lottie stood up. "Bernadette, do you have things that are precious to you? You know, the family Bible, fine china, photographs? Things you wouldn't want lost?"

"What on earth do you think is going to happen, child? The sea is miles away and so is the airbase. We are in the middle of nowhere. This is all such a fuss." Bernadette looked tired and sounded irritated.

"Judging from Manon's hints, I think we could be right in the battle zone." Lottie spoke quietly but the conviction in her voice made Françoise grab little Bertrand and clamp him to her hip.

Bernadette was silent for a moment, then she said, "I hope you are wrong, but I suppose there's no harm in putting a few keepsakes in here. We could use the top cellar for those."

"I'll help you." Lottie followed her up the ladder for what seemed like the hundredth time that day.

Françoise and Bertrand quickly followed them.

"Take the child out into the sunshine while you can, Françoise." Bernadette jerked her head to the door but turned to the staircase. "If you are right, it's good we still have that rifle but I wish we had one each."

"I agree. I'll try and get some. Perhaps I could go to the mill?"

"Don't risk it. We'll manage."

But the seed of doubt had been sown in Lottie's mind. If only the Germans hadn't taken those cylinders. She wished now she'd asked Manon for some firearms. Lucian had probably had some at his farm, but the Germans would have snaffled them by now. From here it seemed the Germans were impregnable, what with their Atlantic Wall and its huge guns, the troops guarding the coast and the villages and towns all around them. Lottie could not imagine how the Allies would defeat them.

They had a cold supper that night. No-one had the energy to cook so they ate some of the cheesy mashed potato with salad from the garden and some boiled eggs.

Afterwards, Lottie got up and switched on the radio.

"Oh, must we have that on tonight? Is there never any peace to be had these days?" Bernadette took up her knitting with a heavy sigh.

"It's important, Bernadette. I must listen to the personal messages from Radio Londres." Lottie sat next to the wireless and tried to tune it to the British station.

"Infernal racket. All I can hear is crackles and whistles."

"Shush. Listen! Can you hear that?"

"I can hear a horrible hissing noise, that's all." Bernadette clicked her knitting needles together.

Lottie bent closer to the wireless set. "It's Beethoven's Fifth Symphony, I'm sure of it. Listen, da,da,da,dhah…"

"Dada to you too."

Lottie held up her hand for silence and concentrated. "It's the first bar. Manon told me to listen out for it. It means 'V' for victory in Morse code."

Bernadette's needles stilled. "Isn't Beethoven a bloody German?"

"He was, but that's irrelevant. Don't you see? It confirms the Allies are gearing up for something."

Françoise clattered down the stairs. "Bertrand has gone out like a light tonight, he's so tired. Oh, and so am I after all that shifting mattresses and stuff."

"Be quiet, Françoise!" Lottie tutted.

"Well, pardon me for living."

"I'm sorry but it's the personal messages. I must hear every word." The other two women went obediently silent.

319

The radio crackled and hissed out its absurd messages. "Listen! It's the *'Chanson d'automne'*." Lottie jumped up from her chair and hunched over the wireless set, holding one finger up for silence.

The radio announcer said, *'Les sanglots longs des violons de l'automne'*.

Lottie froze in her bent posture, then slowly stood up. "They're really coming. Oh, my God, they are really coming!"

"But he only said the long sobs of the violins of autumn. That makes no sense." Françoise looked bemused. "Who is coming?"

Bernadette laid down her knitting. "Do you mean the Allied invasion?"

"Of course, that's what I mean! We only have twenty-four hours to get ready. That last message means I must go to the village to get instructions."

Bernadette frowned. "That would be dangerous, surely?"

"I can't help that. I'm going to bed. I'll go first thing. You two should do the same, and rest while you can. There won't be another chance."

Falling asleep proved elusive that night. Lottie kept thinking of things she should have put in the cellar but didn't dare get up and prowl around in case she woke the other two. She got up at first light and mounted her bicycle. She was in the village not long after dawn and found the square hushed and quiet. Did she imagine that sense of anticipation? The sentry on the bridge was subdued too and barely glanced at her papers. Lottie wasted no time but cycled straight up to the ex-Mayor's house. She propped her bicycle next to the garden gate at the back and unlatched it. She slipped quietly through the doorway and went up to the kitchen door and knocked softly.

There was no answer.

Lottie tested the handle and found it unlocked. She walked inside the kitchen. Everything was tidy and put away. The kitchen looked at rest, the day's busyness not yet begun. She wandered about, feeling hungry after missing her breakfast. The remains of a meat pie sat on the marble counter and she was sorely tempted to help herself to some.

Then she heard a noise. Soft footfalls on the stairs. The maid appeared, still tying her white apron around her waist and yawning.

When she saw Lottie, she shrieked. "Argh!"

Lottie held up her hands. "Shush. I'm a friend. I need to speak to Madame Voclain urgently."

"You are a thief. I will tell my brother, Jules, about you. He's in the Milice now, you know."

"No, no, please don't. I'm not stealing anything. I just need a word with your mistress."

A voice floated down the stairwell. "Who is it, Odette?"

The maid looked at Lottie. "Stay there, peasant girl."

Lottie folded her arms across her chest. While Odette was gone, she caught a glimpse of herself in the mirror above the big side table. Her hair was as short as a boy's, curling crisply above and away from her ears. Her skin was tanned, and she had new, faint lines around her brown eyes and her mouth above her determined chin. She wore an old once-white shirt that had belonged to Bernadette's husband and had tucked it inside his son's corduroy trousers. The whole rustic outfit was held together by baler twine, knotted around her middle. Lottie looked down at her hands. The fingernails were short and black-rimmed and her hands workworn. She realised with a start that she didn't resemble Charlotte Flintock-Smythe at all.

Her study of herself was abruptly truncated by Madame Voclain coming into the kitchen, wearing a pink housecoat as elegant as any of her dresses. It was obviously made of silk and decorated with little blue birds in a Chinese style. What a contrast to her houseguest.

"Odette, go upstairs and get my clothes ready. I'll wear the green silk dress with the pleats today. Don't return until I call you, and make sure you shut the bedroom door."

"But Madame…?"

"Go." Madame Voclain waited until she heard a door shut upstairs and then came close to Lottie. "Are you here about the invasion?"

"Yes. I was told to come here when I heard the message on the radio last night."

"Good. There is an operation to take place when we hear another message. You heard the one about the 'sobbing violins of autumn'?"

Lottie nodded.

"I had thought it would be yesterday but perhaps the bad weather delayed them. You know it means they will invade within twenty-four hours?"

Lottie nodded again. "Yes, of course."

"Very well. Come with me. The next one will also be by Paul Verlaine and speak of 'wounding my heart with a monotonous languor'."

"Yes, Madame, I learned it off-by-heart with Manon."

"Good. You have learned it well."

Madame Voclain lead the way to the pantry where Lottie had seen the jars of honey on her last clandestine visit. Madame fished in her pocket and took out an old, heavy key which she inserted in a door at the very back of the dark, cold room.

"Stay there."

Madame Voclain disappeared behind the ancient door and returned very quickly carrying a folded map. She opened it up and gave it to Lottie. "Take this. When you hear Verlaine's second stanza message, you will know it is your call to action. You must immediately go to the railway track here." She pointed to a place marked with crosses. "Someone will meet you at these crossroads tonight and will have dynamite and guns. Your task is to help blow up the telegraph poles running along the railway track. It will prevent the Germans being able to communicate with each other just before the Allies invade. Can you do it?"

Lottie took the map. "Madame, it will be a pleasure."

Madame smiled and Lottie had a glimpse of how pretty she must have looked when she was younger.

"Very well, go now and be ready. Oh, and, Mademoiselle, do you know if any bees have swarmed lately?"

"None, Madame, that I know about." Lottie folded the map back up.

Madame Voclain looked her age again. "I see. Good luck. May God go with you."

"Thank you. Keep safe yourself, Madame."

Lottie gave a brief smile and left. Before going through the garden gate, she stuffed the folded map down inside the back of her knickers. It rubbed against her backside as she walked, and she was glad to press down on it when she mounted the saddle again.

The village was stirring into life now but without a butcher or baker there was far less bustle than there used to be. Everything seemed to be waiting for something, or was that just her imagination?

She cycled past the control on the bridge. Again, the sleepy Germans didn't seem interested in her and she pedalled fast out of the village before they changed their minds. In the eastern sky the sun peeped over the horizon through a jumbled of confused clouds. Lottie was very afraid it looked like more rain.

Lottie made sure she had everything ready before the personal messages were read out on Radio Londres that evening. She had changed her white shirt for an even tattier dark-brown one to make herself less conspicuous in the dark.

"Here, take this." Bernadette held out a strong leather belt. "It's no good holding yourself together with thin twine, girl. Should have given it to you months ago."

"Thank you, Bernadette." Lottie buckled the belt around the top of her rough trousers. "The holes are too far apart, and I can't fasten it."

"Take it off again. I will use this awl to make a new one."

Bernadette punched a hole into the leather with a little tool like a screwdriver and Lottie tried it on again.

"Ah, that is much better. It's like having an extra backbone."

"You'll need that."

Lottie smiled at the older woman. "You're not wrong." She took the carving knife, having sharpened it for a good half an hour earlier that afternoon, and slipped it inside the leather belt. She had very few bullets left in her trouser pocket for the rifle.

"Take this waistcoat too. It's also made of leather. It's old and worn. It belonged to my son when he was a teenager. I found it in a storage box last night. Might give you some protection. I've rubbed it with leather soap but it's still a bit stiff."

Lottie put her arms through the waistcoat armholes and did up the toggles down the front. The leather smelt of animal and soap and stale sweat. She found it comforting and liked how it fitted snugly, unlike her other garments. It gave her a sense of security, probably a false one.

Françoise came in with something in a closed fist. "Here's my sewing scissors. Thought they might come in handy. They're stronger than they look and sharp too."

"Thank you, Françoise, that is very thoughtful." Lottie put them in one of the handy pockets of the leather waistcoat. "Can you black my face with some ash from the fire?"

Françoise patted the charcoal on her cheeks. "You'd better take my dark blue beret too. I've already cut the pom-pom off."

"Thanks."

Françoise stood back to see the effect. "No one will think you are a girl, you know."

"All the better. Quick, it's time for the announcements."

The three women huddled around the wireless set. Lottie had no need to request silence this time. As soon as she heard the second stanza of Verlaine's poem about the 'monotonous sobs of autumn', she jumped up, slung her rifle over her back and headed for the door.

"Take care, child." Bernadette squeezed her forearm.

"Please be careful, dearest Lottie." Françoise kissed her on both cheeks. The charcoal smudged her friend's full lips.

Lottie gave them each a quick hug and slipped quietly through the door. She had memorised the map tracing the route with her finger so often it was looking thin enough to break, so she had decided to rely on her memory and leave it behind. She settled her beret more firmly on her head and mounted her bicycle. If she saw any German soldiers while out cycling she would be instantly arrested, as it was after the curfew, so she kept to the off-road tracks, weaving in and out of the trees and using the moonlight to avoid roots that might cause an accident.

She reached the crossroads of the two minor roads she was looking for in just over half an hour and slung her bike in a deep ditch which had a hedge behind it. She ran along the bottom of the ditch to avoid being seen and crouched inside it, as near to the crossroads as she could, to wait, as Madame Voclain had instructed, for the others.

The ditch was wet at the bottom, even in June. It had rained all day and the wind was high, making it hard to hear anything above the swishing trees as they rubbed their branches together and flapped their full summer leaves.

Her clothes were soon sodden, making her even more glad of the leather jerkin, which kept the rain off her torso and strengthened both her spine and her resolve. Lottie wished she had more bullets for her rifle that had lain dormant in the cellar so long with its twin, now lost since the train sabotage. Funny, she had hated them on sight all those long months ago, but now would have been glad to have more firepower beside her.

Time passed, the rain fell, the trees danced their noisy ballet and Lottie got colder, wetter and more and more worried she'd gone to the wrong location for the rendezvous. Most of the people she had met through the Resistance had been captured by the Germans. She listed them in her mind. Dear Madame Leroy and her fabulous baguettes and warm hugs; tall Pierre with the loping walk and camera skills; weather-beaten Lucien with his uncanny ability to navigate by the stars in the night sky. They were all in prison in Caen or dead now. Would she recognise the new ones she was due to meet tonight? Would they know who she was? Only Madame Voclain was left amongst her previous acquaintances from the village and Lottie couldn't imagine her with a blacked-up face, handling dynamite. If Jean Everard from the mill came, she would probably smell him before she saw him.

She wished she had a watch but hers was a dainty, jewelled affair and she'd put it away under the attic floorboards years ago, along with her tailored clothes of silk and fine cotton.

She brought her mind reluctantly back to the discomfort of her wet, unpleasant situation in the present and tried to calculate how long she'd been here. Must be an hour since she'd left Le Verger.

Then, above the cacophony of the storm, she heard what sounded like the click of a safety catch being released on a gun. Lottie crawled up the embankment on the road side of the ditch. She clutched at the tussocks of grass at the top and hauled herself up to peep over the edge. She couldn't see a thing. Then the wind hushed and stilled, giving a pause in the background noise and she listened, every nerve-ending straining to hear, but there was nothing.

A man's voice spoke softly right next to her. "Charlotte? C'est toi?"

She reeled around. There was someone in the ditch with her! She hadn't heard him coming, except that click of his gun.

Lottie reached for the carving knife in her belt and drew it out, pointing it at the dark silhouette of the man, no more than three feet away from her. She couldn't see his face, which was blackened up like hers and shielded by his helmet, but she noticed he was wearing glasses and full camouflage battle gear.

She swallowed. "Identify yourself." Her voice had gone all squeaky with fear. She cleared her throat and was astonished to hear the man give a low laugh. He dropped his rifle and came closer, holding outstretched arms to her.

Lottie frowned, concentrating on his face. Then she was enveloped within his embrace and his mouth sought hers.

She broke free. "Thierry? Is it really you?"

He laughed again, soft and low. "Yes, my love, it's really me. I did not recognise you at first. You look like a boy! Are you part of tonight's show?"

"Yes, but Thierry, where have you been? What are you doing here?"

327

"You're lucky I didn't shoot you dead when you poked your head up like that!"

"What a way to greet me! Don't you know I've been worried sick about you? I didn't know if you were alive or dead all this time!"

He didn't answer her but kissed her again. "Oh, Charlotte, I have missed you so much. If only we had time to catch up with everything. Oh, it will be hard to fight now I have seen you again. Please, my darling, take care. I wish you would go home, be safe."

"I'm not leaving you now I've found you, Thierry."

He nodded. "I feel the same way, but we must join the others. We have no time. Follow me and keep your head down. And put that lethal-looking knife away."

He climbed slowly out of the ditch and went across to the shelter of the nearby woods, keeping his upper body crouched low. Lottie followed him and saw two men squatting next to some equipment on the ground.

"You are with the FFI?" The taller of the men stood up and whispered to her as she approached.

"No, but I am in the Resistance and had instructions to be here." Lottie whispered back.

The other man had his back to her and was huddled over a field radio. "So, where's the FFI? They should be here by now. We're on a tight schedule."

Lottie addressed the first man. "Who are you?" She nodded towards the man with the radio. "He is French but you're not."

The man grinned, showing white teeth against his charcoal-covered face. "Let's just say we're on your side, that's if you're not a German spy? Who can vouch for you?"

Thierry turned to his comrade. "I can vouch for this young lady."

"Young lady? I thought she was a boy!"

"Oh, no. She's definitely not a boy." Thierry gave her a quick kiss on the lips.

"What the hell is going on?" The man looked stupefied.

The other man, who spoke French with a strong British accent, had turned to face them and looked furious. "Thibault! What is the meaning of this?"

Thierry cleared his throat. "I beg your pardon, sir. May I introduce my fiancée, Charlotte Perrot."

"Is this some sort damned contrived meeting, Thibault? Because if it is, it's completely against regulations."

"No, sir. I'm as surprised as you are." Thierry turned to Lottie. "But then again, I should have known you would be part of the fight around here."

Lottie looked at all three men. "I had no idea Monsieur Thibault would be here tonight. I am waiting for my French friends. They are late."

Thierry frowned. "D-Day – that's the allied name for the operation - was supposed to happen yesterday, but it was delayed by a day because of the stormy weather. You don't think they came yesterday instead, do you?"

Just then, four other figures appeared through the trees.

Lottie recognised two of them. "Gaspard, oh, and Jean! How good to see you! I thought you must have had trouble along the way."

Jean spoke for them all. "Had to take the long way round, didn't we? Roadblocks all along the Route Nationale since they built that bloody wall. Barbed wire everywhere."

The men crouched down and started talking together, but Thierry took Lottie to one side. "It's so good to see you."

"Oh, Thierry. I can't tell you how full my heart is. What have you been doing? Why are you here?"

"I was fighting down south with the Maquis but then I got in with an SOE agent and was packed off to England for some very uncomfortable training."

329

"To England? Oh, if only I'd known, I could have given you a letter to send to my mother."

"Charlotte, I had no time for anything but the training, believe me. I'm here as part of a Jedburgh team, setting up communications with the local Resistance. I opted to come to my home territory. It's an advantage, knowing the terrain. I can't believe my luck in running into you on the first night. But we can't stay. We're to handover the dynamite to your friends and then we must be away to meet others doing sabotage elsewhere. The invasion will come tomorrow morning."

"Where will you go?"

"Many different places and now, I must get on with it. I don't know where I will end up."

"I understand, but when will I see you again?"

"I don't know, but Charlotte, there will be a massive bombing campaign. There are a lot of Germans at the airbase as well as along the Atlantic Wall. You must get home and stay safe. Hide in that deep, dark cellar." He laughed and went towards his colleagues.

She followed him. "Already set it up. Take care, won't you? Come back when you can?"

He squeezed her hand, then let it go. "I promise."

They joined the others. The British man frowned. "Glad you could spare us some time, Thibault."

"I'm sorry, sir. Won't happen again."

"Better not. Right, we've briefed the locals and handed over the ammunition. We must go to the next rendezvous immediately." He looked at Lottie and said, in his heavily accented French, "Goodbye, Mademoiselle. Please stay focussed on the matter in hand. Your life and many others will be at risk over the next little while."

Lottie answered him in English. She could hear a foreign lilt to her own voice. It had been a long time since she had spoken in her mother tongue. "Thierry and I have not seen each other for a very long time. I'm not in the habit of flirting with soldiers as a rule. Good luck to you."

330

"You're English?" The soldier looked astonished, as well he might.

Lottie grinned. "Yes, stranded in France since 1939 but I have a strong false identity and a safe house here. Please don't wait for me. Go, and keep him safe for me." She turned to Thierry and kissed him briefly on the mouth.

The three soldiers picked up their gear and shook hands with each of the local resistance fighters. Goodbyes were quickly exchanged and then they disappeared silently into the woods behind the road junction.

Jean Everard looked at Lottie and licked his fat lips. "So, seems you're not such an innocent then? Eh?"

Lottie returned his stare. "This is not the time, Jean. Come on, tell me what we must do."

The two other men lay the charges on the ground. There were fifteen bundles of explosives and they handed out three to each person and a rifle with several rounds of ammunition as well.

The tallest man, who went by the name of Christophe, took charge. "Okay, everyone. We will lay a stick of dynamite around each telegraph pole along the railway track. Blowing these means the Germans won't be able to communicate down the line. It's vital we halt any messages about the invasion. Agreed?"

The other men grunted assent. Christophe continued in a low voice. "Good. Lay the sticks near the base, and then undo the bolts on the track itself so that any train that comes along will get derailed. If you see a German, hunker down in a ditch and lay the next charge further along out of his sight. Keep as silent as the grave and don't engage with the enemy. We don't want them to know we're here until the fuse is lit."

Gaspard stroked his stubbly chin. "Are there Germans near here?"

Christophe shook his head. "Not as far as we know, that's why we chose this spot. Now, when you have laid the charge, come back here to the detonator and stand guard for

331

the others. I'll go with Charlotte and then come and tie the fuse wires on this side. Gaspard - you tie the other side. Do not shoot unless you have to. We don't expect to see any Boche, but you never know. Got it?"

Lottie nodded and went to the first pole, running along the base of the ditch, stooping low to keep her head out of sight, trying to focus on the task in hand instead of the wonderment of knowing Thierry was alive, was nearby! Christophe tackled the bolt holding the track together while she tied the fuse around the pole as she had been shown. She felt strangely calm and her hands didn't tremble even though they held explosives. The wood smelled of creosote, acrid and resinous. It was wet and slippery from the rain, but she managed to tie it quickly and ran the fuse wire to the next one. The two others had run on ahead of her in the other direction. She looked up as Christophe ran towards the others and she saw them doing the same manoeuvre. She had a moment of pure exhilaration, knowing she was part of a team of men as determined as her to rid France of the poisonous Nazis and that Thierry was doing the same not very far away. She could still taste him on her lips and that gave her all the strength she needed. She bent low again and went to the next pole, tied the fuses, and onto the next. The other two men were busy getting the bolts out of the track, but Christophe was coming back now and tying the fuse wires together to make a unified whole. Lottie waited for him to catch up and watched as his deft fingers twined the wires together.

"Go, it's done!" Christophe nodded her back to side of the track where Gaspard now waited with the detonator.

When they had all gathered, Christophe knelt down to the detonator. "The rest of you get lost. Disperse through the woods, don't stay together in a group. I will press the plunger in five minutes."

Gaspard protested. "But Christophe, I want to see the fireworks."

332

"It's not a festival, Gaspard. You'll see them on your way home and so will the Boche. You can't do another operation if you get caught. Allez! All of you!"

Lottie didn't need persuading. She ran across to the road, still keeping low, and scrambled back into the ditch on the far side and ran along it till she came to her bike. She lifted it up over the edge of the ditch with some difficulty but managed to set it back on the road before mounting it. By the time she reached the woods, there was the most tremendous crack, followed quickly by another. She looked behind her and saw fifteen telegraph poles crashing down like dominoes, one by one.

CHAPTER FORTY-FOUR
NORMANDY, FRANCE
JUNE 1944

Lottie stirred in her sleep. She didn't want to open her eyes, they felt so heavy. She turned over in her single bed and nestled her weary head into the pillow, craving rest. She had almost surrendered to the bliss of her dream all about train tracks and Thierry's lips on hers and explosions and leaves whispering secrets. She had dreamt she was on a train and it was hurtling along at such a speed, all the teacups were rattling in the dining car. Rattling and clattering. Shaking and vibrating. Her train seat was vibrating wildly too. They were going to crash - it was going too fast. The china would smash onto the floor soon. Why didn't the driver slow up? Didn't he realise the danger? She opened her eyes, momentarily relieved to see she wasn't on a train hurtling into oblivion but laying on her bed in the attic at Le Verger. And yet, the jug *was* clinking against its china basin on the washstand. She clutched the iron railings above her head, shocked to find they were juddering against the metal frame of the bed. Was it an earthquake?

The invasion! It must be that! Fully awake now, Lottie swung her legs to the floor, feeling the house quivering through the soles of her feet. She went to one of the dormer windows and opened the shutters. Lottie craned her neck in the direction of the sea. Her eyes widened in disbelief as flashes of light, more brilliant than the dawn, bloomed on the horizon towards the coast.

She hadn't bothered to fully undress last night so simply grabbed her jumper and pulled on her socks. She opened the other shutters and by the grey dawn light navigated down the ladder and on to the landing on the first floor. Just as her foot touched the first stair down to the kitchen, Bernadette's bedroom door flew open and its owner stood in her nightgown in its frame, staring at Lottie.

"Has it come? Is this it?"

"I think so, Bernadette. Oh, did you hear that? It must be cannon, it sounded so powerful."

The door opposite opened more slowly and Françoise, looking bleary, peered around it. "What's happening?"

Lottie stood on the top step, one hand on the banister. She could feel the wood shaking under her hand. "It's the Allies. They're coming! It's a bloody miracle, that's what's happening!"

She laughed and ran down the rest of the staircase into the kitchen. She unbolted the kitchen door, yanked on her boots and ran outside to look at the spectacle.

Bernadette joined her outside. "Are you sure?"

"Yes, look! It's coming from the coast. There must be ships out there. Ah, I could see better from the attic."

Françoise called from the kitchen door. "Don't stand outside there! You could be killed!"

Lottie turned back and shouted. "No, it's miles away."

Bernadette started to walk to the house. "But it will come our way. We must prepare."

Lottie joined her and they went into the kitchen together.

Bernadette immediately filled the kettle and put it on to heat. "Françoise, see if your son is awake and if so, bring him down. We must stay together and get ready. You," she turned to Lottie, "milk the goats and set them free. I will collect the eggs and do the same with the hens and the rabbits. They'll have to fend for themselves, God help them."

Bernadette went outside to the yard in her nightgown, seemingly unaware she hadn't got dressed.

Lottie ran after her. "Bernadette! Stop! Go and get dressed, I'll sort all the animals out."

Bernadette looked at her and stopped walking. She looked down at her nightgown and then back at Lottie, her mouth hanging open, her face white, her hands shaking.

"Oh, Bernadette!" Lottie reached out and held the older woman's hands. "It will be alright, it will. Soon we will be free. Imagine that! Go now. Get dressed, eat something."

Another cannon boomed in the distance and aeroplanes swarmed overhead, great swathes of them, heading for Caen. Bernadette ducked instinctively under their deafening canopy, but she nodded and trotted back towards the house.

Lottie went to the goats' barn first. The animals were restless, the whites of their eyes showing. She went to each of them, stroking their necks and speaking soothing words directly into their long ears, flattened by fear. There were only two milkers now and it didn't take long to harvest their meagre bags of milk. She talked to them the whole time she pulled on their udders, mostly about seeing Thierry again. She told them all the intimate details of their kisses. Told them he wasn't far away. Told them she might even see him again soon. The goats chomped on the last of the dried feed leftover from winter and listened, stamping their feet and shaking their heads when a particularly loud boom sounded in the distance. Then Lottie slipped off their halters, took the buckets of milk and left the barn door wide open.

"You are free to go, girls. Thanks for listening. Stay safe."

She took the milk straight to the farmhouse kitchen and set them on the stone floor before going back outside again to liberate the rabbits. The little creatures bounded out from their cages, terrorised, and bolted for the woods. Lottie didn't think she'd see any of them again.

She looked for the donkey who had a shelter within the orchard, but she was nowhere to be seen. She must have bolted from fright at the deafening booms resounding all around her. Poor thing.

Last she went to the henhouse. The birds were squawking loudly and flapping their wings in huge agitation. She lifted the latch and they came pouring out.

Lottie widened the door to their run, and they streamed through it, still shrieking their fright and, like the rabbits, made for the woods.

Lottie reached inside the hen house and felt around for eggs. Some of them were still warm. She put them in a basket and ran back to the house, careful not to drop any.

When she got inside the kitchen, Bertrand was bawling his eyes out. Françoise was rubbing his back and looking on the brink of tears herself.

Lottie crouched down to the little boy, who was sitting on a rug on the floor by the window, his favourite spot. His toys lay around him, untouched. "Bertrand? Don't worry, little man. It is noisy, it's true, but friends are coming to help us get rid of the nasty German soldiers. They are soldiers too, you see, and they have great big guns and lots of aeroplanes to scare the Nazis away."

The little boy was sobbing more quietly now as he listened, wide-eyed to Lottie.

Emboldened by this, she carried on. "That's a good boy. No need to cry. They're coming to rescue us but first they have to fight the Nazis and the Nazis aren't going to give up straight away so they will fight back and it's going to be very, very noisy with lots of bangs and planes and soldiers everywhere. But we'll be alright. We're going to hide in the deepest cellar together. Now, you pick up the toys you will need to play with and put them in this basket for me. Can you do that?"

Bertrand nodded and started to put his wooden bricks in the basket Lottie had given him.

"Well done, you are a brave soldier. Mummy will help you." Lottie nodded at Françoise who knelt down with her young son and helped him pack his toys into the basket.

Bernadette came downstairs. Lottie was pleased to see she was as neatly dressed as usual and had tied her plait into a bun at the nape of her neck, just like she always did.

The kettle had come to the boil. Bernadette picked it up and poured the boiling water over some leaves in a pot.

"I'll make a big omelette with those eggs and hard boil the rest. Who knows when we'll eat again?"

"Good idea. The way things are going, they'll scramble themselves if the house shakes anymore."

A huge explosion erupted in the distance.

"They are bombing Caen again. Bound to be a target, it's crawling with Germans because of its port." Bernadette lifted her cup to her lips, and it rattled when it went back down on the saucer.

"Sounds closer. Could be the airbase. That's going to take a bashing too." Lottie gulped down the rest of her omelette and cut some bread. "Good job you baked another loaf yesterday, Françoise."

Françoise came to the table and set Bertrand on the chair next to her, propping him up with cushions. "Sit there and be quiet, Bertrand."

Lottie smiled at the little boy whose chin had begun to wobble again and then announced, "Something amazing happened last night."

"What? What could be bigger than this?" Françoise cut into her omelette and popped a small fork-full into Bertrand's mouth.

"I saw Thierry." Even as she said it, the glow of the memory spread through Lottie's veins, warming them better than any tisane.

"When?"

"Last night. We had only a few minutes together but he's here with some team from the British Army, Jed-something-or-other, I can't remember. It all happened so quickly but he met us at the train track and gave us bullets for the rifle and explosives for the sabotage. Ah, you should have seen those telegraph poles fall like a pack of cards."

Bernadette gave her a hard look. "You have the rifle still – and bullets?"

"Yes, it's in the attic."

"That's good. Only one?"

"Yes, only one, but you're missing the point! Thierry's alive and he's here!" Lottie laughed, throwing her head back but then the feeling overwhelmed her, and she buried her face in her hands instead, choking on a strangled sob.

Bernadette patted her back. "Seems the whole damned world is here right now."

Another explosion shook the building.

"I'm glad he's alive, Lottie, really I am but I think we should get down to the cellar now." Françoise wiped Bertrand's mouth with a tea towel and gathered up the dirty plates.

"Just leave them in the sink." Bernadette picked up the loaf and wrapped it in a cloth. "Oh, my poor goats."

Lottie had never heard Bernadette express emotion for any animal. "I let their barn door stand open, Bernadette. What else can we do?"

"Nothing, there is nothing we can do for them. We must save ourselves."

CHAPTER FORTY-FIVE
NORMANDY, FRANCE
JUNE 1944

All that morning they stayed down in the cellar, not knowing what the weather was like outside, not tasting fresh air by opening the trap door for fear the ceiling would cave in.

"What time is it?" Françoise had been dozing, Bertrand in her arms, also asleep.

Lottie remembered her old watch lying under the attic floorboards so far above them. "I don't know. I wish we'd brought a clock down here. There seems to be a little bit of a lull in the bombing. I'll go and have a look."

Bernadette, sitting on a chair, knitting, stilled her hands. "Don't be a fool. You don't know they've stopped the bombing. It's so close, the house is shaking every time one falls. What if you are killed?"

"I won't be killed. Don't fuss."

"Don't fuss! For goodness' sake, child. We need you." Bernadette laid her wool down and stood up.

"I need a pee, if you must know. And I'm going to get my watch from upstairs. I won't be long." Lottie didn't wait for a reply but mounted the ladder and pushed open the hatch to the upper cellar.

She ran up the stone steps to the kitchen and listened. It was true. The bombing had paused. Not wanting to waste a moment, Lottie ran up the stairs and then the ladder to the attic. There was no need to hide things now. She threw the rug covering the wonky plank to one side and wrenched up the floorboard with the old knife she kept for the purpose by her bed. The wood split apart but she realised with a thrilling stab of adrenalin that it didn't matter anymore. If the Allies kept up this assault, if they *won,* there would be no need for her to pretend to be Charlotte Perrot any longer. She could be herself – at long last. And Thierry was alive. Thierry was nearby. Thierry...

She prised open the box containing her most precious things and strapped on her pretty watch. It had stopped. Of course! She hadn't wound it in simply years. Oh, she hoped it still worked. Lottie grabbed the rifle propped next to her bed and its pouch of bullets, scaled back down the ladder and looked at the clock in the landing. Half past twelve. She set her watch to the correct time and wound it up, holding it to her ear when she had finished. The dainty thud-thud of the hands moving around the little clock-face had the resonance of normality, of regular timekeeping, of minutes and days passing in tranquil formation. It heartened her.

She leapt down the staircase to the ground floor and yanked open to the door to the yard. The sky was obscured by smoke, mostly coming from the airbase and the coast. There must be fires burning everywhere. She looked towards the direction of the airbase and saw, to her dismay, that a large area of woodland was on fire.

So much destruction.

She ran to the goats' barn, but it was empty. The goats must have fled, just like the chickens. She couldn't look for them now but still her eyes were drawn to the orchard to check for them. Something white fluttered in the branches of the apple trees. Unable to resist her curiosity, Lottie ran over and snatched it down. It was a piece of paper. All the words printed on it were in German. Was it from the Nazis? She couldn't make head nor tail of the message. The only bit she could understand was the headline – *'Eine Minute'*. 'One Minute'? What did that mean? Another explosion rent the air. It sounded nearby. More aeroplanes droned overhead, going towards Caen. Lottie screwed up the paper and threw it to the ground. She shielded her eyes and watched the progress of the British bombers, saw their lethal cylinders fall from the sky, heard the impact, watched the smoke pall into the darkened sky. She'd seen enough. Why were the British bombing the

341

French? That last lot looked like it had hit the village of Carpiquet, not just the aerodrome.

She ran back to the outside toilet, used it and, still buttoning her trousers, jogged back to the house. She grabbed the butter dish from the table and took it back down the cellar.

"I've brought some butter. Do we need anything else?" Lottie closed the hatch behind her. How she hated being shut in.

"Thank God you're back. The bombing's started again." Bernadette grabbed her arm and dragged her back inside the deep cellar.

"Yes, they're targeting poor old Caen again. I hate that my countrymen are killing yours."

"There'll be nothing left of the place. They've been pounding it all day, on and off."

Lottie nodded. "Thierry's parents live there. Oh, I wish I knew where he was."

"I'm hungry." Bertrand had woken up.

"Come child, we'll eat our lunch." Bernadette took the towels off the little table and set out some food.

"I don't think I can eat much." Françoise brought Bertrand over to the makeshift dining table.

"Don't discourage the boy." Bernadette sawed through the loaf. "You," she gave Lottie the butter knife, "spread something on it. It will help it go down."

Lottie dutifully plastered the butter on the bread, added a slice of cheese on the top and gave it to Bertrand. The little boy took it and bit into it with his sharp new teeth.

"Good boy, Bertrand. Keep your strength up." Lottie passed another piece to Françoise who took it and put it to one side.

Bernadette frowned at her granddaughter. "Eat Françoise. Think of the boy."

Françoise picked up her snack and nibbled unenthusiastically at the edges.

"How long will we be down here, Maman?" Bertrand had finished his bread.

"I don't know, little one." Françoise stroked his hair.

Bernadette looked at Lottie. "Have you any idea?"

"How should I know? I wish we could listen to the radio down here. You don't have any batteries stashed away, do you?"

"Don't hold with them." Bernadette fetched the cake from the top of the barrel and opened the tin.

Lottie sighed. "I'm going to have a kip. I've only had about two hours sleep. Then I'm going up to the kitchen to listen to the news and no-one will stop me."

"Not even a bomb?"

But Lottie wasn't listening. She lay down on her bed and closed her eyes. She could just about hear the bombers overhead droning away and the crump of their load reaching their target. As far as she was concerned, it was music to her ears.

When she awoke and wondered what the time was, it was a joy to remember she now wore her watch. Lottie squinted at it in the lamplight. "It's six o'clock! I've been asleep for hours. I'm going up to the kitchen to listen to the radio, try and find out what's happening, see if there's more I can do."

Françoise, to Lottie's surprise, got up and joined her by the ladder. "I'm coming too. I need the toilet and some fresh air. Are you coming, grandmother?"

Bernadette put down her knitting. "Oh, I suppose so. It would be good to see daylight."

Lottie already had the hatch open to the upper cellar and drew a deep breath of fresh air. "Oh, that tastes nice." She filled her lungs with hungry breaths as she made her way up to the ground floor.

They all stood together in the kitchen, listening.

"It's much quieter. Just distant rumbles. I'm going outside." The other two women didn't try to prevent her.

"The rain has stopped and the wind has died down." Lottie stood, hesitating in the doorway.

Bernadette came and stood behind her. "Can you see the animals?"

"No, not one." Lottie peered out. She walked over to the barn. The goats had come back inside and were bleating for food.

"Oh, you poor things. Here, have this hay." Lottie stuffed handfuls of dried grass into their feeding baskets on the wall. The two goats tore hungrily at the fragrant hay. Lottie checked their udders. They were full, but not bursting. She settled down to milk them, talking to them all the time to reassure them. Even when she had finished, she didn't tie them up or shut the door. They must find refuge where they could.

Lottie took the one bucket of milk back inside.

Bernadette looked up from her knitting. "Only one bucket? Are both the goats alright?"

"They seem subdued and nervous and gave less milk, but they've survived."

Bernadette picked up the pail and poured the milk into smaller containers. "I suppose that's all we can hope for. It's so long since they were mated, I'm surprised they're still milking at all. Could be their milk will dry up completely with all the damned noise everywhere."

Lottie nodded. "I think you could be right. It's rotten for them. We can't tell them what all the madness is about. Talking of which, let's find out what is happening out there. I'm going to listen to the radio. There may be new instructions for more sabotage. I know they wanted more cables cut, but I haven't heard from anyone else."

"You're better off staying put, if you ask me." Bernadette returned to her knitting.

Lottie switched the radio set on, but no lively crackles answered her. She fiddled with the knobs and then the plug, but the Bakelite box remained stubbornly silent.

Lottie went to the switch for the electric light. The long days of June meant they hadn't needed to supplement the natural lighting in the big room. She flicked it back and forth several times, but nothing happened.

"That's all we need. Bernadette, we have a power cut."

"Well, I won't miss electricity. We have our candles and lamps and the range. There's plenty of logs left outside and the water is from the well. We'll be alright."

"But don't you see? We won't get an update of the fighting! This is more than annoying. We could be in the firing line and not know until it hits us!"

"If that happens, we'll know alright."

"But we won't be able to get out of the way in time. Damn, damn and damn." Lottie flopped down on to a chair. "I'll have to go to the village and find out."

"You will not!" Bernadette laid her wool and needles aside. "We are going to sit tight right here, all of us. If the fighting gets close, we'll go into the cellar."

"But, Bernadette, we won't know who is winning! There's no guarantee the Allies will win! The Germans might overrun the farm and capture us! We must find out in order to protect ourselves."

Bernadette stood up and put her hands on her hips. "We will all stay here until I judge it's safe to go anywhere. Understood?"

"Oh, do come and listen to the radio, Bella, darling!" Cassandra called out, as she leaned out of the sitting-room window.

"Why, what's happened, Mummy?" Isobel looked up from cutting flowers. Her morning sickness had stopped, quite suddenly, a week ago and she now felt reborn with enough energy to do all the things she used to take for granted, like gardening and smiling.

"It's quite thrilling. Listen. D-Day has come at last! I think they landed in France this morning."

"I'll just put these flowers in water."

"Do hurry!"

Isobel ran into the kitchen and shoved the blooms into a jug of water and ran back to the little parlour. To be able to run again at all was enough of a thrill for her but she sat down and concentrated on the announcer's words.

"Who is he quoting?"

"General Eisenhower, you know, the Supreme Commander of SHAEF. He doesn't mince his words, does he?"

Isobel focussed on the words coming through the mesh of the radio.

"...Your task will not be an easy one. The enemy is well-trained, well-equipped and battle-hardened. He will fight savagely. But this is the year 1944..."

Distracted by this announcement about the date, Isobel thought how strange it was that in this year, 1944, her baby would be born, but into what kind of a world?

"...Good luck, and let us all beseech the blessing of Almighty God upon this great and noble undertaking..."

346

"Oh, this is giving me the shivers." Cassandra pulled her cardigan closely around her frame.

"I hope the ATA isn't involved on the front line." Isobel bit her lip.

"Listen, he says His Majesty, the King, will speak tonight at nine o'clock. We must listen in to that. I'll make sure Malcolm is here, I mean, Dr Harris."

"I know who you mean, Mummy."

"They say the fighting is around Caen."

"Whereabouts is that?"

"In Normandy, along the northern coast."

"North of Paris?"

"Thinking of Lottie?"

Isobel nodded. "I'm so worried for her."

"Oh, darling, don't. I can't bear not knowing where she is."

Isobel returned to listening to the broadcast, which seemed to be mostly addressed to Frenchmen and women who might want to join in, but Eisenhower seemed to want them to wait.

"How can the French people do nothing when they are being bombarded? It must be dreadful to be in the path of this massive invasion, don't you think?" Cassandra sat hunched forward on her chair.

"...I call upon all people who love freedom to stand with us. Keep your faith staunch. Our arms are resolute. Together, we shall achieve victory..."

The rest of the bulletin was a list of those countries who would hear it in their own language. When it had ended, Cassandra switched off the wireless and turned to her daughter. "So, it has begun at last."

"Yes, and I wish I knew what Al was up to today."

"Hmm, but he would have said, wouldn't he, if he was going to France?"

347

"Might be sworn to secrecy."

"Ah yes, of course. Well, it's pretty obvious all those American boys are now in France. There's none left here, and the countryside was swarming with them only a few weeks ago. I can't say I miss their noisy ways and all those army vehicles on the road. I think I'll go down to the Katherine Wheel Garage and see Katy after lunch. Want to come?"

"It would be interesting to find out if she knows more about it."

They drove down in the old Sunbeam that afternoon and found Katy and Jem, to their astonishment, sitting on deck chairs in their garden with their feet up.

"Goodness! I never thought I'd ever find you two slacking!" Cassandra kissed her friends. "No, no, don't get up, my dears, it's good to see you relaxing for once. I feel I ought to take a photograph to preserve the memory. It's unprecedented!"

Katy laughed. "We've been working non-stop for weeks, but the last shipment went yesterday and we're taking a breather. Have you heard about the Normandy landings?"

"Yes, we listened to it on the midday news. Exciting, isn't it?"

Jem cleared his throat. "Not if you know someone who's part of the invasion. I wouldn't fancy getting out of them boats into a hail of gunfire."

"Oh, Uncle Jem, I mean, father-in-law, you don't think the ATA is involved, do you?"

Jem shook his head. "Let's stick with Uncle Jem, shall we? No, I should think it's only the RAF. They'll be sending bombers in ahead to soften up the Germans, I dare say. Poor buggers."

Katy got up from her low-slung seat. "Who do you mean? Not the blasted Germans! If it wasn't for those bastards, you would have two arms and our son wouldn't be in danger. I spare them no sympathy."

348

"No, I didn't mean them," Jem replied in his mild way. "It's the French I feel sorry for. Must be awful to get in the way of two armies coming at you from either side, and you caught in the middle."

Isobel looked at her mother, who had gone very pale. "Are you alright, Mummy?"

Cassandra gave her an unconvincing smile. "I'm fine. I just felt funny for a moment. Sort of cold and shivery. Maybe I'm coming down with something."

Immediately, Jem went to her. "Sit down, Cass. I'll put the kettle on." He disappeared inside the bungalow.

Katy turned to Isobel. "We've been neglecting you, dear. Here, you take Jem's seat. How are you, anyway?"

"Much better, thanks."

"That is good news! No more sickness in the mornings?"

Isobel shook her head. "No, thank goodness. Actually, I'm feeling rather wonderful now, except when I think about your son and what he might be getting up to."

Katy patted her hand. "He'll be fine, I know it. A mother always knows if her child's in danger, isn't that right, Cass?"

Cassandra looked back at them both, but she didn't smile back.

349

CHAPTER FORTY-SEVEN
NORMANDY, FRANCE
JUNE 1944

Lottie lay on her improvised bed on the cellar floor, listening to the intimate sounds of the other occupants' breathing through the more distant sounds of warfare. She couldn't sleep through the afternoon again. She tossed and turned on the lumpy mattress, imagining where the fighting was taking place, wondering whose aeroplanes were overhead. She'd rather get up and watch than lie here speculating but opening the hatch was noisy, and she had promised her hostess to stay put. After all that Bernadette had done for her, she felt she must obey her command. Bernadette might be a tough old bird but being surrounded by all this massive firepower was too much for her. Two days of it now.

Eventually Lottie slept. When she awoke, the lamp had run out of oil and the cellar had plunged into total darkness. She had no idea what time it was as she couldn't see her watch-face. Lottie scrabbled about on the floor feeling for the candles and matches she'd left beside her for this very reason. Even striking a match was hard in the utter blackness but she managed it in the end. The glow of the candle flame gave a welcome blessed light into the small space. There was no draught to make it flicker. Upright it burned, illuminating the sleeping forms of her companions. She looked across at Françoise who lay in a foetal position, her son curled up within the curve of her body, as if he was still inside her womb. Bernadette lay facing away from her, towards her granddaughter, one hand under her cheek, its wrinkles less pronounced in sleep. Although they looked peaceful, Lottie could hear renewed sounds of battle way above them. She could no longer resist having a look.

Lottie tiptoed to the bottom of the ladder. She put the lighted candle on the small table against the dirt wall and mounted the steps. She eased the hatch open, wincing as it creaked on its hinges. When she looked back, she saw Bernadette stirred in her sleep but didn't wake. Lottie swung the hatch door wide and let it rest against the upper cellar floor. She quickly mounted the stone steps up to the kitchen, pulled on her boots and quietly opened the back door.

The sun was setting in the west, blood-red and angry as if in protest against all the killing it had witnessed. There was no cannon-fire booming along the coast now, but she could hear other mortars detonating in the near distance, closer than yesterday's blasts. It seemed to be coming from the Caen direction.

She could feel the impact of explosions through her feet. What if the battle came to the farm? Would the cellar really be enough to shield them? She went across to the barn but there was no sign of the goats this time. Was this how it had felt in London during the Blitz? How cavalier she had been back in 1940 about the people she had left behind, how differently she felt now.

A lone aeroplane droned overhead, and she looked up to see the circular insignia of the RAF on its fuselage. Her heart lurched. A British pilot was flying that plane! She waved, not caring he wouldn't see her in the twilight. As if in answer, white squares fluttered out of the belly of the aircraft and spiralled down like giant snowflakes. The wind blew them all over the place, but Lottie managed to catch one.

"I've got it! I've got it! Thank you!" She waved again to the plane, now receding towards Caen where it met ack-ack fire lancing upwards in brilliant white streaks from the city.

"You bastards! Leave them alone! They're not bombing you, this is a leaflet!" She watched the small plane until she couldn't see it anymore, dreading that its dark silhouette might turn into a ball of fire. Then she looked at the paper in her hand.

351

It was too dark to read it. She went inside the kitchen and lit an oil lamp. By its yellow glow, she read the first paragraph.

"People of Western Europe: A landing was made this morning on the coast of France by troops of the Allied Expeditionary Force. This landing is part of the concerted United Nations plan for the liberation of Europe, made in conjunction with our great Russian allies."

"But it wasn't today, it was yesterday." She said the words out loud, unthinking.

In the doorway, Bernadette stood, rubbing her eyes. "What's that?"

Lottie scanned the page. "It's from General Eisenhower."

"Who the hell is he?"

Lottie stabbed a finger at the page. "He, Bernadette, is the Supreme Commander of all the Allies!"

"Humph. What's he got to say for himself?"

"I'll read it out to you." Lottie cleared her throat and read from the pamphlet.

"I have this message for all of you. Although the initial assault may not have been made in your own country, the hour of your liberation is approaching.

All patriots, men and women, young and old, have a part to play in the achievement of final victory. To members of resistance movements, I say, follow the instructions you have received. To patriots who are not members of organized resistance groups, I say, continue your passive resistance, but do not needlessly endanger your lives until I give you the signal to rise and strike the enemy. The day will come when I shall need your united strength. Until that day, I call on you for the hard task of discipline and restraint."

Bernadette broke in. "You see! Even this commander fellow is saying to stay put!"

Lottie scowled but read on.

"Citizens of France! I am proud to have again under my command the gallant Forces of France. Fighting beside their Allies, they will play a worthy part in the liberation of their Homeland."

Bernadette nodded approval at this. "So, we have French soldiers fighting on home soil again. That is good. Let's hope they don't die in the attempt."

Lottie continued, *"Because the initial landing has been made on the soil of your country, I repeat to you with even greater emphasis my message to the peoples of other occupied countries in Western Europe. Follow the instructions of your leaders. A premature uprising of all Frenchmen may prevent you from being of maximum help to your country in the critical hour. Be patient. Prepare!"*

Once again Bernadette interrupted. "Hah! Just what I thought!"

"Bernadette, I'll never finish it if you keep butting in."

Bernadette waved her hand at Lottie to carry on.

"As Supreme Commander of the Allied Expeditionary Force, there is imposed on me the duty and responsibility of taking all measures necessary to the prosecution of the war. Prompt and willing obedience to the orders that I shall issue is essential.

Effective civil administration of France must be provided by Frenchmen. All persons must continue in their present duties unless otherwise instructed. Those who have made common cause with the enemy and so betrayed their country will be removed. As France is liberated from her oppressors, you yourselves will choose your representatives, and the government under which you wish to live."

Bernadette nodded vigorously when she heard this but didn't comment. Lottie smiled and carried on.

"In the course of this campaign for the final defeat of the enemy you may sustain further loss and damage. Tragic though they may be, they are part of the price of victory. I assure you that I shall do all in my power to mitigate your hardships. I know that I can count on your steadfastness now, no less than in the past. The heroic deeds of Frenchmen who have continued the struggle against the Nazis and their Vichy satellites, in France and throughout the French Empire, have been an example and an inspiration to all of us.

This landing is but the opening phase of the campaign in Western Europe. Great battles lie ahead. I call upon all who love freedom to stand with us. Keep your faith staunch – our arms are resolute – together we shall achieve victory."

"Is that it?"

Lottie nodded and looked up from the page.

Bernadette had tears in her eyes. "I like this man. He is very wise to say France must be governed by her own people. So, we've inspired him, have we? Eh, it's not been easy, that's true."

Lottie broke the protocol that had existed in Le Verger for the best part of four years and wrapped her arms around Bernadette. The older woman hugged her back, not for long perhaps but with real affection.

They both had to wipe their eyes afterwards.

In the days that followed, Lottie often grumbled about her imprisonment and every time Bernadette referred her back to General Eisenhower's instructions to stay put until commanded to do otherwise. Battles raged to the north-west of them in the direction of both Caen and the aerodrome. Lottie fretted and fumed within the confines of the farm and, though grateful for its refuge, she came to loathe the lower cellar and the absolute darkness. The oil for the lamp was running low and so were the candles, so they restricted themselves to only one type of illumination at a time. The fumes from the lamp made the small space even stuffier and Lottie's eyes run.

And all the time she thought of Thierry. Was he in the thick of it? He must be. Every day she prayed he would survive but listening to the onslaught made the pit of her stomach go icy cold for fear he wouldn't.

For two long weeks the battles raged all around the farm. Sometimes closer, sometimes terrifyingly close. Lottie ventured out during a lull caused by bad weather one morning around the third week of June. A big storm had brewed up and even in the cellar, they could tell that the guns had stopped.

"Is the war over, Grandmère?" Françoise sat up in bed.

"The guns have ceased blasting us to kingdom come, it's true."

"I'll go and have a scout around. Get out of this dungeon for a few minutes." Lottie needed little encouragement to escape the claustrophobia of the crowded cellar.

Outside the rain lashed her face and she gloried in the water, washing off the fustiness of the last week. The wind whipped her hair around her head. Lottie spread her arms wide to the gale and embraced it willingly. Anything was better than being imprisoned under the heavy earth.

For once, there was no mortar detonating in the distance, no aeroplanes releasing killing bombs above her. She stood in the elemental weather until she was soaked through, opening her mouth and swallowing the raindrops.

The storm lasted two days. Two blissful days without the sound of explosions.

Lottie slept well that second night, they all did. Refreshed, she couldn't resist the impulse to check outside again the next morning and had mixed feelings when she found the sun had come blazing out. Would that mean the bombs would fall again? Everything had that just-rinsed look, as if it was spring, but the midsummer rays shone hot and dazzling and quickly dried the full-blown foliage.

She ran towards the orchard, just for the hell of it, and there she found the goats. Both dead, flies buzzing around their carcasses, they lay at the far end of the orchard. The trees around them had also been blasted and lay in fragments around the corpses of the two animals. Smoke billowed in the distance in the direction of their village. Shocked and dazed, Lottie wandered out of the orchard eastwards, towards Caen. She walked across one field only to stop, dead in her tracks, as she gazed into an enormous crater carved out of the rich Normandy soil by a stray bomb. She stood there, dizzy with vertigo, as she looked down into the depths of the vast hole. Another explosion rent the air. It sounded nearer than ever. It startled her from her daze, and she turned and sprinted back towards the farm. Before she even reached the orchard, the sky ripped open above her. Lottie paused, looked up, and saw two planes, one RAF, one Luftwaffe, in close battle firing frantically at each other. She could see the flash from the fusillade issuing from their guns as they tried to kill each other.

Lottie began to run again, following the duel above her. She was almost in the orchard now, she could see the mounds of the poor goats' bodies, together in death as they were in life. She looked up again as a tremendous boom sounded above her. One of the aeroplanes, she couldn't see which, had burst into flames. It was further away now, hurtling back towards the coast. The terrible machine guns of the planes had ceased their deadly spray. The burning, broken body of the plane exploded in mid-air and fell to earth in a blaze of fire and shrapnel. No-one had jumped out. There couldn't have been time.

She stumbled past the goats, swatting the flies that flew up in her face after she'd disturbed their feeding orgy, and half-ran, half-walked back to the house. As she passed the barn, she saw that the windows on the west side of the farmhouse had all shattered. Lottie looked up at the roof. The top half of the chimney had gone, and tiles slithered down to the gutters, as if the house was crying.

She made it back inside the kitchen and went to the sink to wash her hot face, but the bucket was dry. She picked it up and went to the well outside to fill it. As she lowered the bucket into the cool water, she heard a loud rumbling noise from the road. Lottie climbed up on to the circular wall of the well so she could look over the hedge. She saw the sinister shaft of a tank gun protruding above the hedgerow, and another behind it, but from here she had no idea if they were German or friendly.

Frantically, she pulled up the bucket of water and ran back to the house with it trying, but failing, not to spill any.

She shut the kitchen door fast and bolted it on the inside before clattering down the steps and then the ladder back to the safety of the cellar.

"Where have you been? What's happened? Is the house hit?" Bernadette took the pail of water from her shaking hands.

Lottie spoke between gasps. "Terrible air fight. Plane came down in a ball of fire. Tanks on the road outside. Don't know if they're German or Allies."

"Come, sit down."

Lottie did as she was told and laid down on her bed. "I'll never complain about this cellar again. It's hell up there and I heard machine-guns really close-by."

"Then don't go!" Bernadette ladled some water into a mug and gave it to her.

"And what would we do without water, tell me that!" Lottie drunk it down in one go. She'd never been so thirsty.

Françoise sat up on her mattress. "Thank you for being so brave, Lottie. Bertrand is thirsty too." She got up and dipped the little boy's mug into the cool water and he drank it down so greedily, it dripped off his chin.

Refreshed from her drink, Lottie turned to Bernadette. "Bad news, I'm afraid. Both the nanny goats are dead. Looks like machine gun fire or something got them. They are at the far end of the orchard and some of the apple trees are felled too. There's a bomb crater in the field towards Lucien's patch."

Bernadette wrung her hands together. "Oh, my poor goats. They do not deserve this slaughter."

That night the bombardment got louder and closer. "Sounds like they're in the village itself." Françoise cuddled Bertrand to her while he slept.

"What was that? Are we hit again?" Bernadette clutched her pillow to her chest.

Bertrand moaned in his sleep. "It's alright, little one. Just a dream." Françoise curled her body around her son protectively.

A huge boom made the whole house shake. There was the sound of broken glass immediately afterwards.

"Ow, that hurt my ears." Lottie flattened herself against the dirt wall. "Cover yourselves in your blankets. We must be in the direct line of fire."

Bertrand woke up as another massive crash shook the building. "Maman! I'm scared!"

Instinctively the three women huddled around the little boy.

"Pad your backs with pillows." Lottie grabbed hers and shielded Françoise's back with it.

They held hands as another shell crashed above them.

358

"That was a direct hit. I think it must have knocked the chimney right out this time. You can hear the bricks crashing down through it." Lottie nodded upwards to the centre of the house in line with the fireplace above them.

"My poor house." Bernadette muttered.

"Thank God for this cellar. Your beautiful house is protecting us, Bernadette. We'll put it back together again when this is all over." Lottie squeezed Bernadette's bony hand.

"Thank God I had the thatch removed and replaced with slate or we'd be burned alive."

"The rafters could still burn though, couldn't they?" Françoise whispered above Bertrand's head.

Bernadette grunted. "If they burn my house down, I will kill them."

Lottie chuckled, despite her fear. "I think you might have the disadvantage when it comes to modern warfare. That tank I saw looked as big as your washhouse."

"Was it only one?"

"No, from the sound of it, there were loads of them." Lottie wriggled away from Bertrand's sharp little elbow. It had been digging into her ribs.

"Make it stop, Maman."

"It will, little man, it will."

"Make it stop now!" Bertrand began to whimper.

Lottie could think of nothing more she could say to reassure the little boy. She was terrified herself. The noise continued unabated for a full half an hour and then there was the sound of terrific engine noise.

"The tanks must be driving through the farm itself!"

"Oh my God!" Bernadette looked distraught.

"They won't crush the house, they can't, Grandmère." Françoise gripped her grandmother's thin arms.

The rumbling continued, louder than ever. Lottie held her breath, waiting for the walls to crumble but they only shook. She imagined every stone, every brick rattling

359

in its plaster blanket like a loose tooth. The women held each other tight, Bertrand, in the middle of them all, still crying.

"Listen! They're going! It's getting fainter." Lottie held one finger up.

The women broke apart and sat up. "You're right. I'm going to see what they've done to my house."

"Not yet, Bernadette. It's not safe. You must wait at least an hour."

"An hour? I'm not leaving it that long. They can shoot me if they like, but I'm going up."

"Wait, please. Fifteen minutes?"

A quarter of an hour passed painfully slowly but it wasn't interrupted by more shelling. Lottie looked at her watch in the dim candlelight. "Alright. I'll come with you. Françoise, you stay here with Bertrand."

Françoise nodded. "Don't be long. Be careful."

Up in the kitchen Bernadette stood in the clouds of dust swirling around the big room, her hand over her mouth as she surveyed the damage. Lottie put her arm around her shoulders and found they were shaking.

"What have they done? My house! What have they done?"

For the first time since Lottie had met her, she saw Bernadette break down into tears. Dry, harsh sobs. Lottie looked around the room for a chair that wasn't broken. The settle was still intact by the range, now covered in chimney bricks, and she drew the older woman to it and sat her down. Bernadette lowered her face into her hands and gave way.

Lottie could find no words to ease her pain. The kitchen was devastated. All the glass in the windows had smashed and fallen into shards. The corner of the house had been knocked clean away, exposing it to the air. Motes of dust escaped through the cavity as if it had taken over the chimney's role, great clouds of brick and mortar dust, thick and white, spiralled outside. One of the ancient timbers creaked on its axis, like a broken bone, stuck out awkwardly

360

in the wrong place, dangling uselessly away from the wall it had supported for hundreds of years. The bricks above it shifted ominously. Lottie grabbed a broom and a stout chair and shoved them, with the ironing board on top, under the crumbling plaster where the timber should have been. The bricks above settled on to the flat surface, obscuring the gaudy cotton flowers of the ironing board cover with red dust. She stood back, wondering if it would give way but, miraculously, it held.

Bernadette spoke in a dry, cracked voice. "Do you know how old this place is?"

Lottie turned back to Bernadette and shook her head.

"Five hundred years. Five hundred years! And they destroyed it in five minutes."

"It's not completely gone, Bernadette. It can be mended. We can fix this."

"Not me, this has done for me. I haven't the heart for it."

"You're in shock. You'll recover and so will Le Verger."

In the distance, Lottie heard many more aeroplanes flying westwards. Shortly afterwards she heard more bombs falling on Caen, on other houses and people like them. Lottie wondered if they had cellars; if there was anyone still alive in that beleaguered, beautiful city.

Then she heard machine gun fire coming from the direction of the village. Staccato and in regular bursts it tore through the night air and chilled her very bones.

Bernadette sighed and laid her head on Lottie's shoulder. Lottie looked down on Bernadette's lined face and saw something she never thought she'd find there. Bernadette looked utterly defeated.

Françoise stood up and stretched, then yelped in pain as she bashed her hands on the low ceiling of the cellar. "How long must we endure this, Grandmère? It's been weeks. I can't stand it much longer."

"I have no answer for you, chérie."

Lottie looked across at Bernadette, who had taken to her bed for most of the time since the house had been struck. She was clutching at her chest and her face was screwed up into a grimace.

"Bernadette? Are you alright?"

Bernadette's eyes flew open and she glared back at Lottie. "I'm fine. Why shouldn't I be?"

"Sorry, it's just…"

"It's nothing. Leave it." Bernadette got up and went to the barrel where they kept the food. "There's not much left. We must go and get vegetables, make soup. The child is looking thin."

"I'll go and look in the garden." Françoise stood up. "Come with me, Charlotte?"

"Of course." Lottie was gagging for fresh air and was even prepared to face bombardment for it.

The two girls went upstairs. Françoise had only been out for quick trips to the outside toilet at night after Bertrand had soiled the slop bucket. She never let the little boy go with her. Now, she stood in the doorway, her pretty mouth hanging open, and slumped against the doorframe.

"I wouldn't put all your weight on that, if I were you, Françoise."

"Are you trying to be funny?"

"Sadly, no." Lottie collapsed onto the dusty settle. "God, I'm so tired. What wouldn't I give for a bath; I stink."

"Charlotte, the barn's gone."

"What do you mean, gone?"

"Flattened. Obliterated. Gone."

Wearily, Lottie got up and joined her. "That is close. Could happen to the house."

"Will we be alright in the cellar, do you think, if it does?"

Lottie ran her hand across her forehead. She'd had a headache for days. "Hope so, don't know. Too tired to even care." Another round of cannon sounded in the distance. "Come on, let's see if we can salvage something from the garden. I'm so hungry, I could eat some of your famous snails."

They walked quickly over to the vegetable patch. Most of it was churned up and splattered with debris from the house and barn but Françoise found a patch of courgettes scrambling madly along the ground in happy abandon. "Look, there are loads of these."

"Here, take this basket." Lottie had found some red currants, sparse in number, but gloriously, defiantly ruby-coloured, the sunshine making them glow like the jewels in Granny's tiara. Lottie wondered absentmindedly what had happened to the money she'd put in the bank in Paris when she'd sold it. She sighed; it was too much effort to re-imagine the ordered world she had inhabited then. Her stomach rumbled, prompting her to focus on the task in hand. She picked up the colander she had brought and quickly plucked what was left on the bush.

"Onions! I never thought I'd crave one, but I do." Françoise brandished the aromatic globe above her head by its green hollow stalks.

"And I've found some broad beans, most of them are ruined but there are a few pods." Lottie looked up at the sky. "Damn it, bombers again. Come on, this will have to do."

They ran back into the house. "I'll get some water." Françoise grabbed the pail and went back outside to the well in the yard.

363

More cannon exploded, nearer this time. Lottie went to the pantry door and wrenched it open. It came away in her hand, the hinges broken. She grabbed a tea towel and made it into a bag shape, holding the four corners together. Randomly she took some jars of jam and pickled eggs and threw them into the makeshift carrier. Another explosion rattled the shelves and dust rose, making her cough.

"Charlotte, we must hurry!" Françoise stood there, bucket of water in one hand and the basket of vegetables in the other.

"But we need to cook the vegetables!"

"Not now, not now! And what on, anyway? The range is buried under bricks. Come on!"

Lottie followed her down the stairs and back into the cellar. "Close the hatch, the shelling sounds nearby again."

Françoise handed her cargo to Bernadette and pulled the trap door shut. The house shuddered.

"Was that a direct hit?"

"Don't know, could be."

Bernadette frowned. "Is that all you've got?"

"Not much there, Grandmère." Françoise put the basket down. "I'm afraid the barn is flattened."

"Flattened? What do you mean?"

"It's just rubble."

Bernadette sat down heavily on one of the hard chairs. Her hand went to her chest again in a fist.

"Are you alright, Grandmère?"

"Don't fuss over me, Françoise. I hate being fussed over. Give your child some food and leave me in peace."

Françoise exchanged a meaningful glance with Lottie. "So, Bertrand, look what lovely vegetables we have. See? You can eat courgettes raw, like in a salad. It's delicious."

"Want real food."

"I know, sweetheart, but we can have fun making up new recipes, can't we?" Lottie scooped him up and sat him

364

on her knee. Bertrand was pale, his eyes deeply shadowed underneath their dark pupils. He looked thin and frightened. Lottie hugged him.

There was a whining noise from above them, loud and swift but no impact followed, even though Lottie had tensed ready for it. "Missed!" She laughed, shaking her hand in the air.

"Have we a grater down here?" Françoise smiled at her son.

"Yes, there, look." Lottie pointed.

Françoise found a board and started to grate the courgette and then the onion. "You pod some beans, Charlotte, and we'll make a salad with some pickled eggs."

"I want bread, Maman."

"So do I, Bertrand, but we'll have to make do with this."

The unusual salad was dominated by the strong onion and made Lottie's eyes water. Bertrand spat out his first mouthful and refused point blank to eat any more.

Françoise blinked away tears. "Does anyone mind if I give him the last piece of cheese?"

Both Bernadette and Lottie shook their heads.

Lottie picked up one of the jars of jam. "Have this with it. It's strawberry, your favourite."

Bertrand gave her a smile, his first for days. Lottie opened the jar and dipped in a teaspoon. Bertrand opened his mouth wide.

That night the bombardment was worse than ever. Lottie lay on her bed, feeling the ground around her trembling. Her stomach grumbled from the raw onion. This time there was no let-up in the explosive fight above ground. Only Bertrand slept through it.

"What time is it, Charlotte?" Françoise whispered over the sleeping form of her son.

Lottie squinted at her watch. "About half past eight."

"Is it night or morning?"

"I'm not actually sure. I'll pop up to the kitchen and have a look."

"Oh, don't, please don't. It's worse than ever."

"I must. I've got to know if it's day or night. I'm no longer sure of the date but I want to know when I should sleep."

"For God's sake, child, does it matter?" Bernadette looked more tired than cross.

"Yes, yes it does." Lottie climbed up the ladder and then the stairs. She slipped her clogs on, left by the door in the shoe rack. In the evening light, she could see that all the windows had shattered now. It was a wonder the house was still standing at all.

There was a terrific droning noise. Not bombs. This was the sound of many engines thrumming through the air, steady and consistent. She opened the door and looked up at the sky. Squadrons of bombers flew above her against the dimming light. The sun was already firmly in the west at this time of the evening. Not yet dark, she could see the aeroplanes clearly, as its beams gilded their fuselage and showed her they were all Allied planes. They came in at an angle, flying in close formation, with no gaps; just following each other in wave upon wave. There must have been a thousand or more, heading for Caen, or what was left of it. On and on they flew, blotting out the waning sunlight, making it seem like night had already fallen. And it had, not in a nocturne, but in a dense swarm of killing machines, the worst kind of storm cloud. Lottie quailed at the sheer volume of bombs they must be carrying to that doomed city. She stood there, transfixed, as they carried on through fireballs of shells thrown up at them, streaks of red reaching up to hit them before falling back in black plumes. But the bombers kept coming, remorseless, relentless, not pausing or checking their flight as if they were merely passing through a firework display. On and on they came in their hundreds.

And then came a blast from those huge cannons from the coast, just like on the very first day. What could have such majestic firepower? Was it the Germans own guns turning on them? Had the Germans held the Atlantic Wall after all? Or could it be the Allied naval boats? Could ships deliver such astonishing weaponry? Lottie stood witnessing the spectacle in a sort of dreadful awe, but then the ground began to shake under her as the bombers released their deadly shells. Even from here, she could smell the smoke from the huge pall of fire that hung over the city, like a hellish orange fog.

Some bombs fell nearer – were they targeting the aerodrome again? A shell whistled between the far end of the orchard and the woods. Lottie could see the trajectory of its lethal flame. Too close to home. She turned and fled downstairs and put her pillow over her head.

When Bernadette and Françoise questioned her, she lifted her muffle briefly. "It's too awful. Caen is on fire. It's hell."

"I simply can't stand it anymore." Françoise lay back on her bed, her arms flung up above her head, her hands over her ears and her eyes staring at the dirty brown ceiling.

Lottie scrubbed her face with her dirty hands. "I know how you feel. It's unbearable."

"It's been non-stop for two whole days, Charlotte. How can there be that many bombs in the world? You'd think they'd used them all up in the previous weeks."

"I'm hungry, Maman."

"I know you are, Bertrand, we all are." Françoise turned to her grandmother. "Is there anything left at all?"

Bernadette shook her head. "Not down here. Only the vegetables in the garden."

The house shook again. "If only we could sleep." Lottie's headache had worsened over the last thirty-six hours of continuous bombardment. Sometimes it sounded so close she thought they would be blown to smithereens but in fact they had not been hit again, as far as she knew. Even she had not dared surface from the cellar to find out.

Bernadette rummaged in their meagre food store. "There's a jar of apricot jam and some walnuts here."

Françoise took them. "Look, Bertrand. You love apricot jam."

Lottie passed her the food. "I'll shell the walnuts for him but what we really need is water."

"And lamp oil. I've turned it as low as I can, but we haven't enough for another night." Bernadette lifted up the can of oil and shook it.

"We have candles, don't we?" Lottie felt alarmed at this development. She didn't think she could stand being in the dank cellar in the pitch black without any light.

"There are five left."

368

"But each one only lasts about three hours."

"That's right." Bernadette turned the lamp down further until it spluttered on the lowest flame.

"Oh, don't let it go out completely, Grandmère!"

Bernadette turned the knob up a fraction and the lamp glowed slightly brighter, but the shadows still slunk around the corners of the earth walls.

They fell silent. There was nothing to say and it was hard to talk above the din outside. It was too dark to read to Bertrand or the others, as Lottie had done for hours at a time when the lamp had burned brighter.

Still the crump and thud of artillery vibrated the deep earth around them. Lottie wondered if this was how it felt to be buried in a coffin but then no graveyard would be pounded by mortars and bombs. How did the worms feel about all of this? Were the chickens and rabbits still alive? At least the rabbits could dig a hole and burrow down. Hens roosted up in the branches of trees; were there any left in the woods? The orchard had been decimated already.

Lottie slept. It was the only escape. When she woke, her watch had stopped. She'd forgotten to wind it. It was impossible to stay aware of the diurnal pattern. Maybe it was morning. She lay on the damp mattress. The air was foetid and close. The smell from the slop bucket pervaded most other sensations, even with its lid on and shoved as far in the corner as she could put it. None of them had dared leave the cellar to relieve themselves under the deluge of firepower raging above them. And yet, was it quieter? She sat up in bed to hear better. There were some sporadic explosions but was she imagining they were further away? Was it just wishful thinking?

Her mouth was dry and sore from lack of water, but she licked her lips and tried to concentrate. Her head still thumped but her ears could not detect the normal background noise of incessant artillery. She would get up; she must!

Françoise lay in the middle bed next to her and, as if sensing Lottie's gaze, opened her eyes. "What is it?" She whispered.

"Listen!"

"I can't hear anything."

"Exactly! Françoise, I think it's stopped!"

Bernadette stirred and turned over to look at them. "What's that?"

"They've stopped the bombing. I'm going up." Before they could counsel caution, Lottie was on the ladder and swinging the trap door wide open. "Ah, the air is so sweet up here!"

"I'm coming too!" Françoise poked her head up into the top cellar and inhaled.

"It really is quiet! Can it be over at last?" Lottie stretched her cramped limbs and made for the stone steps up to the kitchen.

Even there, she could hear no bombardment except in the far distance. She called back to Bernadette. "Come up and bring Bertrand. The air outdoors is wonderful!" Lottie grabbed the water bucket and went outside to the well. She lowered the pail and brought up fresh water.

"Bring mugs. Bring four. We must drink!"

Françoise came over with her son and they each drank a great draught of cool, clear water.

"I have never tasted anything so delicious and I doubt I ever will." Lottie lowered the bucket again to refill it.

"My farm, my beautiful farm." Bernadette looked around at the devastation.

"It's no worse than before, though." Lottie put her arm around the older woman. "A few more trees have copped it in the orchard, but the house has only lost that one corner and the chimney. Actually, quite a lot of the roof has gone too, now I look at it. But Bernadette, it could have been so much worse. Your house could have been blown to bits just like the barn. It can be fixed."

"How? By whom? You?" Bernadette turned and went back inside.

"Poor Grandmère. She's in a state of shock. We saw it before, but she's been inside mostly, and I don't think she's seen the barn in daylight."

"I know, but she did see the kitchen earlier. It isn't much worse, like I said, but she loves this place."

"Yes, it's her life."

"No, *you* are her life, Françoise. You and little Bertrand. Never forget that. Houses can be rebuilt. Barns, too. The most important thing is that we are all alive and soon, Bernadette will realise this."

There was a crash from inside the house. Lottie ran into the kitchen and found Bernadette collapsed on the rubble-strewn floor. She crouched by her side and felt for a pulse. Bernadette was blue around the lips and her skin felt cold and clammy.

Françoise joined her, holding Bertrand's hand. The little boy started to cry. "Shush, darling. Oh, Charlotte. What's happened? Is she alright?"

"She's alive. I'm not sure but I think it might be a heart attack. She's been clutching her chest for days as if it's been hurting her. I'm not sure what to do."

"No, neither am I. Grandmère is always the one to look after any illness. Oh, what would she do?"

"Calvados. That's what she gives to people in shock. Get a bottle from the top cellar and bring some water too. Try and find a clean glass or a cup or something, maybe the ones we just drank the water from?"

Françoise dashed off, taking Bertrand by the hand. Lottie got some cushions from the settle and banged the brick dust off them before tucking them under Bernadette's head. She put her ear down to the older woman's chest and listened to her heartbeat, then felt it with the flat of her palm. It was fluttering and irregular. Françoise came back and gave her a mixture of water and Calvados. Lottie held it

371

to Bernadette's lips, propping her head up even more with her arm.

"I'll get a cloth to wipe her face with cool water from the well bucket." Françoise rushed off again.

Lottie managed to get some of the liquid into Bernadette's mouth, but it simply slid out the other side. She remembered the futile attempts she'd made to get *her* grandmother, Lady Smythe, to revive after a heart attack all those years ago, and how utterly she'd failed. Françoise came back and wiped her grandmother's face with the damp cloth.

"Rub her back, Françoise." Lottie's arm was aching, but she pushed Bernadette's limp torso more upright. "Good, now her feet and hands."

Bernadette moaned.

"That's it! She's coming round!" Lottie tipped a tiny amount of the brandy into Bernadette's mouth and this time, she swallowed it. "She's drunk some, Françoise!"

Bertrand squatted next to them, his thumb in his mouth. He took it out for a quick moment. "Will Grandmère get better, Maman?"

"Yes, yes, mon petit chou, I think she will!"

Bertrand replaced his thumb.

They covered her in blankets brought up from the cellar and gradually got Bernadette to take more cognac. After about twenty minutes of hand, feet and back rubbing, soothing words and sips of brandy, Bernadette's eyes fluttered open. She still looked ghastly white, almost grey, but she recognised them.

Lottie relaxed. "Bernadette. Hello. You're going to be alright. I think you might have had a heart attack but you're going to be alright. Really you are." A tear dropped from Lottie's face on to Bernadette's, making a clean streak through the brick dust.

Françoise patted her hand. "Grandmère. We're here. We're all here and we'll look after you. We'll look after the farm too. Don't worry about anything. We'll take care of it all. Just rest."

"Sleepy time, Grandmère," even Bertrand joined in.

Bernadette gave a glimmer of a smile and fell asleep.

"What do we do now, Charlotte?"

"I think sleep's the best thing for her. Let's clean the place up, Françoise. We'll start with making up a bed for her and then clean the sink, get the range working. Try and make things normal again."

Françoise gave Lottie a hug and little Bertrand clamped his arms around her legs.

After a few hours of very hard work, they had transformed the chaotic kitchen. The range was clean, if not yet functional without a chimney, and all the broken furniture had been stacked outside. What was left was brushed, wiped and polished and the floor swept clean of rubble and broken china, glass and bits of plaster and brick. Bernadette slept on one of the mattresses brought up from the cellar and put in a freshly swept corner of the kitchen.

Lottie surveyed the room. "That looks a lot better. God, I'm hungry. Let's see what we can harvest outside."

"What we need is to get the range working again but how can we without a chimney for the smoke?" Françoise joined her outside in the sunshine, with Bertrand trailing behind them.

"No idea, Françoise. I guess we could make some sort of fire outside where the smoke won't matter?"

"Yes, yes of course! Or, what about the washhouse? There's a fireplace in there for heating the laundry water."

"Brilliant!" Lottie kissed Françoise on the forehead. "What an astonishingly good idea! Oh, Françoise, we could make some bread and soup!" Lottie laughed.

"Why are you laughing?"

"I was remembering the first day I came here. It was a sweltering summer's day, just like this one, and

Bernadette made soup and I couldn't believe why she'd done that in the heat! I certainly do now."

They gleaned what they could from the garden and gathered kindling and firewood for the washhouse fire. By evening they were tucking into vegetable soup and chestnut flour flatbreads baked in a frying pan over the comforting flames of the washhouse fireplace.

Just as they were clearing up their meal, Lottie heard footsteps on the lane outside. She froze in the act of washing plates and stared out of the glassless window.

"I think I might have a heart attack myself," she whispered to Françoise, who was stacking the plates in the overhead draining rack.

"What is it?"

"Listen. Those are army boots. We don't know who won that dreadful battle. Could be Nazis."

Instinctively, they crouched below the sink. Françoise gathered Bertrand into her arms.

Lottie looked across at Bernadette, but she was sleeping peacefully on her makeshift bed. "I'm going to look."

"Oh, God, Charlotte, be careful."

Lottie nodded and crept forward on her hands and knees. She peered around the door frame and tried to quell her trembling fear. She saw a solitary soldier walking wearily towards her, limping slightly. He looked exhausted and barely able to put one foot in front of the other. His head was down as if willing his legs to work by looking at them. He was covered in dust and dirt and carried a rifle and rucksack on his back. He looked up and, suddenly, Lottie knew who it was.

She leapt upright and ran to him. "Thierry! Oh, Thierry! You're alive. I can't believe it! You're alive."

He held out his arms and wrapped her up in them. Various bits of his kit dug into her ribs, but she wasn't aware of it. Their mouths searched for each other's and came together in a bruising kiss.

374

"I've found you!" he gasped out.

They hugged fiercely. Lottie felt her breath escaping in the crush of it. She gulped in some air and kissed him again. He held her face in his hands and she gazed into the depths of his blue eyes, behind their glass frames.

"Is it over?" she managed to say.

"Not quite. We've got the airbase, that's all."

"Come in, come in. We have soup."

CHAPTER FIFTY
NORMANDY, FRANCE
JULY 1944

Thierry left behind a packet of aspirins for Bernadette, a bar of chocolate for Françoise and Bertrand and bruised lips for Lottie. She was quite sure she'd had the best of the bargain. He'd stayed barely a quarter of an hour before an army jeep swept up their lane and bundled him back off to his unit.

Lottie watched him go, dazed with delight mixed with longing for him to stay, for the war to be over, to be back in his arms. When even the trail of dust on the lane had settled back on the gravel where it belonged, she'd finally dragged her feet back inside the house.

Stunned, she sat on the settle staring at the empty, scarred range until Françoise found her. "You're lucky, Charlotte."

"How so?"

"At least you know he's alive. I think of Emile every day, you know, but I have no idea where he is or whether he'll come back."

"Had things got that far between you?"

"Oh yes."

"What about David?"

"I see now that was just an infatuation."

"But you have Bertrand."

Françoise looked over at her son, who had found the toy car Emile had whittled for him. He was pretending it was a plane, zooming in the sky and making exploding noises. "Yes, so I shall never regret it. How could I? But with Emile…it's so different."

Lottie stood up. "Then I hope he comes home to you. How's Bernadette?"

"Sleeping still."

"That's good, I think. When she wakes, we must give her one of these aspirins Thierry gave me. He did some training that said they might prevent another heart attack."

"Aren't there doctors with the Allied troops? Maybe one could come and look at her?" Françoise glanced over to where Bernadette lay on the mattress in the corner.

"I think they might be a tad busy. Thierry said there had been bitter fighting over the airbase and many losses. Apparently, they were saved by some RAF Typhoons firing rockets at the German tanks. There was a Panzer division defending it and it was surrounded by bunkers and heavy artillery. He said something about their 'mighty 88 guns', whatever they are."

"I think we know all too well about the heavy guns. We heard them all."

Lottie sighed. "Yes. God knows how many were killed. He said it's all Canadians and Brits hereabouts." She lowered her voice. "There have been some ghastly atrocities. Some Canadian soldiers have been massacred in the woods just outside the village."

"What? In cold blood, do you mean? Why would the Germans *do* that?" Françoise looked shocked.

Lottie shrugged. "Who knows. Violence breeds violence, doesn't it? The Brits are sweeping for mines around the base now. The things people do to each other in war, oh, it makes me despair." Lottie took a deep breath and attempted a smile. "But Thierry came because he wanted us to know that the fighting has moved off from here and we should be able to go to the village for supplies."

"Just the village? Not Caen?"

"No, they haven't conquered the Germans there. That's what he's gone back for. And there's still fighting to the south and west, close-by, so we must be really careful. He said they were mostly Americans further west."

"Does that mean more bombing? I'm not sure I can stand much more of that."

377

"Oh, I know. It's just awful. Thank God we're not in Caen."

Françoise slumped down on to the settle. "There can't be much of it left. I hope its citizens can find refuge somewhere. No-one could survive otherwise."

"Listen, I'll go to the village and see what I can find out. Try and get some food."

"Alright, but Charlotte?"

Lottie looked at her friend with eyebrows raised.

"Have a wash first. You really do stink, you know!"

Lottie, clean and in fresh clothes, mounted her bicycle, thankful it was miraculously unscathed from the bombing damage. The bath in the washhouse, though tepid, had made her feel reborn, that and knowing Thierry was nearby. She couldn't bank on a future with him, she made herself promise that she wouldn't allow too much hope, he still had a lot of fighting ahead. This vow was reinforced as she cycled along the familiar lanes, their hedges burnt away in some places and trees felled, leaving only jagged stumps. American soldiers, looking exhausted and battle-weary, trundled past on tanks and jeeps, their faces breaking into grins when they passed her. There were no German control posts to worry about anymore, but the verges were littered with debris: an over-turned tank, two motorbikes, and a machine gun twisted into uselessness and once, she saw some dead bodies lying in a ditch. German soldiers, their young faces scarred, stained with stale brown blood, eyes staring, their corpses too static, too stiff. Just boys.

Nausea gripped her insides when she passed them. The stench was awful, and a cloud of flies flew up in her face. She almost fell off her bicycle swatting the disgusting creatures away from her eyes and mouth. Within ten minutes she reached the village, or what was left of it.

Lottie screeched to a halt as she turned the final bend and saw the village square. The criss-crossed wooden sides of the bridge had gone but its stone pathway still spanned the river; the walls of Madame Leroy's boulangerie

378

on the other side of the square, Lottie's beloved refuge against the Boche, had been reduced to low, uneven columns. Like jagged teeth, the remaining bricks clung to the earth, their tops reduced to mere rubble in heaps all around it. The house next to it had lost its roof and only its timbers climbed up to the ridiculously blue and sunny sky, naked like a skeleton without flesh. She looked across to the Mairie, surprised to find it relatively intact. She headed for Madame Voclain's house nearby. The front garden was nothing but dust, and its front door stood wide open, hanging drunkenly on its hinges. Lottie wondered if anyone would be inside.

She passed the linden trees, their leaves hanging exhausted and dusty in the heat and noticed two ropes dangling from the stout branches, their ends frayed as if cut with a blunt instrument. Lottie leant her bike against the house - the railings had disappeared under the churned-up soil - and climbed up the steps to Madame Voclain's once immaculate house.

"Coucou! Hello?" Lottie stood at the foot of the stairs, resting her hand on the perfectly curved but dusty newel post. Every door in the elegant hallway had been wrenched from its hinges, just like the front door. One swung in the breeze, creaking like a wheezy pair of bronchitic lungs.

Lottie crunched over the broken plaster covering the beautiful mosaic tiles on the floor into the kitchen, where she had been before. There were no pies on the counter this time. The counter itself had been sliced as if made of pastry; the two halves collapsed down against each other making a 'V' for victory shape. How could all this devastation ever be labelled a 'win'?

Lottie gravitated to the walled garden. Once pretty with organised herb beds and climbing roses, it was hard to see any living plant left. A movement caught her eye and she span around back towards the hallway. Madame Voclain stood in the broken doorway of her salon, smoking a

379

cigarette. She was wearing one of her silk dresses, its fuchsia-pink flowers garish against the drabness of the ever-present pale grey plaster dust.

"Who is there?"

"Madame Voclain? It's Charlotte Perrot, from Le Verger."

"What do you want?"

"I…I heard the village had been secured. I came for supplies." Lottie walked towards the woman.

Madame Voclain gave a harsh laugh. "Supplies of what?"

"I had no idea, Madame, that the village had suffered so much."

"It's virtually levelled. You'll find no supplies here."

"When did all this happen?"

"About a week ago. I don't know. I stayed in the cellar with Odette."

Lottie searched her weary memory. "Odette?"

"Come in here. There's a couple of chairs." Madame nodded at the salon.

Lottie crumped over the debris and joined her.

"Sit down, please. Cigarette?"

Lottie shook her head. "I don't smoke."

Madame took another cigarette from a dented metal box and lit it from her previous one. "Odette is my maid, remember? She has gone back to her mother's house on the other side of the village. You haven't heard about her brother then?"

"Jules Deschamps?"

Madame Voclain drew deeply on her cigarette and retained the smoke. Lottie watched it swirl out of her mouth as she spoke. "Did you not notice the ropes on the linden tree?"

Lottie's skin crawled with dread at what was coming next. "Yes, but…?"

Madame Voclain took another drag. "They hanged him. The villagers. After the battle. When they came back from hiding, crawled out of their cellars, they found him lurking in the butcher's shop."

"With Madame Marchand?"

Madame Voclain nodded, stubbed out her half-smoked cigarette. "They hung her too, you know."

"What?" Lottie couldn't believe what she was hearing. "Why?"

"Said she'd collaborated with him." Madame Voclain shrugged her silken shoulders. "Well, it was true. She and Deschamps were in cahoots all along. People don't forget or forgive something like that. I thought they might get me, but it seems word has got out whose side I've been on all along. Odette ran home before they could catch her, but she's an innocent child. Just naïve. Doesn't have the brains to be devious."

"But Jules?"

"Oh, yes. He had a brain, of sorts. A cunning, conniving one. And absolutely no scruples. He had it coming. Odette hated him, you know. Her own brother." Madame got up and paced around the once lovely room. "Charlotte, where is my son? Have you any idea of his whereabouts?"

Lottie's mind was reeling from what she had just heard. "Emile? No, nothing, I'm sorry. I thought he'd gone to your cousin's in the Auvergne?"

Madame stopped her pacing. "Yes, but I've had no word. He told me he was sweet on your sister."

"My, my sister?" Lottie thought of Isobel. Beautiful, gentle, kind Isobel with the English roses in her delicate cheeks.

"Oh, for goodness' sake! What's her name? Françoise, isn't it? Has some child, hasn't she? Why did he have to fall for a woman like that? Hmm?"

381

Lottie had no answer. Madame Voclain's voice had risen to a high pitch, so unlike her normal composed, deep tone. Lottie let the silence speak for her.

After a few minutes, when Madame turned her back and Lottie saw it heave, Madame Voclain turned around, shoving a fine handkerchief into a cleverly concealed pocket in the seam of her expensive dress. It stayed bulky against her slim outline, ruining the line of perfect pleats into which the skirt was folded.

Lottie looked out of the window at the broken shell of the boulangerie. "Do you know what happened to the prisoners in Caen? To Madame Leroy and the others?"

"No, the Germans are still entrenched in the city. Can't you hear the bombs?"

"Oh yes, we've heard them alright." Lottie stood up. "I'll leave you now, Madame. If I hear anything at all about Emile, I will let you know. Would it be too much to ask that you do the same? Françoise is as desperate for news of him as you are."

"Oh, is she?" Madame turned away again.

Lottie took that as her dismissal.

"Come and sit on the bench under the apple tree, Bernadette." Lottie held out her hand.

"And listen to that pounding? I'd rather stay inside."

"But the sunshine would do you good."

"Sunshine? Huh, never seen so much cloud. Little wonder with all the bombs and smoke and those confounded aeroplanes splitting the skies in two." Bernadette turned her face away and shut her eyes.

Lottie felt nothing but sympathy. Bernadette lay on her day bed, now raised up on some bricks and timbers they had salvaged from the ruins of the barn. It still occupied the same corner of the kitchen so Bernadette could feel part of things. Françoise and Lottie had tried to make the best of it for Bernadette's sake, but the unending sounds of bombardment wore them all down, especially at night.

Lottie gave up trying to tempt Bernadette outside and left her to sleep, which is what she mostly did these days. She found Françoise in the vegetable plot, hoeing the weeds while little Bertrand picked up stones from the debris and popped them, one by one, into his small bucket.

"You are doing a great job there, little man." Lottie picked up a couple of stones and dropped them in his pail.

Bertrand rewarded her with one of his winning smiles. "Heavy."

"Then you'd better go and empty it over there where the barn used to be."

Bertrand dutifully trotted off.

Françoise watched him go, then looked up at her friend. "Couldn't get Grandmère outside then?"

Lottie shrugged. "Don't blame her. It's the incessant planes and cannon fire. It's enough to get anyone down."

"At least they're not targeting the airfield anymore."

383

"But makes you wonder what will be left of Caen. I'd give anything for a quiet night's sleep."

"And some more food. Still, the potatoes are worth harvesting. They're not very big but they should fill us up."

"Oh, lovely. Have we any mint?"

"Listen to the gourmet! There's some by the old henhouse. What we really need is eggs, milk, butter, flour. We can't survive much longer on just vegetables."

"We still have some dried beans, don't we?"

"A little and the apples are nearly ready to pick on the trees that are left."

"I could try in the village again."

"What's the point? From what you told me I can't see they will have any more than us." Françoise returned to scratching the dry dust.

"I'll pick some tomatoes and make something with the courgettes."

When Lottie had enough, she took her basket indoors with some of the potatoes Françoise had dug up.

"You must wash the potatoes more thoroughly than that." Bernadette had sat up to supervise.

Lottie looked round, pleased to see that Bernadette was interested. "I'll get more clean water from the well."

She was pulling up the rope with the full bucket of fresh water when she heard the jeep. Lottie looked down the lane to see Thierry driving towards her, a trail of billowing dust thrown up behind him. Lottie unhooked the pail of water and set it down. She dipped in her fingertips and wetted her hair, which needed a thorough wash, like the rest of her.

Thierry, still in full army battle-dress, leapt out of the jeep and wrapped her in his arms. Neither spoke for a minute or two and Lottie saw Françoise disappear with Bertrand into the farmhouse out of the corner of her eye.

"Come to the bench in the orchard." She took Thierry's hand in hers and lead him to the private spot under the laden apple tree.

384

They sat and kissed again. Lottie wanted to go further; the physical longing almost overwhelmed her but eventually she drew back, gasping for breath. She pressed her hands against his chest and pushed him gently away, but not too far.

"Tell me what's been happening. I went to the village once, but it was virtually flattened. I couldn't recognise some bits. The villagers hung the young Milice policeman and the butcher's wife, Madame Marchand, you know."

"There have been many atrocities. Whole villages have been massacred by the Panzer troops. They're full of Hitler youth fanatics. One Panzer Division massacred a whole bunch of Canadians just up the road from here. I'm surprised you didn't hear it."

"But I did! There was the sound of machine guns rattling through the air one night, terrifyingly close, and I bolted back down to the cellar."

"Thing is, they didn't do it in the heat of battle but in cold blood after they'd captured them. Oh, Charlotte. The things I've seen." Thierry looked away from her and gazed, unseeing, at the orchard.

An apple dropped as if under the weight of this thought and plopped on to the daisy-studded grass.

Lottie had to ask. "Is Caen taken? What about the others – Madame Leroy, Pierre, Lucien...?"

Thierry took a deep breath and gazed deep into her eyes. "Charlotte, my dearest dear. You've not heard then."

Lottie shook her head.

"We didn't find out until July. Some of the prisoners were killed in the Allied bombing on D-Day."

"It's a wonder anyone survived in Caen at all with the thousands of bombs we dropped."

Thierry grimaced. "It's true but when we liberated the city, we found that all the remaining prisoners had been machine gunned in the courtyard."

"Machine gunned? When they were defenceless?"

"It should have been quick but apparently more single shots were heard later so some must have survived and were finished off that evening. Some townspeople heard it all, God help them."

Lottie stood up and tried to quell her sudden nausea. "And the Germans did this?"

"They made the prison guards do it – Russian POW's."

"What?"

"Oh, yes. The Boche destroyed the records themselves though, the cold-blooded cowards. Didn't want to leave a trace. They left the next day."

"And no-one survived? Did they kill the women prisoners too?"

"No-one, I'm sorry. I know you loved Madame Leroy."

A sob escaped Lottie and would not be contained. She turned away, trying to stem the tears.

Thierry's arms stole around her back and he held her quietly. "Pierre was like an uncle to me, you know. He was so clever with cameras. You'd never think it with those big hands he had. And Lucien was a good man. He harboured so many people at his farmhouse – British pilots, Jewish refugees, young men escaping the STO and he got them safely south to the Unoccupied Zone."

"They were heroes."

"Yes."

She turned in his arms and buried her head in the crook of his shoulder. "When will it end?"

"We've made a start, is all I know. You, at least, are a little safer."

"It does seem slightly quieter now, but the cannon fire and aeroplanes never seem to actually stop."

"We've got most of Caen. That's why I'm able to come here. There's fighting in the south now and the Americans are stuck in Falaise, but our victory is inevitable. The Germans don't have replacements like we do, and we have a pipeline for fuel and good food supplies. They are getting weaker and weaker."

"You have food supplies? Oh, Thierry we are so hungry!"

Immediately, Thierry drew out a small bar of chocolate from one of the many pockets in his fatigues. He pulled her back down to sit on the bench. "Here, eat this."

Lottie seized it and snapped off a square. The chocolate melted in her mouth in sweet warm waves.

"How's Bernadette?" Thierry smiled when Lottie closed her eyes to enjoy the chocolate and kissed her sticky mouth.

"I'm giving her one of those aspirins every day and she's accepting it, surprisingly. She sleeps most of the time and doesn't eat much – well, none of us do – but she hasn't had another heart attack, if that's what it was."

"That's good. She ought to see a doctor."

"Lots of things ought to be happening."

Thierry looked across at the ruined barn, or where it used to be. "I know. God, I wish I could stay and help you get this place straight."

"You're going again?"

He nodded. "Plenty of fighting ahead. I don't know when I'll see you again, my darling."

"Oh, Thierry, do you have to go?"

"Yes, I must. I want to finish this. I've been to my parents' house in Caen – the one you were supposed to be visiting when we blew up the train."

"I remember. Seems a lifetime ago."

He kissed her forehead tenderly. "You'll never meet them now."

Lottie watched him swallow painfully. "They've been killed in the bombings?"

Thierry sighed and his shoulders slumped a little. "Yes. Not a brick left of their house. It's just like Bernadette's barn. Rubble. Not a stick of furniture to be seen and no bodies found. A lot of people hid in the crypts

387

under the city or in the quarries at Vaucelles by the railway, but I've checked, and my parents apparently opted to stay home. I met an old neighbour." Thierry's voice gave way.

Lottie held his hands. "I'm so sorry, Thierry. I would have loved to meet them."

Thierry ran his hands through his hair. "I don't know why my parents didn't go to the crypts. Why didn't they? They were such gentle souls, you know, Charlotte. I wish you had met them. I just know you would have got on well with them. I always meant to take you but this war always got in the way."

"Do you have brothers or sisters?"

He shook his head. "No, there was only me. I had a sister, but she died as a baby. I never even said goodbye to them. I'm ashamed of that."

Lottie kissed him. "Don't be. I'm sure they knew you were fighting. Trying to save France from these Nazi butchers."

Thierry brushed his eyes with the palm of one hand. "I hope so. And I must return to it." He stood up and smiled at her, holding out his hand to help her up from the bench.

Standing, she slid back into his arms. He kissed the top of her head; he didn't seem to mind that her hair was dirty. He was none too clean himself.

"I thought you might need some grub. Come and see what's in the jeep."

However hungry Lottie was, she didn't want to move from the spot, didn't want him to start the process of leaving.

"Come on, Charlotte."

They walked, hand-in-hand, back to his jeep. There were some wooden boxes stashed on the back seat. Thierry lifted them down.

"What's this?"

"You'll come to hate it, but it keeps you alive. Bully Beef. Tins of preserved meat. There's some Spam too and dried egg powder and sugar and the worst biscuits in the world."

"Bernadette will be pleased, we all will. Thank you, Thierry. It's very thoughtful."

"Nonsense. It's the same all over Normandy. The army's well fed but the people are starving."

Lottie took another box. "We thought we'd put enough by in the cellar, but the bombing's just gone on and on for so bloody long. Are we safe to leave the house now, do you think?"

"To be really honest, I think not. There are tanks everywhere and it's pretty gruesome. You could easily still be caught in a battle. I'd hate anything to happen to you."

"And yet, you're going off to fight in the thick of it. That hardly seems fair." Lottie put the last box down with a thud.

Thierry turned round and kissed her deeply. "I want us to survive this. I love you, Charlotte. I want to marry you. Start a future somewhere, anywhere."

"I love you too and you know the answer's yes, although you seem to have assumed that I'll hang around waiting for you. You should know by now, that's not my style."

Thierry grinned. "Yes, I should!"

Just then, Françoise came running out into the yard. "Charlotte! Please come! Bernadette's taken a turn for the worse."

Lottie ran into the house and Thierry followed her.

Bernadette was propped up in bed, clutching her chest. Her lips were blue and she had gone deathly pale.

"Give her another aspirin. Under the tongue." Thierry bent over Bernadette.

Lottie went to the cupboard and retrieved the packet of pills and gently opened Bernadette's mouth and slipped the little white disc under her blue tongue.

She felt Bernadette's forehead and found it cold and clammy, like the first time.

389

"She's responding, look." Lottie watched as Bernadette's eyes fluttered open.

Françoise sat on a chair nearby and gathered her frightened-looking son close to her. "Look, Bertrand. Grandmère is coming round already."

Bernadette opened her eyes fully. "What are you all staring at?"

Thierry stood up. "I think she'll be alright. I'm really sorry, but I have to go, Charlotte."

Lottie turned to Françoise. "Will you stay with her?"

"Yes, of course. Go."

Thierry and Lottie went back outside. "Charlotte, she needs a doctor as soon as possible." He took her hand in his. "But she also needs *you*. Françoise needs you too, and that handsome little chap of hers. You must stay here. You are the strong one."

Lottie sighed. "I know all that. Go on with you. Bugger off and get rid of the bastard Boche. I dare say I'll be here when you're done."

"I love you."

She kissed him hard and then pushed him away. "I love you too. See you when you get back. Make sure you do."

Thierry nodded and climbed in the jeep. He reversed it and turned it around, pausing only once to wave goodbye.

Lottie stood amongst the wooden crates he'd brought and watched the dust settle again.

CHAPTER FIFTY-TWO
WHITE WALTHAM AERODROME, ENGLAND
SEPTEMBER 1944

Al pulled back the throttle and allowed the Anson to cruise above the clouds. At last he was going to the theatre of the real war.

He couldn't believe his luck when Trixie had handed him his chit that morning.

"Carpiquet aerodrome, Al. The RAF are short of pilots so we're stepping in."

"Where did you say? Karpeekay? That's in France, isn't it?"

"That's right, Normandy. That Anson on the airstrip is loaded up for a supply delivery to the British airbase there. Here's a map of the area, as you've not done that route before."

Al read the destination on the form. "Oh, that's how you spell it. Didn't know you could speak the lingo, Trixie."

Trixie smiled at him. "You shouldn't judge a book by its cover, First-Officer Phipps."

Al saluted. "Beg your pardon, your ladyship. I'll be on my way. France, eh? What do they say for goodbye over there?"

"Au revoir. It means, 'see you again soon'.

"Oh reevoy, then."

"Oh, get on with you." Trixie laughed and returned to her typing.

Pat McBride, the ground crew engineer who'd been the first person he'd met at White Waltham when he'd arrived as a raw recruit, was in charge of his chocks when he went to board the big plane on the runway. "Morning, Al. Standing in for the RAF, I hear?"

"Yes, off to Normandy at last, Pat. It's going to be very interesting."

"Well, don't be put off by any RAF officer looking down his nose at our lot. Remember, every plane that ever flew in this damn war had an ATA pilot flying her at some point."

Al laughed. "I'll remember that. Thanks."

Soon he was over the channel, heading south. The weather was perfect. Not too many clouds, just cumulus he could fly through easily without losing long distance vision. Late September had always been Al's favourite time of year with just that first hint of the crisp autumn days ahead. This autumn would see a major change in his life. He still couldn't quite believe that he would become a father, maybe even as soon as next month! He wished he could have seen Bella more but, if anything, he'd been busier than ever with ferrying planes for the invasion and then the bombing over Germany and France that had followed. The workload had been even more relentless than before.

He cruised on for a while before he spotted the shoreline of France. Thank goodness he wouldn't be facing a storm of air defence fire, like his RAF colleagues had during D-Day. He wouldn't blame them if they did think themselves better than the ATA, for all Pat's advice. Al was all too aware of the dangers they'd faced and still did when they flew far deeper into occupied Europe in support of the fighting further east.

He checked his map, dipped the wing of the Anson and scanned the coast for landmarks. Yes, there was the Cotentin peninsula pointing its long finger northwards. He could just make out Cherbourg and the road running south from it. Al flew westwards till he cleared the headland and saw the landing beaches of D-Day running in a long, almost straight, line from the west side of the Cotentin peninsula to the big estuary of the River Seine at Le Havre. He pointed the nose of the Anson towards the estuary and dipped the wing again so he could see the sandy beaches to the south. He adjusted his altitude downwards once he saw Bayeux, looking remarkably unscathed and tranquil, and the unmistakable trajectory of the Mulberry artificial harbour at Arromanches, just beyond the city. There were lots of barrage balloons moored here to prevent air attack and still many ships docked at Port Winston, as the Allies called it, which handled the oil supply. Al kept on, steering clear of the balloons and slowing his speed until he spotted the city of Caen, or what was left of it. If it wasn't for the wide river inlet at Ouistreham he might have missed it altogether, it looked so flat. Al lowered altitude further and gasped out loud unconsciously at the devastation below him. Only the cathedral spire rose above the rubble spread out over a huge area where the city had obviously once stood tall. How had anyone survived such total annihilation?

He could see why the Germans had defended it so vigorously, as roads radiated from its ruined core like even spokes of a wheel and of course the river was deep enough to take boats out to sea. A perfect transport hub and route to Paris. All the news reports made so much more sense when you saw the topographical layout in real life. The town resembled a desert rather than the lush countryside surrounding it. Al cast his eyes wider afield and saw that a lot of the satellite villages had also been badly bombed and there were craters pockmarking the ground for miles around. He banked and turned the big aeroplane full circle to face eastwards again where he expected to find the airbase.

Ah, there it was, a clear runway, surrounded by wrecked hangars. It looked busy with other planes parked alongside the tarmac. Landing on tarmac would be a luxury after the mud and dust at White Waltham.

Al prepared for landing, adjusting his speed and altitude and let down the wheels. He was pleased with his first touchdown on foreign soil as the rubber kissed the metalled surface sweetly and he glided smoothly to a halt.

Ground crew ran towards the plane as soon as it had stopped. "Nice landing, sir!"

Al grinned. He could never get used to being called 'sir', but it never failed to make him feel proud to be a pilot.

"Cheers! Get her unloaded, would you, chaps?"

"Yes, sir."

"Is there any building that still has a roof on where you can get refreshments?"

"Only one! Over there, and you check in to the office right next door."

"Thanks." Al walked over to the office and signed the chit with the army sergeant on duty.

"Where are you from, sir?"

"ATA, White Waltham aerodrome, sergeant. Got some medical and food supplies on board. Anything to take back?"

The sergeant made a note in his big book. "I'll have a check, sir. If you'd like to grab a bite next door and come back in say, half an hour?"

"Righto."

"And excuse me, sir, but have you seen any of those V1 flying bombs the Gerries are dropping on London? It's just that I haven't had leave to go home and I've got family there."

"Yes, sergeant. Dreadful things. Started just after D-Day and come out of nowhere. I hope your family haven't been affected."

"Is it right they've no pilot on board?"

"'Fraid so. They've got an awful whine and then the worst of it is when they go silent and you know they're going to drop. Not like an air raid when you've got time to get into a shelter, these doodlebugs are totally random but just as lethal as a conventional bomb."

"Hardly fair on poor old London. I know my Mum thought they'd got through all that sort of thing when the blitz finished. The street next to ours was flattened." The sergeant put his pencil behind his ear and sucked his teeth.

"She's not wrong. Seems very unfair but the Germans are getting their revenge for losing the war in the most cowardly way."

"Do you think we will win?"

"Without a doubt. Now, where can I get a cuppa?"

394

"Just next door, sir. I'll check to see if there's any passengers for your return in the meantime."

"Thanks, sergeant." Al strolled out of the little office.

There were broken down German tanks all around the periphery next to huge bunkers dug out from the soil and the hangars looked like skeletons with no flesh on their bones. He could see that the ground had been worked on next to the runway but further off there were bomb craters everywhere, worse than in London, for all that the sergeant's mother may have undoubtedly suffered. Al had seen London first-hand and only pockets resembled Caen. He'd never seen an entire city wiped out like that anywhere else, and he'd flown all over Britain. The airbase must have been pulverised too. God help anyone living nearby, he doubted they would have had a chance.

That melancholy thought reminded him that Lottie could still be in France, if she was still alive. Neither her mother or sister had ever said so, but he personally doubted that she could be, especially looking at the blasted landscape hereabouts. They hadn't heard from her since 1940. Four very long years ago. What if she'd been in Caen? No-one could have survived that bombardment. The last anyone had heard she'd been in Paris. At least that had been spared the worst of it but if she was still there, surely, she would have got in touch after it was liberated in August? Perhaps messages took longer than three weeks in this chaotic situation.

Ah, if only they knew. If only he could take his plane and search the whole of France for her, but he might as well put a pin in a map and hope he would find her. It was impossible. Even though he was finally in France, he might as well be in Timbuctoo for all the chance he had of finding his friend and sister-in-law.

Maybe his child would never meet his aunt, after all.

Gradually the bombing fizzled out through August and September, but Lottie didn't see Thierry again. There seemed to be just as many aeroplanes overhead as ever, but none were German anymore. Lottie seldom ventured off the farm but when she did, it was noticeable how few American soldiers were around compared to the months following the D-Day landings when they had swarmed everywhere. The countryside was mercifully quiet, and no-one missed the sounds of the bombardment that had wreaked such havoc in the neighbourhood.

She and Françoise concentrated on harvesting apples, making cider and Calvados and nursing Bernadette back to some semblance of health. Stirred by their ineptitude, Bernadette got up and dressed during the apple harvest to bark orders at them. Lottie found this heartening rather than irritating and was grateful for the older woman's lifetime of knowledge in tasks she knew nothing about.

"We must get glass for the windows soon. We can't go through the winter like this. Or do without the range chimney." Lottie shivered as the first whisper of autumn chill penetrated her bones one misty September morning.

"I wouldn't know where to start." Françoise buttoned up her cardigan.

A crackling sound interrupted them.

"What the hell is that?" Lottie spun round and stared at the radio set. "Surely not?" She went to the light switch and flicked it on. "Eureka! We have electricity again!"

Lottie dashed over to the radio and fiddled with the tuner knob. At once, music filled the room. She grabbed Françoise and twirled her round.

"Music! And that means news!"

Bernadette came downstairs, leaning on her stick. "What's that confounded noise?"

"Listen, Bernadette. The electricity's back on at last! We can find out what's going on in the world again."

"Huh, I'd rather not know."

But Lottie wouldn't be dissuaded and listened avidly to the announcements of the progress of the Allied troops as they made their way east. She knew that Thierry had been with the York and Lancaster regiment in June but had no way of knowing where or who he was with now. When they heard that General Leclerc's Free French troops had come south and met up with other French forces coming north from Provence in Burgundy, even Bernadette took notice.

"Shows us French can fight as well as any other country."

"That's right, Bernadette. I wonder if Thierry is with them."

Lottie had taken to sleeping back up in the attic. Françoise left her bedroom door open at night so she could hear if Bernadette needed her in the next room. Bernadette rarely used her day bed now, but they were all missing the protection of glass in the windows. The days were not longer than the nights anymore and every morning was misty unless it was actually raining.

"I'm going into the village to ask about glass. We can't leave it any longer. And that corner must be mended before the frosts come. Every day I think the ironing board will collapse and one day soon, it will."

"You are right, Charlotte. Maybe I should come with you now the donkey's wandered back home." Bernadette rubbed her hands together.

"Are you cold, Grandmère?"

"Always. It's time to repair things."

Lottie stood up. "But I'll go alone. I'm only making enquiries. I'll be back by lunch."

When no-one tried to persuade her otherwise, Lottie knew Bernadette didn't really have the strength to go. She pulled on her coat and boots and set off on her bicycle. It wasn't far to the village, but the debris of the war still hadn't shifted. The tanks she'd seen before, broken and bent out of shape, leaning into ditches, still clung to the tattered hedges but thankfully she neither saw, nor smelled, any rotting corpses.

Occasionally a soldier on a motorcycle zoomed past her and once, she saw a jeep just like the one Thierry had driven to see her that last time. The driver even wore glasses and her heart lurched when she first saw him driving towards her, but she soon saw he was younger, with black hair and a plump face.

Neither of them stopped her to ask who she was. It should have felt liberating and would have done so only a couple of months ago, but Lottie just felt flat, defeated by the waste all around her. Waste of life, animals, plants, machines, houses, trees. It all conspired to emphasise the empty feeling in the hollow of her stomach.

The village had been tidied up a bit in her absence. Some corrugated iron sheets on the sides of the bridge had been tied on with rope to protect travellers from falling into the river and the autumn rain had washed the dust off the piles of rubble, now sorted into neat formations next to the demolished buildings from which they'd been so violently separated.

The boulangerie looked beyond repair. Poor Madame Leroy. Lottie missed her every day.

Lottie cycled past the linden trees where the ropes still swung ominously amongst the browning leaves and over to Madame Voclain's house. This woman was the only one left in the village from her colleagues in the Resistance, except, thank God, Thierry. Long may that continue. Lottie leant her bicycle against a pile of stones and knocked on the front door.

To her astonishment, it wasn't Odette who answered it, but the owner's son, Emile.

"Emile! You're home!" Lottie held out her arms and Emile wrapped his around her.

"Hello, Charlotte. Good to see you."

Lottie held him at arm's length. He looked older, tanned and leaner. "Oh, Emile! I'm so glad you are back safe. Françoise will be over the moon to see you."

"We'll see about that." Madame Voclain now stood behind her son and watched Lottie with narrowed eyes. Lottie noticed that the eyeliner had made a reappearance, along with the pink lipstick.

"Madame Voclain. Good morning."

"Mademoiselle Perrot, the girl from the farm." Madame spoke as if she had a bad smell in her nose.

Lottie wondered if it could be true. Bathing at Le Verger was still difficult with only the wash-house boiler for hot water. Her self-conscious awareness reminded her of the reason for her visit.

"Can I come in?"

Madame Voclain shrugged. "If you must."

But Emile kept his arm around Lottie and kissed her cheek. "How is Françoise? And the boy?"

Lottie smiled up at him. "Both well, I'm glad to say, but Bernadette is a little frail these days and as for the farm, well, it's pretty damaged."

"I'm sorry to hear that."

"It's none of your concern, Emile." Madame Voclain walked ahead into the salon.

Lottie noticed that the floor had been swept and the doors rehung in the elegant hallway. She sat on a tapestry-covered chair, luxuriating in its comfort. She couldn't remember the last time she had sat on a soft seat.

Madame Voclain reached for the cigarette box and opened it. It was full. Lottie wondered how she had managed to obtain them but then, Madame Voclain had always known how to survive.

"You don't smoke, do you?"

Lottie shook her head. "No. I'm surprised you are so well stocked, Madame."

"The Americans are very generous."

Lottie smiled. "That's good to know because we need some help mending the broken bits of the farm before the winter really digs in. We urgently need some glass for the windows. We've got oiled paper on some of the frames upstairs, but it makes it very dark. I see your windows have been replaced, Madame Voclain? Was that also the Americans?"

Madame Voclain shrugged and blew smoke into the room. "The glass makers in Bayeux are operational. Bayeux didn't get bombed, you know. Must have given De Gaulle a false impression when he made his speech."

"He's been here? Really? I haven't been anywhere, and we had no radio until the electricity returned only very recently, so I'm ignorant about what has happened."

"That much is obvious."

"Mother!" Emile smiled an apology at Lottie. "I can help you at the farm. I'm longing to see, um, everyone, and we have a car. The Americans have given us petrol. I could drive you to Bayeux for glass and fit it myself."

"Emile! There is enough to do here without you troubling yourself at Le Verger."

Emile stood up and faced his mother. "I'm not a child anymore, Mother. You are better off than most and can look after yourself. These people are my friends. I probably wouldn't be alive if it wasn't for them. It was Charlotte who got me to the first safe house. I owe them a debt."

Madame Voclain stubbed out her cigarette and shrugged. "Please yourself."

Emile turned to Lottie. "Come, we'll go now and measure up."

Emile roped her bicycle on to the back of the family saloon and Lottie sat back on her second comfortable seat of what had turned out to be a most surprising morning.

Emile started the engine. "You mustn't mind what my mother says. She's pretty shaken up and it comes out the wrong way."

"I understand. It's a wonder we're not all raving mad after suffering that bombardment. It was truly awful, Emile."

"I can see that." Emile drove carefully over the narrow bridge. He smiled. "I think this bridge was designed to carry donkeys rather than cars."

"When did you get back, Emile?" She looked across at him. He seemed so relaxed as a driver. He'd changed from a boy into a man since she'd seen him last.

Emile steered around an abandoned machine gun. "A few days ago. I was going to visit Le Verger soon."

"Have you been with your mother's cousin in the Auvergne?"

"No, I saw her only briefly before I went to join the other Maquis in the forest in Mont Muchet."

"Did you see any fighting?"

Emile looked back at her. "You could say that." He closed his mouth firmly.

Lottie didn't press him. "Françoise will be so glad to see you."

When they drove up the little lane to the farmhouse, Françoise was outside in the vegetable patch, digging up potatoes. She looked up at the sound of the car and froze, her spade in mid-air, her face comical with surprise.

Emile leapt out of the car without putting on the handbrake. Lottie yanked it on from the passenger side and stayed inside the luxurious vehicle.

Françoise threw down her spade and ran to meet Emile. They wasted no words, but he swept her up in his arms and twirled her round before kissing her soundly. Lottie felt a pang of jealousy mixed with pure joy at her friend's reunion with her young lover. She got out of the car and shut the door quietly and went around to the boot to unknot the rope that tied her bicycle to it. She didn't want to disturb the moment, so propped her bike against the farmhouse wall and went into the kitchen.

"Who is that?" Bernadette sat with her back to the draughty open window, a woollen shawl around her bent shoulders.

"It's me, Charlotte."

"I meant, who is in the car I heard."

Lottie came and sat before her on the settle by the empty range. "It's Emile come home, Bernadette."

Bertrand, who had been playing quietly at Bernadette's feet, jumped up. "Emile?"

Lottie smiled at the little boy. "Yes, he's back."

"I go see him!"

Lottie put out her hand. "Leave it a minute, Bertrand. He's talking to your mother."

But Bertrand shook off her arm and ran outside.

Bernadette hitched her shawl tighter around her frame. "Don't stop him. Those three belong together."

402

"No, I'm fine. Really, I am, Al. No, no sign of the baby coming. It's not due for another week, remember. Yes, I'm looking after myself. Miss you too. Alright, take care, Al, darling. Love you with all my heart." Isobel replaced the telephone receiver into its cradle.

She levered herself up from the chair they kept by the telephone in the narrow hallway of West Lodge. She didn't really feel a hundred percent, if she was really truthful, but she wasn't going to let Al know that. If only he was here with her. She longed to see him so much.

Her back ached. Everything ached. She couldn't even walk properly anymore. Just waddle. Maybe it was as well Al couldn't see her in this state. She felt enormous. As big as a whale. Bigger. Her backache was worse standing up, but sitting was uncomfortable too, there wasn't a position she'd found this last two weeks that had given her any degree of comfort.

Isobel looked down at her swollen stomach. "Listen, baby, I'm getting fed up of waiting. You're very heavy, you know, so if you want to turn up early, that's fine with me."

She had the house to herself, for once. Her mother had barely left her side for a week, in case she went into labour, but this morning Cassandra had a meeting with Mrs Andrews about the domestic arrangements at the manor house she said she could not postpone. Isobel hadn't bothered to inquire what it was about.

She wandered into the kitchen to make herself a drink. It was too much effort to put the kettle on, so she swigged some milk, straight from the bottle. No-one would see her lack of manners. Oh, that backache! Isobel went to her bedroom and lay down on the bed, shoving a pillow between her knees and trying to concentrate on a book she was reading. She read a paragraph three times without

403

taking in a word before her eyes grew so heavy, she gave up resisting and let them close.

She dreamt she was up in an aeroplane with Al flying it. White fluffy clouds drifted past them and the sky was periwinkle blue. Al was laughing and showing off and she told him to stop being so silly. He didn't reply but took the plane into a swooping nose-dive, making her stomach lurch and her head spin. Feeling they were going to crash as the ground loomed up to them, Isobel started to shout. "Stop it, Al, you're hurting me!"

She woke up perspiring, with her heart pounding, and became instantly aware that her backache had worsened considerably, and she felt sick. She groaned and tried to turn on to her back, to ease out the hollow in it, but the baby was too heavy. She felt her skin crawl over her huge belly and then the tingling feel built up into a rippling crescendo.

What was happening? Did birth feel like this? Isobel waited for the sensation to abate and heaved herself up on to her elbows before swinging her legs over the edge of the bed. She must reach the telephone!

Another contraction swept through her body and she gasped for breath. She must get up! As soon as the feeling passed, she tried to rise again. It took a few goes but she managed to stand and lean her weight against the bedroom wall. She heard the sound of splattering water. Had she knocked over her glass of water in her clumsiness? She exerted pressure against the wall with her hands and lurched towards her bedside cabinet. No, the water stood there silently in its tumbler, its calm meniscus undisturbed. Isobel looked down at the floor, alarmed to see a pool of liquid spilling around her feet. It was coming from *her*! Mummy had said this would happen and that it was perfectly normal, but Isobel never dreamt events would unfold so fast.

She *must* get to the telephone! Another contraction, much stronger this time, threatened to overwhelm her. She braced herself against the wall and pressed her hands to its flat surface. Breathe, wasn't that what everyone had said to

404

do? Breathe through the pain. Isobel was panting now and drenched with sweat. She couldn't do it. Couldn't get to the hall. She shuffled backwards and fell back on to the bed. She would just have to wait until Mummy came home.

Isobel looked at the clock beside her. It was only just gone eleven, Cassandra had said she'd be home for lunch. That could be two hours away! Another ripple of her abdomen muscles took her mind off her mother and everything else besides. Isobel grabbed her pillow and bit into its cotton softness, hating the dryness of the cloth against her tongue.

Oh, why had this happened when she was alone? The wave of pain subsided and she lay back, exhausted. She looked at the clock again. Eleven fifteen. By midday, the contractions were coming every ten minutes and Isobel was desperately frightened. By half past twelve, they were seven minutes apart and it was all she could do to recover between them. Then, at quarter-to-one, she finally heard the front door open.

"Cooee! I'm home!" Her mother's voice called out. "Just getting some things from the car, back in a sec!"

"Mummy," Isobel whispered the words. "In here, please!"

But her mother had obviously gone outside again and didn't hear her.

She heard her mother's footsteps in the hall, as she called out cheerily, "I'll put the kettle on, darling. I'm gasping for a cup of tea."

Isobel listened with increasing frustration to Cassandra clattering about in the kitchen. "Please, oh please, listen to me."

Another contraction took hold of her so strongly, Isobel yelled out with the pain. In seconds, her mother was in the room.

"Oh, my darling! It's the baby, isn't it?"

Isobel could only nod as she bit her lip against the torture.

405

"How often are the contractions coming?" Cassandra held her hand on Isobel's brow.

"Five minutes apart now. Ooh! Make that four." Isobel's back arched as the spasm took over again.

"I'll phone Dr Harris and be right back. Hold on!" Cassandra left the room again.

Isobel screamed out loud with the next birthing spasm.

By the time it had waned, her mother was back. "Malcolm is coming, darling. He'll be here in five minutes. You are doing brilliantly, my love. Really marvellous."

Isobel gripped her mother's hand as her belly muscle hardened up again. "Might not be in time." She just got the words out through gritted teeth.

Ten minutes later the front door opened again, and within seconds, Malcolm Harris stood at the bedside. He immediately took charge. "Cassandra, get some hot water and clean towels, please."

Cassandra instantly vacated the room.

"Now then, Isobel, may I call you Bella? Let's have a look at you. I'll have to cut your underwear away, I'm afraid."

Isobel only felt relief without the constraint of her pants and too far gone to worry about embarrassment. "Want to push, doctor."

"Well, you *are* ahead of me, aren't you?" The doctor put his hand on her belly as the next contraction took hold. "You are doing very well, my dear." He went to the foot of the bed and lifted the sheet she'd drawn over herself earlier. "Right, Bella. I want you to raise your knees. That's it. Good, I can see the baby's head. Steady, now. You can push next time."

Isobel was vaguely aware of her mother beside her, bearing a sheaf of white linen and looking terrified, before she forgot everything and pushed downwards.

Dr Harris smiled at her. "Splendid, my dear. I have the baby's head. Push gently again next time and you'll be there."

"Arrgh!" Isobel pushed.

"That's it! The baby is born, Bella!"

Isobel flopped back against the pillow, her body trembling with spent effort.

Cassandra came to her side. "It's a boy, darling. The most beautiful, perfect, wonderful baby boy. You are such a clever girl."

Dr Harris was fiddling about with a pair of scissors and then he placed a red, squirming, noisy baby in her arms, wrapped up in a white towel. The baby stopped crying and stared into her eyes. Isobel fell in love for the second time in her life.

She smiled at her son, who looked very much like his father. "Hello, gorgeous."

Lottie leaned back against her chair. "I couldn't eat another thing. That was delicious."

Françoise grinned. "I never thought I'd ever have a full stomach again, after the last few years. Thank you, Veronique, for bringing the pork and wine."

Madame Voclain, invited for the special occasion, inclined her head in acknowledgement. She'd been visiting often lately and, to everyone's relief, seemed to have accepted that her son was in love with Françoise instead of railing against the liaison, now the trauma of the invasion had faded. It wasn't the first time she had brought presents either. Madame Voclain had a knack of knowing where to locate food, equipment or building supplies in a way no-one else could.

Emile sat beside Françoise; they were holding hands openly on the table-top. "It's a good feeling when you have enough to eat."

Lottie looked at Bernadette, pleased to see her thin cheeks flushed and rosy. Even it was down to the Calvados, she looked stronger than she had for many weeks.

Madame Voclain stood up. "I give a toast! Merry Christmas everyone, and let's hope it will finally be a happy new year!"

Lottie took another sip of the smooth Calvados. "Here's to the end of the occupation throughout all of France!"

Emile raised his glass. "And to victory in the rest of Europe."

"Hear, hear."

"May it happen soon."

As they clinked their glasses together, Lottie wondered where Thierry was now. The only letter she'd had from him said he was in the Ardennes forest, deep in snow and freezing cold. He was with some American outfit now, translating for them with the local people and the fighting was as hard as ever. Thierry wrote that the Germans were really dug in and bitterly determined to prevent the Allies from entering Antwerp and supplies were very depleted. It had been a worrying letter, short and to the point and obviously written in haste. Lottie could read the fatigue Thierry suffered between his lines of unconvincing optimism.

She drew her attention back to the warm room and the faces around the table. Ever since Emile had come back from the Auvergne, battle-hardened and determined, he'd spent most of his time at the farm, repairing the damage inflicted during the battle of Normandy.

The ironing board propping up the timber frame of the kitchen corner had long been replaced with new, sound wood and plastered back over. You would hardly notice the crack now, unless you looked for it. The barn had taken much longer and the additional help of Emile's friends, also back from hiding from the enforced labour order. Monsieur Voclain had not been of their number and Emile privately confessed that he did not expect his father to return.

Lottie had enjoyed the young company of Emile's friends and worked with them rebuilding the stone walls and re-slating the roof through the darkening days of autumn. The donkey looked grateful to be back under its shelter when the first snow had fallen in early December but had kicked out in disgust when new goats had been bought and introduced to him in his private lair.

Since the goats had arrived, Françoise had undertaken the milking every day. She said she enjoyed it and little Bertrand helped his mother with surprising eagerness. "He's turning into a proper little farmer, Grandmère."

Bernadette had smiled at her great-grandson and ruffled his hair. Lottie had felt left out, not being a family member, and she no longer felt indispensable, now that

Emile had taken on many of her former roles. Looking at the smiling faces around the table, laden with the debris of a very good Christmas lunch, she felt alien once more and wished she could be at Thierry's side instead, whatever the hardships.

Veronique Voclain stood up again. "I have a special announcement to make. It's important, so pipe down, Bertrand, and listen."

Françoise shushed the little boy, who had been running around with his new toy aeroplane, making loud engine noises and releasing pretend bombs onto the flagstones of the kitchen floor, with an all too realistic imitation of their explosions.

"What is it, Maman?" Emile eyed his mother a little apprehensively.

Lottie looked at Madame Voclain who was, as ever, dressed elegantly, this time in a red and green tweed suit, which chimed perfectly with the festive season. Lottie hadn't been able to upgrade her own attire. The only dresses she had brought with her from Paris were thin summer ones, so she kept her man's trousers on but had donned a clean shirt and tied a colourful silk scarf around her hair to make up for her humdrum style.

Madame Voclain cleared her throat. "My husband, as you may remember, was a solicitor."

Emile butted in. "Let's hope he still is. We do not know if Father is dead, Maman."

Madame Voclain inclined her head. "This is true, and I hope you are right, Emile. But, in his absence, I have been dealing with some of the most pressing local affairs of law. Sadly, Lucien Dubois died valiantly in defence of France, God rest his soul, but before he did, he changed his will."

There was a sudden hush in the room as everyone concentrated on Madame Voclain's next words.

"Monsieur Dubois has left his farm to Bernadette. I have the papers here. It is my Christmas present to you,

410

Bernadette." Madame Voclain fished in her bag and brought out a formal-looking document which she passed to her hostess.

Bernadette took it, her mouth hanging open in surprise, and undid the red ribbon that held its cylindrical shape together. She spread out the parchment and read it out loud.

Lottie, fluent though she now was, found the legal French hard to follow but she could guess the contents by everyone's joyful reaction.

"Grandmère, that is wonderful! You will have more than twice the land you have now and another farmhouse!"

Madame Voclain smiled. "Your granddaughter is right, Bernadette. You are a woman of property now. I'm glad that Lucien left things this way. You deserve it for all you have done for the Resistance. He wanted it in French hands – good hands."

Bernadette leant on the table for support as she stood up. She straightened her bent shoulders and gave one of her rare smiles. "I never expected this, Veronique. It will make a big difference." She turned to Emile and Françoise, sitting to her left. "I shall change my will, too. Your mother is lost to me now, Françoise. It doesn't matter to me whether Mireille is alive or dead. You will inherit it all, Françoise. I'll make sure of it."

"Thank you, Grandmère. I'll always be here for you, you know that."

Bernadette turned to her granddaughter and kissed both her cheeks. Looking exhausted, she sat back down again amidst the spontaneous applause that had broken out around the table.

Madame Voclain frowned. "I don't understand. Is Charlotte to receive nothing? Isn't she your granddaughter too?"

Bernadette looked at Lottie with raised eyebrows of enquiry.

Lottie took the hint. "Veronique, you surprise me. I thought you knew everything about everyone!"

Veronique Voclain stared at her.

Lottie laughed softly. "Well, you may as well know the truth about me, now the Germans are at a safe distance. I am not Françoise's cousin or the daughter of Charles and Sylvie Perrot. I'm not even French!"

Both Emile and Veronique Voclain gasped out loud at this statement.

Lottie spread her hands out in a truly Gallic expression and shrugged. "You are surprised. I take that as a compliment because you are not easily fooled, Madame Voclain. I love Françoise as a cousin, it's true but she is only my friend. A long-standing friend and a true one. My real name is Lottie Flintock-Smythe and I'm English. Françoise and I were pen-pals when we were schoolgirls and I was visiting her in Paris when war broke out." Lottie turned to Bernadette. "This wonderful woman took me in and housed me throughout this dreadful war and I can never repay her hospitality."

Bernadette waved her hands. "Nonsense. You already have."

Veronique looked around the table. "I confess I'm shocked and impressed, Charlotte. Your disguise certainly fooled me and that doesn't happen often. I suspected you were not a member of the Perrot family, but I had not guessed you were English. I raise my glass to you."

They all cheered and took a sip of wine. Veronique still looked stunned and she opened her mouth to speak again but her son interrupted her. Lottie was glad when Emile pushed his chair back and stood up.

"It seems this is an occasion for important announcements, so why not another?" He smiled, nodding his head to Françoise. "I am proud to tell you that Françoise has agreed to become my wife."

Lottie looked quickly at his mother, but Veronique didn't look cross, as she'd expected. It seems this pronouncement had not come as a surprise to Emile's mother, unlike her own. Had she engineered that change of will of Lucien Dubois? Was that legally possible? Veronique Voclain met her gaze and winked discreetly. Lottie realised it didn't matter anyway. She knew Lucien had no family of his own, he'd told her so himself. Why shouldn't it eventually go to this young couple, who were so in love with each other, once Bernadette had gone?

Lottie got to her feet. "To Françoise and Emile! Good luck to you both and congratulations!"

"What about me?" Bertrand tugged at her trousers.

Lottie picked him up. "And to Bertrand! Health and happiness and may you all have a long, happy and above all, peaceful life together!"

Lottie slept well that night, replete with food and wine and knowing that Françoise's future was secure. How Veronique Voclain had connived that inheritance she didn't know. Perhaps it was genuine. Lucien Dubois was no fool and he would have made sure the Boche didn't get his land. Emile and Françoise could live in his farmhouse, if they wanted to, but Lottie knew they wouldn't desert Bernadette.

But the next morning, her sense of contentment slowly evaporated with the morning mist and her hangover headache also took a while to clear. Françoise might have a cosy outlook but what of hers? She was no longer needed here at Le Verger. Emile had supplanted her and quite right too. She was fond of them all, but they weren't her family. Not for the first time, she wished she'd gone with Thierry and endured the privations of war alongside him.

Having nothing to do, all the chores being already assigned elsewhere, Lottie decided to go for a bike ride. The weather looked promising, despite the season. A slight frost rimed the hedgerows and the rusting metal of warmongery still littered the lanes, but she'd almost got used to them now. She let her intuition guide her direction and gravitated northwards. Perhaps a view of the sea would lend her perspective. She had some serious thinking to do.

413

After half an hour she realised she had the aerodrome within sight. There were quite a few planes on the runway, all marked by the distinctive circular insignia of the RAF. But that meant they were British! Of course, why hadn't she thought of it before? Lottie stood up on her pedals and powered her way forward. At the gates to the airbase, a British soldier stopped her and asked for her papers.

Lottie answered him haltingly, unused to speaking in her native language. She braked and got off her bicycle to retrieve them from her coat pocket. "Um, it says I'm French here on my ID card, but actually, I'm British. I've been living in France throughout the occupation under an assumed name. Is there anyone I could talk to about getting a letter home on one of your planes?"

"I think you'd better go and see the officer-in-charge, Miss. This way." The soldier started to walk off to the one building still intact. All the other hangars had been wrecked by bombs and there were craters and broken German planes scattered all around the periphery of the base.

Lottie followed the young man into the office, wheeling her bicycle alongside her. She propped it against the wall and went inside.

The soldier saluted the burly man at the desk. "This young lady needs to speak to someone about getting some post back to England, sir."

"Is that so? Well, come in, Miss. Thank you, Forbes. You can return to sentry duty now."

"Yes, sir." The soldier saluted his senior officer smartly and left.

"Would you like a seat, Miss?"

"Yes, thanks."

"Want to tell me your story, then?"

Lottie briefly explained her situation.

"Blimey, if you'll excuse the expression. I think you'd better see the Commanding Officer."

414

"Oh, no! Really, there's no need for all that. I just wanted to know if I could send a letter home."

"Just wait there a moment, Miss."

The sergeant went into an interior office. Lottie heard a muffled exchange, before the sergeant called her in, then he left and shut the door behind him.

Lottie suddenly felt very aware of her old trousers, her scuffed leather jacket and her worn beret.

The officer stood up and extended his hand. "Captain Reid, at your service. Please, sit down and tell me how I might help you."

Lottie was regretting her impulse now. "I just want to get a letter home to my mother."

"That seems simple enough. Can I ask your name?"

"I'm known here as Charlotte Perrot, but my real name is Lottie Flintock-Smythe."

"And you've been in France throughout the occupation, is that right? How extraordinary."

"Well, yes. It has been challenging at times."

"Wouldn't you rather go home in person than send a letter?"

"Oh! I didn't know that was possible!"

"I'm sure it could be arranged. Do you still have your British passport?"

"Why yes, it's at home, I mean, at the farm where I'm living."

"Well, then. Perhaps you need some time to make arrangements? Let us know when you're ready and we'll arrange transport. We've got ATA planes flying back and forth every Monday, Wednesday and Friday. They ferry our planes and bring supplies, so you wouldn't be taking any RAF pilots out of active service."

Lottie was lost for words.

"Well, Miss Flintock-Smythe. Have a think about it. And, when you're ready, let us know. I'm sure you have a great deal you could tell the Home Office about your experiences here in France. They would be very interested in your story. It might be indelicate to ask, but did you engage in operations with the Resistance?"

Lottie wasn't sure how much she should divulge. Some of the things she'd done could be considered criminal in other circumstances. "A little."

"Listen, it's not my job to investigate, don't look so alarmed! If you decide to hop back to Blighty, just pop back here and let me know. I'll do all that I can to assist you. You must have had a pretty tricky time hereabouts with the carpet bombing."

"Yes, that's been truly horrendous, to be honest with you. I…I don't know what to say. It's so much to take in. I should have come before, I suppose, but I've been busy on the farm, trying to put it to rights. I don't know why it didn't occur to me to come here before."

"War does strange things to people." The officer stood up. "Come back when you're ready. I'll make sure we get you home."

Lottie stood up. "Thank you. I'm a bit non-plussed! But I'll come back soon."

"I'll show you out. Have you cycled far?"

"No, not very."

Lottie grabbed her bicycle and wheeled it back to the sentry post at the gate.

"All sorted then, Miss?"

"I think so. I'll come back soon, maybe tomorrow."

"As you like, Miss. Look after yourself now."

Lottie clambered on to her bicycle, still dazed from the suddenness of events and wobbled off back towards Le Verger.

That Captain somebody-or-other had called her Miss Flintock-Smythe. Lottie was no longer sure who that was. She forgot all about cycling to the sea and arrived back at the farm with the instinct of a homing pigeon.

She found everyone, including Emile, busily preparing lunch.

Bernadette, as observant as ever, gave her a hard look. "What's the matter. What's happened?"

Lottie sat down at the table without offering to help. "I've been to the airbase. It's full of British soldiers and airmen. They've offered me a lift home to England."

There was a moment's silence when everyone stood stock still, pausing in their tasks, and stared at her. It made Lottie want to laugh because it reminded her of the game she used to play at parties as a child when the music would stop suddenly, and they'd all had to pretend to be statues. A strangled sound did escape her, but she wasn't laughing.

Immediately, Françoise unfroze and put her arm around her friend. "Oh, Charlotte, I mean, Lottie, do you want to go?"

"Yes, no, I don't know!" Lottie rubbed her hands over her face, trying to clear her jumbled thoughts.

Bernadette came and sat next to her, took her hands and pressed them gently but firmly. "Charlotte, your mother has not known what has happened to you for years. You *must* go to her, now you have the chance."

Lottie looked into Bernadette's shrewd grey eyes, trusting the wisdom of this woman she felt she knew as well as any member of her real family. "You have been like a mother to me, Bernadette. I'm so grateful but I know you are right."

Bernadette withdrew her hands. "That's settled then. You'll need to pack. We'll find your suitcase. Eat first and then we'll get organised."

Over lunch, of which Lottie ate little, Emile offered to take a message up to the airbase. "When do you want to go, Charlotte?"

"Tomorrow, I suppose. What day is it today?"

"It's Tuesday, 26th December."

"Oh yes, of course. They said they flew Mondays, Wednesdays and Fridays, I think."

Bernadette looked at her sternly. "Don't make your mother wait another day, child. If they fly on a Wednesday, then you can go tomorrow."

Lottie sighed. "I will miss you all so much. You are like a second family to me."

Bernadette nodded. "We know, Charlotte. It's the same for us."

Lottie blinked away tears. "Thank you." She took a deep breath. "Alright then, I'll leave tomorrow."

Emile smiled. "I'll borrow your bike and cycle to the airbase this afternoon and let them know. Françoise and I will miss you too, you know."

"And me! And me!" Bertrand leant across and gave Lottie a sticky kiss.

Lottie hugged him back. "Thanks, little man."

Bernadette cleared her throat. "Right, I'll clear the table. Emile, off you go with the message. Françoise? Help Charlotte find her things. Her suitcase is in the top cellar. Allez!"

Emile returned later, not only having delivered the message and told Lottie that her trip was confirmed for tomorrow, but also with his mother's car. "I strapped the bicycle on the back again, Charlotte. You shall arrive in style in the morning."

"Thank you, Emile. What time do I have to be there?"

"Eleven o'clock, they said. They have to wait for the incoming flight to be unloaded before you can board."

Butterflies jittered in Lottie's stomach the next morning as she sat beside Emile on the front passenger seat. Her face was covered in the imprint of kisses, not only from Françoise and her son, but also from Bernadette, who had crushed Lottie to her chest and held her for some time.

"Goodbye, Charlotte. Thank you for all you have done for me and the farm and for Françoise. I shall never forget you, child, not for as long as I live. That may not be for long, so I may not see you again, but, know this, you are

418

truly loved." Before Lottie could say her own thank-you's, Bernadette had turned away and gone, leaning on her stick, back into the house and shut the door.

Françoise and Bertrand piled into the back of the car and chattered all the way to the airbase, but Lottie was quiet, remembering Bernadette's sincere words and acknowledging the truth of each of them.

They reached the airbase very quickly, too quickly for Lottie to regain any semblance of poise. The sentry waved them on, and Emile drove right up to the little office and drew up alongside. Lottie got out of the car, but Emile wouldn't let her carry anything and ushered her inside as if she was royalty. Françoise followed, still wittering excitedly and clutching little Bertrand, his mouth a perfect 'o' of awe as he gazed at his unfamiliar surroundings.

"Morning, Miss. Got everything you need?"

"Um, yes, thank you, Sergeant."

"Righto, just need to check your passport."

Lottie handed over her British passport which had lain under the floorboards in the attic of Le Verger for so long. The four of them clustered around the sergeant's desk while he scanned the document. The door banged as someone else came in, but Lottie didn't look round to see who it was.

The sergeant handed back her papers with a smile. "All present and correct. Ah, here's your pilot, Miss Flintock-Smythe. Have a safe journey home, won't you?"

"Thank you, I…"

"*Lottie*! I don't believe it! Can it really be you?"

Lottie span around to see who could possibly be addressing her by her old name. She opened her mouth, but her voice wouldn't work, so she opened her arms instead.

If Bernadette had nearly crushed the breath out of her, it was nothing to the bear hug she got from Al Phipps. Lottie clutched him to her, unable to believe it was him.

A spontaneous round of applause made her drop her arms and speak to the company at large. "It's Al! My childhood friend! My *best* friend!"

Al was grinning from ear to ear as he shook everyone's hands. "Not just your friend, darling Lottie, but I'm your brother-in-law now and you're an auntie!"

"What?" Lottie felt faint.

"Quick, get her a chair." The sergeant bustled over and pushed a chair under her knees, which were shaking visibly.

Captain Reid appeared at her elbow. "Water, get her some water. At the double, Sergeant!"

"Yes, sir. Right away sir."

Al squatted down in front of Lottie. He still hadn't let go his hands. "Lottie, darling Lottie. I saw your name on the passenger list and I couldn't believe my eyes. I was determined to do the Carpiquet run this morning and find you at long last. It's so good to know you're alive! Bella and your mother will be over the moon!"

Lottie gulped some water from the tumbler that someone had shoved into her hand. Her teeth rattled against the glass and someone else took it away, but her throat was no longer sandpaper dry. "Al, I can't believe my eyes. What did you say about being an aunt?"

Al laughed. "Bella and I are married, Lottie, and we have a son. Charles Albert. He was only born in October! Ah, you've missed it all and there is so much to tell you."

"A *baby*? Why, that's wonderful! And is Bella alright? When did you get married? Is Mummy well? Oh, tell me everything!"

Captain Reid stepped between them. "You've obviously known each other a long time and I'm very happy to see you reunited, but the daylight won't last for anyone and we must keep to our schedule. First-Officer Phipps, I must insist that you board that Anson on time and talk to your passenger on the way. Sorry, and all that, but there is still a war on, you know, and the days are at their shortest right now."

Al stood up and saluted the Captain. "Yes, of course, sir. I'll make sure Miss Flintock-Smythe is well enough, first, if that's alright with you."

Lottie staggered upright. "I'm fine, really I am. Please, don't let me mess things up for you." She turned to Françoise and hugged her. "Goodbye, dearest Françoise. Look after that gorgeous boy of yours."

"I will, oh Charlotte, how I will miss you! How wonderful that someone from your family is here to greet you and take you home. I will worry less now."

"Yes, I have dearest Al by the most extraordinary chance. It's nothing short of a miracle. Ah, but you have Emile now and I know you will be very happy together. Give my best love to Bernadette, won't you?"

Lottie kissed them all over again until Captain Reid coughed loudly and looked at his watch.

Al put his hand gently on her back. "Think we'd better head off, Lottie."

Emile handed him her suitcase and Lottie picked up her handbag. She was wearing one of her summer frocks with her coat tightly buttoned up against the cold, but her legs, despite her woollen stockings, were covered in goosepimples from the December chill as they crossed the tarmac and climbed up to the plane. She gave one last wave to her French friends, now gathered outside by Madame Voclain's car, then climbed inside the aeroplane and Al followed her in and sat in the pilot's seat.

"Well, I must say, this is the most important mission of my life, Lottie. Let's get you home."

Lottie was very impressed when Al landed the plane without a hitch or a bump. As they climbed down from the Anson onto the runway, he carried her case for her. "I would love to spend the day catching up with you, Lottie. There is still so much I want to learn about your time in France and to tell you about what you've missed here, but I have to get back to work. I'll get a car to take you to the station. You mustn't waste a minute in getting home. Your mother will be as astonished to see you as I am! We've all missed you so much."

Al escorted her into the office where she had to sign a chit and show her passport, and he was given another mission to complete before the daylight finally faded. He ushered her to a taxi at the base and told the driver to take her to the station at Paddington. Al gave Lottie some British banknotes and Lottie leaned out of the car window to say yet another goodbye.

Al leaned in and kissed her cheek in a very brotherly fashion. "I wish I could come with you, dearest Lottie. I'd love to see their faces when you walk in! I used up my leave when Charlie-boy was born."

"It's alright, Al, I understand. The train journey will give me a chance to take it all in. Thanks for everything."

"I still can't believe you're here. It's bloody marvellous, it really is! Take care, old girl. I'll telephone tonight to make sure you've arrived safely."

"Look after yourself too, Al. You know, flying and everything. It's amazing you're a pilot! And thanks for bringing me home safely."

"Get on with you, I'm just glad that I'm on the routine run for Carpiquet. Give my love to my wife, won't you?" Al laughed and waved as the car moved off.

Lottie waved for as long as she could see him. They'd had so little time to exchange their news. The flight had been much quicker than she had anticipated, and Al had to concentrate on flying for most of it. The noise of the engine had made any conversation hard work and much had been left unsaid. Now she had been bundled into a taxi without having time to catch her breath.

Lottie found it difficult to navigate her way at Paddington station. There were so many people, more than she'd seen in years. She bought a ticket and waited on the platform for only a quarter of an hour before the Woodbury train was announced. Relieved she had boarded the right train, Lottie climbed into a compartment with only one other passenger and sat back against the plush seat. It smelled of stale dust and old tobacco smoke. The train slid slowly out of the station, past the raggedy town houses of yellow London brick. There were gaps in the streets where bombs had fallen, and children played in craters amongst heaps of rubble in the ruins. As the early twilight fell, the buildings thinned out and the blacked-out night took over. Then, all she could see in the glass was her own reflection.

She'd kept her French beret on against the cold winter air and wore her old tweed coat that she'd brought with her from England back in 1939. She noticed that many women wore the same dated style and looked as shabby as she did. She missed her corduroy trousers and the strong leather belt that lent support to her backbone. Her grey woollen stockings, lent by Bernadette and loose around her ankles, were no substitute against the draught whistling around her legs for the manly garb she'd worn for so long.

It had been such a shock when Al waltzed into the office at Carpiquet airbase. He didn't look much older but there was an air of confidence about him now that he'd never had before. Lottie smiled at her own face in the train window as she remembered how smart he'd looked in his ATA uniform. Al had always been a bit of a scruffy kid. It's funny, she already thought of him as her brother and he

423

really was now he'd married Isobel. Love was strange. If someone had told her that Al wasn't the love of her life back in 1939 when she'd bolted for Paris, she would never have believed them.

The man in a greasy suit sitting opposite her lit up a cigarette and offered her one with a smarmy wink. She declined and shut her eyes, pretending to sleep. With the day she'd had, she had no energy to fend him off. He seemed to take the hint and before long she was genuinely dozing.

When she woke up, the annoying man had gone and had been replaced by a middle-aged woman who was placidly knitting a scarf, and a younger one sitting with two school-aged children playing cat's cradle.

The older woman smiled at her. "Had a nice sleep, dear?"

Lottie stifled a yawn. "Thank you, yes."

"Hope you haven't missed your stop. Where are you off to?" The needles clacked together.

"Woodbury."

"That's lucky then. Woodbury's next."

"Gosh, already?" Lottie smoothed down her coat and rubbed her eyes.

"Are you foreign, dear? I hope you don't mind me asking but you don't sound like you're from round here."

"No, I'm English. I was born near Woodbury."

"Well, I never. Could have sworn you was French or something exotic like that!" The woman tittered and swopped her needles over.

"I…I've been in France for a while."

"Ooh, I knew it. Say no more, duckie. I expect it was hush-hush. How exciting!"

"It wasn't the least bit exciting, I just got stuck there. Oh, never mind." Lottie jumped up from her seat and retrieved her case from the netting on the parcel shelf above her.

"Sorry, I'm sure. Didn't mean to cause offence."

424

The conductor shouted out. "Woodbury. All passengers for Woodbury please alight now."

"Excuse me." Lottie slid the compartment door open. "Good night."

"Night, dear. Good luck."

Lottie slid the door shut again and went down the corridor to the lobby with the outside door. She pushed down the sliding window and leaned out to open the door handle when the train wheezed to a standstill. Woodbury station looked a lot less crowded than Paddington.

Lottie walked across the platform and down the steps into the yard outside, pleased to find a taxicab parked there.

The driver sat at the wheel with his arms folded across his chest, snoring loudly. When she tapped on the window, he jerked awake and wound it down.

"Yes, Miss?"

"Cheadle Manor, please."

"Right you are, hop in and we'll have you there in a jiffy."

Lottie clambered into the back of the cab. She felt nervous, like she had at the beginning of this bewildering, endless day, and clutched her case on her lap to steady her nerves.

When the car swung through the gates of the manor house and up the long drive, her heart lurched uncomfortably above her diaphragm and her throat felt tight. She fumbled with some money, trying to remember the British coinage. She gave up and handed a pound note to the driver. "Just keep the change."

"Thanks, Miss! Very generous, I'm sure. Bless your heart." He turned the car back around and was gone.

Lottie stood at the foot of the stairs to the big front doors of the manor house. Everything was dark and it was hard to see. Not even a chink of light escaped the long windows, but she could just make out the walls in the moonlight, smothered in swarming ivy, and looking uncared

425

for. She climbed the steps up to the front door. She lifted up her hand to the bell-push and noticed the paint was peeling around it.

She pressed her finger on the button and heard the ringing of the bell inside. Her heart was pounding now. Would old Andrews still be alive to answer the door?

The door opened and she was bathed in light. Blinking in its rays, it took Lottie a moment to realise that a nurse, in full uniform complete with starched white apron and a preposterously tall cap, had answered the bell, not her ancient butler.

"Yes, who is it? I hope it's an emergency at this late hour." The nurse had a hard, professional demeanour and gave no hint of a welcoming smile.

It was not what Lottie had expected. "Is Mrs Flintock-Smythe at home? Is she unwell? Why are you here?"

"Mrs Flintock-Smythe does not live here anymore."
"What?"

The nurse frowned. "Look, who are you?"

"I'm her daughter."

"No, you're not - her daughter is Mrs Phipps and you don't resemble her at all."

"I really shouldn't have to explain this to you. My mother has *two* daughters. My name is Charlotte Flintock-Smythe and I demand to see my mother!" Lottie hadn't realised she was shouting.

A tall, middle-aged man in a white coat joined the nurse in the hall. He spoke with a soft Scottish burr. "What's all the commotion, Nurse Heatherley?"

"This young woman claims to be Mrs Flintock-Smythe's daughter, Dr Harris."

"I see, leave this to me, Nurse. Please, Miss Flintock-Smythe, do come in."

The nurse marched off, sniffing loudly. Lottie entered the hall and looked around while the man shut the door behind her. There was a strong smell of antiseptic and

426

the beautiful octagonal space was bare of any painting, plant or a single stick of furniture.

The whole effect chilled her. "What has happened to my home?"

"Please, won't you come into my office?"

Lottie followed the tall man into her grandfather's old study. This room at least looked a bit like it used to, but all the family portraits were missing. "I don't understand. This isn't *your* office, it belonged to my grandfather, Sir Robert Smythe. Why are you here?"

"Let me explain, my dear. Cheadle Manor has been requisitioned as a hospital for the duration of the war. I'm a psychiatrist, specialising in trauma. My name is Dr Malcolm Harris and Mrs Flintock-Smythe is…is a good friend of mine. She now lives in West Lodge, by the front gates."

"West Lodge! But that's where Al's grandparents lived! Why didn't he tell me?"

Dr Harris looked concerned. "Ah, so you've met young Phipps?"

"Yes, he flew me home this morning. I've been in France."

"Then you must be Charlotte. I can't tell you how extremely pleased I am to meet you. This must be very disorientating. I expect you will want to see your mother at the earliest opportunity. She will be thrilled to see you. Will you allow me to escort you down the drive?"

The gravel crunched under Lottie's old court shoes. She hadn't worn anything but boots for years and they pinched her toes. She couldn't focus on anything but the discomfort. She tried to pay attention to the doctor's monologue about his work at the hospital in the house she'd once called home, but she couldn't take in a single word. Dr Harris offered to carry her suitcase, but Lottie refused and gripped it firmly. He'd already taken her home away.

Cheadle Manor a hospital? She looked back at the house. It stood in silhouette against the moonlit sky, brooding and unhappy, as if it wanted her back. She told

427

herself not to be fanciful, that she was tired. Houses didn't have feelings.

Lottie stood back while Dr Harris rapped on the front door of West Lodge. After a couple of minutes, it opened a crack and then was thrown wide. Lottie stayed in the shadows looking on while her mother greeted Dr Harris with a full-blown kiss – on the lips! Dr Harris pulled Cassandra's arms away from his neck and held her at arm's length.

"My dear. I have a monumental surprise for you. Shall we go inside?" Dr Harris guided her mother back indoors and then nodded back at Lottie, who had hung back even further at this shocking development.

Lottie clutched her bag and her case tightly and walked forward slowly into the tiny hall of West Lodge. Dr Harris stood between her and her mother, his bulk obscuring her from view. He reached behind with his foot, kicked the door shut, and only then did he get out of the way.

Lottie put her luggage down and stared at her mother. "Mummy?"

Cassandra's enthusiastic smile of welcome for Dr Harris slipped away and her face became ashen white. "It can't be…Lottie?"

Lottie nodded, unsure what to do.

Cassandra looked at Dr Harris as if needing confirmation that this was her daughter.

He gave a slight nod and stood back. "I'll go into the parlour, my dear. Join me when you are ready."

Cassandra didn't appear to notice him go. She stared and stared at Lottie until Lottie feared she didn't know her.

Then her mother gave a sob and opened her arms as wide as the narrow space would allow. "Oh, my darling, darling girl. You've come home at last. I thought you were *dead*! Come here, Lottie. Let me hold you, so I know you are real and that I'm not imagining this. God knows I have wished for this moment so many times."

Lottie gasped with relief and joy mixed together and ran into her mother's arms. "Oh, Mummy! It's so wonderful to see you!"

Cassandra covered her face in kisses, holding it between trembling palms. "I can't believe you're here! How did you get here? Where have you *been* all these long years? Oh, I've been so worried about you."

Lottie laid her head on her mother's shoulder and hugged her tight. Tears streamed down her face.

"Come in and sit by the fireside. You must be exhausted! Are you tired? When did you get here? Oh, I have so many questions!" Cassandra kept her arm around Lottie as they squeezed through the sitting-room doorway together.

A bright fire flickered in the small grate. Dr Harris immediately got up from one of the two fireside chairs and beckoned Lottie to sit down in it. Just then, there was a wail from another part of the house.

Lottie couldn't think what it was for a moment.

"It's Charles. The baby. Do you know about the baby?" Cassandra sat opposite her on the other chair by the fire.

Lottie nodded. "Al brought me home in his plane."

"What? That's amazing!" Cassandra leapt up again. "So, you know that Bella and Al are married then?"

Lottie nodded again. "Yes, he told me. Oh, do let me meet my nephew!"

"Of course, of course! Oh, my goodness! This is overwhelming!"

"Shall I fetch Isobel?" Dr Harris went to the door.

"Oh, yes please, Malcolm."

Before he could reach the door, Isobel was in the room, holding a baby to her chest, patting its back and saying soothing words in an attempt to stop its raucous crying.

She stopped stock still in the doorway. "Lottie! Is it really you? Oh, heavens, it is!" Isobel rushed over to her, baby and all, and wrapped her spare arm around her sister.

Lottie caught a whiff of the unique, tender smell of a young baby and kissed her sister. "Oh, let me see his face, Bella!"

Isobel turned the baby over and Charles reached out his chubby hand and touched her face. Lottie took his little fist in hers and kissed it. Miraculously, the baby stopped crying and stroked her cheek.

"You have the magic touch, Lottie. Oh, it's so good to see you!" Isobel kissed her again.

Cassandra came and put an arm around each of them. "My two darling girls. Together again. I never thought I'd ever see the day. All my dearest wishes have come true tonight."

CHAPTER FIFTY-SEVEN
CHEADLE MANOR, ENGLAND
DECEMBER 1944

Unused to sharing a bedroom after having the attic at Le Verger to herself for so long, apart from those desperate days in the cellar, Lottie couldn't sleep at West Lodge that first night. Isobel's bed was quite close to hers and the baby constantly snuffled and stirred in his sleep. From time to time, Isobel picked him up and fed him at her breast and once, apologising profusely, she had to put the light on to change his nappy.

Lottie had been oblivious to all this nocturnal nursing when Françoise had been at this stage with Bertrand. She was beginning to wonder how any mother survived with so little rest.

Eventually she dozed off and it was daylight and quite late when she awoke. She hadn't a clue where she was when she first opened her eyes. The small bedroom was unfamiliar and had a distinct aroma of soiled nappies. Blinking, she sat up and looked across at the other single bed. It was empty, only the imprint of her sister's body remained. The cot beside it was empty too. Lottie got up and drew the curtains. The day was dull with sulky clouds squeezing out a cold-looking drizzle. Very uninviting, but she was so tired, so muddled in her head, she didn't really care.

The latticed window looked out on the garden of West Lodge. Beyond it, Lottie could see Cheadle Manor above the tree line. At this distance it still looked imposing and majestic. Its three gables still pointed to the sky but the ivy she'd noticed strangling its foundations was below her line of vision. Smoke billowed up from its chimneys to add gloom to the already grey sky. Lottie shivered involuntarily but whether from the chilly morning or her frisson of déjà vu, she wasn't sure.

431

Not having a dressing gown, she pulled her tweed coat on over her nightgown, rubbed the sleep from her eyes and went to see who else was in the little house. Did Dr Harris sleep over? Had things progressed that far with her mother? Her weary mind couldn't grapple with *that* thought.

She found Cassandra, Isobel and baby Charles in the kitchen, sitting at the small gate-leg table in the centre of the square room, the remains of what looked like a pretty meagre breakfast between them.

"Oh, it's lovely and warm in here." Lottie stood in the doorway contemplating her relatives.

Cassandra immediately vacated her chair - there were only two. "Come and sit down, darling. You look cold. Didn't you sleep?"

Isobel put baby Charles over her shoulder to wind him. "I hope we didn't keep you awake, Lottie. This young man is so greedy. I can't remember when I last had a good night's sleep. Sometimes the days and nights just blur together."

Lottie sat down. "I am a bit tired, it's true, but I doubt I would have slept anyway. It's so strange being here and not in our real home."

"Have a cup of tea, darling. It will help you wake up." Cassandra poured dark liquid from a big, brown teapot, not unlike Bernadette's, into a chipped mug.

Lottie felt a pang of sadness that Bernadette wasn't here to meet her family. The big kitchen of Le Verger had been a lot more comfortable than this boxy room. For a guilty, fleeting moment, she wished she was back there.

"Drink up, Lottie."

"Oh, yes, thank you. Lovely." The tea was strong, almost bitter and had been brewed too long. The milk was cloying and sweet, poured from a punctured hole in a tin of evaporated milk. It didn't have the refreshing tang of fresh goat's milk she usually enjoyed.

"Would you like a cooked breakfast? We have two rashers of bacon leftover from the rations this week. I was

432

saving them for a pie, but you are very welcome. I could mix it up with some powdered egg into an omelette, if you'd like?" Cassandra stood by the range, hesitating.

"Um, no. Just a slice of bread and butter would do."

"No butter, just jam, I'm afraid. We used up the butter ration on Christmas Day."

"Oh, well, jam is fine, thank you."

Cassandra cut a thick slice from the square, shop-bought loaf and smeared a thin-looking red jam on it.

"Thank you. That's great." The bread was bland and tasteless, and the jam sour from lack of sugar. "Mm, lovely." Lottie swallowed the sticky bolus in her mouth and chased it down with the stewed tea.

A pungent smell wafted across the kitchen.

"Oh, dear, he's filled his nappy again. I'll have to go and change him. Don't say anything important till I get back! I want to hear everything you've been up to, Lottie." Isobel got up and took the baby back to the bedroom.

Cassandra took the empty seat. "You're not finding this easy, are you, darling?"

Lottie shook her head and pushed her plate away. "No, no I'm not."

The telephone rang in the hall. "Oh, drat! I'll have to answer it." Cassandra got up and went into the hall. Nothing was far from anything else at West Lodge so Lottie could hear every word her mother said.

"Yes, still here. No, no idea what her plans are. She seems rather confused and tired. Yes, it is understandable, of course but…what's that? Yes, you're right. Of course, you can, about seven o'clock? It's Spam fritters and cabbage again, I'm afraid! Alright, darling, yes, I will. See you later."

Lottie drank the dregs of her tea. The overheard conversation had made her feel like a displaced parcel that nobody really wanted.

Her mother came back into the room.

"I think I'll go out for a walk, Mummy."

433

"In this weather?"

"I don't mind a bit of drizzle. It's not heavy rain."

"Want some company?"

"No, not at the moment. Sorry."

Cassandra nodded. "I understand, darling."

Lottie found this compassionate acceptance disconcertingly annoying and knew it was unjust of her. She got dressed quietly in the bedroom, relieved to find Isobel absent. Lottie went to the lean-to bathroom and looked at herself in the mirror, but it was so cold the glass steamed up and she couldn't see anything but an oval blur in the condensation dripping down its surface. She splashed water on her face, got dressed and went out to the back porch. She found some wellington boots by the back door and pulled them on.

The soft rain was cold. Not icy but cold enough and deceitfully penetrating. Lottie pulled her folded beret from her coat pocket and shoved it over her short hair. Funny how Mummy and Isobel were so fair and she so dark. It emphasised their differences.

Cheadle Manor drew her up the hill like a magnet. How strange to be excluded from her old, familiar home. An ambulance passed her on the drive, its siren bell clanging; its wailing discord jangling her already overstretched nerves. She watched as it drew up outside her old front door and Nurse Heatherley came down the steps Lottie used to play hopscotch on to greet it. Two soldiers, one on crutches, one with bandages around his head, shuffled up the steps, with the ambulance driver helping, and the nurse shut the door behind them.

Her door.

She shouldn't mind. They were helping brave soldiers to heal their wounds and, if Dr Harris was a psychiatrist, presumably not just the visible injuries.

War. There was no escaping it anywhere.

Lottie wandered around the grounds of the big house. She had no choice, being banned from its interior.

She was shocked to see some of the lawn had been dug up and vegetables planted in it. Being winter a lot of the exposed soil was bare. The whole effect was utterly depressing. She wondered what they had done to her old bedroom and the dear old nursery. What had become of all her precious beloved childhood things? She hadn't even known she'd cared about them, that holding them in her hands again would have meant so much. What had they done to the room in which Granny had died? Had young men now also become ghosts in that huge bedroom with the heavy, dark blue curtains?

Somehow, she gravitated to the bare-limbed orchard. She sat down on the old, rusting loveseat on the lawn between the apple trees and the ancient grey stone walls of her home. This had been her father's favourite spot. She had few memories of him but she could remember him sprawled on this seat, his long legs spread-eagled out on the grass; his arms draped across the figure-of-eight shaped back, her mother invariably beside him, necessarily close because of the size of the bench and because she loved him so much. Lottie closed her eyes and pictured them here together. In her mind's eye, her father was laughing, throwing his head back and surrendering to mirth in that all-or-nothing way he'd tackled everything. She'd forgotten his eyes were blue, you couldn't tell from a photograph.

The family photographs! Where were they now? Where was anything? And where did she fit in this new upside-down world?

One thing was for sure, it no longer felt like home.

Lottie sat for a good while on the loveseat. In her mind's eye she remembered the chain of events leading up to this moment; Granny's horrible death; the crazy way she'd left her will; her own anger at her rejection by both her mother and Al and subsequent impulsive dash to Paris; the dizzy days with Mabs; joining the exodus out of Paris; the horror of the elder Bertrand's death on the road; meeting Bernadette; Mireille going off with that fat German;

435

blowing up the train with Thierry; ah, Thierry – those kisses! That night when she'd bathed him by the fire in the kitchen of Le Verger returned in vivid images. Her yearning for him became a physical ache as she remembered the flickering firelight over his lean body. Everything would be different if he was here. Or even if she was with him, wherever he was. Would she ever see him again?

Eventually, she started to shiver from the cold and wet and got up, rubbing her arms to get some life back into them. She took one last, lingering look at Cheadle Manor, then turned away from it and started to walk back down the hill to the tiny lodge house which guarded its magnificent pillared gates.

She must think about her mother. About Isobel and the baby. They were the ones who needed her now. Bernadette had Emile and Françoise to care for her. She must let go of this feeling of responsibility for everyone at Le Verger. Emile was a very capable young man with a formidable mother of his own. Now Lucien Dubois had left his farm to them all, their futures were assured. Thierry – no, she couldn't reconcile herself to not knowing his fate, but she had to unwillingly admit, there was absolutely nothing she could do about it. She was here and must make the best of it.

Lottie squared her shoulders, wiped the rain from her face and walked more purposefully down to West Lodge.

When Lottie arrived back at the lodge, she entered the porch quietly and took off her borrowed wellington boots.

Her sister's voice floated out from the kitchen. "Honestly, Mummy, I feel I'm walking on eggshells. I'm longing to find out about where Lottie has been, but I dare not broach the subject – or any subject, come to that – because she looks so sort-of shutdown. Is it me, or do you feel the same?"

"Malcolm says we must give her time. She might be in shock, he says."

Lottie seethed inwardly. Didn't her mother have an opinion of her own these days?

She almost pulled the boots back on to go out again but then Isobel came into the porch. "Oh, hello Lottie, didn't hear you come in. I'm just getting some leeks for lunch." Isobel looked flushed and awkward.

"Hello."

"You look cold, come in and dry off." Isobel picked up some leeks from a box under the counter.

"Alright." Lottie followed her sister indoors.

Cassandra took her wet coat. "I'll hang it over here near the range to dry it out. What a filthy morning. I hate this time of year, don't you?"

Why was her mother talking to her as if she was a stranger?

"I'm going to make potato and leek soup, darlings. Bella, why not make us a cup of tea?" Cassandra stood at the sink, a leek in each hand.

A monumental tide of emotion welled up in Lottie at the sight of her elegant mother, washing leeks with red, careworn hands. She felt as if a dam was bursting in her

437

chest. "Oh, Mummy, just look at you!" A sob erupted. "You're just like Bernadette!"

"Oh, my darling girl." Cassandra dropped the leeks, wiped her wet hands on a tea towel and sat down next to her. Lottie turned into her mother's arms and let the floodgates open.

"I'll make the tea." Isobel bustled around them while Lottie cried all the tears she could not shed before.

Lottie regained her composure within a few minutes and blew her nose on the handkerchief offered by her mother.

Cassandra wiped her own eyes with bare hands. "Why don't you tell us all about it, Lottie?"

Lottie drew in a rattling breath and nodded. "It was the soup. We always had soup, every single day, whatever the weather. In fact, the first time I met Bernadette it was so hot and I'd driven all the way from Paris, you see, and Bertrand was killed by the Luftwaffe on the road and I was sick in a ditch and…"

Cassandra nodded. "Take your time, darling. Sounds like you've been through a lot."

Isobel put the teapot on the table and covered it with a home-made knitted tea-cosy. "Oh, Lottie, you've been to hell and back, haven't you?"

All that afternoon, Lottie talked, and her sister and mother listened, exclaiming and sympathising, cooking, and tending to the baby in between. They drifted into the parlour after lunch as Lottie continued her story and she listened to theirs.

Lottie was astonished to learn that her sister had toughed it out as a Land Girl in north Wales and at Home Farm and congratulated Isobel on her new skills.

"Oh, I loved it really, well I did at Home Farm." Isobel laughed. "It wasn't so great up at the Williams's hill farm. Short rations, you see!"

Cassandra frowned. "Oh, and I must tell you that your American grandfather and Aunt Cheryl were killed in a car accident back in 1942. I don't suppose you remember them much."

"Not really."

"No, well, why should you? You were so young when you met them. Aunt Rose is still going strong. It's funny how she's outlived them all and has produced five children, would you believe!"

"That is a lot."

"Yes, and Aunt Katy's factory is going great guns. You wouldn't believe how much it has expanded. She has a lot of orders for the services of course. All sorts of kit need rubber, it seems. She has a much bigger workforce now."

"Is the Katherine Wheel Garage still going? I couldn't see from the taxi last night, it was too dark."

"Oh, yes, but Jem runs it mostly and he still finds time to grow all those vegetables. They are an incredibly resourceful pair, those two."

"And Lily?"

"Oh, Lily is just like her mother. If it wasn't for the age difference, you'd think they were twins! She loves working on the machines too. Clever girl."

The short winter's day soon drew to a close and Cassandra drew the curtains and banked up the fire. "I think this calls for sherry, my darlings. Tell us more about your experiences, Lottie. There's so much more I'd like to know."

"Yes, me too. I mean, who organised the sabotage on the train, Lottie? I'm not sure I would have had the courage for that!" Isobel picked up her baby, who had started to whimper.

"I haven't told you about Thierry, have I?"

Cassandra handed them each a glass of amber sherry. "He sounds important."

Lottie sipped the sweet alcohol. "He is. I'm going to marry him, if and when he comes back from the front."

"My goodness, then he is the most important person in the world!" Cassandra lifted her glass. "To Thierry."

Isobel unbuttoned her frock and put Charles to her breast. "Don't mind me, will you? Greedy little monkey. Please tell us about Thierry."

"He's a schoolteacher - or was. He's so good with children. He was defending his flock when I first saw him. The Germans had taken over the village, you see, and one of the kids was mocking their silly goosestep. The soldiers pointed their guns at the children – can you imagine – and Thierry stepped between them. One of the villagers, a man I came to know and love, Lucien Dubois, feigned a fit and distracted the German officer and I helped Thierry get the children safely into school. The bastards still came after him and beat him up though."

Lottie told them about hiding the rifles, getting the wireless and joining in with the sabotage when Thierry had been shot in the leg and she'd had to get him back to Le Verger. She was still talking when there was a knock at the door.

Cassandra got up to answer it and came back with Dr Harris. "Oh, my goodness, I've forgotten all about supper! Are you starving, Malcolm?"

"A bit peckish but I can wait. How are you, Charlotte?"

"Hoarse! I've been talking so much."

Cassandra poured a whisky for Malcolm and topped up everyone else's glass. "It's been fascinating, Malcolm. I'm so proud of my daughter – both my daughters, of course, but Lottie's been incredibly brave. She's been part of the Resistance, helping the Free French!"

"That's very impressive, I must say. I salute you!" Malcolm raised his tumbler of Scotch to Lottie.

"We must break off our storytelling and feed ourselves. A scratch supper of Spam sandwiches and the rest of the soup will have to do!" Cassandra disappeared into the kitchen.

"I must change this chap before we eat. Excuse me." Isobel took the baby and left the room.

440

"I'm glad to hear you've been able to talk about your adventures." Malcolm took the fireside chair opposite Lottie.

"I wasn't on a school trip, you know. It wasn't adventurous. It was life and death."

"I beg your pardon."

"So you should. It's still life and death for the friends I have left in France. War is truly hellish."

"Did you lose many friends?"

"Yes, I did, and I shall never forget them. It's impossible for you to understand the daily terror of living in an occupied country with a false identity. How could you? Not ever knowing if you'd be carted off to a labour camp - or shot. Every day, can you understand that?"

Malcolm was silent. Lottie found it infuriating.

She got up and started to pace around the room. "Did you know that Canadian troops were massacred just up the road from the farm where I was living? Did you know that Caen is nothing but rubble now? That our barn was flattened? The beautiful, gentle nanny-goats killed? And Madam Leroy, dear, kind, wonderful Madame Leroy! They burned her arms with cigarettes. Oh, don't look like that!"

"I'm sorry." Malcolm had turned round in his chair and his eyes never left her face.

"Are you? *Are you*? I saw it, you know. Saw the smoke rise up from her arms, the red circles left behind on her skin. And what for? Did you know they were all shot the day after D-Day? Shot in the back. And the bloody Boche didn't even do it themselves. They got the Russian prisoners-of-war to man the machine-gun and kill them up against the prison walls." Lottie ran her hands through her hair the way Thierry always did. "Oh, no, they were not childish adventures. Murder in cold blood is not something you'd find in a kid's storybook, Dr Harris."

Someone coughed in the hallway. Lottie looked towards the door. Both Isobel and Cassandra stood there, holding hands and gazing at her with such compassion in

441

their eyes that Lottie's anger deflated like a pricked balloon. Suddenly, she felt exhausted.

Cassandra came into the room. "Sit down, sweetheart. You don't have to say anymore. We may not understand exactly what you've been through but both Malcolm and I served in the last war, you know, so we do know something of the horrors you've talked about."

Lottie sat back down and rubbed her face with her hands. "I'm sorry."

Cassandra knelt in front of her. "Don't be sorry, my darling. You've suffered so much. I'm so glad you're home."

CHAPTER FIFTY-NINE
THE KATHERINE WHEEL GARAGE, CHEADLE,
ENGLAND
MARCH 1945

Al got down from the train at Woodbury Station and scanned the platform. Yes, there was his mother, waving like mad. He rushed over to her and enfolded her in a hug.

"Oh, Al, it's so bloody wonderful to see you."

"And you, Mum."

Katy hooked her arm in his. "I've got your son and Bella in the car."

"Oh, good. I can't wait to see them, and you of course."

Katy laughed. "Don't worry, I'm happy to play second fiddle these days."

They clattered down the station steps and walked outside to where the Baby Austin was parked. Bella was sitting in the back, so Al got in beside her and kissed her soundly.

"Hello gorgeous. God, I've missed you."

"You too, Al."

His baby son immediately protested at this monopoly of his mother with very loud crying.

"Blimey! He's grown so much!"

"Babies do that, Al." Katy started up the car.

Al laughed and stared at Charles, who stared back from his mother's knee, his face all red and scrunched up like on the day Al had first seen him as a new-born baby. "He's a little corker, isn't he?"

"Takes after his Dad." Isobel kissed Al's ear, which was the only bit she could reach.

"Does he sleep through the night now?"

"Only wakes once, usually." Isobel winked at him.

Al winked back, delighted to find his wife as keen as him to spend a night together again.

443

Katy accelerated away from the station yard. "You could stay at ours, while Al's home, if you like. Lily could go in with my Mum."

Isobel answered for them both. "Thanks, Aunt Katy, but we'll be alright at the lodge. Lottie's offered to sleep in the sitting-room. It's only for two nights."

"Worse luck." Al took Charles on to his lap and the baby immediately started to cry again and reached for his mother.

Isobel held out her arms. "Give him back to me, Al. He's not used to you."

Katy stopped at a junction. "This bloody war. Makes everything wrong side up. Still, I see that our boys have crossed the Rhine now, shouldn't go on much longer."

"I hope not, Mum. That battle of the Bulge was a close call, though, but the Wehrmacht haven't put up such a fight since."

"It's those V2-rockets I worry about with you so close to London."

Al nodded. "They are the worst, it's true. Croydon's had a bad time of it. It's when the bloody engine noise stops that's so awful. Who'd have thought silence could be so terrifying?"

"Oh, I can't bear the thought of it, with you up there. I can't sleep some nights for thinking about it. So, let's forget about the war for two whole days, while we can." Isobel bounced Charles on her knee, and he changed his tone from whining to giggling.

Al put his arm around Isobel, loving the feel of her. Knowing she thought about him all the time made him feel both sad and happy. He'd had a close shave with one of those V-2 rockets only last week when he'd gone shopping in Oxford Street, but he wasn't going to tell either of these women about only just making it to the shelter in the nick of time.

"He enjoys that, doesn't he?" Al smiled at his son. "If he keeps this up, I could almost get to like him."

Katy glanced in the rear-view mirror at them. "I'll stop off at the garage and we'll see your Dad and everybody. Gran is dying to see you. She's gone very downhill these last few months."

"Sorry to hear that, Mum."

"I think she's had another minor stroke, but she won't hear of going to the doctor's. She won't even let Dr Benson call. Says he's not a patch on his father."

"That must be a worry for you."

Katy put the car into gear and moved off again. "I could do without it, it's true. The factory is as busy as ever. We're sending stuff out to the Pacific now, which is ironic because that's where the rubber came from in the first place, though supplies have been very erratic. Good job the government stockpiled it before the war started. Now it's going back like a boomerang."

"But the rubber's going back to the East in a different shape, of course." Al met his mother's eyes in the rear-view mirror.

Katy laughed. "Somewhat different, yes. We're sourcing some new supplies from Ceylon now which has saved the day and the Americans have come up with a good substitute too."

Al gave his son an index finger to hold. "You have to hand it to the Americans when it comes to new ideas."

Katy nodded. "Yes, it's impressive, but it still seems daft to me to be sending the stuff back east where they are bombing the plantations it came from. Still, I'm not complaining. We're a lot better off than we were but I hate all the destruction this war has brought to the world."

His Dad was waiting for them at the bungalow when they arrived and his grandmother was ensconced in a comfy armchair by the sitting-room fire, surrounded by pillows. She looked very frail.

"Hello, Gran. It's smashing to see you."

Agnes spoke in a cracked voice. "Oh, Al, my lovely boy. How good it is to see your bonny face again. Give us a kiss."

Al leaned in and kissed her withered cheek. It felt like parchment.

"How long have you got, son?" His Dad came in bearing a tea-tray.

"Only two days."

Agnes shifted against her bank of pillows. "That's no time at all. They work you too hard in that ATA of yours."

"It's the same for everyone, Gran. But it'll soon be over, you mark my words. The Allies are in Germany now, you know. We've got the Nazis beat alright."

"I still don't hold with being up in the air in a machine like that. 'Tisn't natural."

"I'm as safe as houses up in my aeroplane."

"And who says houses are safe anymore? Judging by the news, no-one's safe anywhere, especially with them rocket-things. I don't know what the world's coming too, I really don't. As if the last shout wasn't bad enough." His Gran looked tired already.

Katy put a cup of tea by on the little table by her elbow. "There you are, Mum."

"Thanks, love." But Agnes was asleep before it had cooled.

They stole away to the kitchen, taking the tea-tray with them. Al told them about his flights over Europe. "Some days I go to Brussels twice in one day. It's amazing how quickly you can get somewhere in a plane. It's a beautiful city, hardly been touched, except for the airfield. Lost a few Ansons of our own there.

"Have you seen much bomb damage elsewhere?"

"Oh, yes, you wouldn't believe some of it. Caen is the worst, where Lottie was. It's as flat as pancake except for the cathedral. Apparently, that was only saved because they made a red cross from sheets dipped in blood during the carpet bombing."

"Good God." Jem looked genuinely shocked.

Al took a sip of his tea. "Don't know how she survived it. How is she, Bella?"

"Well, I can talk about it as she's not here but she's not happy, Al. Seems really depressed all the time. Keeps complaining about the hospital being up at the big house and she hasn't really taken to Malcolm very well. It makes it very awkward at the lodge."

"That's a shame. Must be tough on your Mum."

Katy put her cup down. "You know Aunt Cass though, never complains, but I can see it's a strain. Can't be easy for you either, Bella."

"Oh, I don't mind. We all thought she was dead, you see, how could I possibly resent her now? If I'd been through what she has, and I'm sure she hasn't told us the half of it, I'd be a total wreck. She isn't horrible to anyone, just, sort of, absent, if you know what I mean. Maybe she'd talk to you, Al."

Al and Isobel stayed chatting for a couple of hours and then Katy drove them up to the lodge. When pressed by Cassandra, she refused an invitation for more tea. "You don't need me cluttering up the place when you have my son! See you soon. Got to get back to work anyway."

Cassandra greeted Al with all the affection any son-in-law could wish but Lottie's welcome was more muted. Cassandra had put on a spread of sorts, and they sat down to a lunch of meatloaf, marrow chutney and jacket potatoes in the kitchen.

Afterwards, Isobel picked up Charles and wiped his face. "Got to put him down for his nap, Al. why don't you take Lottie out in the car for a drive?" She gave Al a meaningful look over the baby's head.

Cassandra started to clear the table. "Oh yes, good idea. I'd like you to have a listen to the engine. Your mother never has time these days, but I think the timing's off. See what you think, Al."

Al dutifully turned to his sister-in-law. "Come on, Lottie. Let's go for a spin in the motor, shall we? Just the two of us?"

"What about Bella?"

"Oh, don't mind me. I need to put my feet up as well." Isobel smiled at her.

"Sounds like you all want to get rid of me." Lottie fetched her coat and they went out to the car.

"Where to?" Al revved up the engine of the old Sunbeam.

"Oh, up on the downs, please."

They drove in silence until they reached the top of the hill. Al cut the engine and pulled on the handbrake. The ploughed downland spread its shades of dun-coloured soil out before them, pierced by green shoots of wheat pushing up in serried rows.

The silence continued. Lottie broke it. "Oh, it's so nice not to make polite conversation. To be with someone who's seen the carnage and understands."

"Bella understands and I'm sure your mother does too."

"Oh, I know they *think* they do, Al, but only you have actually seen it."

Al lit up a Woodbine and wound the window down to let out the smoke. "Well, only from up in the air and the immediate bits around the airbases."

"It makes a difference."

"Want a fag?"

"No, thanks."

They were quiet again for a few minutes and it was Al who spoke this time. "Bella says you've fallen in love?"

"Yes."

"I'm glad."

"Glad I'm not still pining for you, you mean?"

448

Al laughed softly. "No, although it would have been awkward, let's face it. No, I'm pleased that you've found someone."

Lottie blinked rapidly and looked away. "Yes, he's wonderful, Al."

"I'm sure. He'd have to be, to deserve you."

Lottie frowned. "Oh, I don't know about that."

Al smiled. "I bloody do."

Lottie turned her head and looked at him properly for the first time. "Thanks."

"What did he do for a living before the war?" Al knew the entire story of Thierry from Isobel's letters, but he wanted to hear it from Lottie.

"He's a teacher. He's French. His name is Thierry Thibault. He was fighting in the Ardennes around Christmastime. I don't know where he is now, though. Haven't had a letter since I got home. For all I know, he could be injured, or even dead. There are so many dreadful things still happening – look at what the Russians found at that awful camp in Auschwitz. I worry he's been caught up in it all."

"He's hardly likely to be with the Ruskies, is he?" Rain started to patter on the windscreen and Al wondered if he should switch the engine on to clear it, then thought better of it. "Why not write to Françoise? Does she know your address?"

Lottie tutted loudly. "Of course, she does, stupid! We've been pen-pals for years!"

Al chucked his cigarette stub out of the window and wound it up a bit against the rain. "Yes, silly me. Still, I'll bet she'd like to hear from you." Al sneaked a look at his watch. He was longing to get back to his wife, but he'd promised to talk to her sister and knew he wouldn't be welcomed back unless he returned with some sort of result.

Lottie shrugged. "Yes, you're right. I've been in such a slump. Haven't been able to stitch two thoughts together. You see, in France, I was the kingpin of the farm

449

and the Resistance kept me busy too. Being in danger all the time somehow made you feel more alive. Though the winters were pretty dreary, I can tell you."

"Winters always are."

"Not like that. We didn't have enough to eat for the last couple of years and the goats were giving less and less milk. Bernadette killed the oldest one because she had run dry."

The rain beat harder now, drumming on the metal roof sheltering them from the spring shower. Al wound his window up tight. He'd left it open a crack to stop condensation building up. "Blimey. That must have been grim – killing the goat, I mean."

"Strangely, it wasn't. Bernadette is very skilled at all sorts of things. She mended Thierry's leg – he'd been shot escaping the Boche. She had a couple of heart attacks, you know. It was the Allied bombing. She couldn't stand all the destruction – or the terrible noise. The orchard was felled, the barn demolished, even a corner of her medieval farmhouse was taken out. Everything she'd worked for. But then, when Emile came home, I wasn't really needed anymore. To be really honest, and, strictly between ourselves, Al, I feel like that here."

"Do you?" Al thought about how busy he was at the ATA, how useful he felt. "Yes, that must be hard. But I'll bet they miss you in France. Don't you want to know how Bernadette is now?"

Lottie sighed. "You're right. I'll write soon. Françoise is good at writing letters."

"Good idea. And make sure you ask about Thierry."

Lottie spread her hands in a gesture that was entirely French to Al's eyes. "She won't know about him. He could be anywhere, if he's still alive."

"He might write to the farm, trying to find you. In fact, he probably thinks you are still there. He doesn't know you've come back to Blighty, now does he?"

Lottie dropped her hands and stared at him. "Oh, Al! Do you really think so?"

"Worth a try."

Mission accomplished, Al pressed the starter button of the old car, which as far as he could tell was running as smoothly as ever. He flicked the one wiper on and cleared the windscreen.

Lottie's face broke into a genuine smile. "Oh look! The rain's stopped."

Al pointed to the east. "And see there? It's a rainbow. A good omen, don't you think?" Al turned the car around and drove back to the lodge to make the most of the little time he had left with his wife and baby son.

Lottie went straight to the sitting-room when they got back. Energised, she searched in the bureau for pen and paper and sat down to write to Françoise.

As the ink flowed across the page, she found it easier and easier to think in French again. As she pictured Françoise receiving her letter, she could remember little details of Le Verger and wondered how much it had changed. Why *had* she left this for so long?

The letter was completed in less than an hour. Lottie went into the kitchen and grabbed her coat. "What time is it? I think I'll walk down to Lower Cheadle and get a stamp straight away at the Post Office."

"You'll be lucky, they shut in half an hour." Cassandra lifted a saucepan of potatoes and put it on to boil.

"Here's the coal." Al came in from the garden with the coal hod. "Where are you off to, Lottie?"

"The Post Office. I've written that letter we talked about."

"Oh, you don't need to post it. I'll take it back with me to White Waltham. Someone's bound to be flying to Carpiquet and they can easily take it to the farm for you. It would be much quicker than the postal service."

"That's a great idea!"

"Oh, I'm full of 'em, me!" Al laughed.

Lottie couldn't wait for Al to go back to work, once he had her letter. It was selfish of her when Isobel looked so happy, but she couldn't help it. The thought of hearing from Thierry was like seeing that rainbow after the rain.

When a letter addressed to her in Françoise's hand arrived a few weeks later, Lottie grabbed it from the mat and tore it open, then and there. She scanned the contents quickly but there was no news of Thierry.

"Got that letter you've been hoping for?" Cassandra came into the hall, carrying a basket of dirty linen.

"Yes," Lottie let her hand holding the letter fall.

"Not bad news, I hope?"

"Oh, no. Well, some. They found Lucien's farmhouse had been flattened by the Allied bombing. Nothing but a crater left, apparently. But the rest is rather good news, actually. Bernadette is much better, Françoise says, and she and Emile got married on the first of March. She's full of plans for the extra land and sounds really happy."

"Then why the long face, darling?"

"Oh, nothing, I was hoping she'd have heard from Thierry, that's all."

"Ah, yes, that must be disappointing." Cassandra went into the kitchen with her soiled laundry.

Lottie re-read the letter several times, but she couldn't squeeze anything different from its single page. She folded it up and went to help her mother with the washing.

"You know it's April next week?" Cassandra scrubbed a sheet against the wooden washboard with the bar of carbolic soap.

"Yes, what of it?"

"Why, it will be your birthday on the 26th, of course!"

Lottie dipped the soapy cloth into a bucket of rinsing water. "Oh, yes, I suppose so."

"Your twenty-fifth birthday, Lottie." Cassandra plunged her sore-looking hands back in the sink of hot, soapy water. "You, know, when you'll inherit the manor."

"Oh, that, yes, I'd forgotten. It'll be a bit pointless, won't it? We can't even go inside the house without Malcolm's say-so."

"Now you know that's only temporary and it's hardly Malcolm's fault."

"I suppose you're right. Should I visit Mr Leadbetter or something?"

453

Cassandra handed her another sheet for rinsing. "I'm not sure. We'd better give the old boy a ring, once we've put these sheets through the wringer and hung them out to dry."

A fortnight later, when they were gathered around the radio, they learned of the sudden death of the President of America.

"Well, I knew he was in poor health, but I didn't see this coming, did you, Malcolm?" Cassandra put down her mending.

"No, and I'm a doctor."

"And we're never allowed to forget it." Lottie muttered under her breath.

Cassandra turned to her eldest daughter. "What was that, darling?"

"And we must never forget how suddenly things can happen." Lottie crossed her fingers.

Malcolm gave her one of his quizzical looks. "Cerebral haemorrhage is a good clean finish for an invalid like him."

"Oh, Malcolm! How grisly!" Cassandra picked up her workbasket and extracted a sock with a hole in its heel.

"Well, I'm sorry for it. He's been a good leader and it's not an ideal time for a change in the presidency."

"Thank goodness we have dear Winston."

Lottie sighed. "And anyone's better than old Pétain."

Mr Leadbetter agreed to meet them a week before Lottie's birthday to go through the papers beforehand. They all went together, Cassandra, Isobel and Lottie, and left young Charles with his other grandmother, Katy, who came to the lodge to look after him.

"Goodness. I don't know about you, Cass, but I can't believe I'm a grandmother!"

"Oh, I know, Kate darling. Life is catching up with us." Cassandra handed the little boy over.

Katy hugged the baby tight. "What a lump! Gosh he's heavy, what are you feeding him, Bella?"

"He's the greediest little piglet! Thank goodness he's on solid food now or I would be a wraith!"

Cassandra drew her driving gloves over her reddened hands. "Are you sure you can manage the little monster, Kate?"

"Oh, don't worry about me. We'll be fine, won't we, Charlie?"

Charles answered by tugging at Katy's greying curls.

"Ow! I think it's just as well I'm here to teach you some discipline, young man!" Katy laughed and waved them off in the doorway.

"Oh, life is strange." Cassandra got behind the wheel of the Sunbeam and pressed the starter button.

"What do you mean, Mummy?" Lottie waved back.

"When I think of Katy being a house servant at the manor, growing up in that little lodge house and now she's standing there holding our shared grandchild and is a celebrated local industrialist, while I'm doing my own laundry in her mother's kitchen sink."

Lottie sat back against the seat as Cassandra swung the car out through the gates onto the London Road in the direction of Woodbury. "Yes, when you put it like that, it is pretty extraordinary." She turned to Isobel, who was sitting on the back seat. "You have a very remarkable mother-in-law, Bella."

"Don't I know it! I can never live up to her."

Cassandra frowned. "No-one says you must, Bella."

Isobel sighed. "No, I know that, but she's achieved so much, sometimes I feel a bit useless."

"What utter drivel, darling." Cassandra changed gear. "You have given both Katy and I the best thing we could ever have and that's a stake in the future when this ghastly war is over."

Lottie looked out of the window. Would she ever bear Thierry a child and be able to give her mother the same joy?

The meeting with the solicitor was over and done with surprisingly quickly.

"It's only a formality, Miss Flintock-Smythe." Mr Leadbetter's hair was mostly gone now and his bald pate shiny. When he looked over his old-fashioned pince-nez at Lottie, she felt she was looking at someone from the previous century. The solicitor still wore a stiff collar, just like Chamberlain's.

Mr Leadbetter cleared his throat and looked at her sternly, as if sensing her critique of his anachronistic outfit. "Until the hospital vacates the premises and you are released from the conditions of its requisition by his Majesty's government, you will not be able to claim your rightful possession of Cheadle Manor, of course. I shall keep the deeds here for safekeeping in the meantime."

"Thank you, Mr Leadbetter."

"All we can do now, ladies, is to hope for a swift cessation of hostilities."

He shook hands with them all and ushered them out with grave civility.

Lottie stood on the pavement outside. "Well, that was a bit of an anti-climax."

"Want to do a bit of shopping or have a cup of tea somewhere to celebrate?"

Isobel shook her head. "If you don't mind, I'd like to go straight home and see if my little piglet's behaving himself."

Lottie walked to the car and opened the door. "Of course, you do. Nothing's really changed, anyway. Let's get home."

That night, they gathered around the radio as was their nightly ritual, with Malcolm Harris amongst them.

456

Lottie was reflecting on the day's legal milestone, how momentous it perhaps should have been and yet didn't feel it, when her train of thought was eclipsed by the War Report.

Cassandra crossed her legs and sat back in her armchair. "Oh, good. It's Richard Dimbleby. I like him. Good diction."

"Ssh, Mummy. Let's hear what the man says." Lottie strained her ears to hear every detail of the broadcast which tonight was coming from some camp in Germany called Bergen-Belsen. She was desperate for news of Thierry. Maybe this journalist would interview him, and she would hear his voice again. Then, even Lottie forgot about anything personal, as they all listened in shocked silence to the young journalist's report.

"I passed through the barrier and found myself in the world of a nightmare. Dead bodies, some of them in decay, lay strewn about the road and along the rutted tracks. Inside the huts it was even worse. I've seen many terrible sights in the last five years, but nothing, nothing approaching the dreadful interior of this hut at Belsen. The dead and the dying lay close together. I picked my way over corpse after corpse in the gloom, until I heard one voice that rose above the gentle, undulating moaning. I found a girl. She was a living skeleton, impossible to gauge her age, for she had practically no hair left on her head, and her face was only a yellow parchment sheet, with two holes in it for eyes. Babies were born at Belsen, some of them shrunken, wizened little things that could not live because their mothers could not feed them."

Isobel gasped out loud and clamped her hand over her mouth. Lottie went to her and sat on the arm of her chair, one arm around her sister's shuddering shoulders.

The man's voice, laden with emotion, continued his story. *"One woman, distraught to the point of madness, flung herself at a British soldier who was on guard in the camp on the night that it was reached by the 11th Armoured Division. She begged him to give her some milk, for the tiny baby she held in her arms. She lay the mite on the ground, threw herself at the sentry's feet and kissed his boots. And when, in his distress, he asked her to get up, she put the baby in his arms and ran off, crying that she would find milk for it because there was no milk in her breast. And when the soldier opened the bundle of rags to look at the child, he found that it had been dead for days. I have never seen British soldiers so moved to cold fury as the men who opened the Belsen camp this week, and those of the police and the RAMC, who are now on duty there trying to save the prisoners who are not too far gone in starvation."*

"I can't listen to anymore." Isobel got up and ran out of the room, and her mother hurried after her.

"Oh, Malcolm. This is dreadful. The worst yet." Lottie wiped tears from her eyes with the palms of her hands. She looked across at the doctor, shocked to see his own face wet.

He took out his handkerchief and blew his nose. "I think I've heard enough. Mind if I switch it off?"

"Please do."

Lottie made herself read the full report in the newspaper the next morning. Apparently, the BBC had been unwilling to broadcast the Dimbleby report because of its shocking content but he had threatened to resign unless they did.

"Do you know they've edited that report about Belsen because it was even more grim than we thought?" Lottie lowered the paper and took a gulp of tea.

Isobel looked at her. "Please, Lottie. Don't read it out loud. I simply can't stand the thought of what those poor people have been through."

"I thought it was bad enough when they carted men off for the STO."

Cassandra poured more tea. "What was that?"

"Oh, 'Service du Travail Obligatoire'. They took Emile's father because Emile had run off and was hiding at Le Verger. Often it was to a slave labour camp in Germany. Some of those poor people in Bergen-Belsen would probably have got there from the STO round-ups. Monsieur Voclain hasn't come home. I doubt he survived. I helped Emile get away to the Maquis in the south." Lottie drained her cup.

"These Nazis are truly wicked. I thought the Gerries were bad enough in the first war but this…" Cassandra shivered visibly.

"I'm taking Charles out for a walk. Want to come?" Isobel got up, scraping her chair.

Lottie shook her head. "No, I'll try sending another letter to Françoise. This will be hard for Emile. His father could have been at that horrific camp."

"Oh, surely not, Lottie?" Cassandra had begun to clear the table and paused.

"Why not? It's a wonder Françoise wasn't caught. Bertrand's father was Jewish. I'll bet he was taken to one of those dreadful camps. David Blumenthal was his name. Handsome boy. A musician, you know, played the violin."

Lottie went into the sitting room and sat in front of the bureau, staring out of the lattice window at the drive. How could Isobel and her mother understand? They still hadn't witnessed what she had. The brutality, the injustice, the starvation, the rubble after the bombing; its deafening volume. They had suffered, of course they had, but sometimes she felt they were in a cosy, insulated bubble here at Cheadle Manor.

She dashed off a letter to Françoise and walked down with it to Lower Cheadle and the Post Office.

Susan Threadwell weighed the envelope. "Oh, writing to someone in France?"

459

"Obviously, Miss Threadwell."

"Well I never. I heard you were out there for ever such a long time."

"You heard right."

Miss Threadwell took the envelope off the scale. "Must have been dreadful, being occupied and that."

"Yes, it was."

"Made friends, though, did you? You know, to write to, like?"

"How much is it, Miss Threadwell?"

Miss Threadwell sniffed. "I'm sure I don't mean to offend."

Lottie passed some coins over. "Do you know how long it will take to get there?"

"I couldn't say, I'm sure."

"Well, thank you, anyway. Good day."

"And good day to you too, Miss Charlotte." Miss Threadwell shut her till drawer with a forceful hand.

Lottie loitered as she climbed the hill on the way home. The blossom was beginning to bud on the trees and the lengthening days were definitely warmer. It made it harder than ever to picture that death camp in Germany when pink petals were tenderly unfolding in the quiet Wiltshire countryside.

Her mother was in the garden when she got home, and the baby's pram was parked under the blossoming cherry tree in the dappled sunshine. "Nice walk, dear?"

"Lovely, thanks." Lottie sat on a stool against the house wall, where the sun warmed the stone.

"Fancy doing something to celebrate your birthday on Thursday?"

"Oh, I hadn't thought. I'm not really bothered about it."

"Come on, it would be nice to do something to mark the occasion. How about I bake a cake?"

"Oh, Mummy, you are so kind when you already have so much to do. You never stop these days. Who would

460

have thought you'd have to grow your own potatoes and cook them! And live in this ridiculously small house."

Cassandra stood up and rubbed the small of her back. "I'd be quite happy for you to plant these potatoes, darling. Quite frankly, it would be better than hearing you complaining. There is still a war on, and we all have to make the best of it."

Lottie got up and hugged her. "I'm sorry. Do forgive me. I can't seem to settle to anything."

"Maybe, when your inheritance is real, you'll feel more like taking up the reins again?"

"How can I? Your Dr Harris is in charge of the house and it's mad that it will only be mine, anyway."

"Well, you have a point there." Cassandra looked like she would say more, but then Lottie noticed the postman stopping by the gate and checking through his mailbag.

"Look! We have post!" Lottie ran to meet the postman, and when he said there was one for her, she snatched it from his hand.

The envelope was smeared with dirt and battered from travel. The initial address of Le Verger had been crossed out and replaced with Cheadle Manor's. She didn't recognise the handwriting underneath, but the English address had been written in the familiar hand of her French pen-pal.

The postman coughed ostentatiously. "Morning to you, Miss Charlotte."

"Oh, sorry, yes, good morning, and thanks." Lottie took the letter inside and went into the sitting room, glad to find it empty.

She ripped open the envelope with trembling fingers. When she read the opening words in French, *"Ma chérie amour, Charlotte,"* she sat down on the nearest chair to concentrate on the scrawled words.

"I miss you. I need you. I long for you. What I have witnessed, Charlotte, no human should ever see. Such misery, I cannot describe it. Such evil! These Nazis are not people but monsters. Thousands of them, thousands, my darling. Starving, dying, stinking, innocent people. Huts and huts of them, both dead and alive.

The smell is indescribable. Rotting corpses. Shit. Disease. Oh, I should not tell this to you, but you are the other half of me. So many times, I longed to write and ask you to join me but always we were on the move and in danger.

I am very distressed by what I have seen. I cannot write more.

All my love, Thierry. Xxxxxxxxxxxxxxxxxx"

Lottie read it over and over again, searching for an address. He must have been in Belsen or it could have been Buchenwald or Dachau. The newspapers and the radio bulletins were disclosing new camps being liberated by the Allies almost every day, as they marched on towards Berlin. How could she go to him when she didn't know where he was?

She ran into the bedroom and pulled down a suitcase. Frantically, she started throwing clothes into it.

Cassandra came into the room, carrying folded clean nappies in her arms. "What are you doing?"

Lottie didn't even look up at her mother. "I must go to him."

"Go to who?"

"Thierry of course! He needs me. I must find him!"

"But, darling, where is he? Did you get a letter at last?"

"Where's my comb? Ah, here it is. Yes, yes, the letter is there on the bed. Read it, if you like."

Cassandra put her linen down and picked up Thierry's letter. It didn't take her long to scan the short note.

462

She sat down on the bed, next to the suitcase into which Lottie was still flinging her belongings.

"Poor man. He is obviously very upset."

Lottie paused in her chaotic packing. "Well, wouldn't you be, after what he's seen?"

"Do you think it might have been Belsen, like on that War Report?"

"Could be anywhere. Those bastards set up camps all over Europe."

"Then, my darling girl, how could you possibly find Thierry?"

Lottie stopped hurling things into her suitcase. "The envelope! I must look at the postmark." Lottie dashed back to the sitting room for it and her mother followed her. "Oh, no! I can't see where it's from, it's all blurred and crossed out because of being forwarded. What can I do? Mummy? Oh, what can I do?"

Cassandra put her hands on her daughter's shoulders. "You can calm down, for one thing. This isn't like you, Lottie. Come on, sit down."

She guided Lottie to a fireside chair in the sitting-room and sat down opposite her. "Now, listen to me, young lady. It's obvious you love this young man very much and he loves you. He's written to you once to say he wants to see you. I'm very sure he'll write again. You can't go chasing all over Europe trying to find someone without knowing where on earth they are!"

Lottie put her face in her hands. "Oh God. You're right. I'm just going to have to sit tight and wait, aren't I?"

"I'm afraid so."

CHAPTER SIXTY-ONE
CHEADLE MANOR, ENGLAND
MAY 1945

"Hitler's dead." Lottie put the newspaper down.

Isobel blinked. "What did you say?"

"The bastard's dead. Killed himself and that woman, what's-her-name? Eva Brown or something."

"I don't believe you."

Lottie passed the newspaper to her sister. "See for yourself."

"Surely this must mean it's the end?"

"Well, they've hung Mussolini upside-down in Italy so who's left to lead the Nazis now?" Lottie got up from the breakfast table and looked out over the back garden of West Lodge. The three stone gables of her house looked back down at her from above the treetops.

"I hope it means Al will be home soon and never have to go back." Isobel spooned porridge into her son's open mouth. Charles banged his highchair table for more.

A week later, when they were listening to the BBC's Home Service on the radio one evening as usual, the programme was interrupted by the radio announcer telling them jubilantly that the Germans had surrendered unconditionally in Berlin.

"The war in Europe is over."

Malcolm stood up, knocking his cup and saucer over. "Hurrah!"

Isobel came hurrying in from the bedroom. "What's all the commotion? I've only just got Charles off to sleep."

Cassandra was busy kissing Malcolm, so Lottie wrapped her arms around her sister and hugged her tight. "It's over, Bella. It's really over!"

"Ssh, listen, he's saying something else." Cassandra leaned over and turned up the volume.

"And so tomorrow, Tuesday, the 8th of May 1945, will be declared 'Victory in Europe Day' and will be a day

of national holiday. The prime minister, the Right Honourable Winston Churchill, will give a national broadcast on the BBC Home Service at three o'clock tomorrow afternoon."

"This calls for a highland jig!" Malcolm linked arms with Isobel and Lottie and Cassandra joined in. They hopped and skipped around the tiny sitting-room until the telephone rang in the hall.

"Oh, no! Who can that be? Charles will never sleep through all this!" Isobel stood panting, hands on hips.

"I'll go. It could be the hospital with an emergency for you, Malcolm." Cassandra left the room.

Lottie heard her mother's voice floating back into the room.

"Hello, Katy, yes! We've done it! We've bloody done it! Isn't it marvellous? What's that? What time? Oh, yes, we'd love to! What can I bring?"

"I don't think that's the hospital!" Malcolm smiled at Lottie.

"No, sounds like Aunt Katy. News spreads fast."

"Good news moves quicker than bad on this occasion, thank goodness."

"Oh, damn it. It's spread to Charles now." Isobel went in answer to the wail from her bedroom.

Cassandra came back, smiling broadly. "Trust Kate to be organised. She's setting up a street party at the garage for tomorrow. Starts after Churchill's broadcast. I've said we'll all go, if that's alright?"

Malcolm frowned. "I may have to stay at the hospital during the day, I'm afraid and organise something with the patients. In fact, I ought go back there now and speak to the staff."

Cassandra put her hand on his arm. "Oh, do try and join us at the garage later tomorrow, won't you, darling?"

He leaned down and kissed her. "I'll do my very utmost. Sounds like a party not to be missed! Goodnight all, and it really is a good one at last."

Lottie watched Malcolm and Cassandra go. Alone, she sat by the dying embers of the fire and wondered if Thierry knew about the end of the war.

The next morning flashed by in a flurry of sandwich-making and cake baking.

"It's impossible to get a sponge to rise with powdered egg. Look! This Victoria sponge is half the height it should be!" Isobel prodded the cake with her index finger.

"Well, don't flatten it even more then!" Cassandra was whipping cocoa powder into margarine. "We'll put plenty of this chocolate filling in and no-one will notice the difference."

"Don't forget the sugar!" Lottie passed the packet over.

"Lottie, dear, can you grate some carrot and cheese – go very sparingly with the cheese – for these sandwiches? And add a dab of chutney to give it some flavour. I'll cut the bread as thin as I can. Now where is the dratted breadknife?" Cassandra lifted all the various tea towels covering things they'd already prepared and still didn't find it.

Then the telephone rang for the sixth time that morning. "Who can it be now?" Cassandra wiped her hands and disappeared into the hall.

"She's never off that damn telephone. I'll cut the bread then." Lottie found the breadknife, exactly where it should be, in the knife holder on the draining board.

By a quarter-to-three, Cassandra declared they could not possibly make another thing to take with them and they abandoned the kitchen for the sitting-room and the all-important Prime Ministerial broadcast.

"Gosh, we only just made it!" Lottie sat down on the hard chair by the bureau and let Isobel and Charles share the fireside one opposite their mother, as the chimes of Big Ben rang out and the announcer said, *"This is London. Here is an announcement by The Prime Minister, The Right Honourable Winston Churchill."*

Cassandra smiled at them both. "This is it, girls, the moment we've been waiting for."

Lottie listened to the Prime Minister's distinctive, lisping voice, telling them of the Germans' unconditional surrender and that, although hostilities wouldn't end until midnight, the ceasefire had already been sounded at every base in Europe. That surely must include Thierry, wherever he was. If he was with British or American troops somewhere in Germany itself, he might even be listening to this very broadcast. Thrilled with this notion, Lottie concentrated all the harder and when Churchill talked of 'gallant France' and 'our Allies', she could have wept.

"We can allow ourselves a brief period of rejoicing but let us not forget for a moment the toil and efforts that lie ahead. Japan, with all her treachery and greed, remains unsubdued."

Isobel chipped in, "I wish we could forget about blasted Japan. Oh, why won't they just give up and let the world get back to normal."

"Ssh, dear, let's hear dear old Winnie." Cassandra frowned at her youngest daughter.

"...We must now devote all our strength and resources to the completion of our task, both at home and abroad. Advance, Britannia! Long live the cause of freedom! God save the King!"

"I think he's finished now. What a rousing speech, as ever." Cassandra got up and switched off the radio. "Come on, girls, get your best bibs and tuckers on and let's party!"

"Hello, Cass! Hello, you two!" Jem and Lily waved to them as they tumbled out of the Sunbeam in the Katherine Wheel Garage forecourt, laden with trays of food, half-an-hour later.

The street party had been set up in the yard between the garage and the factory. Tables had been slung together and covered in white sheets and bunting was strung from tree to tree on either side.

"Goodness, Kate! You have been busy!" Cassandra kissed her old friend.

"Nonsense! Many hands make light work, and all that." Katy turned to Lottie. "Hello, sweetheart, how are you?"

"I'm fine, Aunt Katy." Lottie kissed Katy who waved her to the table where Lottie put down the tray of triangular sandwiches she'd made.

"Hmm, if you say so." Katy turned to her grandson, who held out his plump arms to her. "Shall I take him, Bella?"

"Oh, please do! He weighs a ton!" Isobel relinquished her burden and went back to the car for more cakes.

Soon, all the guests were seated at the tables. Lottie looked around at the happy faces. There was Agnes in an armchair, propped up by cushions, at the head of it all. She looked frail but was beaming goodwill at all the younger people around her. Lottie didn't know some of the other faces, they must have been factory workers and their families, but she recognised a few. Len Bradbury sat next to a slight woman of his own age, whom Lottie assumed was his wife and two younger girls sat on either side of them whom she guessed were his daughters. Then there was Billy and Daisy Threadwell and their brood, and his spinster sister, Susan, smiling broadly for once.

Katy turned to Cassandra. "I wish Emily and Jack could have been here and Jem's brothers and sisters but they're all going to parties of their own."

468

"I think you've quite enough already, Katy!" Cassandra raised her glass of squash and addressed the entire gathering. "Here's to peace!"

Jem raised his glass. "Here's to Victory in Europe!"

"Hip, hip, hooray!" They chorused.

Katy stood up and addressed them. "I want to say a huge thank you to everyone here for keeping the factory and the garage going through this dreadful time. Without you, and people like you, we wouldn't have won this damn war. To prosperity, and your good health!"

Everyone raised their glasses a second time and then fell on the food. A general buzz of conversation followed the speeches and the May sunshine added to the general mood of benevolence. Lottie drank in all the goodwill and joined in with the rest of them, but her private wishes remained hers alone.

When all the guests had drifted off, and the plates and the cloths had been tidied away, only The Phipps and the Flintock-Smythes remained.

"That was a fantastic party, Kate." Cassandra told her friend.

"Wasn't it just? Boy, I'm tired now, though. Want to come in for a cuppa and listen to His Majesty?"

"What do you want to do, girls?" Cassandra turned to her daughters.

"Well, Charles is asleep already, so it won't make much difference to him." Isobel laughed.

"Yes, let's stay a bit longer, it's been such a lovely day." Lottie agreed.

Jem smiled. "Good, let's go inside then. It's getting a little chilly."

Cassandra fell into step beside him. "Oh, but hasn't it been glorious?"

Agnes went off to bed and Lily helped her. Isobel laid Charles on Lily's bed in the other room and left the door open so she could hear if he woke up and then they all settled in the front room of the bungalow and Jem lit the electric fire. "The King will be on in half-an-hour. I'll make a brew, shall I?"

Jem disappeared back into the kitchen but reappeared ten minutes later. "Look who's turned up!"

Isobel jumped up from her seat. "Al! Oh, how marvellous!"

Katy elbowed her out of the way for a kiss of her own. "How did you manage to get home, Al?"

Al grinned his hello to the general company. "Hitched a lift with someone and walked the rest of the way from Woodbury. Thought I'd stop off here and see if anyone was home."

"Oh, what a pity you missed the party." Katy pulled him to sit in the best armchair.

Al plonked down heavily. "Been having a jolly without me, shame on you! Ah, but it's good to be home."

Jem said, "How long have you got, Al?"

"Three days this time!"

Isobel squeezed into the chair with him. "That's the best thing on an already wonderful day."

"Oh, before I forget, I've something for Lottie." Al fished in his breast pocket and drew out an envelope.

Lottie got up and took it from him. "What's this?"

"I only got it at the last minute. It was in my pigeon-hole at the office. It's a bit bashed about, I'm afraid, but it looks like it's from France. Hope it's good news, Lottie."

Lottie turned it over in her hand. "Thanks, Al. Excuse me everyone. I'm going to read this somewhere quiet."

Cassandra looked at her. "But, darling, you'll miss the King's speech!"

"I've heard enough speeches for one day, I don't mind." Lottie was already halfway through the door.

She clutched the envelope to her chest. She felt the thin paper was burning her fingers. Having had one letter from Thierry, she now knew his handwriting.

470

She went into the garden, amongst the neat rows of vegetables. There was an old dining-room chair in the western corner, which caught the last rays of the sunset. She gravitated to it without even thinking and sat down on its warm, gilded seat.

She kissed the envelope and stared at it for a few moments before she tore it open.

Thierry's writing was more even this time, more measured and therefore easier to read, even in the fading light.

The first thing he'd written was an address.

"c/o British Army, DP Camp, Celle, Near Bergen, West Saxony, Germany"

"Ma Chérie,

I have stopped fighting, thank God, and am now saving lives, something that suits me much better. I hope my last letter did not distress you, if you received it. The opening of the death camp here was a life-changing experience. I am changed."

Lottie looked up from the page when she read this. Was he about to say it was over between them? She could hardly bear to continue.

"I am not the man I was and will never be again. I want to devote the rest of my life to caring for these innocent victims of war. Victims of such unspeakable evil, Charlotte, such that you cannot (I hope) imagine. Never before did I know that humankind was capable of such wickedness. I have seen both the depths and the heights that man can reach here. The doctors and nurses who cleaned and bathed the survivors are true heroes. I would say more so than the soldiers whom I saw killing each other in their thousands. At least those were clean deaths, although I did not think so then.

471

Ah, Charlotte. Man's inhumanity to man has known no bounds in this wretched fight.

So, I am staying here in Germany to help. I am working as a teacher again, which feels right. As you know, my parents were both killed in Caen by the Allied bombing. I feel there is nothing to return to there."

Again, Lottie looked away from the pages trembling between her fingers and at the distant view of the river valley beyond the garden. She remembered the green waters when she'd tumbled into the weir as a child, all those years ago. She felt she was drowning again now.

"I have not heard from you these long months, Charlotte. I don't even know where you are or if you will receive this letter. I am sending it to Le Verger, into Françoise's care, in hopes you are still there. The war in Europe will soon be over, that much is certain. It may even already be over by the time you receive this, and you may be home with your English family now, in your beautiful manor house that you described so well to me.

Charlotte, I will understand if you want to stay there, to take up your inheritance and the duties that will come with it. I will understand if you want to stay with Bernadette and her family and make your life there. I will understand if you do not want to come and see me in this desolate place but, and I hardly dare write this, I want you to know that I love you as much, no, more, much more, than I did before and I would like to share this new life with you, as my wife, if you will have me. Not many women would desire such a life. It's hard, very hard, and facilities are rudimentary to say the least. It's barely sanitary yet and there is much suffering.

But you are not like other women, are you, my love? Could you find it in your heart to be a part of this life with me? The most important part? For I long for you still, with all my heart. It's a big decision, in the circumstances. It's

472

not a conventional proposal or a normal life that I'm asking you to share but, if you do still love me, please, at least think about it and let me know your thoughts."

With my dearest, fondest love, Thierry. Xx"

Lottie remembered how she had held the receiver to her ear, wincing at Al's strident tone. "I insist that I take you myself, if you must go to Germany. There's an airbase at Celle. I'll make sure I'm on the rota for that route. I'll let you know when. I'm not letting you go to that hellhole alone."

Despite her resistance, Al hadn't taken no for an answer.

Now, here she was, looking down over northern Europe through the clouds, sitting next to him in the cockpit. They hadn't talked much on the flight, except about the devastated cities they flew over. The industrial areas around Rotterdam had been especially hard hit and Lottie remarked on it.

"Huh, you should see Cologne or Dresden. They are just as bad as Caen but bigger." Al shook his head. "I'm not convinced about the Allied bombing strategy. Makes us as bad as the Gerries, if you ask me."

"Do you really think so?"

"Afraid I do."

Lottie looked back down at the ruins. "Yes, Al, I think you're right."

But they didn't talk about much else. Al's mouth was set hard the whole way. He'd not held back about his doubts about her decision. A decision she'd made in an instant after that second letter from Thierry.

"You can see the barracks now. Look, down there." Al pointed down to the ground beneath them.

"I can't see, Al. There are too many trees." Lottie strained her eyes.

"To the left, Lottie. Look, see the wooden huts, all in rows?"

"Oh yes, I can see them now."

474

"Doesn't look very inviting. Are you quite sure about this?"

"Completely."

He tipped the wing and started to bank towards the ground. "You don't have to get off this plane, you know. You could change your mind."

"I've told you, Al, my mind is quite made up."

"I think you're mad, you know that."

"You said."

"I mean, I know you love Thierry and all that, and I admire what he's doing but why not wait until it's a bit more civilised? Some of the things I've heard…"

They dropped altitude and Lottie watched the ground rise up to meet them. "The whole point is to help him when it's not so easy."

"Rather you than me. Bella cried buckets when she told me."

"I know. She and Mummy tried their best to make me stay but they understood, in the end." She could see the huts now. They did look bleak.

"And what about Cheadle Manor? After all, it belongs to you now."

"Oh, I'll think about that when the war's over, Al. It's still a hospital. We can't access it yet. And Malcolm will look after it for me."

"I can't persuade you, even now you've seen it, can I?"

"No, you can't."

It was a bumpy landing. Al looked upset and distracted but eventually the Anson came to a halt and they clambered out. Ground crew came running towards them and trucks drew alongside ready to unload the medical supplies in the hold.

Al drew off his leather helmet. "Right, let's meet your man, then."

They walked across the tarmac towards the hangars clustered together about three hundred yards from the

475

landing strip. Lottie saw him first. He was wearing a uniform with a red badge she didn't recognise but she picked out his blond head easily and started running towards him.

They didn't speak, just held each other. Al stood to one side, once he had caught up with her. Lottie saw him standing awkwardly and released Thierry. "Please, Thierry, meet my oldest friend and pilot, Albert Phipps."

Thierry held out his hand and smiled warmly. "Enchanté, monsieur."

"Call me Al." Al shook the outstretched hand.

"Oh, it's so good that you two have finally met." Lottie grinned at them.

"Want some coffee?" Thierry spoke English with a strong French accent. Lottie loved the sound of it.

"Please." Al followed him towards the hangar.

While Al was signing off his paperwork, Thierry brought three mugs of coffee and set them down on a table outside.

Alone with Lottie, he reverted to French. "I cannot say how glad my heart is to see you. It is too full to form words."

"I know. It's impossible, isn't it?" Lottie picked up her mug and sipped it. The coffee was strong, foreign-tasting.

"We will have time soon. I have managed to secure lodgings for you in the women's quarters – the staff ones - of course. Oh, Charlotte, what have you come to? It's certainly not the Ritz."

"I don't care. I'm with you."

"I love you." Thierry's blue eyes behind his spectacles never left her face.

Al joined them and picked up his drink. "Sorry to butt in. Seems I've got to get straight off. Return trip with some VIP for London. No peace for the wicked."

Thierry stood up. "I'm sorry. I'd hoped we could get to know each other a little. Perhaps next time?"

476

Al drained his mug. "Perhaps. Well, goodbye, Lottie. Take care, won't you?"

Lottie hugged him. "Goodbye Al, give my love to everyone. Tell them I'll write soon."

Al nodded. "Of course." He shook Thierry's hand again. "Nice to meet you, mate. Promise me you'll look after her?"

"With my life."

"Make sure you do, or you'll have me to reckon with." Al gave an unconvincing laugh.

"Monsieur, I understand completely."

"Righto, I'll be off then."

Thierry and Lottie watched as Al strode across to his plane which had already been refuelled and loaded. A senior-looking officer with some people in plain clothes followed him and climbed aboard. Soon, the plane had turned around, zoomed past them, and risen up into the sky.

Tears pricked the back of Lottie's eyes as she looked up at the Anson receding into the clouds above her. Her last connection with home.

Thierry, sensitive to her mood, put his arm around her shoulders. "Come, my love, let me take you to your new quarters."

The dormitory reminded her of her schooldays, except those walls had been made of stone and these merely consisted of thin planks of wood.

She turned to Thierry and fibbed. "It's lovely. Any particular bed?"

Thierry gave a Gallic shrug. "No idea. Have to ask someone."

"This one's free." A tall, dark-haired American woman, wearing a feminine version of the same uniform as Thierry, came in and pointed to a unmade-up bed. "And there's a window above it. Sometimes one is glad of a little air."

"Thanks." Lottie put her suitcase on the bare mattress.

477

"I'm Lorraine, by the way." The tall American held out her hand.

"Charlotte." Lottie shook it and smiled. "And this is my fiancé, Thierry."

"Oh, I know Thierry Thibault. Everyone does." Lorraine smiled more broadly at Thierry.

Lottie, secure in Thierry's affections, didn't let it rattle her. She knew her man.

"Come, Charlotte, let me show you around the rest of the base." Thierry steered her towards the door.

"I'll get you some clean linen. You have to know who to ask." Lorraine called out as they left.

"Thanks, Lorraine." Lottie gave her a wave as she departed that she hoped looked friendly.

"This isn't very romantic, I'm afraid, Charlotte."

"I didn't expect it to be, Thierry. It's alright."

"Let's go for a walk. I have so much to tell you." Thierry showed her around the base camp which consisted of rows of huts, which she'd already seen from the aeroplane. What she hadn't seen from the sky were their emaciated occupants. Wan, skeletal people sat in the sunshine outside the simple houses. They looked at them with suspicion, those that were animated enough to show any emotion. Army personnel, looking ridiculously robust in comparison, busied themselves around the camp, some in medical uniforms, some in khaki, all looked serious and worn-out.

"I think I've seen enough, now, Thierry."

"Let's get off base and walk in the woods, shall we?"

"Please."

Lottie breathed easier outside the perimeter wire fence. "It's funny, the air is the same, but it smells sweeter here. There's so little birdsong around here. The silence is a little uncanny."

"Oh, they are coming back, slowly. Like the health of the camp survivors but these things take time."

478

Thierry took her hand in his as they walked along, and Lottie noticed he still had a slight limp. "It's hard to see all this, I realise that. Many hardened soldiers wept when we liberated Belsen. Many retched their guts up. I'm glad you did not witness it."

"We heard a report about it on the radio from a BBC journalist that left little to the imagination. What can have reduced the Nazis to behave in this bestial way, Thierry? What stripped them of kindness, humanity, empathy?"

"I wish had the answer but it confounds me too, mon amour."

There was a fallen tree just inside the line of pine trees and they sat down together. Thierry ran his hands through his hair. Lottie loved the way the blond fibres stood up on their own when he did that.

"What have I brought you to? Seeing you here, makes me realise how selfish it was of me to ask you to join me."

"I came of my own free will."

Thierry shrugged. "Perhaps but I should have been strong enough to manage on my own."

"Why? We belong together. We both know it."

Thierry was silent. He reached out and cupped her face in both his hands. Lottie took his glasses off and laid them down on the tree trunk. They drew closer until their lips met for a long time.

"Tell me about what you hope to achieve here, Thierry." Lottie withdrew at last, her senses reeling. She needed to return to the real world for a moment.

Thierry ran his hand through his hair again and replaced his glasses. He took a deep in-breath and grinned at her. "You are more composed than I!"

Lottie laughed and the last bit of tension dropped away. "I don't feel it, believe me! But being with you makes me feel calm. It always did. That was how I knew I loved you."

"Come on, let's walk again before I ravish you where everyone can see us."

Lottie stood up, smiling and linked arms with him. "That's a tempting thought but this definitely isn't the right place or time. It's very sobering, seeing the camp."

"I know. The suffering is unbearable to witness."

Lottie tugged his arm. "I suspect you have a plan to relieve some of it. Come on, tell me what I'm in for."

"Well, I do have an idea, as it happens."

"I knew it."

"Most of the kids here are either Jewish or Poles and have their own teachers emerging from the adults among them. I'm not sure where I fit in or even if I'm needed here. I don't speak Polish for a start and my German is barely adequate. However, through an American friend, I got to know about an organisation called UNRRA."

"And you're already working for them?"

"Yes, they pay my wages now, hence the uniform."

"Is it a new organisation? I've never heard of it."

"It was set up in 1943 to relocate and house the millions of refugees this war has displaced."

"Oh, so that's what your badge is about. What do the letters stand for?"

"It's a bit of a mouthful. It's the United Nations Relief and Rehabilitation Administration and I joined up as soon as I heard about their work from the Americans working here. Remember Lorraine who you met in the dormitory? She works for them and told me about a place in Bavaria that is for abandoned and lost children and they want someone with good English skills to teach them. Their children have no ties, unlike the ones here."

"You mean the children still have their families here at Belsen?"

Thierry shook his head. "Sadly, no, in many – even most - cases but they do have their strong Polish and Jewish cultures with good leaders they can identify with."

"I see, but you said that's not the case at this orphanage in Bavaria?"

Thierry pulled her arm tighter through his. "It's just starting up, of course, but they have a different approach to the other Displaced Persons camps where they just bundle the kids together and hope for the best. I've heard that the staff at this particular place are really trying to help the children readjust psychologically after the severe trauma they have experienced. It used to be an orphanage run by nuns, till the Nazis disbanded it. Now, it's a forward-looking enterprise that could really make a difference to these kids and, I must admit, I've been impressed by what I've heard about it."

Lottie nodded all the time this poured out of Thierry. She could hear the passion in his voice. "So, you want to work in this place in Bavaria for this organisation?"

"I think so, yes."

"Would there be room for me? What could I do?"

"Charlotte, you've only just got off the plane, but will you marry me here? Soon? Then we could go as man and wife. I know you will be valued and find plenty to do there. You have many skills. I've seen you with the children from my school back in Normandy – in that other life."

"You don't waste an opportunity, do you? I think that's the third time you've asked me."

"So, will you?"

Lottie looked through the wire fence surrounding the boarded huts, watched weak, emaciated men and women – it was hard to tell which was which – shuffle between them. A group of children sat in a pool of sunlight in the dirt. They were listening to a story by the looks of things. Another group of people stood in line, bowls in their hands, beseeching looks in their eyes, as food was doled out along the queue. They ate ravenously, their hands clawing at the white gloop. They looked barely human.

She swallowed the lump in her throat. "I'd be proud to be your wife and I'll do anything I can to help make a better world."

"But, Charlotte, you would be giving up so much. I don't have anything to go home for, but you do. What about your family, your responsibilities, back in England?"

Lottie inclined her head in agreement. "Yes, there is that. Let's just see what happens next, shall we? Whatever we have to face, let's do it together from now on."

CHAPTER SIXTY-THREE
GERMANY
AUGUST 1945

Lottie decided she couldn't even make a token effort to be conventional for her wedding, as she would be wearing the only summer dress she had brought with her; the one she had bought in Paris in 1940 with Mabs goading her on to buy it.

"Do you think it matters that I'm not wearing white?" She'd asked Lorraine that morning, as she'd got ready in the women's staff quarters.

"God, no. You look ravishing, darling. I adore that yellow colour on you."

"But the red jacket looks a bit much, doesn't it?" Lottie shrugged on the little silk jacket over her saffron dress.

"Personally, I love a good colour clash, and with your dark hair you can carry it off. Do you have a hat?"

"Didn't think to bring one with me."

"Here, take this red beret. Much more stylish than a boring old veil."

Lottie took it and put it on her head at a rakish angle.

Lorraine clapped her hands. "Perfecto! You'll take Thierry's breath away."

"You're right. I've never been one for lace."

"It's your wedding, Lottie. You decide what you're going to wear, no-one else." Lorraine held up the only small mirror the room possessed.

Lottie smeared her lips with the red lipstick she'd bought at the same time as the dress and jacket. She'd kept it in the attic at Le Verger under the floorboards for years and had hardly used it. It was exactly the same shade as her bolero jacket.

"I think you're ready to get married, Charlotte."

483

Lorraine offered her arm and they walked off to the makeshift chapel in the Polish sector. "Is Thierry a practising Catholic, then?"

"Yes, it still means something to him." Lottie's shoes pinched. She never wore high-heels anymore.

"But you're not?"

"Oh, no. We were always Church of England, but I've never been that devout, I must admit."

"You're going to need faith where you're going. It's run by nuns, isn't it?"

"I think it used to be and there are still some there, but they're so desperate for help, I don't think they'll turn me away."

They entered the hushed gathering and walked up the aisle, still arm in arm. Thierry was waiting for her.

The Polish priest spoke in heavily accented English through the short ceremony. After they had exchanged their vows, he said, "I now pronounce you man and wife. You may kiss the bride."

Lottie heard the cheer roaring behind her as she kissed her husband. It was no less loud than the roaring in her ears.

"And may I add that I think it is a very auspicious omen for your marriage that it coincides with the end of the war in the Pacific. None of us will forget the fifteenth of August 1945."

Thierry smiled at the priest. "You certainly may, Father. I never will forget the day I married Charlotte, or the day peace broke out across the whole world."

"Yes, my son. Let us pray it stays that way."

Lottie and Thierry turned to face the congregation. Lottie looked at the smiling faces as she walked back down the aisle, this time on the arm of her husband. American and British officers and servicemen, Red Cross doctors and nurses, a few of the less gaunt survivors from the concentration camp: all were beaming goodwill at them.

Outside, more people had gathered to wish them well, even though they were leaving in the morning for Bavaria.

A British officer came up and shook Thierry's hand. "May I kiss the bride?"

"You had better ask her!"

Lottie liked that. She might be married but she was no-one's property, not even Thierry's. She presented her cheek to be kissed by the soldier. His moustache tickled her nose.

"I've got a surprise for you two. Got a couple of my men to vacate their room so you can have it to yourselves tonight, hey? Can't have you separated on your honeymoon."

Thierry inclined his blond head in thanks. "That is most kind of you."

"Well, it's only for one night and my lot will be boozing well into the small hours to celebrate beating the Japs, so I don't suppose they'll need much kip." He winked at Thierry. "Hopefully neither will you, old man." He elbowed Thierry in the ribs.

Lottie looked up at her husband, who bowed stiffly. "You're very kind."

"Think nothing of it, old chap. Congratulations and all that. Now, I'm off to organise the beer."

The afternoon and evening passed in a blur for Lottie. The camp residents, many of whom were still too weak to do anything but survive another day, did not join the party in great numbers but she could feel the quiet easing of tension throughout the camp. The sense of relief everywhere was almost tangible. The soldiers ate well and insisted they join them, raising a glass or a beer bottle to toast their futures, but Lottie kept longing for the night to fall so she could be alone with Thierry.

They stole away once the dancing began. The little room had two single beds that had been pushed together and some kind soul had picked some woodland flowers and put them in a jam-jar on the chest of drawers in the corner.

"Well, it's better than Bernadette's cellar." Lottie laughed when they shut the door behind them.

"It's hardly a plush hotel room, though, Mrs Thibault." Thierry took her in his arms.

"Who cares. Do you know, this is the first time we have been really alone since you left Normandy?"

"Oh, my darling wife, I'm very aware of that."

They undressed each other slowly, with delicate precision, taking turns. Lottie took Thierry's spectacles from his nose last of all and put them down on his pile of clothes.

"I adore every inch of you." Thierry picked her up and Lottie wrapped her legs around his lean thighs.

Lottie chuckled. "Prove it."

The morning sun found them entwined still, its rays licking their naked limbs. Lottie blinked when the golden light flickered across her face and made her wonder why her arm had pins and needles. She looked down to see Thierry's tousled blond hair lying on it and gently prised her arm from under his head.

"Hmm?" Thierry looked up and grinned. "Morning, my love."

"Good morning. Fancy a trip to Bavaria?"

"What a good idea."

The camp was quiet as they boarded the plane.

"Seems everyone's sleeping it off, bud." The American pilot helped them up by taking their suitcases.

"Tough for you that you have to fly us."

"Oh, I'm not much of a one for drinking anyways. Need a clear head to fly this old bird. So, off to the American zone we go."

They settled down on some seats on the side of the plane, next to each other. There were no other passengers, only boxes of freight and no windows to see the view below. Lottie was glad. Tired from their lovemaking, she rested her head on her husband's shoulders and dozed through the short flight.

They landed at the airbase near Munich and caught a bus to Markt Indersdorf. There was much evidence of RAF carpet bombing around the city but as they travelled north, away from the industrial areas, the savage scarring diminished. As they neared their destination and Lottie looked out of the window at the greenery, the white houses with their red roofs and she was heartened at the normality of it.

The bus driver pointed them in the right direction for the orphanage. It wasn't far or difficult to find. Kloster Indersdorf dominated its town with its white spires gleaming and pointing to heaven as befitting the convent it once was. They walked under one of the cloisters that enclosed its imposing square façade and knocked on the door.

A young woman in a uniform like Thierry's answered the door. "Can I help you?"

Lottie knew a thrill of pride when Thierry answered. "Monsieur and Madame Thibault. We've come to help."

She spoke in a soft American accent. "Ah yes, we had a telephone call. Please, follow me and I will show you to your room."

They followed her along a long corridor and up some broad stairs until she opened a door and ushered them inside.

"I will leave you to unpack and refresh yourselves. There is a bathroom down the corridor. We ask people to be quick in there! You will find a towel each on the bed. Dinner is served at six o'clock in the refectory. Ask anyone to show you the way." The pleasant young woman bowed out of the room and left them alone.

"What a lovely room, Thierry." Lottie looked around the white-washed space. A double bed took up most of it, with a tall wardrobe and a dressing table along one wall. There was a bedside cabinet on either side of the bed;

one bore a bible, the other, two glasses and a carafe of water.

"Yes, it's very clean." Thierry sat on the bed. "Feels comfortable too. We have come to a good place."

"Yes, I think so. I'll go and freshen up in the bathroom."

Thierry laughed. "Well then, you'd better be quick!"

Lottie smiled back and took her white towel along the corridor and had a speedy wash in the spotless, simple bathroom.

At six o'clock they descended the stairs. There was quite a racket coming from the other side of the entrance hall and they walked towards it.

They entered a large, vaulted hall, teeming with children and adults. Long refectory tables lined the walls as well as one down the centre of the big room. A savoury smell wafted over everything. At the top table, a middle-aged woman with a tired, kind face stood up and rapped her spoon against her glass.

Many of the children ignored her, wriggling and restless, the young ones screaming to be fed. They squirmed on their chairs and shouted for food but eventually, encouraged by the adults among them, quietened down.

"Good evening everyone. Please be seated if you are not already. Put your hands together and we'll say grace."

Lottie and Thierry found two empty chairs and complied.

"For what we are about to receive may the Lord make us truly grateful."

Then a lot of the adults, including a couple of nuns, got up and disappeared through a door in the back of the hall, reappearing moments later with huge dishes of food which they placed on the tables at regular intervals. Lottie watched, horrified, as some of the children grabbed hot pieces of meat or vegetables and crammed them into their mouths with their fingers. Others surreptitiously sneaked morsels of bread into their pockets, their scared eyes darting here and there in case they were seen.

A young man sitting next to them tried to serve the food onto the children's plates. He turned to Lottie. "They have been starving so long, they cannot help themselves. The ones who steal bread think it will be taken from them. You must forgive them."

"Oh, I understand. We have come from Bergen-Belsen. It's the same there." Thierry smiled at the earnest young man. "My name is Thierry, and this is my wife, Charlotte."

"Hello, I'm Bruno. A lot of these children were in Dachau, not far from here. Some came by death march. They witnessed their parents, siblings, friends, dying along the way from starvation. Our first priority is to simply feed them. Manners, and knives and forks, will come later, we hope."

After the meal, which was simple but generous, Bruno took them to meet the woman who had said grace.

"Mrs Fischer, let me introduce Monsieur and Madame Thibault, who have just arrived from Bergen-Belsen."

"Good evening and welcome. Come into my office and I'll sign you on to the register for staff and tell you a little of our work here."

They followed Mrs Fischer down the long hallway into an office, simply furnished with some filing cabinets, bookshelves and a large desk with one chair behind it and three in front.

"Please, do sit down."

Mrs Fischer took some details from them and they signed the register. "I'm not sure if you know, but Kloster means monastery and this wonderful building used to be run as an orphanage by the Sisters of Mercy of Saint Vincent de Paul but the Nazis commandeered the building and closed the orphanage.

489

"At the end of the European war in April this year, UNRRA, who employ you, Mr Thibault, charged our Team – number 182 – with reopening Kloster Indersdorf specifically to help orphaned children displaced by the war. We have more every day, and already have more than the hundred initially intended. So, we are very glad of new staff."

Thierry raised his eyebrows. "Hopefully we have arrived at a good time."

"Indeed. Now, let me explain our philosophy. Our commitment is to give each child a feeling of security along with an understanding that he or she is desired and loved. Coming from a death camp yourselves, you will understand the trauma these children have suffered. Here, at Kloster Indersdorf we are trying not just to simply house them, but to help them recover to the extent they can lead fulfilled lives so they will be able to serve the world in their turn, and make a better future for us all."

"That is a big ambition." Thierry had nodded all the way through Mrs Fischer's introduction.

Lottie chimed in. "But a wonderful one. We saw how the children grabbed their food and looked emaciated."

"That's right. Some have been starved, literally, at concentration camps. Some have come from Nazi orphanages which were no less brutal. Many are the inevitable result of rape during the war and have no idea who either of their parents are. All have been separated from their mothers, many of whom have died."

Lottie leaned forward in her seat. "These are dreadful experiences but it's good that at least some of the children who've suffered such hardships have come here."

Mrs Fischer inclined her head in assent. "First of all, we must delouse, worm and clean them. They arrive with scabies, tuberculosis, diphtheria, as well as starvation and trauma, and dealing with these illnesses is our first priority, of course. If they have identification papers, we make every effort to trace their biological families, but this is often

490

impossible. We sometimes get foster families coming forward, but no-one really wants these children."

"If they do find their families, their reunion must be very emotional." Thierry clasped his hands together on his lap.

Mrs Fischer nodded. "Oh, there's no deeper joy, believe me, but it is all too rare. There is a Central Tracing Agency in Frankfurt who are very good, but often the children don't remember their background until they have had time to heal – both physically and mentally."

Thierry nodded. "Of course. That must take time."

Mrs Fischer became quite animated. "Exactly. Now this is the core of our philosophy. We do not solely aim to find these children homes - we aim to restore their *humanity*. Do you see?"

Thierry nodded, his face grave. "Completely, Madame."

Mrs Fischer continued, "We believe the children must be allowed to talk about their experiences. We encourage them to do so by listening with compassion and, something you will find you will need huge amounts of - patience."

Lottie, stirred by this woman's obvious passion for her work, ventured, "Mrs Fischer, my husband is employed by UNRRA, but could I also apply? I would like very much to work here too, in any capacity. I'm a good listener."

Mrs Fischer gave a tired smile. "We would be delighted to have you on our staff. Have you any qualifications?"

"No, I'm not trained in anything. I left my school in England with a Higher Certificate in 1939 and went to Paris. Then, when the Germans invaded, I went with my host family to Normandy and lived – and worked – on a farm there. I can speak English and French. I can milk a goat, look after hens, do most of the jobs you'd do on a farm. I'm not a trained teacher, like my husband, but I'd love to help them learn to read – anything, really."

491

Mrs Fischer screwed the lid back on her fountain pen. "My goodness, you're a woman of many talents. I'm confident we can find you work, and it would be especially useful to have another English teacher. Here are the papers to apply for a post. That way, you'll have a wage. Our regime here is simple. Each member of staff is assigned twelve to fifteen children under their wing in a parental or mentor role – like a surrogate family. Regular meals, exercise in the fresh air, good hygiene and, only when the children are ready, lessons. Do you think you could undertake such a role?"

Lottie and Thierry spoke as one. "Yes." "Definitely."

Mrs Fischer gave a tired smile. "Good, and you have found your room comfortable, I trust?"

Lottie and Thierry spoke together again, then laughed. "Very, thank you."

Lottie added, "It's much more comfortable than a lot of places I've stayed in during the war, I can tell you!"

Mrs Fischer got up and extended her hand to each of them in turn. "Then, welcome to you both. No duties for you tonight but you can start in the morning. Mr Levy – Bruno – will come for you at eight in the morning and show you around, starting with breakfast, of course!"

Sleeping next to Thierry in that clean, bare room felt like heaven to Lottie. She snuggled up to him after kissing him goodnight, and completely relaxed. She was safe here. Safe with the man she loved, safe because no bombs would be falling from the sky, safe in a huge stout building with very strong walls. She closed her eyes and didn't wake until morning.

Breakfast was substantial but the children still fought over it. After Bruno had given them a tour of the extensive building and its grounds, Thierry went off to meet the other teachers and Lottie was assigned work in the kitchen gardens.

Bruno introduced her to Sasha, a Russian girl of about seventeen, who was in charge of growing the vegetables.

"Hello, Madame Thibault."

Lottie took to Sasha immediately with her shy smile and grubby, work-worn hands. She pointed to herself. "Charlotte."

Using sign language and lots more pointing, Sasha took Lottie to a vegetable bed of peas. Sasha took a green pod and pinged it open, and offered it to Lottie, miming eating the peas. Lottie took it and chewed on the green, round seed, nodding and smiling. Sasha then gave her a big hessian sack and indicated Lottie was to pick the ripe pods and gather them into it.

"Okay, I understand." Lottie took the sack and demonstrated she understood by started to glean the harvest.

Sasha waved goodbye, pointing to the kitchen door and mimicking a full sack.

"Yes, take it to the kitchen when it's full. Okay, I will." Lottie got to work immediately. The sun was bright and warm and the clear sky an unbroken alpine blue. She could see mountains in the distance and the air smelled so clean it was almost antiseptic. It was a perfect spot for these tormented kids to heal.

She worked contentedly in the garden all morning and knew a moment of real satisfaction when the peas made their appearance at the dinner table. The afternoon was spent in similar tasks and the evening meal was welcome at the end of it.

Lottie, like the children, took comfort in the structured days and weeks that followed. Gradually she became absorbed in the life of the orphanage and helped teach them to grow vegetables and keep hens, remembering all the while to listen to their stories. All of them were shocking and heart-breaking as the children learned to trust her and unfold within the sanctuary of the orphanage. Sometimes it would all come out in a rush, sometimes in small, staccato reveals, sometimes it would take all day but each time, Lottie could see how the children's spirits would lift a fraction more.

One day, she was tying onions whose stems had dried. She now had a few children under her own wing, as Mrs Fischer would say. She was teaching them English in formal lessons now and one boy, Miklos, was really getting the hang of it.

Miklos was determined to go to America. "I know if speak English will help."

"Here Miklos, you plait the stems of the onions like this, see? One over the other."

"Onions, plait." Miklos always repeated the words carefully until he memorised them.

"Good, that's it!"

"We have onions in Hungary. My father grow them in garden."

"Grew them in the garden."

"Grew them in the garden." Miklos repeated carefully.

"Did your father grow lots of vegetables?"

"Oh yes, he good gardener but deported. Never see again."

Lottie listened and waited for more.

"My mother, sisters, brothers all go to Auschwitz last year but men one way, woman another. Never see again."

"I'm sorry."

"Yes, I go work in Buna labour camp, but SS bastards made us march to Dachau. Many die on way. No food. They shoot weak ones. My brother shot. He too weak. Hungry."

Lottie wanted to reach out to him, but she kept her hands working along the plait very slowly, to make it last and not disrupt the flow of Miklos's disjointed speech.

"Hide in woods, barns, sheep huts, but American soldiers find me. Come here. Safe now."

494

"Yes, Miklos, safe now."

In October Mrs Fischer called a staff meeting. "An American photographer, Mr Charles Haacker, from the United Nations is coming to take the children's photographs. I want each child to have a complete dossier before he arrives, as far as it is possible. Then we will put the photographs with each dossier and use these documents to try and find them safe locations in their home countries. Some children, of course will have no verifying identification but let's do what we can. Listen especially to their accents, those of you who are good at languages, and see if you can place their country of origin."

Lottie redoubled her efforts to listen carefully to the children's stories and painstakingly wrote down any scrap of information she could glean about each one. When she watched Mr Haacker taking their photographs as they stood before him with their nameplate, she was choked with emotion at seeing such hope in their faces. Each child's face showed the transparent, desperate longing that someone would see their picture and come and scoop them up into a new, happier life in America.

After the exercise, Lottie talked to Thierry as they got ready for bed.

"You know, most of these kids don't want to stay in Europe. They want to go to America – to the 'free world' as they call it."

"It's hard to get visas if you don't have a relative."

"I know. I've been thinking about that."

"Oh? Got some long-lost aunt who could adopt them all?" Thierry undid his tie and laid it over a chairback.

Lottie untied her laces and slipped her shoes off. She wiggled her freed toes. "That is uncannily accurate, Thierry. I do have an aunt in Boston and of course, I'm half-American myself."

"Are you?"

"Yes, my father was American." She pulled off her skirt and hung it in the wardrobe with her shirt.

"I never knew that; I assumed both your parents were English."

"No. And you'll think me mad…"

He kissed her. "Never."

Lottie chuckled. "I wouldn't bank on it."

"Tell me your idea."

Lottie stood in her petticoat within her husband's arms. "It's strange, Thierry, but I'm not sure I want to go back to England. I want a new start. Do you want to go back to France?

"No, not really. I don't know where I want to go. Just stay here for now perhaps."

"And why don't you want to go back? I'll tell you. Because all this hatred and fighting happened there. The old world - England, Germany, France - is where this evil was born, wasn't it?"

"Yes, that's true, I suppose."

Lottie went to the dressing-table and brushed her hair. "I don't want to stay where the old hatreds might resurface and they so easily could, Thierry. People are set in their ways. They don't accept strangers easily, especially foreigners like these abandoned kids. All the same old prejudices still hold."

"Hardly!" Thierry got into bed.

"No, well, obviously not genocide and Fascism but more subtle forms of prejudice. I should know, my grandmother was the worst offender. Do you remember Al, the pilot and my old friend? The one who brought me to Bergen?"

"Yes, of course. I wish I'd got to know him better."

"Well, his mother, Katy, was a housemaid at Cheadle Manor when she was a girl. She was born in the little lodge house my mother's been camping in throughout the war while the manor house was used as a hospital. She made a play for my uncle – oh, he's long dead – First World War. His name was Charles – Al and Bella have named their boy after him and Al's father so he's Charles Albert."

496

"Is this story going somewhere, Charlotte? Only I have a class to give first thing in the morning and I'm very sleepy."

"Don't be rude. This is important." Lottie sat on his side of the bed.

"I beg your pardon." He leaned forward and kissed the tip of her nose.

Lottie carried on regardless. "The point of the story is, that Granny threw her out without a reference. That was a big deal in those days and Katy was on her uppers."

"But I thought she had some enormous factory – and isn't there a garage too?"

"Yes, that's right. The Katherine Wheel Garage. Oh, this is a long story!"

Thierry lay back on the bed, hands behind his head and eyes on his wife. "Then I'm going to settle in and get comfortable."

"Katy married Jem after that."

"Who is Jem?"

"He's Al's father. He was a gardener at the manor. Everyone who had a job worked at the manor, pretty much."

"It must be a big place, an important one."

"Yes, or at least I thought so until I saw more of the world."

"Jem went off to fight in the war and Katy followed him after a while. She worked for the WAAC and learned to be a mechanic. When she came back, she started up the garage from an old Nissen hut on the London Road."

"And how did she finance this enterprise?"

"Ah, that's where my father came in. He had money from my other grandmother's tobacco franchise in America but when she died, all the money was cut off from him and the funding for the factory was lost too. Mummy says that's why he drove so madly in that fatal race."

"Hold on, you're going too fast."

Lottie grimaced. "So was he, sadly. Katy had designed some new type of brake seal and wanted to showcase it at the races to get sponsorship money to replace what my father had lost. Daddy was their driver and he came off at a bend. Mummy said it was the worst day of her life. She grieved for him terribly after that."

"This is fascinating, my love, but what is the point you are trying to make?" Thierry yawned.

"The point is I want a fresh start, Thierry. A new life, with you and maybe some of these kids no-one wants."

"How would you fund your new life?"

"That's the bit I can't work out. I have some money in a bank in Paris. I sold Granny's tiara."

"Would it be enough to get us somewhere to live this dream of yours?"

"No, not nearly enough. But Thierry, seeing those kids having their pictures taken, the hope in their eyes, the stories they've told, I just know they are right to seek a new life in America. I can feel it, in fact, I think I share it."

"Don't you think you should talk this over with your family?"

"You're right. Let's go back to England and see if we can find a solution. I'd love you to meet them, anyway. Mrs Fischer will let us have a little holiday, wouldn't she? I'm sure we could hitch a lift with the RAF or something?"

Lottie got off the bed and went to the chest of drawers and drew out a pen and some paper. "I'm going to write to them now."

When the taxicab swept past West Lodge instead of pausing outside it, Lottie knew a moment's misgiving. Things had changed at Cheadle Manor in her absence. For the first time, she questioned her decision.

Thierry looked at her. "Excited?"

"Hmm."

"Charlotte, are you having second thoughts?"

"No, it's just so strange to be coming back to the manor itself after all this time. Did you notice that little house by the gates?"

"Yes, of course."

"That's where Mummy and Isobel were living last time I was here. Our home was still a hospital then. Looks like it's gone."

The taxi parked outside the steps by the front door of her old home. Lottie barely had time to register that the ivy clambering up its walls had grown up to the first floor. In some places it looked like it was the only thing holding the house together, as the rest of it was so unkempt and neglected. Then the big front door swung open.

"They have been waiting for you, ma chérie." Thierry paid the driver and got out of the car, holding the door open for her.

Lottie clambered out and ran up the steps into her mother's arms. "Oh, Mummy, it's so good to see you."

"Hello, darling Lottie. I hope you didn't mind me sending a taxi to pick you up, but I've been so busy getting things ready here."

"No, of course not. It's lovely to be here."

"Come here, you!" Isobel hugged her next and then Al appeared, carrying a little boy.

"Oh, my goodness! This can't be Charles? He's so grown up!"

499

Al gave his son to Isobel and kissed Lottie heartily on the cheek. "He's had his first birthday now and is tottering about on his own two feet. We need eyes in the backs of our heads!"

Lottie turned around. "This is Thierry, my husband." She couldn't keep the pride from her voice.

"Oh, come in, come in. Al, can you grab the bags? Oh, let me kiss, you Thierry. It's wonderful to finally meet you." Cassandra grabbed Thierry and kissed him on both sides of his face, French style. "A very warm welcome to you. Now I have two handsome sons-in-law! I count myself very fortunate."

Thierry gave one of his transformative grins. "Enchanté, Madame."

"Oh, call me Cass. We're family now, Thierry."

"I am charmed to do so, Cass, but I will assist Al with the cases before I come in." Thierry went back down the steps, shook hands enthusiastically with Al, and picked up the two cases.

Al looked in the boot of the car. "Is that it?"

Lottie called down to him. "We haven't brought much."

Cassandra looked at her eldest daughter quizzically. "Not staying long?"

"Oh, Mummy, I have so much to tell you!"

Isobel fell into step with her sister as they went inside. "It's lovely to be back in our real home, isn't it, Lottie? I'm just loving living here with Al and Mummy. It feels like we are finally getting back to some sort of normality." Isobel beamed at her and then at the child on her hip. "You love being here in the big house too, don't you, my darling?"

Little Charles nodded and treated Lottie to a beautiful smile, showing four tiny front teeth, two at the top and two at the bottom.

"You're looking very well, Bella. Being a mother suits you."

"Thanks, Lottie, and being married suits you, I think. Did you know that Al and I had moved into the manor as well as Mummy?"

"No, I hadn't realised. And it sounds like it's working out well for you all?"

Isobel kissed her son's nose. "Oh yes, very much so. I feel I'm home at last."

Cassandra pointed up the stairs. "You go on up, Lottie darling, and show Thierry your old bedroom. I've had a double bed put in there. Katy and Jem are coming to supper, with young Lily. Agnes is too frail to leave home these days, but Susan Threadwell has offered to sit with her for this evening. We'll serve drinks in the drawing room. Come down when you're ready. You must be tired after such a long journey."

"Thanks, Mummy. We won't be long." Lottie showed Thierry up the grand staircase that dominated the octagonal, marbled hall. "Turn right at the top."

They reached the galleried landing and Lottie opened the door of her old bedroom.

As they entered the big room, Thierry's eyes widened behind his spectacles. "Mon dieu, I did not realise you came from such a wealthy background, ma chérie. I cannot imagine why you married such an ordinary Frenchman like me." Thierry put the suitcases down.

Lottie kissed him. "This is why."

Thierry returned her kiss passionately before walking around the room. He stopped at the big window that overlooked the orchard. "Apple trees. It reminds me of Bernadette's farm. Now I see where you come from, it is hard to remember you there, wearing a man's trousers held up by twine, and milking goats. Are you really sure you want to leave all this splendour and luxury behind you?"

Lottie joined him at the window, where the daylight was fading rapidly. "It's funny, I've been away so long, changed so much, I don't really feel I'm Lottie Flintock-Smythe anymore, and of course, I'm not. I'm Madame

501

Charlotte Thibault and that's who I want to be. After all we have been through, Thierry, I don't want to stay here, cocooned in an easy life, marooned in a backwater. I want a big life, one with purpose and meaning, and with you in it."

"I feel the same but I'm not renouncing a grand house. Are you sure you don't want to be here because you feel I won't fit in?"

"Good God, no! How could you even think so? You are as cultured and clever a man as anyone who came into this house. Believe me, Thierry, my grandfather wasn't exactly a thinker or even that polished. He preferred a bottle of claret and a good hunting horse to reading a book. Just because people have wealth, it doesn't mean they are exceptional at all. And anyway, I'm not sure that the estate is wealthy anymore, judging by the house being throttled by all the ivy worming its way into every crevice in the mortar." Lottie turned from the window. "Don't ever think you're not good enough for me, Thierry. You're the best thing that ever happened to me."

She opened her suitcase and pulled out her saffron dress.

Thierry watched her put it on. "I shall never forget you walking towards me in that lovely outfit on our wedding day."

"I'm glad you like it."

"I prefer you without it."

"No time for that, monsieur! Now come on, let's go downstairs."

A roaring fire was blazing up the chimney in the large drawing room and everyone, including the Phipps, was sitting on the sofas around it.

"Lottie! Ah, how marvellous to see you, my dear." Katy got up to meet her.

"This is Thierry, Aunt Katy."

Katy released Lottie from her embrace. "You have a good woman, there, Thierry."

"I am very aware of it, Madame."

"This is my husband, Jem, and my daughter, Lily."

Thierry bowed and shook hands with Jem. "Pleased to meet you, sir."

Lottie watched with pride as she could see he'd noticed Jem's wooden arm, but no-one would have guessed from the way he shook the good one.

Thierry turned to Lily, who looked very pretty in a pale blue dress with her dark curls bound in a matching ribbon. "Enchanté. Your daughter is as beautiful as yourself, Madame."

Katy laughed. "Now, listen Thierry, if you are going to flirt with me, I insist you call me Katy."

Thierry laughed. "I would be delighted."

Cassandra pulled the bell rope. "Now, we must all celebrate with a proper drink. I have got Andrews to resurrect some champagne he'd hidden in the cellar. Unbeknownst to Malcolm, it's been lurking down there throughout the entire war!"

Lottie laughed with the others. "Where is Malcolm, Mummy?"

"Oh, he's back in London, working in a hospital up there. Sadly, there are still soldiers who are badly affected by the war but not so many that they need dear old Cheadle Manor as a hospital any longer, I'm glad to say. The old house is pretty battered but it's still good to be living here again." Cassandra smiled at the gathered company. "It's so wonderful to see everyone together at last. Where *is* Andrews? Oh, he's so slow these days but he refuses to let a younger man take over!"

A few minutes later, Andrews, the butler entered the room. "You rang, madam?"

"Yes, Andrews, remember our little discussion about the champagne?"

"Indeed." Andrews bowed his grey head.

"Now is the time! Make sure we have enough glasses."

"Of course, madam."

503

"It's good to see you back at the manor again, Mummy." Lottie sat down facing the fire in her grandmother's old armchair, now frayed on the arms, which looked greasy and shiny from use. She looked around the room, noting the stained curtains, the worn rug, the peeling paint.

Her mother turned to the door. "Ah, here's Andrews. Please serve the champagne straight away. And Andrews?"

"Madam?"

"Take a bottle down to the kitchen and share it with the staff, would you? You all deserve to celebrate too."

"Thank you, madam, but I think we shall celebrate *after* we have served dinner." Andrews gave a thin smile that Lottie thought looked more like a remonstrance.

She whispered to her husband. "Do you see how stuffy it all is? That the servants have to have their tipple separately?"

Thierry whispered back. "Why is that? Why don't they just come in here for a drink?"

Lottie shrugged. "That's the custom. Separation of the classes."

Lottie caught her mother's eye. Cassandra was glaring at her breach of etiquette.

Andrews brought the full champagne flutes around on a silver tray.

"Has everyone got a glass?" Cassandra lifted hers up. "Then let's give a toast! To Mr and Mrs Thibault!"

Everyone echoed her and drank a sip.

"To young Charles!" Lottie raised her glass to the little boy on Isobel's knee, now dressed in pyjamas and obviously fighting sleep.

"And finally, I'd like to propose another toast." Jem waved his glass to include them all. "Peace, good health and prosperity to us all."

"Hear, hear!"

"Long may it last."

"May it last forever!"

Lottie sipped her champagne and looked at all the faces around her. Her mother looked well and was wearing a new dress in a shade of turquoise that really suited her colouring. "I like that new way you have with your hair, Mummy."

"Thank you, darling. There's a new hairdresser in Woodbury who's got a bit of style. Oh, was that the doorbell? I wasn't expecting anyone else."

Andrews shimmied out in that silent way Lottie remembered so well. The butler might be ancient, and slightly bent, but no-one could shoe-shuffle like him.

"Dr Harris, madam."

"Malcolm! Oh, now I'm completely happy. Do join us for a glass of champagne. Come and meet my charming new son-in-law."

Dr Harris entered the drawing room. "I couldn't resist getting the train down after we spoke on the telephone earlier, my dear."

"Lottie and Thierry have just arrived from Germany, as you know." Cassandra gave Malcolm a quick peck on the cheek and Andrews handed him a full champagne flute. "And of course, you know Katy and Jem and their daughter, Lily."

Malcolm Harris nodded a greeting at the Phipps family and then turned to shake hands with Thierry. "Germany, eh? That's somewhat surprising."

Both tall, and of a slim build, Lottie thought how alike they were. "We'll tell you all about it later. I think you'd find it particularly interesting, Malcolm."

Butterflies competed with the bubbles in Lottie's empty stomach. She looked at her husband, who stood beside her and raised his eyebrows in inquiry.

He gave a Gallic shrug and blew her a kiss and whispered in her ear. "It's up to you, chérie."

Lottie swallowed. It was now or never. She went to stand next to the grand piano from where she could see each face. "Um, I've something to say to you all. As we're all together here tonight, it seems a good time to tell you my plans."

Cassandra turned around to see her properly. "Lottie? Goodness, this sounds important."

"It is, Mummy." Lottie cleared her throat. "As you know, Thierry and I have been working for UNRRA."

"Oh, do remind me what that is, darling, I have no idea what it stands for." Cassandra took a deep drag on her cigarette.

"What's the full title, Thierry, I can't for the life of me remember?" Lottie looked at her husband. She was so focussed on her forthcoming announcement the question had made her mind go blank.

"United Nations Relief and Rehabilitation Administration."

Jem looked genuinely interested. "Is this a world-wide outfit, Thierry? I mean, who heads it up?"

"It's mostly run by Americans but represents forty-four nations altogether, I believe."

Malcolm chipped in. "When was it set up, Thierry?"

"In 1943, I believe, when more and more people became displaced in the European theatre of war."

Jem looked solemn. "The writing was on the wall, even then."

Lottie sensed the mood of the room change and darken at the mention of the war. Now, all eyes were upon her, and serious. She swallowed and told them all about the work they had been doing.

"So, you're going back to Germany?" Cassandra stubbed out her cigarette.

Lottie nodded. "That's right, Mummy. There is so much more to do."

"But what about Cheadle Manor? After all, it belongs solely to you."

"I was coming to that. Thierry?" She couldn't do this alone.

Thierry got up and joined her, so they stood together by the grand piano. Lottie looked down at its polished surface and saw the old photograph of her father in his racing gear, head thrown back, laughing. She picked up the silver frame that housed the image. "You see, I've had an idea."

Everyone was listening intently now. Lottie glanced around at each of them, staring back at her. Cassandra sat next to Malcolm Harris on one sofa and Jem and Katy had Lily between them on the other. Al and Isobel perched on a single chair together, their arms loosely linked and their son asleep on his mother's lap. She wished her heart would calm down. Thierry quietly held her other hand.

"Go on, Lottie, dear. Don't keep us in suspense." Katy nodded encouragement.

Lottie took a deep breath. "I want to open an orphanage of my own," she looked at her husband, "of *our* own."

Cassandra leaned forward on her chair. "You mean, you want Cheadle Manor to become an orphanage?"

Lottie shook her head. "No, that's just it. I don't think it would work back here in Wiltshire. The children are difficult, sometimes their behaviour is bizarre, and they are disorientated. I can't see them being accepted around here. And, more than that, they all desperately want to go and live in America. They want a new start in the new world. A world they see as the 'land of the free' and different from the old one where they have suffered and lost so much. They want a fresh start, away from all the bitter memories, and who can blame them?"

Lottie paused, looked up at Thierry standing so close beside her, she could feel the warmth from his body seeping into hers. "And that's what we want too. A fresh start in a new place." Lottie looked down at her father's photograph again. "After all, I am half-American. I look at you all here, and you look so at home. You belong here but I don't feel I do anymore."

"Lottie, darling, of course you do!" Casandra looked upset and Malcolm put his arm around her.

"I'm sorry, Mummy, I love you all, of course I do, but my destiny lies elsewhere."

Isobel frowned. "But Lottie, you own Cheadle Manor. It belongs to you!"

Lottie looked directly at her sister. "Yes, I know but I want *you* to have it, Bella. You and Al and Charles, and Mummy too. When I look at you, I can see you are part of the landscape, you fit these old walls. I've decided I'm going to renounce my inheritance and sign it over to you. The will that Granny made was wrong. I always felt so."

"What?" Cassandra stood up now, looking distressed. "Don't you *want* to be with your family anymore?"

Lottie put her father's photograph back on the shiny wood of the grand piano. "Thierry is my family now and our future is in America."

Isobel frowned. "But Lottie, we can't just take your inheritance away from you without giving you something in return!"

Al shifted in his seat and leant forward. "Bella's right. You would have to be recompensed for at least your half of the value of the estate."

Cassandra still looked troubled. "Yes, you can't just *give* Cheadle Manor away! And where will you live? How will you fund this orphanage?"

"I was hoping Aunt Rose could find us somewhere to rent in Boston. You see, you have to have a relative resident in America before you can apply for a visa and it's bound to help that my father came from there too. Once we have set ourselves up there, we can invite the children to come and live with us. Adopt them or foster them until they can fend for themselves. Some are so young; they would need us for many years. After all Thierry and I witnessed and went through in the war, we both feel we need to be part

508

of a new order that will bring justice to its victims, in our own small way."

Cassandra sat back down again. "This is all very confusing. I don't know what to think."

The gong sounded and Andrews was once more at the door. "Dinner is served."

"Thank you, Andrews." Cassandra stood up. "I think we'd better discuss this momentous proposal when our stomachs are full of more than champagne."

Everyone got to their feet in an embarrassed silence. Lottie felt awkward, wishing she had left her speech until later, but her mother took a deep breath and put on the bright, social face Lottie remembered from her childhood when Cassandra had been feeling low with grief for her father and was determined no-one would guess.

Cassandra smiled at the assembled company. "This is just like old times. Thierry? Give me your arm, and you must sit at my right hand. Malcolm, will you take Lottie in?"

Lottie exchanged meaningful looks with Thierry, who raised one eyebrow at her smile. She could see he understood now how English country houses still clung to their stuffy conventions. How her mother had dodged the question and pretended it hadn't happened at all.

Katy took Al's arm and Isobel and Lily filed into the dining-room last, with Jem between them.

Andrews had obviously recruited new staff and the meal was served by him and two younger men in black suits with stiff, white collars, who were hesitant and kept looking at the aged butler for their cues.

Lottie listened as best she could to the news about Al leaving the ATA now the war was over, Charles cutting his first teeth, the winding down of the factory and, from her mother, the difficulties of evacuating the hospital and retrieving bits of old furniture from the attics, but all the time she felt ill-at-ease and at odds with these people she loved so much. What were they really thinking?

At the end of the meal Cassandra tapped her wine glass. "Andrews - do give Mrs Andrews our compliments and tell everyone below stairs they have performed a miracle with tonight's dinner. Considering we're all still on rations, it's been a triumph!"

"Very good, madam. Shall I set out tea for the ladies in the drawing room?"

"Not tonight, I think. You may retire for the evening and let the staff relax too. We can get ourselves off to bed."

Andrews withdrew. "Goodnight madam and, may I say, welcome home, Miss Charlotte?"

Lottie gave him a little wave. "Goodnight, Andrews, and thanks for everything."

"Let's go into the drawing room together, shall we?" Cassandra got up and lead the way across the marbled hall and through the double doors. "Do help yourselves to a drink, everyone."

Katy Phipps, whom Lottie thought the best dressed woman in the room, in her red velvet evening gown and genuine milky pearls, stood by her friend. "Cass, dear. That meal was scrumptious. You'd never guess it was bought with coupons."

Cassandra touched the side of her nose with the tip of her finger. "I think a little poaching could have been involved. I've always been partial to pheasant."

Katy winked at her friend. "Anyone mind if I smoke?"

"As long as I can, too!" Cassandra laughed and withdrew a cigarette from the box on the piano. "Well, now that the servants have departed for the evening, perhaps we can talk more freely again."

Katy got up and Jem followed her. They stood together at the grand piano just as Thierry and Lottie had done before dinner. "I've been thinking about everything you said, Lottie, and Jem and I have had a quiet word together about it, haven't we, Jem?"

Jem nodded. "Yes, we are both in agreement about what we'd like to do."

Katy continued. "I understand about your plan, Lottie, I really do. I had to break the mould to start up the Katherine Wheel Garage and it wasn't easy, but, just like you, I felt it was my destiny. Like you, I was pretty determined! I made it work," she reached for Jem's good hand, "with the help of my lovely husband. I'm sure you and Thierry will too, and I admire your ambition. I think you've got real guts and a very big heart."

Lottie smiled at Katy and Jem. "Oh, thank you, Aunt Katy! I'm so glad you understand."

Jem smiled back. "She's right, you know, Lottie, my Katy always is, though I don't always let on."

Everyone laughed at Jem's honesty, including his wife.

Katy turned to face the others. "I have an idea that might work for everyone. Cheadle Manor is in a right state after being requisitioned as a hospital, begging your pardon, Malcolm!"

Malcolm inclined his head in acknowledgement. "Guilty as charged."

Katy smiled at him. "There's no getting away from the fact that it needs some serious money to set it straight. Lottie will need funding for her enterprise too. Well, we have plenty of money, as it happens. The rubber factory has made us a fortune, quite literally, with all the work that came through the war. Jem and I having been thinking about the future and we had already decided we can afford to help out, even before Lottie came up with her new idea."

Katy looked at Jem, who nodded in his grave way. "We'd like to give Lottie half of what Cheadle Manor is worth so she can set up her orphanage in America, in return for her relinquishing her ownership of the estate to Al and Isobel, as she has already said she would like to do."

There was a gasp from the others and Cassandra started to speak. Katy held her hand up. "We'd still have enough left to help Bella and Al to refurbish this lovely old house and would give them an equal amount. That way, Isobel and Al could become the owners of Cheadle Manor, which would then in turn go to young Charles. Of course, darling Cassandra must also be provided for, but that's between you three to work out."

Cassandra looked non-plussed. "But, Kate, dear, why would you do all that? That must amount to a huge amount of money."

Katy nodded at her friend. "You forget, Cass, Charles is my grandson too. Can't you imagine how wonderful it would be for me and Jem to see our grandchild inherit the very place we used to work in as humble house servants? It would make my whole life make sense. All the hard work that Jem and I have done these long years would have been worthwhile."

Katy's beaming smile embraced them all. "It would give us great joy to enable these young people to achieve their dreams, now we have realised our own."

EPILOGUE
THE BEACH HOUSE, CAPE COD, AMERICA
JUNE 1948

Lottie stood on the wooden veranda, gazing at the breakers pounding the shore and the sun setting on the waves. How she loved this place. Once her momentous decision had sunk in, it had been her mother who had suggested this Beach House at Cape Cod.

Cassandra had telephoned Aunt Rose the very next day and she had told them that she would be only too happy to help Thierry and Lottie come to America but they couldn't stay with her as she now had five children of her own and her husband's ministry in the church kept him busy but hardly affluent.

Lottie remembered the thrill of excitement she'd felt when she heard her mother say, "Rose, what about the old beach house? Do you still own it?"

It had been a torment waiting for the reply, but Lottie guessed from her mother's response that her dream would come true. "You do? Would you sell to us? Yes, of course we'll pay the going rate, we'd be glad to. Yes, it's this crazy idea Lottie has to set up an orphanage for the war refugees. You'll help? Oh, that's marvellous, Rose. Alright, dear, yes, I'll be in touch soon. You get it valued and let me know. Yes, alright, bye, bye! Love to the children!"

Cassandra had put the telephone down and turned to her eldest daughter. "It's still there, Lottie, darling, if you must go through with your mad scheme."

"I must, Mummy, really I must. What is the beach house like?"

Lottie would never forget the faraway look in her mother's eyes at that moment. "Oh, Lottie. It has such special memories for me. The short time I spent at that glorious place were the happiest days of my life." She turned to face her, and Lottie saw tears welling up and trickling down her mother's face.

"Mummy? Are you alright?"

Cassandra nodded. "Oh yes, do you know, Lottie, it would give me the greatest pleasure on this earth to know that you are living there, where I was so blissfully happy with your father." She wiped her eyes.

"Really? You don't mind?"

"No, I don't mind. I'm very fond of Malcolm but I shall never love another man the way I loved your father. I shall have Bella and Al here to keep me company and look after the old place, and you will be just across the ocean in the new one. I can come and visit you there, can't I?"

"Of course! As often as you like!"

"Then I shall be with my darling Douglas again. Ah, my dear, he would have been so proud of you!"

The sun had slipped down below the horizon now and Lottie shivered. Thierry came and joined her. He stood behind her with his arms around her and kissed the back of her neck.

Lottie nuzzled against him. "Is everyone asleep?"

"Just about. Had to break up a pillow fight in the boys' dormitory."

Lottie laughed. "High spirits. That's good. Are the girls quiet?"

"As little mice. That clam bake knocked them all out."

"Peace at last, my love."

Thierry pulled her closer. "That's what I thought. We have a full house but tonight belongs to just us two."

"Not quite."

"Hmm?"

Lottie pulled his hands down to her belly. "Us three."

THE END

Find out more about Katy and Jem's lives before and during World War One in <u>Daffodils.</u> Find out how Jem and Katy got together in the first place and the reasons they joined up to fight for their country. And just who is Lionel White?

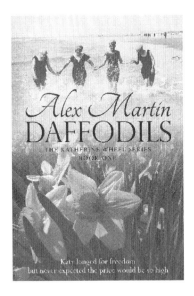

"Katy dreams of a better life than just being a domestic servant at Cheadle Manor. Her one attempt to escape is thwarted when her flirtation with the manor's heir results in a scandal that shocks the local community.
Jem Beagle has always loved Katy. His offer of marriage rescues her, but personal tragedy divides them. Jem leaves his beloved Wiltshire to become a reluctant soldier on the battlefields of World War One. Katy is left behind, restless and alone.
Lionel White, just returned from being a missionary in India, brings a dash of colour to the small village, and offers Katy a window on the wider world.
Katy decides she has to play her part in the global struggle and joins the war effort as a WAAC girl.

She finally breaks free from the stifling Edwardian hierarchies that bind her but the brutality of global war brings home the price she has paid for her search."

"Impressively well-researched and vividly imagined."
"A fantastic story which was written beautifully. I have not read many books based around WW1 and this was just right. The characters have some hard times and I found myself in tears at times, but overall the story was told in a way I could relate to and understand. Highly recommended for fans of historical fiction."
"Probably one of the best books I've read of this genre. Took me to the First World War as never before. Will certainly read the second with great anticipation. Only chose it because of the price and picture on the front but what a find and such a treat !!!"
"Daffodils is an extraordinary story of commitment and enduring hope which teaches us the power of resilience, integrity and true honor. This book was a deeply emotional experience that managed to reach the inner core of my being. This is such a powerful story! Highly recommended."

Daffodils is also available as an audio book, narrated by the author

Peace Lily, the second book in The Katherine Wheel Series is also available in both kindle and paperback.

Sequel to Daffodils
Book Two of The Katherine Wheel Series

Although the war is over, its aftermath is anything but peaceful

After the appalling losses suffered during World War One, three of its survivors long for peace, unaware that its aftermath will bring different, but still daunting, challenges. Katy trained as a mechanic during the war and cannot bear to return to the life of drudgery she left behind. A trip to America provides the dream ticket she has always craved and an opportunity to escape the strait-jacket of her working class roots. She jumps at the chance, little realising that it will change her life forever, but not in the way she'd hoped. Jem lost not only an arm in the war, but also his livelihood, and with it, his self esteem. How can he keep restless Katy at home and provide for his wife? He puts his life at risk a

518

second time, attempting to secure their future and prove his love for her.

Cassandra has fallen deeply in love with Douglas Flintock, an American officer she met while driving ambulances at the Front. How can she persuade this modern American to adapt to her English country way of life, and all the duties that come with inheriting Cheadle Manor? When Douglas returns to Boston, unsure of his feelings, Cassandra crosses the ocean, determined to lure him back.

As they each try to carve out new lives, their struggles impact on each other in unforeseen ways.

"Daffodils' sequel Peace Lily is as enthralling and fresh as its predecessor."
"Great follow on book. Couldn't put down till finished."

The third book in The Katherine Wheel Series

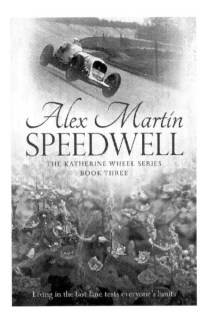

Living in the fast lane tests everyone's limits

Katy and Jem enter the 1920's with their future
in the balance. How can they possibly make their new
enterprise work? They must risk everything, including
disaster, and trust their gamble will pay off.
Cassandra, juggling the demands of a young
family, aging parents and running Cheadle Manor,
distrusts the speed of the modern age, but Douglas
races to meet the new era, revelling in the freedom of
the open road.
Can each marriage survive the strain the new
dynamic decade imposes? Or will the love they share
deepen and carry them through? They all arrive at
destinies that surprise them in Speedwell, the third
book in the Katherine Wheel Series.

"I really enjoyed the stories. Read all three books in the series while on holiday. Her writing style makes for comfortable reading. Her characters are credible and in the main her story lines are unpredictable and powerfully descriptive."

"A fascinating set of characters weave their magical story through a daring enterprise just after the end of the Great War. The story travels from humble but daring beginnings in a small Wiltshire village with Katy and Jem and takes us to Boston in the USA and back."

"Wow!! To put it in the vernacular of the era of Speedwell, what a rip-roaring book! I loved it."

<u>Willow i</u>s a short novella that bridges the generational gap. Book Four in The Katherine Wheel Series may be small, but it packs in many surprises for the children of Katy and Jem, and Douglas and Cassandra.

"This is a very well written and descriptive novella with the children and the idyllic countryside setting, well observed and portrayed. You feel you are there experiencing it first-hand. It draws you into a totally believable world, perfect material for a film or a Sunday evening drama series."

"This tale brings to life their distinctive well-rounded characters; the dialogue distinguishes each child's voice and fits exactly into the era it represents. The descriptive narrative sets the scene perfectly and moves the plot along in gripping speed."

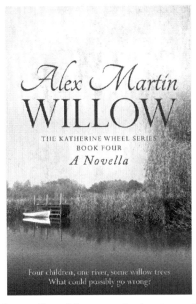

The stifling heat of a midsummer's day lures four children
to the cool green waters of the river that runs between
Cheadle Manor and The Katherine Wheel Garage.
Al captains the little band of pirates as they blithely board
the wooden dinghy. Headstrong Lottie vies with him to be
in charge while Isobel tries to keep the peace and look after
little Lily.

But it is the river that is really in control.

Lost and alone, the four children must face many dangers,
but it is the unforeseen consequences of their innocent
adventure that will shape their futures for years to come.

Woodbine is the fifth book in The Katherine Wheel Series.

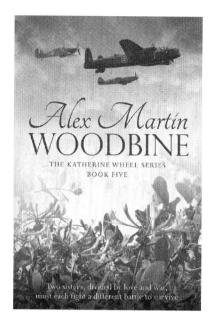

Lottie, her sister Isobel and Al, the man they both love, are
on the brink of adulthood and the Second World War in
Woodbine, the fifth book in The Katherine Wheel Series.
Trapped and alone in occupied France, Lottie must disguise
her identity and avoid capture if she is to return and heal the
bitter feud over the future of Cheadle Manor.
Back in England, Al is determined to prove himself. He
joins the Air Transport Auxiliary service, flying aeroplanes
to RAF bases all over the country.
Isobel defies everyone's expectations by becoming a Land
Girl. Bound by a promise to a dying woman, she struggles
to break free and follow her heart.

IVY, Book Six, concludes The Katherine Wheel Series

Alex Martin's debut book is based on her grapepicking adventure in France in the 1980's. It's more of a mystery/ thriller than historical fiction but makes for great holiday reading with all the sensuous joys of that beautiful country.

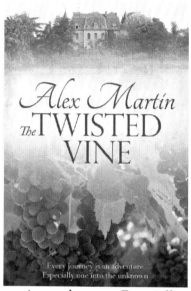

Every journey is an adventure. Especially one into the unknown.

The shocking discovery of her lover with someone else propels Roxanne into escaping to France and seeking work as a grape-picker. She's never been abroad before and certainly never travelled alone.

Opportunistic loner, Armand, exploits her vulnerability when they meet by chance. She didn't think she would see him again or be the one who exposes his terrible crime.

Join Roxanne on her journey of self-discovery, love and tragedy in rural France. Taste the wine, feel the sun, drive through the Provencal mountains with her, as her courage and resourcefulness are tested to the limit.

The Twisted Vine is set in the heart of France and is a deeply romantic but suspenseful tale. Roxanne Rudge escapes her cheating boyfriend by going grape picking in France. She feels vulnerable and alone in such a big country where she can't speak the language and is befriended by Armand le Clair, a handsome Frenchman. Armand is not all he seems, however, and she discovers a darker side to him before uncovering a dreadful secret. She is aided and abetted by three new friends she has made, charming posh Peter, a gifted linguist; the beautiful and vivacious Italian, Yvane; and clever Henry of the deep brown eyes with the voice to match. Together they unravel a mystery centred around a beautiful chateau and play a part in its future.

"The original setting of this novel and the beauty of colorful places that Roxanne visits really drew me in. This book was a lot more than I'd expected, because aside from the romantic aspect, there's a great deal of humor, fantastic friendship, and entertaining dialogue. I strongly recommend this book to anyone who likes women's fiction."

"This is a wonderful tale told with compassion, emotion, thrills and excitement and some unexpected turns along the way. Oh, and there may be the smattering of a romance in there as well! Absolutely superb."

The Rose Trail is a time slip story set in both the English Civil War and the present day woven together by a supernatural thread.

Is it chance that brings Fay and Persephone together? Or is it the restless and malevolent spirit who stalks them both?
Once rivals, they must now unite if they are to survive the mysterious trail of roses they are forced to follow into a dangerous, war torn past.

"The past has been well researched although I don't know a lot about this period in history it all rings so true – the characters are fantastic with traits that you like and dislike which also applies to the 'present' characters who have their own issues to contend with as well as being able to connect with the past."
"A combination of love, tragedies, friendships, past and present, lashings of historical aspects, religious bias,

527

controlling natures all combined with the supernatural give this novel a wonderful page-turning quality."

" I loved this book, the storyline greatly appealed to me and the history it contained. Fay has always been able to see spirits. The love of her life is Robin, whom she met when she was 11 at school. She trains to become an accountant and purely by chance meets up with an old school friend. The book develops into an enthralling adventure for them both as they slip back and forth in time."

"I love the cracking pace, with surprising jolts. It's a great gripping read!"

All Alex Martin's stories are available as ebooks as well as paperbacks and make great gifts!

Alex writes about her work on her blog at
www.intheplottingshed.com
where you can get your FREE copy of Alex Martin's short story collection, 'Trio', by clicking on the picture of the shed.

Constructive reviews oil a writer's wheel like nothing else and are very much appreciated on Amazon, or Goodreads or anywhere else!

Alex Martin, Author

Facebook page:
https://www.facebook.com/TheKatherineWheel/
Twitter handle: https://twitter.com/alex_martin8586

Printed in Great Britain
by Amazon